"We're onto him," Jax said, grinning.

"There's just one problem," Keara told him.

"What? That we probably haven't found everything?" There was one time gap big enough that they'd agreed there was probably at least one more connected crime. "I'm sure another one will surface eventually."

"Not that," Keara said. "Every single one of these cases is in a different jurisdiction. Hell, every case is in a different state."

"Okay, but—"

"Jax, he set off this bomb in Luna, left behind this symbol. This pattern suggests he commits one crime and then leaves. He's probably already gone."

He stared back at her, his grin slowly fading.

Beside her, Patches whined and nudged her leg.

They'd found the criminal's trail, but had it already gone cold here?

Boom!

A sound like thunder directly overhead exploded. Then the silence following the loud noise was replaced by screaming.

K-9: TRACKING THE TARGET

ELIZABETH HEITER

2 Thrilling Stories
K-9 Cold Case and *K-9 Hideout*

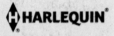

ISBN-13: 978-1-335-42999-5

K-9: Tracking the Target

Copyright © 2022 by Harlequin Enterprises ULC

K-9 Cold Case
First published in 2021. This edition published in 2022.
Copyright © 2021 by Elizabeth Heiter

K-9 Hideout
First published in 2021. This edition published in 2022.
Copyright © 2021 by Elizabeth Heiter

Recycling programs
for this product may
not exist in your area.

For questions and comments about the quality of this book, please contact us
at CustomerService@Harlequin.com.

Harlequin Enterprises ULC
22 Adelaide St. West, 41st Floor
Toronto, Ontario M5H 4E3, Canada
www.Harlequin.com

Printed in U.S.A.

CONTENTS

K-9 COLD CASE   7

K-9 HIDEOUT   247

Elizabeth Heiter likes her suspense to feature strong heroines, chilling villains, psychological twists and a little romance. Her research has taken her into the minds of serial killers, through murder investigations and onto the FBI Academy's shooting range. Elizabeth graduated from the University of Michigan with a degree in English literature. She's a member of International Thriller Writers and Romance Writers of America. Visit Elizabeth at elizabethheiter.com.

Books by Elizabeth Heiter

Harlequin Intrigue

K-9 Defense

A K-9 Alaska Novel

K-9 Defense
Alaska Mountain Rescue
K-9 Cold Case
K-9 Hideout

The Lawmen: Bullets and Brawn

Bodyguard with a Badge
Police Protector
Secret Agent Surrender

The Lawmen

Disarming Detective
Seduced by the Sniper
SWAT Secret Admirer

Visit the Author Profile page
at Harlequin.com for more titles.

K-9 COLD CASE

This book is for my husband, Andrew,
who gives me my own HEA every single day.

Acknowledgments

A special thanks to everyone at Harlequin
for helping me bring my K-9 Alaska series to life,
especially my editor, Denise Zaza, and
assistant editor, Connolly Bottum, for managing all
the details, and my publicist, Lisa Wray, for sharing
the stories with bloggers and reviewers. My sister,
Caroline Heiter, brought her beta reading magic to
this book, and my husband, Andrew Gulli,
kept me fed and working! A special shout-out to my
#BatSignal writer pals, especially Tyler Anne Snell,
Nichole Severn, Regan Black, Louise Dawn and
Janie Crouch, who brought motivation and inspiration
during virtual writing sessions.

Chapter 1

You have to be the calm in their chaos.

Jax Diallo repeated the mantra in his head, the words he always reminded himself of when he was sent to the scene of a tragedy. Being an FBI Victim Specialist wasn't for the faint of heart.

As the FBI vehicle he was riding in slammed to a stop, Jax closed his eyes for a few seconds, tried to center himself. Tried to prepare to walk into the aftermath of a bomb.

"Let's go!" one of the Special Agents said, hopping out of the vehicle with his partner, two Evidence Response Technicians on their heels.

With the doors open, the bitter Alaskan wind penetrated the vehicle. So did the unnatural quiet of nature, as if all the animals had taken off. The silence was punctuated by staccato bursts of sobbing, from victims or family members still on the scene. Or maybe a first responder or law-enforcement officer who'd never seen anything like this.

In the distance a phone rang and rang, before going silent and then starting up again. A friend or family member searching for a loved one, desperately hoping for an answer to a call that would never be picked up.

"You ready, Patches?" Jax asked quietly.

His Labrador retriever stared up at him steadily, the soft brown eyes that always reassured victims also working their magic on Jax. She'd transitioned fast from a scared, abandoned puppy into one of the FBI's best therapy dogs. Right now she could read his mood as well as any victim's she'd been sent to help.

He gave her a reassuring pet, then climbed out of the SUV. Twenty feet ahead the beautiful greenery of a park was littered with the twisted metal skeleton of what had probably once been a park bench. Pieces of metal had blown into the street, and were still smoldering. Directly beside the park, a small freestanding building—maybe a bathroom—had collapsed, the front wall gaping open. Crumbled concrete, support beams and insulation spilled out of it. Around the edges of the park, one tree was pierced with a metal fragment, like a spear. Others were singed black and missing huge limbs.

As Jax got closer, he saw the detritus from first responders: abandoned needle covers, wrappers and blood-soaked gauze. The concrete walkway was stained a deep red.

The scent still lingered, too, burned metal and charred trees, and something worse underneath. A scent Jax recognized from too many other crime scenes.

The bomb had gone off just over an hour ago in the

sleepy town of Luna, Alaska, on an otherwise peaceful Saturday morning. When it happened, Jax had been
four hundred miles away, sipping his morning coffee
on his back deck, with Patches asleep at his feet. Then
his FBI phone had gone off and he'd grabbed his go bag
and raced to the tiny nearby airfield, where a jumper
plane was waiting.

The briefing on the plane had been short and infor-
mation-light. A single bomb had detonated. At least six
were dead and thirteen more injured. Right now the
tiny Luna Police Department had no suspects, no obvious motive and no idea whether to expect more bombs.

Jax looked around the small park, with butterfly-
shaped benches around the edges and a couple of trails
leading into the woods. It wasn't an obvious spot to set
off a bomb. There'd been no events here, except for an
impromptu soccer game. All locals, no news coverage.
If the bomber had a specific target, the park seemed like
an odd place to go after them, because a bomb here was
too likely to miss that person and take out others. If he
hadn't been targeting a specific person, it still seemed
like a strange choice, without the volume of spectators
that mission-oriented bombers favored.

Not your job, Jax reminded himself. The agents
would search for the perpetrator. He needed to help
the victims and their families.

Kneeling down, he slipped special shoes onto Patches's feet that would protect her from bomb fragments
and other sharp items in the rubble. Ideally, they'd stay
out of the blast zone entirely, but that wasn't always possible. Then he stood, holding his arm out straight, directing her toward the park. "Come on, Patches."

She followed his direction, walking past the gawkers

on the outskirts of the scene. She headed straight toward the woman sitting alone on one of the intact benches, with a vacant gaze and blood smearing her sweatshirt. When Patches reached the woman, she sat next to her, and the woman—girl, really, Jax decided as he reached her—seemed to refocus. She reached out a shaky hand to pet Patches, who scooted closer.

Ignoring the chaos behind him as the FBI agents and evidence specialists coordinated with Luna police, Jax knelt in front of the girl. He pegged her at nineteen. The shock in her eyes suggested she still hadn't processed what had happened. The grass stains on the knees of her pants suggested she might have been part of the soccer game. Or maybe she'd skidded to the ground from the force of the blast or in desperation to help someone she loved. There were a couple of bandages visible on her arms where she'd rolled up her sleeves, but nothing that would have caused the amount of blood on her shirt.

"I'm Jax Diallo," he said softly, not wanting to startle her. "I'm a Victim Specialist with the FBI."

Her gaze skipped to his, then back to Patches. She pet his dog faster, and Patches moved even closer, putting her head on the arm of the bench and making the girl smile.

"What can I do for you?" Jax asked. "Is there someone I can call? Do you need to get to the hospital to see someone?" He hoped the person whose blood coated her shirt wasn't in the morgue.

She glanced at him again, surprise and wariness in her eyes. "You're not going to ask me about what happened?"

"We can talk about that, too, if you want. I'm here for you. So is Patches."

Her gaze darted to his dog, at the mix of brown and black that had earned her the name, and smiled briefly.

"What's your name?"

"Akna." Her voice was croaky, quiet enough that he had to lean forward to make it out.

She'd inhaled smoke when the bomb went off. Or the blast was still impeding her ability to tell how loud she was speaking, even an hour later. Probably both.

"Akna, I'm a Victim Specialist. It's my job to help you and anyone else who needs me today or in the future. Right now that means getting you any resources you might want, or helping you contact someone."

She stared back at him, her gaze still slightly unfocused. But as she pet Patches, the fear and confusion on her face slowly started to fade.

Most people had no idea his job existed. But he was the lifeline between victims and their families and the Special Agents, who often didn't have the time or know-how to manage victims' many needs. Part of his role was to help victims navigate the criminal justice process, making it more likely they'd find the perpetrator and put that person behind bars. But the other part was simply helping victims get the resources they needed to move on with their lives.

"Akna, were you here alone?"

"Yeah." She shook her head. "No. Sort of."

"You were here for the soccer game?" he guessed.

"Yeah. We've got an online community board. Someone wanted to play." She shrugged, a fast jerk of her shoulders. "It was a nice day. I wanted some exercise." A strangled sob broke free. "How could this happen?"

"Is there someone you want me to call? To let them know you're okay? Or to pick you up?"

"I helped carry her over there," Akna said, gesturing vaguely toward the edge of the park. "I saw a couple of the players trying to lift her, carry her away from the rubble." Her voice picked up speed, picked up volume. "She was right by the building and big pieces of it fell on her. We thought it would be better. But—"

"She was a friend of yours?" Jax asked, keeping his voice calm, letting Patches do her own work as Akna continued to pet her, probably not even aware she was doing it.

Akna shook her head. "I didn't really know her. But she was on my team." Her eyes met Jax's and instantly filled with tears. "I think she was dead before we carried her over there."

"I'm sorry, Akna."

"Who would do this?"

"We don't know yet. But we're going to find out."

"We were just playing the game. I was running down the field, heading for the goal—it was supposed to be those trees." She pointed, her hand shaking uncontrollably. "No one thought to bring a net. And then…and then, there was this huge *boom*. It was so loud I could *feel* it. I don't remember falling, but then I was on the ground and people were screaming and then…" She sucked in a violent breath.

"Akna, you're okay," Jax said softly, in the same even tone he'd used with hundreds of victims. "You're okay. It's over."

"Akna!"

Akna leaped to her feet, making Patches stand, too. The tears she'd been persistently blinking back suddenly spilled over as she whispered, "Mom."

Then a woman with the same dark hair, the same

deep-set eyes, rushed over, enveloping her in a tight hug. "I heard about the bomb. And I couldn't get a hold of you. Your phone kept going straight to voice mail."

"It broke," Akna sobbed. "I fell on it and it broke. And then I was trying to help Jenny and—"

"It's okay, it's okay," her mom soothed, smoothing back her daughter's hair. "I'll take you home."

"Akna," Jax said, holding out his card. "You call me if I can help you, okay? Anything at all. Anytime."

She took the card with a shaky hand, nodded.

Akna's mom looked at him questioningly, even as her gaze skimmed over his coat, emblazoned with *FBI.* "You're investigating the bombing?"

"I'm a Victim Specialist, not an investigator. I'm here for your daughter. If she saw anything that could help the investigation, she can talk to me. Or if she wants information about the status of the case. Or if she wants help finding someone to talk to about what happened today. The same goes for you, ma'am."

Surprise registered on the woman's face as she glanced at the card in Akna's hand, then back at him.

Akna swiped the tears off her face with the sleeve of her bloody sweatshirt, then whispered, "Thanks, Jax." Then she gave his dog a shaky smile. "Bye, Patches."

Woof!

Her happy bark made a handful of Luna police officers glance their way.

Akna let out a surprised laugh, then she left, her arm looped around her mom's waist.

Jax pulled out a notebook and jotted down the details Akna had mentioned, before tucking it back into his FBI jacket. Then he raised his arm to gesture toward the other group of civilians gathered at the edge of the park. "Let's go, Patches."

She headed toward them without pause, used to her role of calming people.

As he followed, snippets of their conversation drifted toward him.

"Why would anyone set off a bomb here?"

"...nothing here, man!"

Right now Jax needed to focus on the victims' immediate needs, on information he could gather to help them later and on the details that might matter in the investigation. But he had a background in psychology and he'd never quite been able to turn off the analytical side of his brain that sorted through why a person did the things they did. It had helped him back in his therapist days. As an FBI employee, it sometimes made him clash with the investigating agents.

But right now he couldn't stop wondering: What had a bomber been doing in this small park?

Jax had been to the sites of several bombs since he'd joined the FBI. Usually, they fell into two categories: big spectacles meant to cause widespread panic, or small explosives meant to kill a certain person. This didn't seem like either one.

This crime scene was different from anything he'd experienced. Even though knowing the motivation behind a crime didn't necessarily make it less scary, for Jax, it made it easier to comprehend. And usually, easier to comprehend meant a starting place for him, for the victims, even for the Special Agents in their investigation.

He squinted at the destruction in this once-beautiful

place and dread settled in his gut. Was the bomber finished or was he just getting started?

Being police chief in a remote Alaskan town was supposed to be quiet. It was supposed to be simple.

Today Keara Hernandez had spent the day reassuring scared citizens that they were safe in Desparre, that the explosion in the town next to them was under investigation. That she'd have more information over the next few days, that it would be solved soon. She hoped her reassurances were true. But she'd been unable to get through to her colleagues in the Luna PD all day.

So now, instead of going home to rest, she was on her way down the mountain that separated Desparre from Luna. Getting to Luna was a two-hour venture if you went around the base of the mountain. Trekking up and then down the mountain again took half the time. In winter that trip could be dangerous. Right now, with May a few days away and the snow melted except in the highest parts of the mountain, it was much easier. But Keara felt every minute of the drive.

Her throat was sore after talking to more citizens in a day than she usually did in a week in her town full of recluses. Her shoulder ached from one of her regular calls, close to her own house. A belligerent drunk who liked to scream at his wife. At least once a week Keara was out there, talking him down and occasionally tossing him in a cell. Today he'd taken a run at her and she'd had to cuff him, bring him in the hard way.

She wanted to soak it off in a tub, relax in her quiet house, set apart from her neighbors by a few miles. She wanted to continue to live in the fantasy that a small town like Desparre would never face the same types of threats a big city like Houston saw.

The thought of her hometown made her chest tighten and Keara pushed it out of her mind, punched down on the gas. This was a fluke. She'd lived in Desparre for six years and although bar fights and domestic violence weren't unusual, big, complex cases were few and far between. Other than the kidnapping case that had given Desparre way more attention than it had ever wanted five years ago—and a rehash six months ago when one of the kidnappers reappeared—Desparre and its neighbor Luna were places people came to stay below the radar. Not to set off bombs.

The idea made her shudder as she navigated off the mountain and toward downtown Luna, toward the quaint little park where she'd come more than once over the past six years. The first time she'd seen it, she'd thought what a fun place it would have been to take kids. Which was irrelevant for her, since that part of her life had ended before it ever got started. But right now she prayed the park hadn't been hosting one of their toddler play groups when the bomb had exploded.

The news had reported six dead and at least thirteen injured, but they hadn't offered many more details. The hospital was keeping media out and police weren't talking, other than to say they were contacting next of kin and working with the FBI to investigate. And typical of the people who chose to live in this remote Alaskan area, the residents weren't interested in their own fifteen minutes of fame.

It had been twelve hours since the bomb went off, but Keara parked down the street, not wanting to get in the way of investigators if any were still on scene. As she hurried toward the site on foot, she pulled up the collar on her lined raincoat, wishing she'd opted for something heavier. The temperatures were already dropping into the thirties, the sun casting an array of pinks and oranges across the sky as it settled behind the trees.

Her footsteps slowed as the park came into view and the sharp scent of smoke invaded her nostrils. The front of the building housing the public restrooms was blown out, a metal bench shredded to pieces, the once-green field charred black in places. But it was the blood-stain splotches on the ground, on the benches, even on the side of the building, that made her stomach flip-flop. Made memories rush forward that she ruthlessly pushed down.

The area was cordoned off, but she didn't see any evidence markers, suggesting all the obvious evidence had already been bagged up and taken to the lab. There was likely more searching to do. Bomb fragments could fly a long distance, into the woods behind the park or buried under the rubble of the building.

Keara scanned the park, her gaze moving quickly over the civilians on the outskirts of the scene. She was looking for an officer who would give her straight information about the status of the case. All she saw was one Luna officer she didn't know and another who didn't like anyone from Desparre PD after a debacle six months ago with one of her officers. She frowned, looking for friendlier faces, but she mostly saw FBI jackets, plus a handful of people covered from head to toe in white protective gear. Evidence technicians, probably more FBI. All of them flown up the four hundred plus miles from the FBI's Anchorage field office.

Movement off to her side caught her attention and

then an adorable black-and-tan dog plopped down at her feet, staring up at her expectantly. Behind the dog was a man with dark curly hair, perfectly smooth light brown skin and hypnotizing dark brown eyes. He had more than half a foot on her five-foot-six-inch frame, was probably a few years older than her thirty-five years and he wore an FBI coat.

"That's Patches," he told her, in a smooth, deep voice that would have put her instantly at ease if it hadn't made awareness clench her stomach. "And I'm Jax."

He tilted his head, and she had the distinct feeling he was cataloging everything about her.

She stood a little taller, feeling self-conscious in her civilian clothes—comfortable jeans with a warm sweatshirt under her jacket, and a pair of heavy-duty boots that could kick in a door.

"Did you know one of the victims?" he asked as Patches nudged her hand with a wet nose.

Keara smiled at the dog, petting her head as she told Jax, "No. Well, I don't know. Maybe." She cleared her throat, held out her hand. "Keara Hernandez. I'm the police chief in Desparre." She gestured vaguely in the direction of the mountain. "We're Luna's neighbors."

His eyes narrowed slightly, assessing her without any of the visible surprise she was used to from Alaskans when they heard about Desparre's female police chief. Then his big hand closed around hers, warm and vaguely unsettling. "Jax Diallo. Victim Specialist for the FBI. Patches here is a therapy dog."

"Therapy?" She looked down at Patches, who stared back at her calmly. "I assumed she was a bomb-sniffing dog."

"Nope. Patches and I are here to help the victims."

"Well, maybe you can give me some details, as a professional courtesy." She showed him her badge, just in case he thought she was lying, but he barely glanced at it. "I've got to answer to my citizens tomorrow. They want to know if they're safe."

"I can't really answer that, Keara." He drew out the *e* in her name slightly, *Kee-ra.* It was almost Southern, and it made her flash back to another case, another man, another time in her life entirely.

She'd been a brand-new patrol officer, assigned to partner up with a man who would eventually become her husband. Juan had frowned at her that first day, and although he hadn't said anything, she'd seen it all over his face. He didn't like being assigned to work with a woman.

Keara glanced away from Jax, not wanting him to see the emotions that were hard to keep off her face whenever she thought about Juan. But when she redirected her gaze to the right, all she saw was that blood.

It was a dark smear across the concrete, nothing like the thick, pooled mess that had surrounded Juan when she'd found him behind their house seven years ago. His eyes had been open, glassy, his cheek already cold to her touch.

"Keara?"

She jerked at the feel of Jax's hand on her elbow, the concerned tone of his voice. Shaking off the memory, she forced her gaze back to the Victim Specialist. "Is there someone I can talk to about the case?"

"Not right now. But I'm here if you want to talk about—"

"Sorry. I've got to go." Keara gave Patches one last pat, then spun back the way she'd come, suddenly uncaring that she'd driven all this way and hadn't gotten any answers. Because right now what she needed most was to get out of here.

Away from the bloodstains and the bomb remnants. Away from the unexpected memories.

Hopefully, the FBI would do their job fast. Hopefully, the people of Luna would get the answers they deserved about the person responsible for this bomb, the closure that would help them move on with their lives.

Without it, they could try to move on. She'd tried damn hard. She'd left behind everyone in her life and moved across the country, given up the job she'd dreamed of as a detective to become the police chief in a sleepy little town where she might spend six months of the year snowed in.

But she'd never actually found the peace she'd desperately searched for, the peace she'd almost convinced herself she'd achieved. Not if the sight of one smeared bloodstain could bring it all rushing back like this.

She'd never found her own closure. Not with her husband's killer still out there somewhere.

Chapter 2

Desparre's police chief walked away from him at a pace that looked purposeful, rather than desperate, the stomp of her boots echoing behind her.

Jax stared after her, intrigued. Even dressed down, she looked like someone who was used to being in charge. The dark hair she'd pulled back into a severe bun highlighted the sharp lines of her face, the thick eyebrows and exaggerated Cupid's bow of her lips. She looked like she had Mediterranean heritage, with perhaps a hint of Irish. It was hard to downplay beauty like hers, but she was obviously trying, with little to no makeup. Probably an attempt to get people to take her seriously. Women in law enforcement were the minority; women in high-level law-enforcement jobs even more so.

She was young for a police chief, although a place

like Desparre probably didn't get a lot of crime. It was the sort of town where people came to disappear. Usually, those people weren't dangerous. They were running from a tragedy in their lives or from someone who meant them harm. Hiding out in the vast Alaskan wilderness, in somewhere like Desparre, which rarely rated mention on a map, would be a good option.

Keara probably didn't see much crime of this scale. When a tiny town like Desparre—or Luna—faced a threat, they often didn't have the resources to handle it. Their police forces were small, too; their training often less than ideal.

But Alaska could be tough. With the constant threat of natural dangers, like blizzards or avalanches, frostbite or even wild animals, the people here learned to get tough, too, or get out, Jax had discovered.

Until six months ago Jax had lived in DC, working on the FBI's Rapid Deployment Team. Victim Specialists on that team worked a three-year term responding to mass casualties all over the country. When his time was up, Jax had been more than burnt out. Working as a private therapist for trauma victims had been intense in its own way, but it couldn't compare to the sheer volume of victims he could see in a single day, at a single site, with the FBI.

Moving to the Anchorage field office had felt like his chance to slow down. A chance to relax in Alaska's wild open spaces instead of DC's city center. He'd just finished training the puppy he'd found abandoned and scared, teaching her to work with victims. Coming to Alaska had felt like the right time to get her started as an official FBI dog.

He was the first Victim Specialist in the Anchorage

office. Although they'd been unsure what to do with him initially, that had changed fast, putting him and Patches in high demand. Still, he hadn't been to any mass casualty events in Alaska until today.

Shaking off his exhaustion, Jax turned away from Keara Hernandez's retreating form as two agents jogged his way.

Ben Nez was a couple of years older than Jax's thirty-eight, with years of experience working in Alaska, since he'd spent most of his FBI career here—and before that, a good chunk of his life. His partner, Anderson Lync, was four years younger than Jax, and the office's designated "FNG." As Ben had explained it the first time Jax heard the term, Anderson was the "effing new guy." Because even though Anderson had been at Anchorage six months longer than Jax, they only gave agents the FNG designation, not mere Victim Specialists.

"We've got seven dead," Ben announced without preamble.

Anderson knelt down and pet Patches, probably as much to comfort himself as to be friendly. The younger agent looked worn out, his normally perfectly styled blond hair sticking up, exhaustion leaving half-moons under his eyes.

"Six died at the scene, one more at the hospital," Ben continued, speaking rapid-fire like he'd been mainlining coffee all day.

Or maybe after more than a decade with the Bureau, an agent just gained the ability to set aside the horror and exhaustion and be fueled simply by the desire to find those responsible. Whether it was getting numb after seeing a huge volume of tragedy or knowing from experience that pushing through was the only way to find answers, Jax wasn't sure.

"Twelve others are being treated in the hospital, and some are critical. Given the location choice..." Ben paused to gesture around them meaningfully, and Jax realized how serene this park must have been before the bomb. "We're probably looking at an intended target—or maybe targets—rather than someone trying to create fear or make some kind of statement. We'll need to get a lot deeper in this investigation to be sure, though. What have you heard from the victims, Jax?"

"Not much about a possible motive." Besides Akna and her mom, he'd spoken to a pair of locals who'd come by to see for themselves if it was really true, the parents of a victim who'd already been transported to the hospital and a handful of people who'd been near the park when the bomb exploded. Then he'd fielded calls from various family members asking for updates on the case's progress and collected as many details as he could about the victims so he could follow up with them personally. "So far all I'm hearing is shock. No mention of anyone with enemies. But right now my focus is getting them help."

"What about the soccer game?" Ben asked, not sounding surprised.

Normally, when Jax got called to a scene, he'd go with the investigators to interview victims, not do it himself. But often information came out when victims or family members were talking to Jax about details they didn't think were important or had forgotten to mention to the agents. Sometimes, it was one of those small details that led them to the perpetrator.

"It was posted on some kind of online community

board." Jax repeated what Akna had told him. "Sounds pretty last-minute, but we can pull it up and check the time stamp."

"I already did," Anderson said, standing up, while Patches scooted over to Ben, and the veteran agent took his turn petting her.

What most agents didn't realize was that while the therapy dogs were there for the victims, they helped the investigators cope, too.

Anderson pulled out his phone and scrolled through notes, his lips moving silently until he finally said, "Eight a.m. About half an hour before the game started and an hour before the bomb went off."

"Not much time for someone to plant it if they were targeting one of the players," Ben mused. "Not to mention that not everyone who responded used their real names. Some of them are just screen names. Unfortunately, the guy who posted the idea about the game, Aiden DeMarco, died at the scene."

"But not all of the players were killed," Anderson said. "Maybe the bomber was going after one of the other people at the park. Or even someone who was supposed to be here, but left once they saw a game in progress."

Ben nodded slowly. "Or they'd been targeting one of the soccer players and they planted it quickly when they learned that person would be here this morning. That game drastically increased the number of people who were hurt or killed today."

"Was the bomb on a timer?" Jax asked. "Or did someone set it off remotely?"

"Looks like it was set off remotely," Ben replied. "Probably with a cell phone, but we'll know more after the lab techs get their hands on it. We sent it to the lab six hours ago. Hopefully, we'll have the answer tomorrow. In the meantime…" He stared meaningfully at Jax.

"You want me to come with you to the hospital? See if any of the victims saw anything?"

"The fresher it is in their minds, usually the better," Anderson said.

"No problem," Jax agreed, even though he knew that was only partially true. Sure, memories faded over time. But with trauma, the mind could block out pieces. Sometimes, those details only returned later.

He gave Patches an encouraging smile. "Want to go help some more people?"

Woof!

Ben jerked slightly at Patches's enthusiastic reply, but Anderson just smiled. "She handles this part of it better than any of us."

"Kind of," Jax replied, but Ben and Anderson were already heading toward the SUV.

The truth was, dogs were susceptible to depression from this kind of work, too. They needed breaks, just like people did. But there was no denying that Patches loved cheering people up. Right now she was staring at him expectantly, then glancing toward the SUV, knowing she had more work to do.

He smiled at her, then lifted his arm, directing it toward the vehicle. "Okay, Patches, let's go."

The hospital was going to be his next stop anyway. He ignored the growl of his stomach reminding him he hadn't eaten anything since the quick sandwich he'd grabbed four hours ago. He had hours left before his day would be over.

Hopefully, one of the victims at the hospital would

have answers that would get them closer to the bomber. Because if Anderson was right and the intended target of the bomb hadn't been on scene, would the bomber try again?

After seven long years alone, the memories shouldn't have been so close to the surface.

Keara stared into the whiskey she'd ordered hours ago, but had barely touched. The amber liquid reflected back a distorted version of the hand under her chin, a hand that had once worn a thin gold band, no diamond to get in the way on the job.

She hadn't had such a vivid flashback to Juan's murder in years. The bomb scene was nothing like her husband's murder. The thick jagged slice across her husband's neck, the blood pooled underneath him, the crickets chirping happily in the background. Her scream echoing through the tiny yard, making a neighbor call the police, because she was too traumatized to move. Too shocked to do her own job because she'd known with a single look that he was already gone. And she'd never even suspected there was a threat.

When the investigation began, she'd been told repeatedly to stay out of it. It was her husband, but it wasn't her case. She'd understood that, believed in her fellow detectives, believed Juan would get justice. But a year later the case had gone cold, the detectives insisting they'd done all they could, that they'd loved him, too. In that moment she'd known she couldn't stay. Not with the Houston PD, not in the life she and Juan had built together. Not if she wanted to be able to move forward.

It's over, Keara reminded herself, squeezing the whiskey glass but not lifting it to her lips. She'd made her choice when she moved to Alaska. Let go or drown in it. Those had been her options six years ago and she'd picked *let go.*

At least she thought she had.

Except here she was, failing to do her job because of the past. Pushing the whiskey away from her, Keara glanced around the old-fashioned bar on the outskirts of Luna. Between the claustrophobic closeness of the booths jammed together and the heater turned up to battle the chill that slid underneath the ill-fitting door, the air was stuffy and beer-scented. She'd chosen it because she'd wanted to be alone in a room full of people, rather than truly alone in her vehicle and then her house.

Although it was nearly twice the size of tiny Desparre—in terms of population, if not geography—there weren't many options late at night in Luna. She'd hoped a quiet booth and a short glass of whiskey would calm her nerves. Instead, she'd choked on the only sip of whiskey she'd taken. And there was nothing quiet about this bar.

Since moving to Alaska, she'd become a loner. It was a trait many of her citizens shared, for myriad reasons. For her, it was partly because of her job. A chief of police didn't fraternize with colleagues or civilians too much. Especially not a female chief of police who was new to Alaska and wanted to be taken seriously.

The rest of it, of course, was Juan. Although people in Desparre usually let you keep your secrets—because they often had their own they didn't want to open up about—real friendship dictated honesty. After living here for six years, Keara still wasn't sure if she was ready for honesty.

Now she glanced around the bar, wondering if all

the small decisions she'd made to isolate herself had brought her right back to where she'd started. Sinking into grief.

She needed to go home. But there was something vaguely calming about having people around her, people she didn't know, who mostly left her alone. The bar was closer to Luna's lone hotel than it was to downtown. She didn't recognize anyone, and the snippets of conversation that reached her said most of these people were outsiders.

There was a group of guys in jeans and T-shirts who'd been drinking since before she'd walked through the door and already hit on her more than once. A loner at the bar drinking soda water and eyeing the hard stuff. And a couple at the other end of the bar who'd jammed their stools as close together as possible while they flirted. She'd bet a week's pay that none of them had been in Alaska longer than a few days.

Still, they weren't immune to what was happening here. In between lewd jokes from the group of drinkers, the alcohol-tainted conversation beside her would shift to the bombing.

"I heard a couple more died in the hospital."

"No one else died, man. But I think one of them had to have a leg amputated because it was blown mostly off in the explosion."

"Someone was trying to kill one of those soccer players."

"Nah, this is terrorism. You'll see. They'll start hitting bigger parks next, take out more people."

Only the two men hunkered down near the door sharing a couple of pints looked like locals. One of them periodically patted his friend's shoulder awkwardly and glared at the out-of-towners. The guy getting the sympathy had red-rimmed eyes, ruddy cheeks and a knocked-over pile of shot glasses beside him.

She'd recognized the look as soon as she walked into the bar and chosen a seat on the opposite end of the place. Against the wall, where she could see everyone, but she tried to avoid glancing their way. One of them had lost someone they loved tonight. Keara couldn't bear to hear about it.

She dragged her gaze away from him and tried to focus on what she needed to do next. It was after eleven, well past the time when the Luna Police Department shut down for the night. But after the bombing—even with the FBI on the case—maybe someone would still be there. She could stop by on her way home, hopefully get some real answers she could share with her officers, with her town.

Setting aside her whiskey, Keara stood. She wasn't ready to face the drive up and down the mountain, or the emptiness of her house that she knew would feel more lonely than usual tonight. But she was still the chief of police. And she had people who needed answers.

"Hey, at least there's only six dead," one of the guys at the rowdy table slurred. "Could have been way worse."

Before Keara could maneuver free of her booth, the big guy who'd lost someone he loved was up and screaming.

Then he was diving across the small bar, leading with fists and grief. His punch landed, sending the guy who'd spoken to the floor. Then the guy's friends jumped on his attacker, and suddenly, everyone seemed to be in the fray. Even the loner at the counter grabbed an abandoned beer bottle off the bar and chucked it. The way he swayed violently when he did it told her that although he'd been drinking soda water since she'd arrived, he'd imbibed plenty of alcohol beforehand.

Only the couple near the door leaped up and ran out of the bar, away from the fight.

The bartender reached under the counter and Keara knew what was coming. She tried to get ahead of it, holding up her badge and screaming, "Police. Stop!"

But the bartender was quick, yanking his shotgun up and over the top of the bar, racking it loudly.

Keara heard it and flinched, but no one else paid any attention, not even when the bartender yelled, "Stop it or I'll shoot!"

"Sir, put the shotgun away!" Keara yelled at him, but the bar had gotten louder.

One of the men in the group closest to her spotted her badge and yelled, "Cop!"

Then the group was shifting, a furious mob coming for her fast.

She backed up, trying to protect her weapon as she pulled out her mace and sprayed it across the group. The noxious fumes spilled back toward her, clogging her throat and making her eyes water.

The group kept coming, too drunk or unthinking.

Keara backed up another step, but then her back slammed into something protruding from the wall and there was nowhere left to go. The four men who'd been hitting on her were rushing her from one direction. The two men who'd been grieving got in the mix, too, still going for the drunken group.

She was about to get overrun by them all.

Chapter 3

Twelve hospital rooms, filled with pain and fear and disbelief. Twelve victims, trying to recover from burns and deep cuts and in one case, an amputation. Twelve families, furious and scared and feeling helpless.

Jax and Patches had visited them all this evening. Some as briefly as five minutes, when the victims or the family didn't have the energy or inclination to talk to the FBI. Others as long as half an hour, the longest the agents would allow since they wanted to talk to everyone before the night ended.

Jax glanced at the base of his bed back at his hotel, where Patches had the right idea. Her tongue lolled slightly out of her mouth, her feet periodically twitching in her sleep. As soon as they'd returned to the hotel, she'd hopped up into bed and fallen fast asleep.

He needed to do the same. But despite being emotionally worn out, he was still hungry, since he hadn't ever found time for dinner. Part of him was still amped up, feeling the pressure from all directions. A need to help the victims and families move forward. A need to help the investigators get information to find the person responsible.

Slipping quietly out of the hotel room, he slid on his coat and trudged down the stairs. The hotel didn't have its own restaurant, and as far as he could tell, the only thing nearby that was open was a bar. He didn't want a drink, but maybe they'd have food. At this point he'd settle for peanuts.

He zipped his coat up to his chin and huddled low in it. Springtime in Alaska was beautiful, but it wasn't warm.

On his way out, he waved to Ben and Anderson, who were still slumped in the lobby chairs, trading case notes.

"Where to?" Ben asked, raising an eyebrow when Jax answered, "Bar down the road."

Jax looked them over, in the same spot he'd left them after they'd returned from the hospital. "Did you two ever eat dinner?"

"Power bars," Anderson said. Without looking up from his phone, he tossed one to Jax. "I always travel with them."

"Thanks." The protein-heavy power bar was probably better than anything he'd get in the bar, and Jax hesitated, debating returning to his room. But he was too antsy to sleep and although he liked Ben and Anderson, he needed a break from the case. "See you later."

When he stepped through the door out into the frigid Alaskan air, Jax knew it was what he needed. A walk

probably would have been better than the bar, but he
didn't know the area and he didn't want to get lost or
run into a wild animal. So instead, he walked quickly
toward the log-cabin-style establishment. The walk was
long enough to make his nose and ears sting from the
cold, but not long enough to clear his head.

He heard it when he was fifteen feet away. Yelling
and crashing sounds. Probably a fight, definitely too
many people involved.

Then a couple holding hands darted out of the bar
and ran toward him.

"What's happening?" he asked.

"People are mad and drinking," the woman said, only
pausing briefly as they continued past him, toward the
hotel. "It turned into a big fight. I wouldn't go in there."

Yanking out his cell phone, he texted Ben and Anderson a message.

Bar fight. Call the Luna police? Or earn your community badges today...

A bar fight was a local PD problem, not the pur-
view of the FBI. But the agents were close and Luna
police had a lot to manage right now. Jax didn't know
which option Ben and Anderson would choose. But he
figured doubling up couldn't hurt. He'd just started to
dial the Luna police chief directly when a female voice
cut through the yelling. A voice he recognized, slightly
husky and naturally commanding. But right now underlaid with definite panic.

Dropping his phone into his pocket, Jax raced inside.

Five angry and obviously drunk men were crowded
near the side wall, some of them holding beer bottles

aloft like weapons. All of them were yelling, most of it incoherent, but what Jax could make out were a mix of violent threats and juvenile insults. Two were facing off against each other, shifting back and forth, glowering.

A sixth was passed out half on a table, half on the floor, and looked like he needed stitches. A seventh stood near the bar, holding his own beer bottle and watching the spectacle with a wide grin. The bartender stood behind him, brandishing a shotgun but looking uncertain.

Where was Keara?

Jax strained to see, then realized. She was behind the pack of men, ordering them to back up. From the way his eyes started watering and his throat was suddenly on fire as he took one step farther inside and the door slammed shut behind him, he realized she'd sprayed them with mace. It seemed to have only made them angrier.

Fear tightened his chest, knowing she was trapped behind the angry group. Could he wade into them, give Keara a chance to slide free?

He rejected the idea immediately. There were too many of them, fueled by alcohol and fury, likely to take any physical contact as an invitation to resume fighting.

Still, he had to do something. The two who'd been circling each other had turned toward Keara, and from the way they shared a sudden look of agreement, they were about to rush her.

Jax wasn't armed. Even if he was, it probably wouldn't help, based on the bartender's worried shake of his head.

"I already called the police," the bartender yelled at him. "If I fire this now, it might go through those guys and hit the lady back there. She's in trouble."

Jax swore and looked around for something he could

use as a weapon, even though he knew it was useless. What he needed was Ben and Anderson, a way to even the numbers.

Leaping on top of the bar, Jax bellowed, "FBI!"

As one, the group turned toward him, but they only lowered their fists and bottles for a split second. Then they were up again, and the group was turning back toward each other.

Faster than he would have thought possible, while the men were distracted, Keara slid along the wall, breaking free of the group. She had her pistol out and leveled at the man who seemed to be the primary instigator.

"I'm chief of police in Desparre!" she yelled. "And the man on the bar is with the FBI. Put the bottles down and back away right now!"

For a moment it seemed like it might work.

Then the big guy in front swayed a little and yelled back, "You can't get us all, bi—"

"People died today!" Jax cut him off as Keara took a slow step backward, closer to him.

They froze, their attention redirecting his way. "We're searching for a *bomber* right now! You really want to end up in jail for threatening a police chief?"

Two of the men shook their heads, set down their bottles and stepped away from the group, holding up their hands.

Two of the others hesitated, their bottles lowering slightly.

But the big guy in front flushed an even deeper, patchy red and announced, "You're not FBI! You're not even armed!"

A flash of movement below Jax caught his attention. Too fast for Jax to move out of the way, the loner who'd been watching with glee grabbed hold of his leg and yanked hard.

Jax flung out his arms, trying to brace himself, hoping his head wouldn't smack the top of the bar as he crashed downward, sliding awkwardly, painfully, off it. Broken glass sliced through his arms, and his back scraped the edge of the bar as his legs slammed into the bar stools, knocking them over.

Then he was on the ground, trying to catch his breath and focus through the pain in his head, and a bottle was crashing toward his face.

Knowing it wouldn't be fast enough, he tried to roll away.

The guy over him suddenly stiffened, his eyes going unnaturally wide. Then he toppled over, the bottle crashing down inches from Jax's face and luckily not shattering.

Behind him, Keara had her gun trained on the group who'd frozen again, and her other arm directed his way, wires extending from the Taser in her hand to the guy on the ground beside him, still stiff and moaning.

Then the door burst open and Ben and Anderson were there, weapons out, yelling, "FBI!"

As they rushed into the room, giving Keara an approving nod, Ben glanced down at him with a mix of concern and amusement.

"You've got to stop playing agent, Jax."

She'd gotten lucky.

Although no officer was immune to the danger of being caught alone and outnumbered, at least in Houston, backup tended to be relatively close. You might get caught in a dangerous situation—and it wasn't uncommon—but you'd probably be in the thick of it with other officers. In Alaska, the danger was far less persistent. But you were way more likely to be caught alone. The distance it could take the closest officer to come to your aid could be deadly even if you held off the threat for a long time.

Keara had been reaching the end of that time when Jax had walked into the bar.

She glanced at him now, sitting across from her on a couch in the lobby of the hotel down the street from the bar. He was grimacing in a T-shirt, his bloodied sweater in a bundle next to him along with his coat, as one of the agents—a tall, lean blond guy who'd introduced himself as Anderson—wrapped his arms with gauze.

"There's no glass left behind," Anderson said. "I was SWAT for a while in DC, so I had to get some basic medical training, but you still might want to go back to the hospital. Most of these cuts will close up, but this one—" he pointed at the last, deepest cut he'd bandaged "—might scar unless you get it stitched."

"I'm fine," Jax said tightly.

"Yeah, I get it. I wouldn't want to go back there, either," Anderson said. "That was a rough evening, talking to all those victims. Especially the one who lost her leg, whose fiancé died in the blast. I don't know how—"

"You should have stayed outside," Ben cut his partner off. "You keep forgetting—you're not an agent." He glanced at Keara, eyes narrowing as he studied her. "Was this all drunken, overemotional idiocy or did you hear anything we might want to know for our investigation?"

She didn't have to glance at Jax to feel his embarrassment, but the truth was, she'd needed him tonight.

Law enforcement or not, his presence—and presence of mind—had definitely saved her from getting hurt. Maybe even from getting killed.

"Idiocy," she confirmed, trying not to cringe as she subtly probed her lower back with her fingers. Between the time she'd maced the group and Jax had arrived, she'd been shoved into the wall, right where some kind of decoration hung. The bruise ached with every quick movement.

"And grief," she added, remembering the man who'd burst into tears when Luna police arrived and cuffed the whole lot to escort them to cells. His younger sister had died in the explosion.

Her hand shook as she stopped pushing on the bruise and it wasn't all from pain. The bruise was nasty, but she didn't need medical care, just time to heal. It was also adrenaline, still pumping as if she hadn't left that bar. As if she hadn't gotten away from the crowd of men towering over her with bottles and fists and anger they were willing to redirect at the nearest available target. Especially one who'd just sprayed them all with mace.

With six years on the police force in a big city like Houston—five of them on patrol—Keara had faced plenty of dicey situations. Most of them with a partner at her back, but a few alone. Back then she'd lived with a different level of awareness at all times.

In Alaska, she'd gotten used to needing to be wary of the elements more often than the people. She should have positioned herself near the door. Should have ignored her emotional desire to avoid the grief-stricken man there and picked a spot near the exit. She still might have been overrun, but she probably could have gotten to a safe distance to pull her weapon sooner. Maybe stopped the brawl faster, without anyone getting hurt.

"So Keara," Ben said as Anderson finished patching up Jax, "you were at the scene a few hours ago."

When he stared at her assessingly, as if waiting for her to confirm what he already knew, she nodded.

"Did you notice anything unusual? Anyone hanging around who seemed off?"

Ben didn't need to clarify as all three of them stared at her, waiting for an answer.

At the scene of a bombing, in a small town full of people who liked their business to be their business, it would be easy to slip into the edges of a group. Pretend to be sympathizing. Pretend to be there out of safety concerns or empathy for neighbors, while actually reveling in your handiwork.

Police officers—especially someone like her, who'd spent years on patrol in a busy city—learned to spot the outliers. People who were trying to blend in, but were just a little too focused. On the woman alone, walking in front of them. Or the fire blazing in a building, origins unknown. Or the devastation of an attack, like a bombing.

Keara mentally reviewed the people she'd noticed at the edges of the scene, near the hastily assembled memorial made of candles and flowers and stuffed animals, or down the street, pointing and shaking their heads. Everyone had looked the way she'd felt. Shocked. Horrified. Like a veneer of safety had just been ripped away, revealing a vulnerability they'd never expected.

She shook her head. "I don't think so. I don't know everyone here. Not even close. But many of the people on scene I recognized at least vaguely. If the bomber was there, he's a good actor."

"Or she," Anderson put in.

Keara shrugged, acknowledging that truth, although as far as she knew, bombers were more likely to be male. Running murder investigations in Houston had told her that men liked to kill violently: strangulation, bullet wounds, stabbing. Women were less likely to murder in the first place, but more likely to use arson or poison. And they were more likely to kill a single person; men were significantly more likely to kill multiples or commit mass murders. Of course, those were generalizations. Bombings weren't something she'd ever investigated.

"What about this?" Ben asked, sounding like he already expected the answer to be negative. "This is a bomb fragment. Does the symbol on it look familiar? Does it mean anything to you?" He held out his phone, zoomed in so she could see the detail, the series of interconnecting loops.

Distantly, she felt Jax leap up and grab her arm as she swayed. She heard Anderson's surprised "You know it?"

But she couldn't focus enough to answer. The lobby around her spun in dizzying circles as her whole body seemed to catch fire and her lungs couldn't get enough oxygen.

She'd seen that symbol once before, seven years ago. On the wall at a murder scene in one of Juan's last investigations before he was killed.

Chapter 4

Could their bomber be connected to a case Keara's husband had investigated seven years ago?

Jax's heart thudded too hard as he watched Keara, her olive-toned skin too pale, a sudden tightness around her eyes and mouth. The knowledge that she was a widow surprised him, filled him with sadness for what she'd experienced, along with a tinge of jealousy. Ridiculous and inappropriate, but he was self-aware enough to recognize why. He'd been instantly intrigued by her, attracted to her. Seeing her in trouble in the bar, then seeing her in action, had only increased those feelings.

None of that mattered. Not when she was staring back at them, trying to get it together after she'd announced that her dead husband had investigated a case with the same symbol. Not when she might have the key to the investigation.

Ben and Anderson were staring at her, too. Ben's fingers tapped a frantic beat against his chair and Anderson was leaning toward her, hanging half out of his seat. But both of them were experienced enough not to rush her.

Finally, her fingers loosened the death grip they'd had on the couch since he'd helped her sit. "I haven't seen that symbol in seven years."

"Are you sure it's the same symbol?" Ben asked.

She held out her hand for his phone, then zoomed in and stared at it a long moment. "I'm pretty sure. It might not be exact, but it's close enough to look connected."

"Tell us about this case," Anderson requested.

"It was a murder," she said and some of the intense energy radiating from Ben and Anderson instantly deflated.

Jax had been part of enough investigations—even though he was on the periphery—to know why. A murder was pretty different from a bombing.

"The victim, Celia Harris, was fairly well-known in Houston. She owned a popular chain of bakeries and was always volunteering her time to local charity events. The press picked up news of her murder fast, maybe because she had two young kids and was killed in a back alley in a bad part of town. Probably also because the murder was violent. That symbol was spray-painted on the wall behind her. I didn't work the case, but I know Juan and his partner suspected it was going to be the start of a series of killings."

"They thought it was a serial killer?" Ben asked. "Why?"

"None of the obvious suspects panned out. There were signs Celia had been abducted and probably not by someone she knew. They thought the symbol was a serial killer's signature."

Anderson scooted back in his seat, looking less anxious the more Keara spoke. "But..."

"But there were no more killings that matched. They never saw the symbol again. Well, Juan's partner didn't. Juan died a few weeks into the investigation."

Jax didn't ask the question he most wanted to know the answer to right now: What had happened to her husband?

Instead, he glanced from Ben to Anderson. He knew them well enough to recognize their waning interest. They didn't think this was connected. But the symbol was unusual, an odd series of interconnecting loops that he'd heard the agents say earlier didn't mean anything they could identify.

"Any idea what the symbol means?" Jax asked Keara.

She shrugged. "Juan and his partner thought it was the killer's own design."

"How sure were they that the killer actually drew the symbol? Couldn't it have been spray-painted before the murder happened?"

Keara shrugged, suddenly looking exhausted. "I didn't ask for particulars. I just knew they'd determined it was put there by the killer. You can contact the Houston PD for more details. Juan's partner is still there, as far as I know. I don't keep in close touch with the department, but I don't think the murder was ever solved."

Ben nodded and Anderson wrote down the contact information for Juan's partner, but Jax didn't need to ask to know it was low on their list of priorities. They'd follow up—they were both good agents—but despite the strange symbol, they didn't think it was connected.

And he understood why. The symbol was too generic, the crimes too different. Besides, there were too many variables. They couldn't even be sure the murderer in Keara's husband's case had been the one to draw the symbol. Alleyways were often filled with random graffiti, especially in a big city like Houston.

Keara stood, flinching in a way that told him that he wasn't the only one who'd left that bar with injuries. The closed-off expression on her face said she wouldn't welcome him asking about it, so instead he asked, "Are you okay to drive home? Desparre isn't exactly close."

"Out here, it's about as close as you get," she replied, her chin tilting up just slightly. "Thanks for the help," she added, her gaze sweeping the three of them, lingering briefly on him before she headed for the door.

"The symbol is unusual," Jax said once she'd left the hotel and it was just him and the agents in the brightly lit lobby.

"It's not connected," Ben said, rubbing a hand across his eyes.

"I'll call the partner and follow up anyway," Anderson added, "but Ben is right. It's strange, but coincidences happen."

"I don't know—"

"Jax, you want to talk to her about this more? Be my guest," Ben said, glancing at his watch and standing. "But you know as well as we do that it's unlikely there's a solid link here. Yeah, the symbol is odd, but it's not particularly unique. And we can't even be sure the killer in her husband's case is the one who drew it. She said it was spray-painted on an alley wall. Could have been some random tagger practicing. Our symbol was literally on the bomb fragment. That's pretty different."

"Maybe, but—"

"An alley in downtown Houston at a murder site. And a bomb fragment in the middle of nowhere, Alaska. A single murder and a bombing that's already killed seven and injured at least twelve more. You've got the psychology background, so you tell me: How likely is it that a violent murderer turned into a bomber?"

"Not very," Jax agreed, trying not to be distracted by the way his arms stung, the way his back and legs and head throbbed. The two aspirin he'd gotten from the hotel desk hadn't done much to ease the pain.

From the type of murder Keara had described, the killer had wanted to get up close. He thrived on the brutality, on causing someone else to suffer, on watching that suffering up close and personal. He'd probably loved the attention, the big press coverage in a big city. A bomber was a different personality type. Someone who *didn't* want to be hands-on for the actual kill. Someone who wanted to see more destruction, but choosing a place so far off the map meant maybe he wasn't looking for the intensity of news coverage.

"Still…"

"What?" Anderson prompted when Jax went silent.

Jax's specialty was working with trauma victims, helping them reclaim control over their emotions and their lives. He'd spent time analyzing the motives behind the perpetrators, but only if it was in service of the survivors.

But the more time he'd spent working for the FBI, the more he'd realized that the specialty translated. And not just as a Victim Specialist, but also in providing real insight into the way the perpetrators thought.

He didn't know enough about the case Keara's husband had investigated to be able to say if it was connected or not. But something about it kept nudging his brain.

"The symbol was on the bomb fragment," Jax said. "That means it's important. But maybe the bomber didn't expect it to survive the blast. Maybe he drew it for himself."

"Maybe," Ben agreed.

"So maybe he never expected it to be connected to a seven-year-old murder."

"Is there any news on the Luna bombing?" Tate Emory, an officer she'd brought on to the Desparre PD just over five years ago, leaned his head into her office.

Tate was one of her most easygoing officers, with a calm under pressure none of her veterans had expected. Of course, they only knew Tate's cover story, believed he'd been a true rookie when he joined the force. But Keara knew he'd been a police officer before hiding away in this remote Alaskan town. Because she'd kept his secret, he was one of the only people here who knew anything about her past.

Still, she wasn't about to share the possible connection to one of her husband's cases. Not when the FBI had grown less and less interested the longer she'd spoken. Not when the light of day was bringing her own doubts.

Last night she'd been so certain. This morning, back at work in Desparre and fielding calls from concerned citizens about their neighboring town, she wondered if she was wrong.

It had been seven years since she'd seen that symbol. Yes, years on the force had enhanced her skills of observation and memory. But maybe it wasn't the same. Even she had to admit it didn't look like much beyond doo-dling. Or maybe both a murderer and a bomber had seen the same symbol somewhere and used it themselves.

"The FBI is managing the investigation." She told Tate what he'd surely already seen on the news. "I couldn't get anything useful out of them."

An image of Jax, crashing down from the top of that bar after he'd tried to help her, filled her mind. There was something compelling about him. And it was more than the tall, dark and handsome thing he had going for him, or the adorable dog who followed him around.

It was the eyes, she realized. The way they'd fixed on her, given her one hundred percent of his attention. A psychologist's trick, surely, but it had felt personal.

"They have no suspects?"

Keara shook off thoughts of Jax and focused on Tate. The officer was only a few years younger than her own thirty-five, but the way he carried himself made him seem like he'd seen a lot over those years.

"If they do, they didn't share the details with me." She thought about the exhaustion on the two agents' faces in the lobby of the Luna hotel last night, going over evidence after a full day at a bomb site. "I think they're struggling to figure out a motive."

"That was a big blast. Seems like it was someone who had experience making bombs," Tate said. "Then again, these days any criminal-minded sociopath can find a recipe to make a bomb on the internet."

Keara nodded, her gaze moving to the open door of her office. Resisting the urge to ask him if he'd dealt with bombings in his previous job, she said, "I got cards from several FBI agents and their Victim Specialist. I'll stay in contact."

"Sounds good."

As Tate turned back for the bullpen, Keara said, "Close the door behind you, please."

Once she was alone, she dialed a number she hadn't called since she'd moved to Alaska. For all she knew, he'd changed it. A small part of her—the part that really did want to leave the past behind her—hoped he had changed it.

"Fitz," he answered on the first ring, his voice a deep grumble created by years of smoking and drinking.

The familiar voice instantly took her back to the swampy summers in Houston, to responding to a dangerous call one last time with Juan before he took the promotion to detective and partnered up with veteran Leroy Fitzgerald. Leaving her to work with a rookie for a year, before she made the jump to detective herself. But by then, they were engaged and rules prohibited them from working together anymore.

"You talk or I hang up," Fitz snapped.

"It's Keara Hernandez," she blurted, relieved when her voice sounded only slightly strained.

She and Fitz had never gotten along. She'd tolerated him because he was Juan's partner and a partner's trust on the force could be the difference between life and death. He'd tolerated her for the same reason.

"Keara."

His voice softened in a way she'd only come to know after Juan had died, when Fitz had been sidelined like her, and two other detectives were assigned to investigate. Unlike her, Fitz had been allowed to stay close to the investigation, even tag along at the end.

"How's Alaska?"

His voice was neutral, but she'd always suspected

he was glad when she left Houston. When she stopped hassling him and everyone else for details on her husband's case. When she'd stopped making all of them feel guilty for failing, no matter how hard they'd tried. She'd been the final holdout, the last person to accept the case would never be solved.

If the sudden pain burning its way up her chest was any indication, she'd never truly accepted it. She'd only run from it.

"Peaceful, mostly." She got right to business, not wanting to hear about life on the force she'd left behind—assuming he was still on the force. "I'm calling because there's a case up here with a symbol that I think matches the one from that murder you and Juan caught at the end. The one you thought was a serial?" She was purposely vague about the Alaskan case, phrasing it in a way that wouldn't be lying if she had to admit it wasn't her case at all, but hopefully not inviting questions.

"Really?" He sounded surprised, but only vaguely interested. "Another murder?"

"Not exactly. Could you fax me the details? I want to see if my memory is as good as I think it is. See if the symbol really is the same."

There was a pause long enough to make Keara silently swear, before Fitz asked slowly, "I'm guessing since you called me on my personal line that this is an unofficial request?"

"Yes."

"Is this about Juan?"

The pain that had been creeping up her chest clamped down hard. "Why? What do you mean?"

"Nothing. I just… I figured if I ever heard from you again, it would be because you'd finally started investigating Juan's death on your own." He let out a forced laugh. "You always were dogged. Kind of a rule-breaker."

It was a much more polite version of what she'd overheard some of her colleagues in Texas saying about her when she'd been a patrol officer, even after she'd become a detective. They were traits she'd tried hard to tame when she'd come to Alaska.

Follow the rules, for the most part. Definitely not date anyone within her ranks. She'd barely befriended them, determined to keep her distance. Not just to maintain her authority, but also to protect herself. Being a police officer was a dangerous profession, even in a quiet little town like Desparre. The officers here had become her responsibility and she took that seriously. If someone died on her watch, she needed to be able to stay removed enough to do what had to be done, to keep the rest of the team going.

Of course it was important to be persistent, to chase down the truth no matter what. But there was also value in learning when to let go.

It was something she thought she'd succeeded in.

"Is there some reason to think Celia Harris's murder was connected to Juan's death?" she asked tightly. If there was, they'd all kept it from her back then.

"No," Fitz replied.

"Are you sure?" she demanded, suddenly certain he was keeping something from her.

"Yeah, I'm sure. As sure as I can be. I mean, we don't know who the hell took Juan out. Just because Juan's case went cold six years ago doesn't mean we all gave up on it."

It was only the hurt underneath the anger in Fitz's

voice that kept Keara from snapping at him. When the case had officially gone cold, she'd done the only thing she could do to survive it. She'd tried to shut down that part of her life entirely, remove herself from any reminders that she'd ever been married, that she'd ever faced such a loss. And she'd done it in spectacular fashion, by running as far away as she could.

"Have you found anything?" she demanded, anger seeping into her own voice. Whatever Fitz thought of her decision to leave Houston, she was still Juan's wife. She still deserved answers.

"No."

In that single word, she heard all of the defeat she'd felt six years ago, when the chief had officially called off the active investigation, told the detectives on Juan's case they had to move on.

Closing her eyes, Keara let out a long breath, trying to regain her composure. "Tell me about Celia Harris's murder, then. Please. You never found any likely suspects, did you?"

"Well…"

Her eyes popped back open. "Who?"

"Your husband went to talk to someone whose car was near the scene of the murder. A hospital orderly with some minor criminal history named Rodney Brown."

A mix of dread and anger made her pulse speed up. "You remember the name all these years later? Why?"

"Juan talked to the guy on kind of a long-shot lead. I didn't go with him. He said it didn't look like anything, but that Rodney kept insisting the whole thing was a mistake. That he hadn't taken his car out at all. It struck Juan as a little weird, but he thought maybe

Rodney was just nervous about being interviewed by a police officer. I wouldn't have thought anything of it, either, except Rodney disappeared a few weeks later."

Keara let the timeline sink in and her anger intensified. "A few weeks later. So you're telling me this guy disappeared right after Juan was killed?"

"We looked into it," Fitz insisted. "We couldn't find any evidence that he was involved in Juan's murder."

"You couldn't find any because it didn't look like he'd done it or because he disappeared and you couldn't find him?"

When Fitz didn't immediately respond, Keara jumped to her feet. Through the glass walls of her office, she saw some of her officers staring at her with curiosity and concern.

She turned her back on them, knowing there was no way she could hide the horror she felt. "You think it was him."

"I did," Fitz said quietly. "But no one else agreed, Keara. And seven years later I wonder if I was just reaching for anything. For anyone I could blame. He was my partner. It eats me up every day that we couldn't solve his murder."

"Why the hell didn't you tell me?"

"What would you have done?"

Investigated on her own. She would have done whatever it took to find Rodney Brown and figure out if he'd killed her husband.

"That's why I didn't tell you," Fitz said, without her saying a word. "Because we chased that lead as far as we could. It was a dead end. And…" He let out a heavy sigh. "You deserved to move on. Juan would have wanted that."

Keara grit her teeth, trying to hold back the tears suddenly threatening. "Just send me the file, Fitz."

She hung up before he could say anything else, then planted her hands on her credenza for stability. Seven years. Someone who might have killed Juan had had seven long years to run. Seven long years for the trail to go cold.

Was it possible he'd shown up here, stepped up the volume of his kills by becoming a bomber?

Chapter 5

"Does this symbol look familiar to you?" Jax held up the digitally enhanced image that had been found on a bomb fragment.

Gabi Sinclair winced as she hauled herself up higher against the headboard of the hospital bed. Her sheet slid downward and she immediately hiked it up, avoiding looking at the leg that had been amputated below the knee yesterday. Her light brown skin was tinged with an ashy gray, her eyes bloodshot.

When Jax had met her last night, she hadn't been able to stop crying about the fiancé who'd died in the blast. Today she was all gritted teeth and desperate determination, wanting any information she could get about the investigation. A mix of numbness and anger that would only last so long before the grief bled through again.

Hopefully, when that happened, he'd be able to help her.

She stared at the symbol intently for a long minute, her free hand dropping down beside the bed to pet Patches, who'd been patiently waiting. Finally, she shook her head. "I don't know it. What is it?"

From slightly behind him, Jax sensed Ben and Anderson's disappointment, heard their suit coats slumping against the rough hospital wall. They'd taken the lead today, but asked him along to make the victims and their families feel more comfortable. The more rooms they visited, the more questions Jax asked. Technically, it was the agents' job to ask about the symbol, but for some of the victims, he suspected it would be easier to talk to him.

Gabi was their final hospital visit. None of the victims they'd spoken to had recognized the symbol.

"This was drawn on one of the bomb fragments," Anderson spoke up, stepping forward in the tight space. "We don't know what it means. It might be nothing. But we're checking everything."

Gabi frowned slightly, directing her gaze at Patches, who scooted closer to the bed and made the tiniest smile quiver at the corner of Gabi's lips.

"When we have some answers, we'll tell you what we can," Jax said, not wanting to overpromise what he might not be able to deliver, but also wanting to help start the healing process. If Gabi felt like she was cut off from real information, it would only increase the helplessness she felt.

She nodded at him, her hand stalling against Patches's head, her brow furrowed like she was trying to puzzle it out, too.

Despite research done by Ben and Anderson—and some curiosity searching Jax had done himself on publicly available sites—none of them understood it.

They'd found symbols that were similar, but nothing close enough and so far, nothing else tied to a crime like this. If the bomber had been trying to send a message with the symbol, it appeared to be one only he understood.

Maybe the case Keara's husband had investigated would provide the break they needed. When Jax had pressed him on it that morning, Anderson said he was waiting for a call back from the Houston detective.

"Is there anything else you can remember from yesterday morning?" Ben asked, stepping up next to Jax, crowding him just slightly, like he wanted Jax to step back.

Gabi glanced from him to Ben, then shook her head. "Not really. Carter and I were just going for a walk." Her voice trembled on her fiancé's name, then she cleared her throat and kept going. "We'd stopped to sit on the bench for a few minutes when it happened."

"And you didn't notice anyone behaving strangely?" Ben asked. "No one leaving the park or staring at it from a distance?"

The FBI had gotten news back from the lab that morning that the bomb had been set off remotely. That made it more likely the bomber had been nearby, watching for the exact moment he wanted it to detonate.

Gabi shook her head quickly, but she'd answered these questions before.

"Thanks, Gabi," Jax said. "I know this isn't easy. But if you think of anything—even if you're not sure it matters—you can call any of us. And if you need to talk, I'm just a phone call away, day or night. You know Patches is always excited to come and see you."

Beside her bed, Patches let out an affirmative *woof!*

Gabi startled at the sudden noise, then gave his dog a tiny smile.

Anderson shot him a look, but Jax ignored it. Technically, telling a victim they could call in the middle of the night was dangerous territory. He'd known Victim Specialists who'd fallen into roles halfway between personal therapist and best friend by being too available. But he worried more about not helping enough than being overwhelmed by a victim's needs.

As Jax and Patches started to follow the agents out of the room, Gabi's voice, more tentative than before, reached him.

"You're going to catch the person who did this, right?"

"That's why we're here," he assured her. "The FBI brought us in all the way from Anchorage because Agents Nez and Lync, and their colleagues, have a lot of experience. This case is the only thing they're investigating right now. It's our biggest priority."

"That's not an answer," she said, more grief than anger in her words.

He nodded soberly. "I'm not going to make you a promise I can't guarantee. But I'll tell you this—we're putting everything we have into this investigation. And when it comes to finding bombers, the FBI is *very* good. I'd bet on us."

He stepped a little closer, wanting her to read on his face how much he believed it. "I can also promise to I'll keep you informed. I believe we'll get this person. You let us worry about that. You focus on getting better. Deal?"

She swiped a hand across her face, wiping away a rush of tears he pretended not to see. "Okay."

He gave her an encouraging smile, then followed Ben and Anderson into the hall.

It wasn't until they were outside the hospital that Ben halted suddenly, turning to face him and making Patches stop short. "You want to act like these victims' personal therapist, that's your business. I know you're good at your job, so I'm not going to question your methods. But Anderson and I know what we're doing, too. So let us do our jobs."

Jax put his hands up, pasted an innocent look on his face.

"We asked you to come along because it makes the victims more comfortable. They connect with you and it reduces the stress of feeling like they need to give us information or we won't find the person who killed someone they love. Or the stress of having to relive what happened to them. We're happy to have you with us. But you're not an agent, Jax. You need to remember that."

Ben shook his head and spun around again, striding for the SUV.

Anderson gave Jax a sympathetic look, but he didn't disagree with his partner, just followed.

Patches stared up at him, reading the tension, and Jax stroked her soft fur. "You did a good job, Patches. I'm the one who's in trouble."

She shifted, pressing all sixty pounds against him. She wasn't that big, but she was strong.

He laughed, giving her an extra pat on the head. "Thanks, Patches. Let's get going."

She strode alongside him, her gait full of puppy energy. Sometimes, he forgot that at a year old, technically she still was a puppy. Despite the tough job he'd given her, despite the difficult start in life she'd had—being tossed onto the street to fend for herself at a few weeks old—she was always cheerful.

The perfect fit for a job like this. But sometimes the job still got to her.

Right now it was getting to him. And it wasn't talking to the victims, as hard as that was.

He'd come to the FBI from private therapy to help stop perpetrators before they could become repeat offenders. He knew he made a difference here. But despite his training, despite how much he loved what he did, sometimes being a Victim Specialist felt too far on the sidelines.

Sometimes, it just didn't feel like he was doing enough.

The station was empty and dark.

Normally, Keara would be gone by now. Actually, if things were normal, she probably wouldn't be working at all on a Sunday. But with worried citizens needing reassurance, and a town that needed extra vigilance because of a nearby bombing without an obvious motive, she'd come in early and stayed late.

Heading home didn't mean she was off the clock. In a small town like Desparre, there was no such thing as truly off the clock. If something happened after the station was officially closed for the night, the officer—or chief—who was closest to the action would get the first call.

Tonight she didn't want to get on the road. Didn't feel like making the relatively short drive to her house.

She'd been distracted all day, moving on autopilot. In a job like hers, that was dangerous. But knowing that didn't make it any easier to focus.

After she'd returned home from Luna last night, images of her life with Juan had taunted her sleep. She'd woken on a scream, on the memory of returning home from work that horrible day.

She'd been exhausted, frustrated by a case she hardly remembered, one she'd subsequently solved. She'd wanted nothing more than to settle on the couch in front of the TV with a delivery pizza and a bottle of red wine. To simply snuggle with her husband and forget the argument they'd been having on replay every few weeks.

The house had been lit up, the front door locked, no sign that anything was wrong. She'd walked inside and headed straight for the shower, a holdover habit from her days on patrol. Forensics said the timing wouldn't have mattered, that Juan had been dead before she even arrived home, but the shower still bothered her. The fact that she hadn't suspected for a second that anything was wrong, that she'd had no idea the man she'd loved so deeply was already gone.

And then, afterward, the hint of annoyance when she'd walked through the house and couldn't find him. The sigh she'd heaved as she'd realized the back door was open, that he hadn't bothered to come in from the garden when she'd arrived. The way she'd desperately tried to suck in gulps of air once she'd fallen to the ground beside him, but her lungs still screamed, telling her she wasn't getting enough oxygen.

The investigation had determined that someone had hopped the fence into their backyard while Juan was relaxing on a lawn chair. They'd slipped up behind him and slit his throat.

If he'd realized anyone was there, the knowledge had come too late. There were no defense marks on his arms or hands. No awkward angle to the slice across his neck, which might have happened if he'd tried to turn at the last minute.

She hoped it meant that it had all happened too fast for him to suffer. But even an instant of pain, even a flash of insight that everything he'd fought for in his life was over, was too much.

It was too much for her, too. For six years being in Alaska had kept the memories at a survivable distance.

Now the bombing was bringing it all back. But if the person who'd killed Juan had come here and set off a bomb, why had he chosen such a different crime?

Fitz hadn't sent her the case file from Celia Harris's murder yet, but if that killer was responsible for the bomb, too, something drastic had changed. She'd seen the evidence photos from Celia's murder; the whole office had. They'd been gruesome enough, with such an unlikely victim, that Juan and Fitz had consulted briefly with the rest of the detectives.

Celia hadn't been killed in the alley where she'd been found, and her killer had taken his time murdering her. Although Keara's cases tended to be the standard sort—motivated by more obvious reasons like greed, jealousy or anger—Houston wasn't immune to serial killers. She'd understood immediately why Juan and Fitz had thought there'd be more murders.

But a bombing seven years later? Even if the bomber had stood nearby and watched the pain and death his handiwork caused, was it really the same as wielding a knife? She'd never heard of a violent killer becoming a bomber.

Maybe she was reaching, grasping at a similar symbol because she still needed answers, despite how far she'd run.

The crackle of the intercom from outside the entrance of the building, followed by a familiar voice asking "Keara? Er-Chief Hernandez?" startled her.

The distinctive voice made goose bumps prick her arms. Keara rubbed them away as she stood and strode to the front of the station, swinging the door wide.

"How did you know I was here?"

Woof! Patches answered, making a smile break through the mask of competence and calm that Keara used automatically on the job.

"Yours is the only civilian car in the lot."

He'd noticed what car she was driving? She studied him more closely, taking in the focused stare belied by a relaxed stance. Maybe psychologists were more like police officers than she'd thought, both needing to be observant and analytical.

"You have news on the bombing?" As she asked it, she realized the only reason he'd tell her in person was if it was connected to her past. Bracing her hand on the open door frame, she asked, "Is it connected to my husband's death?"

"What?" Jax's too-serious expression morphed into concern as he took a step closer.

Too late, she remembered that he knew her husband had investigated a murder where the symbol was found, but not much more. He didn't know anything about Rodney Brown, or the fact that her husband's murder had never been solved. Or even the fact that her husband's death had been a murder.

She took a step back, losing the stability of holding on to the door frame, but also escaping Jax's cinnamony scent. She didn't know if it was aftershave or cologne or if he just liked to mainline chai, but it was the sort of scent she wanted to keep breathing in.

It was distracting. *He* was distracting.

Something bumped her leg and Keara looked down, finding Patches there. The dog had followed her inside. Jax was coming, too, but moving more slowly.

Keara kept her gaze on Patches, petting the dog while she tried to come up with a way to redirect Jax, a way to avoid talking about what had happened to Juan.

"I don't have anything new to share about the bombing," Jax said, his voice slow and soft. "And Anderson is still waiting on that file from Houston PD. Is there more you need to tell me? Some other connection we should investigate?"

When she didn't immediately answer, he put his hand under her elbow.

The contact startled her, warmth from his hand making her realize how cold the rest of her body felt. She jerked her gaze back up to his. "Maybe. I'll know more once I get a look at that case file."

Jax stared at her, his dark brown eyes hypnotic. Finally, he nodded, stepping just slightly closer.

She had to tilt her head back to hold eye contact and she put a warning in her gaze. She liked Jax, but she'd been a police officer too long not to see what was coming. He was trying to make a connection, sympathize with her so she'd trust him enough to tell him what he needed to know.

A slight smile tilted his lips and Keara wondered if she needed to put a different kind of "back off" vibe out there. Nerves fluttered in her chest and she put it down to how long it had been since she'd had to let anyone down easy. Since she was their police chief, thankfully, people here mostly considered her off-limits as a woman.

"I'm not an agent."

His words were so far from what she'd expected to hear that it took her a few extra seconds to digest them.

"And you have no jurisdiction in Luna," he continued.

She crossed her arms over her chest, refusing to take a step backward and let him know his closeness affected her. "And?"

"The case you talked about feels psychologically different—the MO, the location, everything. But I can't get that symbol out of my head. It might have been an accident that we were able to recover it on the bomb, but it wasn't an accident that the bomber made it. It means something to him. That suggests the cases are connected somehow. I can't let this go. And since you're waiting on a case file you really shouldn't be requesting, I'm guessing you can't, either."

Keara frowned, trying to keep her expression neutral as Patches nudged her leg, looking for attention. Despite all the memories that had resurfaced tonight, she couldn't help but smile at the dog, with her tiny matching brown spots at the top of each eyebrow, and bigger spots on her muzzle and chest. Keara silently pet Patches again as she waited for Jax to continue.

"I think we should work together," Jax finished, staring at her expectantly. "Quietly, on the side. If we come up with anything, we share it with the agents."

It was a mistake for a lot of reasons.

Keeping information from the investigating agents— no matter how small or seemingly inconsequential— could be the difference that prevented the case from being solved. Besides, if she and Jax worked outside the official team, they wouldn't have all of the information.

After this was over, Jax would go back to Anchorage, but she still had to live in this community. She'd have to answer to her citizens if something went wrong, and she'd lose the support of their closest neighboring town, too.

Then there was Jax himself. Although she had no concerns when it came to her self-control around the handsome Victim Specialist, she couldn't deny that he ignited a tiny flicker of attraction whenever he was near.

Juan had been gone for seven years. She wasn't totally closed off to the idea of moving on someday. But it didn't feel like the time, not even for a fling. Not if this case could be the key to solving his murder.

"Okay," she agreed, the word bursting free before she could hold it back. "Let's work together."

Chapter 6

Something was wrong.

Jax could see it through the window of the tiny diner on the outskirts of Desparre, somewhere Keara had told him they were less likely to attract attention. It had been an hour drive for him after spending the day all over Luna with Ben and Anderson, talking to victims and families. He'd left discouraged and exhausted, with the bruises on his back and legs aching, but judging from the unguarded torment on her face, Keara's day had been worse.

He pictured the look on her face yesterday when she'd asked if the bombing was connected to her husband's death. That meant her husband had been murdered—and presumably, that the murder had never been solved. He'd desperately wanted to ask about it, but he couldn't turn off years of working as a psychologist. It had been the wrong time. But maybe today would be different.

"Come on, Patches," he said, leading the way into the diner. Keara had told him that the owner was low-key and didn't mind letting working dogs inside.

True to her promise, the diner was mostly empty and the waitress who nodded a greeting just cooed "aww" when she spotted Patches.

By the time Jax joined Keara at her booth, she looked serious and in control. The ability to mask her emotions that fast was probably a necessary skill for a police chief. But it still surprised him. And if he was being honest with himself, he was a little disappointed that she felt the need to hide from him.

You barely know her, he reminded himself. Yes, people usually opened up to him faster, probably because knowing how to reach people was a job requirement he couldn't just turn off outside work. And yes, last night they'd agreed to work together, so he'd expected more honesty. But mostly, he was just intrigued by her. He had no idea how long he'd have to get to know her before the case was solved and he had to go back to Anchorage.

"Is anything wrong?" Jax asked, keeping his voice neutral.

Patches took the more direct route. She went to Keara's side of the booth and put her head on the seat.

From the surprise and amusement on Keara's face, Patches had looked up at Keara with her soft puppy eyes, a tactic that rarely failed.

The smile twitching at the corners of Keara's lips burst into a true grin as she pet Patches. "She really knows how to put on the charm, doesn't she? Is that something you taught her when you trained her to work for the FBI?"

"Nah, she came by that naturally. I was biking home from work one day and—"

"You *biked* to work in Anchorage? Must have been summer."

"This was almost a year ago. I was working in DC then. Getting to and from FBI headquarters took forever in traffic, so I bought a bike. Anyway, I was on my way home and I saw something moving in the bushes and then this tiny little puppy jumped out. She gave me this look like she wanted me to take her home."

He'd had to swerve his bike, had almost tipped it. But he'd always felt like she'd been waiting for him to come along.

Growing up, he'd had a dog, so he'd known instantly that Patches was too young to be away from her mother. But she'd been totally alone, so he'd scooped her up, walked his bike the rest of the way home and then taken her to a vet.

Keara's smile curled downward. "Someone left her out there?"

"Yeah."

She shook her head, still petting Patches. "Kids and animals," she muttered. "Those are the worst calls, because they're trusting, relying on someone to care for them. Not that I want to get called to any scene where someone is hurt, but at least as an adult, you've seen enough of the world to know. If you're paying attention, there are threats everywhere."

She was staring at his dog when she spoke, letting Jax study her more closely. He'd worked with law enforcement long enough to know how terrible their jobs could be. He wondered how being a chief in Desparre compared to being a detective in Houston. The latter was surely bloodier, but the former put a lot of responsibility on her shoulders.

Deciding to keep the conversation light, he continued, "It's lucky I found Patches when I did. The vet thought she was about six weeks old. But she was feisty and determined from the start. I'd been working for the FBI for two and a half years by then and there are a few Victim Specialists who have therapy dogs in DC. I immediately thought she'd be good at it. She officially started at six months. Youngest dog they've ever used."

He heard the pride in his voice as Keara's gaze finally swung back to him. There was something pensive in her gaze, something that made him want to lean across the table and get a little closer.

"Can I get you anything?"

The nasally voice startled Jax and he realized the waitress was standing next to their table.

"Just a coffee would be great."

"Make it two, please," Keara said.

"And for her?" The waitress nodded at his dog, then smiled. "Does she want a bowl of water? Or we can bring her a dog c-o-o-k-i-e."

Woof! Patches's head appeared over the top of the table, swiveled toward the waitress.

The waitress laughed. "I see she spells. Okay, two coffees and a dog cookie it is!"

When she left, Jax returned his attention to Keara. But whatever he'd seen in her eyes was gone now, replaced by a seriousness that told him they were about to get to work.

"So the woman who was murdered seven years ago?

Celia Harris? Apparently, Juan, my husband, and his partner, Fitz, had a possible suspect. I mean, they looked at a lot of people and I guess this guy didn't stand out more than anyone else, at least not initially. But then, a week after my husband was murdered, Fitz went to talk to him again. I think it was kind of a distraction assignment, honestly, to reinterview any witnesses or suspects that Juan had talked to alone. You see, Fitz wanted to be part of the investigation into Juan's death and the chief wouldn't let him."

She didn't have to tell him that she'd also tried to insert herself into the investigation of her husband's murder. Just talking about it was making her eyes narrow and her lips tighten.

"What happened to your husband, Keara?"

"He was murdered." Her expression became even more pinched. "In our own backyard."

"I'm sorry."

"Me, too." She straightened, and he saw her game face come on. "It was never solved, which is why…" She took a visible breath, shook her head and started over, her voice calmer. "So about a week before he was killed, Juan went to talk to Rodney Brown. His car was pictured close to the scene near the time of Celia's murder. Fitz said Juan returned from that interview without feeling like he'd gained much, but the guy lied about the car being near the scene. And when Fitz went back—a week after my husband's throat was slit—the place was totally cleared out."

Jax felt himself cringe at Keara's description of how her husband had died. He could tell from the anger and pain wrapped up in those few words that she'd been the one to find him. An ache formed in his chest as he watched her, trying to be clinical. How much worse must it have been, as an officer of the law, knowing the person who'd killed him had gotten away with it?

"Fitz spent a lot of time trying to track down Rodney Brown. Apparently, he worked as an orderly at a hospital in Houston, but he just stopped showing up. His work history before that was a little spotty, so it wasn't totally out of character. And his family told Fitz that he was flighty and not great about staying in touch. Back then none of them were all that surprised that he'd just cleared out of his apartment. Fitz has been checking for signs of him over the years, even got a warrant to watch his credit report to see if he popped up somewhere else in the country. But there's been nothing."

"So you think he killed Celia Harris and your husband, too?"

"It's pretty suspicious timing to disappear."

"Yeah, it is."

"And now there's a bomb here with the same symbol. But…" She frowned, shook her head.

"You're thinking the same thing the FBI is," Jax concluded.

Her eyes narrowed at him, but she held off on saying anything as the waitress dropped off their coffees, and Patches started greedily chewing on her dog biscuit.

After the woman was gone, Keara demanded, "What do they think?"

"They don't know about your husband. No one from Houston mentioned that angle. And I'm guessing Rodney Brown's name is in the file, but he didn't stand out. The main thing is that—"

"A violent killer—someone who obviously enjoys the kill itself—is unlikely to become a bomber?"

"Pretty much," Jax confirmed. "You're right that the symbols are eerily similar. But if it's the same person, why a bomb? And why here? Why *now*, so many years after the murder in Texas?"

Fitz was right. Rodney Brown was a ghost.

Keara leaned back on her couch and took a sip of red wine. It had been another long day, full of questions from her citizens that she couldn't answer, full of worry about a case she wasn't even supposed to be investigating. She wasn't usually much of a drinker, especially while she was pondering a case, but tonight she was on her second glass.

Maybe that was why she reached for her wedding album, instead of returning to her laptop. In those first months after Juan's death, she'd sobbed over the pages. But since moving to Alaska, she'd tucked it into the corner of her bookshelf and hadn't opened it again.

Now she ran her finger over the shape of Juan's face, frozen in a slightly nervous smile as he waited at the altar for her. When she'd first met him in that Houston roll call, seen the way his shoulders slumped and his mouth tightened at hearing he'd be partnered with her, she'd been sure they'd never be friends. But after a year of tough calls, patrolling a dangerous area together, they'd developed a mutual respect that had slowly blossomed into more.

Now he was gone. The constant, overwhelming grief she'd felt in that first year after he died had slowly dulled into something she could push to the back of her mind. But with each day that passed since she'd seen that blasted symbol, the gnawing ache was returning, along with the certainty that she'd failed Juan.

Fitz was right. She'd played by the rules in Houston, let her fellow detectives handle the case because she'd been sure they'd find justice for one of their own. And because it had been hard enough to function at all during those early days and months, let alone constantly look at pictures and details of what had happened to Juan. When the case had gone cold, she should have taken it up herself and damn the rules, damn the consequences. Instead, she'd run away.

Since coming to Alaska, she'd followed the rules, too. She'd tried to be a by-the-book chief. But not anymore.

She took another long sip of wine and closed the album, pushed it away from her. Tipping back the rest of her glass, she yanked the laptop into her lap and stared at the notes she'd compiled on Rodney Brown.

The guy was a loser. He'd had a handful of arrests as a minor for getting into fights. More of the same as an adult, usually bar fights. Plus a single sexual assault charge that had later been dropped. From what Keara could tell, it was more because the victim didn't want to go through a trial than for lack of evidence.

Serial killers were often sexually motivated. But Celia Harris hadn't been sexually assaulted. Fitz's investigation had never turned up any similar kills. Although Rodney Brown clearly had a violent streak and a problem with women, there were no signs he'd ever crossed paths with Celia Harris. And he didn't seem sophisticated enough to have pulled off the risky abduction and then committed such a violent murder without leaving behind useful evidence.

Juan's murder had been almost professional. A quick hit and then the killer had disappeared. No one in her neighborhood had noticed anyone who didn't belong or seen anyone running away at the time of the murder. Yes, it made sense that a violent killer of women who thought the police were onto him might try and take out the detective who'd questioned him.

But Rodney Brown had only been questioned once. After a few weeks of silence, would he seek Juan out and murder him? The closer she looked at the details of the case, the more unlikely that idea seemed. Taking all of the pieces together, she understood why Fitz had decided the two weren't connected.

Except the timing was pretty hard to ignore. And the fact that Rodney Brown had so completely dropped off the map suggested a sophistication that perhaps he'd hidden in the rest of his life.

As for the bomb, sure, anyone could dig up the basics on the internet. But pulling it off was another thing. And no matter how she looked at it, the long gap in time and the change in MO made it pretty unlikely that all three crimes were connected.

Cursing, she tossed her laptop onto the couch beside her. Tears of frustration blurred her vision, but she blinked them back.

Yes, cold cases were harder than fresh investigations. The adage of the "first forty-eight hours" was true. Over time, memories faded, witnesses forgot, evidence that had been missed the first time often disappeared for good. But that didn't make them impossible.

Keara pictured the symbol from Anderson's phone, with the series of interconnecting loops, drawn onto the bomb with a thick black marker. Different enough from the symbol over Celia's body in that alley, spray-painted onto the stucco wall of the adjacent building in bloodred. But the design itself was the same, the loops that looked almost childish. If all of this was connected, if she had a shot at solving her husband's murder, that symbol was the key.

The melodic ring of her doorbell startled her, made her glance at the credenza in the corner where she'd stashed her weapon. Few people knew exactly where she lived. Even fewer would visit.

She considered ignoring it, but curiosity got the better of her and she strode to the door. When she peered through the peephole, there was Jax on her front porch, shivering in a dark coat and looking tired. Patches was at his side, her head swiveling from him to the door, as if she knew Keara had stepped up to the other side.

It had been a long time since she'd felt attracted to someone. Sure, she'd had brief flashes of awareness in Alaska when she crossed paths with someone, but nothing that lasted more than a few minutes. With Jax, the attraction seemed to grow each time she saw him, with each new detail she noticed. The surprising muscles in his arms when he'd stripped down to a T-shirt in the hotel lobby, the intuitiveness of his gaze when she was holding something back, the hint of a dimple that popped on his right cheek when he gave a full-blown grin, usually at Patches.

More than simple attraction, though, she felt a *connection* with Jax. Some invisible pull, a desire to simply sit beside him and soak in his presence. She'd tried to ignore the feeling, but right now she felt that pull even more than usual.

"It's the wine," she muttered, resting her forehead against the door, anxious at such a simple decision. Open the door and let him in? Or pretend not to be home?

Woof!

A smile burst free and Keara had to smother the giggle that wanted to follow. Any man who could inspire such loyalty from a dog like Patches had to be a good one. And maybe the fact that he lived so far away was a plus. Anchorage was definitely past the point of being practical for a relationship, so that alone should avoid any awkwardness when it was time for him to leave.

He might be FBI, but he wasn't a law-enforcement officer. He wasn't in the thick of danger, wasn't someone she'd have to constantly worry about.

Not that it really mattered. She didn't want anything serious. Not now. Probably never again.

But a fling with a handsome, intelligent, sensitive man? Maybe it was time.

Taking a deep breath, Keara opened the door.

Chapter 7

The door swung open and Keara swayed forward, her gaze locked on his and lips parted. He'd never seen her hair down before, but right now it hung long, silky and loose, perfectly straight over her shoulders. She was dressed casually, in jeans and a well-worn long-sleeved T-shirt that looked soft to the touch and showed off curves her police uniform hid. Even her expression was less guarded, softer.

"Come in," she said, her voice huskier than usual.

Patches bounded inside at the invitation, but warning bells went off in Jax's head, despite the desire stirring in his belly.

He could see it in her low-lidded gaze. She thought he was here for a totally different reason than the agreed-upon plan to investigate together. Of course, she'd never given him her address, never invited him over. It had been foolish to show up without calling. Especially at nine o' clock at night.

But after yet another day of nonstop visits with victims and family members, feeling no closer to bringing any of them real closure, he'd just wanted to see Keara. To sit across from her and watch the way her lips pursed when she was deep in thought, see the determination in her gaze and posture when she thought she was onto something. To soak up her presence and soothe his own frustrated nerves.

So he'd managed to get her home address out of Luna's police chief, under the pretense that he was keeping her apprised of the investigation, and she was keeping them informed of anything suspicious in Desparre.

It had been stupid and selfish, he realized now as Keara raised her eyebrows at him, the corners of her lips twisting up in an expression that looked like a dare. Red wine stained her lips with a hint of purple.

He tried to come up with an excuse to leave, but then she licked those lips and he was moving forward without conscious intent.

She pushed the door closed behind him, leaning against him as she did it, and the brief contact made his mouth go dry.

This close, he could see the ring of slightly lighter brown at the center of her coffee-colored irises. He could smell a rich cabernet, subtle enough that he doubted she'd drank a lot. And it wasn't just her well-worn T-shirt that was soft; it was also her skin.

She blinked up at him, her chest rising and falling faster, and he could feel his own breathing pick up in response.

He'd been drawn to her from the first day they'd met.

So when she swayed forward again—or had he leaned toward her?—he ignored the voice in his head telling him this was the wrong time. Threading his fingers through hers, he tugged gently and then she was pressing against him, up on her tiptoes.

The first contact of her lips sent a spark through his body like he'd given himself an electric shock. Then he closed his mouth around her bottom lip and tasted the cabernet she'd been drinking.

She let out a noise that was half-sigh, half-moan and pushed higher on her toes, her free hand tangling in his hair and pulling him closer. Then her tongue was in his mouth and her kisses turned fast and frantic.

Jax wrapped his free hand around her back, molding her body to his, and his heart rate skyrocketed. He had a solid seven inches on her and yet somehow, the fit was perfect.

Woof!

Patches's bark registered in the back of his mind as Keara kissed him harder.

Then Patches let out several more, higher pitched barks.

The insistent sound returned him to reality, helped his mind take the lead back over from his body. He pulled away slightly, trying to catch his breath as he stared over Keara's head and down the hall.

Patches stood in Keara's hallway, leaning slightly forward, as if ready to bark again or run toward them.

Unwinding his arm from around Keara's back, Jax tried to calm his pounding heart. The scent of her—a mix of that wine with something sweeter and more subtle—invaded his senses, making it hard to focus, especially when she leaned in again.

He stepped back, quickly enough that she stumbled toward him before righting herself.

"This probably isn't a good idea," he forced himself to say.

Keara blinked at him a few times, then that professional mask slipped back over her features. But not before he saw a flash of hurt in her eyes.

She was as attracted to him as he was to her. But he'd be a terrible psychologist if he didn't recognize that they were both acting on it for the wrong reasons.

Flings weren't his thing. They never had been, but at thirty-eight years old, he felt way past them. And even if Keara was emotionally available, she lived four hundred miles away. He might be here for a month or a break might come in the case tomorrow and that fast, he'd be on a flight home.

Besides, Keara hadn't kissed him because of that attraction. She'd kissed him because she was emotional and frustrated, probably over the thread-thin connection between her husband's death and the bombing.

He took another step away from her, as the idea of her kissing him because she missed her dead husband cooled the rest of his desire.

"You came to talk about the case?" Keara asked, her voice as detached and remote as the expression on her face.

When he nodded, she spun and headed into the interior of her house. "Come on, then."

As soon as she reached Patches, the dog turned to walk with her. Keara stroked Patches's head as they strode away, his dog's tail wagging.

Running a hand through his hair, straightening the spots where Keara had tugged and tangled it, he followed. With every step, he took a deep breath, trying not to watch the sway of her hips as she led him into her living room.

It was exactly what he would have expected her personal space to be. Cozy, with a fireplace centered in the room. Comfortable, with a couch that looked perfect for curling up on. There was even a wool blanket thrown over the back of it. And peaceful, with big curtained windows diagonal from the fireplace that had to open to a spectacular view of the forest behind her.

There was an open bottle of wine and a single empty wineglass on the live-edge wood coffee table. Beside it, a laptop and a wedding album.

A mix of regret and pain—some for her, some for himself—tensed his chest and then dropped to his stomach.

Her gaze went from him to the album, then back again. "If there's a connection between all of this, it's that symbol. We need to know what it means." Her expression gave nothing away, but her voice was slightly shaky as she sank onto the couch. "You've got a psychology background, right? Any ideas?"

Jax settled on the big leather chair beside the couch, not surprised when Patches pushed past him to sit beside Keara. His dog always knew who needed her most.

"That's profiler territory," Jax said. "I used to be a psychologist, so yeah, I definitely have insight into some of these criminals. But this symbol doesn't represent anything I can decode."

"It's the only thing connecting the crimes," Keara said, the frustration in her voice edged with grief. "Nothing else is similar. Fitz sent me the file from Celia Harris's murder. And I know everything about Juan's murder. The only possible link is the timing and the fact that Juan questioned a possible witness shortly before he was killed—and shortly before that witness disappeared. But the bombing? Nothing about it seems remotely connected. Except this damn symbol."

Jax leaned forward in his chair, resting his forearms on his thighs. "What if that's because the murder—or possibly murders, if your husband's case is also connected—were the anomaly? What if he was always a bomber?"

Keara twisted slightly to face him, her eyebrows twitching inward. At her interest, Patches pivoted, too. "What do you mean?"

"Maybe the kill was personal. Maybe the bomber knew Celia Harris. Maybe bombs are his thing and this was the exception." He could hear the excitement in his voice as he turned it over in his mind. "It could make him easier to track if he's really a bomber. Maybe there have been others."

Keara's shoulders dropped, her excitement obviously waning. "I don't think so. Juan thought Rodney was suspicious mainly because he so vehemently denied being near the crime scene when it happened. But he couldn't find any personal connection between Rodney and Celia. If this was a serial killer, that wouldn't matter so much. But a personal kill?" She shook her head. "After Juan died and Rodney disappeared, Fitz dug deep, looking for a connection. He never found one, either."

"You said Rodney was flighty, right? That he didn't tend to stay in one place for long, that even his family wasn't all that concerned when he cleared out?"

"Sure, but it's pretty coincidental timing," Keara insisted.

"Exactly," Jax agreed. "What if Rodney leaving *is* just a coincidence? Maybe Celia's murder and this bombing are connected. And it's possible your husband's death is, too. *Maybe.* But what if it's not Rodney? What if we're looking for someone else?"

"What if it's not Rodney?"

Jax's words from last night had run through Keara's mind during a restless night of sleep and again during her drive into work this morning—when she wasn't distracted by memories of kissing him. She'd been attracted to him from the start, so she'd expected to enjoy those kisses. What she hadn't expected was the intensity.

The man kissed with a singular focus, until she'd felt consumed by the feel of him, by the taste of him. He might not have been law enforcement, but after plastering herself against him, she suspected he worked out with his agent colleagues, because his chest was rock-solid.

It was better that he'd stopped it before things went too far.

He was a colleague. He was also her best chance at connecting the Luna bombing to her husband's murder—if in fact they were connected.

He was also dangerous. A fling was one thing. A fling was temporary, a distraction from the fact that she'd chosen a profession that sucked away a lot of her personal time. A distraction from the fact that even if she had more personal time, she had no one to spend it with. But a single kiss from Jax and she'd felt herself wanting. Physical wanting, of course. But emotional wanting, too. And that was territory she didn't want to revisit.

"Everything okay, Chief?"

Keara looked up from her desk.

Tate Emory was standing in her doorway, too-perceptive concern in his dark eyes. He was the closest thing she had to a friend on the force. Not that she didn't like just about everyone on her team, but Tate was different. She knew his secret, had given him a job in a tricky situation, so it was easier to share things with him in return. She'd kept his confidence, so he'd keep hers.

But not this. Not the guilt that filled her like nausea when she thought about kissing Jax when she should have been focused on getting justice for Juan.

She forced a smile. "It's been a tough week. We're four days out from that bomb and neither the FBI nor the Luna police have much more to go on than they did when it went off."

By Wednesday morning—a full ninety-six hours after the bomb had detonated—she'd expected a solid suspect, maybe even an arrest, but at the very least, a manhunt. Instead, the FBI's semiregular news conferences beside Luna's police chief focused more on reassuring a scared public that they were working on it, and asking them to come forward if they had information that could help.

What the public didn't know—what Keara had learned from talking to her colleagues in the Luna Police Department—was that the FBI still had a long way to go. They still had no idea who or what the intended target was, or what goal the bomber was trying to accomplish. Was there a message? If so, no one knew what it was. They still weren't even sure if the bomber had been going for a bigger death toll by waiting until the impromptu soccer game happened or if that was unintentional and he'd expected few—or maybe even no—dead.

"Hey, at least it's finally May," Tate said, his tone more enthusiastic than the forty-five-degree weather warranted.

It would be a while before they hit temperatures that didn't require a coat. But at least it was sunny.

She gave him a halfhearted smile, acknowledging his attempt to cheer her up.

"I'm going to take a trek up the mountain today," Tate said, apparently giving up on that.

"Take Lorenzo and Nate with you. I doubt we're going to magically run across someone who knows something, but let's be honest. If Desparre is a good place to hide out, the mountain takes it to the next level."

The mountain that separated Desparre from Luna was a great place to get lost, even more lost than the relative isolation offered by the rest of Desparre. Five years ago they'd discovered kidnappers had hidden five kids on that mountain for many years. They'd also found a murderer, running from a decades-old charge in Kansas. It wasn't a stretch to imagine a bomber hiding there, too.

All of her officers were using their extra time between calls to chat with citizens, both to reassure them that the bombing investigation would be solved and also to see if anyone had useful information. So far it hadn't borne any fruit, but there had to be a reason the bomber had targeted such a tiny park. Luna and Desparre weren't that far apart, at least not in Alaskan terms. So there was a good chance someone around here knew something, even if they didn't realize it.

Lorenzo Riera was one of her veterans, a steady officer who'd once faced down a grizzly bear who'd gotten a taste for people food and wandered downtown four years ago. He'd just as readily had her back at a more standard bar fight breakup last month. His partner, Nate Dreymond, had barely passed a year on the force. Since Tate's partner, Peter, had left a few months ago, Nate was the force's rookie.

Having Lorenzo at his side would be good backup for Tate if he ran into trouble, and having Nate tag along would give the rookie a chance to watch two great officers at work.

"Got it," Tate agreed. "But you know, maybe you should reconsider the K-9 unit. If I had a K-9 partner, you wouldn't have to keep putting out those failed job postings for another officer."

It was a request Tate had been making almost from his first day on the force. Usually, Keara cited their lack of funds. But after seeing Jax work with Patches, she wondered if the cost might be worth it. "I'll think about it."

Tate's mouth opened and closed, as if her response had totally thrown him.

"Let me know if anything pops," she said.

He nodded and took the cue to leave.

She should do the same. Being chief meant a certain amount of politics and paperwork, but in a town as small as Desparre, it still required her to be out on the streets, too. Or maybe that was just the kind of chief she'd chosen to be.

She'd been out in her town every day since the bomb

had gone off, reassuring citizens and doing the same kind of low-key investigative work as her officers. But right now the question of Rodney Brown's involvement was still messing with her focus.

Jax's claim that Rodney's leaving was just coincidence could be right. Twelve years in law enforcement had taught her that stranger coincidences happened. The problem was, it had also taught her to always be suspicious of them, because too much of a coincidence usually meant it wasn't actually a coincidence.

Then again, maybe something bad had happened to Rodney, too. But what? And why?

Rodney Brown killing Celia Harris and then killing Juan was a real possibility she couldn't drop. But the bombing connection felt more tenuous.

What if they were two different people? The idea made Keara jerk straighter in her chair, making it roll slightly backward and bump the credenza behind her.

Two different people didn't mean they weren't connected.

The theory made her heart rate pick up, sent a familiar rush through her body. The thrill of the chase, when her gut was screaming she'd hit on something. She'd felt it regularly as a detective. As a chief, she had less opportunity to be in the center of a case in the same way.

Grabbing her cell phone, she hit redial on a number that had started to appear constantly on her list of recent calls.

"Jax Diallo."

The deep, relaxing tone of his voice sent a little thrill through her that Keara tried to ignore. "Jax, it's Keara."

"Keara."

The way he said her name, the way she could practically see his slight smile, made her stomach clench. Pushing forward, she told him her new theory. "What if you're right about Celia Harris's murder being personal? What if the person who killed her is still out there, but it's not Rodney Brown?"

"I don't—"

She kept talking, adrenaline pumping, her words spilling out faster as the idea continued to take shape. "What if the killer knew Rodney, knew the symbol he liked to use, and spray-painted it above Celia's body to lead police in the wrong direction? Or maybe they'd had a falling out and it was a 'screw you' kind of move?"

"So you're suggesting Rodney is the bomber?" Jax asked, not sounding anywhere near as excited by the theory as she felt.

"Yes! When Juan came to talk to him about the murder, he was pissed because his symbol was used. He killed Juan to keep him from connecting it to his own crimes. Then he left town."

"So you think Juan is the one who let it slip about the symbol? But what about Rodney's car being near the murder scene?" Jax asked, still sounding confused.

"We know Rodney was near there at the time of the killing. Maybe it really was coincidence. Or maybe he knew what was going to happen and drove by, but he wasn't the killer."

"Then, the real killer told Rodney he was going to murder this woman? Why would he do that?"

"Maybe they had a sick friendship. You can't tell me you haven't seen criminals connect before, give each other ideas, trade stories about what they've done, even cooperate with each other. Maybe give each other alibis. Maybe play a one-upmanship game."

"Well, sure," Jax said, his tone still skeptical.

"Maybe that's what happened here," Keara said, holding in her frustration. "And whether or not Juan mentioned the symbol, Rodney knew about it. So maybe that was his real worry. He wouldn't know that Houston PD isn't like the FBI. We don't have bomb databases. We wouldn't know if he'd used that symbol before, not if it was outside our jurisdiction."

She blew out a heavy breath, tried to slow her adrenaline along with the speed of her words. "What I'm saying, Jax, is that maybe the killer and the bomber *aren't* the same person. But maybe they know each other, even schemed together at one point. And Rodney killed my husband because he was onto something bigger than a single murder."

Jax sighed. "It's a good theory, Keara, but there's a problem."

"What?"

"The FBI ran the bombing details through our database, specifically that symbol. They finished reviewing everything today and confirmed it. We've never seen a bomb with this symbol before. Not in Houston, not anywhere."

Chapter 8

With every large-scale crime scene, Jax found at least one person whose resilience awed him. From the Luna bombing, that person was Gabi Sinclair.

The young woman was a fighter. She'd lost a leg, lost a fiancé. She was definitely angry, grieving and in pain, but she was also strong. She had a lot still to get through, but he knew she'd come out the other side of it.

He went to see Gabi at her mom's house in Desparre, where she was staying while she healed. He was hoping she might remember something more, since she'd been at the edge of the park, maybe at a good vantage point to see the bomber leave the scene. But she had nothing new to offer him, just like he had nothing new to share about the investigation. The most he was able to do was return her fiancé's watch, which had been processed by the FBI.

"They told me in a month, I'll get a preparatory prosthetic," Gabi said, fighting through the pain as she settled herself on her mom's couch, with Patches beside her good leg. "After a few months I'll be able to get fitted for something permanent. Then I'm going to learn to run again."

She said it all with her chin tipped high, with her mom clutching her hand and fighting tears. Gabi only broke down once, when he handed her the watch and she told him about her fiancé's funeral, which had been put on hold long enough for Gabi to be released from the hospital.

As Jax and Patches climbed into his rental SUV, Gabi's broken words echoed in his head. "I thought Carter and I had so much time. We had so many plans. Now all our dreams for our future together are just gone."

Instead of seeing Gabi's tearful gaze, he pictured Keara, stoic and frustrated as she tried to get closure, seven long years after her husband had been murdered.

It wasn't his job. Not to investigate the bombing outside his role with the victims. Definitely not to try and connect it to an old murder case. But he'd seen what a good investigation could do for those left behind. Knowing who was to blame, being able to see justice done for those they loved. It made a difference. It was why he'd left private practice to join the FBI. Maybe he could help Keara find her own closure.

"Call Keara Hernandez," he told his phone as he started up his SUV, heading toward downtown Desparre instead of back to Luna. Even before she picked up, his pulse increased at the thought of seeing her.

"Hello?"

Her tone was cautious, as if she wasn't sure what to expect, and he wondered if it was because of their kiss last night or his less-than-enthusiastic response to her theory this morning.

"I'm in Desparre and I was hoping we could grab a coffee before I make the drive back to Luna," he told her, surprised at the nerves in his belly, like he was asking for a date instead of a chance to talk about the case.

He could have just swung by the police station, but he didn't want word getting around that he was spending too much time talking to the Desparre police chief. Ben and Anderson were already suspicious. As much as he respected them, he wasn't in the mood for their only-partially joking jabs at him "playing agent." Especially since he didn't plan to stop. Not for this case, and not when it might help Keara.

When the pause on the other end of the phone went on too long, Patches chimed in. *Woof! Woof!*

Keara laughed. "Okay, Patches. I can do that." Then her voice got more businesslike. "This isn't Anchorage. We don't have a dedicated coffee shop in Desparre. But there's a spot we can go outside downtown with good coffee. You have a new idea about the case?"

"I wish I did. I just thought we could talk it over again, see if we can come up with something new." He didn't say the rest of it: he wanted to see her.

There was another pause, like Keara was reconsidering, but then she said, "Okay," and gave him an address.

It was actually closer to Gabi's mom's place than driving all the way into downtown, and Jax pulled into a gas station and did a quick U-turn to get onto a different street. According to his GPS, it was a quicker route to The Lodge, the spot where Keara had recommended they meet.

"You ready to see Keara?" he asked Patches, glancing at her in his rearview mirror.

As she barked an affirmative, Jax frowned, squinting at the huge dark blue truck behind him. It looked like the same vehicle that had been behind him on the road from Gabi's. But why would it now be going this way? Had it also turned around at the gas station?

Was someone following him? And why did that vehicle seem slightly familiar, like he'd seen it before today?

He eased up on the gas, slowing to ten miles below the limit, hoping the truck would pass him on the otherwise deserted road. But it slowed, too, staying just far enough behind him that Jax couldn't get a good look at the driver.

His heart rate picked up, even as he told himself he was being paranoid. Why would anyone follow him?

It was probably just a coincidence. Still, when a street appeared to his right, Jax yanked the wheel that way.

Patches barked and he could hear her sliding across the seat at his sudden turn.

"Sorry, Patches," Jax said, his gaze darting back and forth between the road ahead and the rearview mirror.

After a minute passed and the truck didn't appear again, Jax let out a heavy breath and eased his foot slightly off the gas.

Despite telling himself he'd been overreacting, he didn't fully relax until he reached the restaurant Keara had chosen. Apparently, it had once been a lodge and even the outside looked more like a log cabin than a small-town restaurant.

As he let Patches out of the SUV and scratched her ears, an apology for his erratic driving, he couldn't help glancing around for the big blue truck. Then he shook his head and muttered, "I think I needed a longer break, Patches."

She stared up at him, her soft brown eyes telegraphing sympathy.

He'd considered taking a vacation between finishing his term on the Rapid Deployment Team in DC and moving out to Anchorage. But the job opening had seemed perfect and the idea of Alaska had felt so different and enticing that he'd jumped on it. He'd been sure the cases he'd see here would be tiny compared to the mass casualty events that had burned him out over the previous three years. But this bombing was bringing it all back.

Apparently, that stress was making him imagine threats where there were none.

Movement in the distance made him jump and his gaze darted to the woods bracketing the restaurant. Then he froze in awe.

A moose, much bigger than he'd imagined the animals to be, paused and stared back at him.

When Patches took a slow, curious step forward, Jax grabbed her collar and his rapid movement sent the moose running.

Letting go of a breath along with Patches's collar, he said, "Let's go see Keara."

Woof! Woof!

Grinning at his dog's suddenly wagging tail, echoing his own feelings, Jax led her into The Lodge. There were small tables scattered throughout the main space, centered around a fireplace. Near the front was a section that carried food, like a small specialty grocery store.

It wasn't very big, so he could tell immediately that despite his detour, he'd still beaten Keara here. Probably due to his erratic driving. Good thing there hadn't been a cop around to pull him over for speeding. That would have been embarrassing—and not just because Keara would have heard about it.

Jax ordered himself a chai latte, while the teenage girl behind the counter cooed at Patches, and then he sat at one of the cozy tables. It looked like a spot to take a date, not the sort of place you'd sit and talk about an old murder and a new bombing.

His nerves picked up again, for an entirely different reason, as Keara entered the restaurant. She spotted him across the room, a hesitant smile tipping her lips before she turned and ordered herself a drink.

Then she was walking toward him and Jax couldn't stop himself from cataloging all the differences from last night. Her hair was tied up in its typical tight bun and as she unzipped her coat, he discovered she was wearing her police uniform. Everything about her—including the serious look on her face—broadcasted that today was all business.

He tried to respond in kind, but he couldn't stop his gaze from dropping to her lips. Couldn't keep his mind from revisiting the feel of those lips against his, the taste of her mouth as she'd kissed him. The sudden desire for a big glass of cabernet filled him.

When he dragged his gaze back to her eyes, they were slightly narrowed. The hands around her mug whitened at the knuckles. Her gaze drifted to his mug and then a smile quirked her lips. "Are you drinking chai?"

"Yeah."

That smile quivered again, making him wonder if he'd missed something, and then Keara cleared her throat, her expression turning serious.

"So there are no other bombs with this symbol?" she demanded. "Not anywhere in the country over the past seven years?"

Woof! Patches went to Keara and nudged her, making her reposition her mug to prevent her drink from spilling.

From the smell that wafted toward him, she'd opted for hot chocolate. He tried not to wonder what that would taste like on her lips.

"Sorry, Patches," Keara said, taking a seat and petting his dog.

Finally, she turned back to him with raised eyebrows.

"No. And when it comes to bombs, since the FBI has the biggest lab in the country dedicated to bomb evidence, we probably would have seen it. Unless—"

"Unless the other bombs exploding destroyed the symbols," Keara finished for him. "Maybe we were never intended to see that symbol at all. Maybe that's why Rodney had to kill Juan, because even if Rodney didn't kill Celia, the crime was now connected to the symbol."

"Killing Juan doesn't change the case file," Jax reminded her.

"No. But Juan was the only one showing any interest in Rodney," Keara shot back, her expression as desperate as it was determined.

Jax stared at her, dread sinking to his stomach. This tenuous connection between the murder in Texas and the bomb had reignited Keara's hope that her husband's case could be solved. Based on the way she'd responded to the symbol the first time she'd seen it, that was something she'd given up on until now.

This new chance could be making her see connections where there weren't any. Was his hope that she could move on making him do the same?

If so, were they both fooling themselves that they could possibly solve Juan's cold case?

She needed to keep her distance from Jax.

Maybe not physically, since he was helping her investigate the bombing—and hopefully her husband's murder. That was giving her access to information she'd never be able to get from the FBI otherwise. So simply staying away from him wasn't an option. But separating herself emotionally was.

Sighing, Keara signed another document in the huge stack of paperwork on her desk and set it in her out-box. Being chief, even in a small town, meant a lot of paperwork. It had taken her several years to get used to the amount of time she spent at her desk, rather than out in the field. A small town in a place like Alaska—with more than twenty percent as much land as the whole of the lower forty-eight, but the lowest population density anywhere in the country—meant she still had to take calls personally. That fact had made the transition easier.

Slowly, she'd gotten used to being the boss. Of maintaining a certain distance between herself and her colleagues. Of being tougher on her officers than she would have wanted in their place, because she knew how important it was not just to maintain her authority, but also to keep them safe.

It wasn't easy. Not just the loss of the camaraderie she'd had when she was just one of the force, but also being hard on her officers. She'd even fired one, a rookie who'd had tons of promise and she'd liked personally, too. But he'd ignored direct orders, actually broken the law. Yes, he'd done it to save someone, and in his place, she might have done the same. But that didn't matter. Not now.

She had to do whatever it took to make sure none of her officers' spouses ever faced what she'd experienced. It was a responsibility that weighed heavily on her every day.

Still, most days she loved being a chief in Desparre. She loved the way a town known for its self-sufficient, independent citizens would pull together and look after each other when needed. And she was proud of the officers who worked for her, proud to call herself their chief.

There were definitely days when she missed being a detective. Missed working closely with a partner, unraveling a puzzle to give someone justice. She'd made the conscious choice to put that role behind her after Juan's death had gone unsolved. But now...

She shook her head and pushed her chair back from her desk, then stood and stretched. She'd been dealing with paperwork for hours, ever since she'd left The Lodge.

Coffee with Jax and Patches had felt more like a date than a professional meeting, despite the fact that they'd only talked about the case. Her fingers pressed against her lips, remembering the feel of his kiss, wishing she could get it out of her head.

She hadn't dated since Juan had died. Not really. Sure, she'd gone on a few "you'd get along so well; what's the big deal; give it a try" kind of setup dates. The kind where she'd met a guy for a drink, tried not to feel uncomfortable as he asked her what it was like being new to Alaska, what it was like being a police chief, then finally gone home. A couple of times, the guy had called for a second date and she'd let him down easy.

She'd told herself it was just too awkward to date in a town where she was the top law-enforcement official. She'd told herself that one day this would feel more like home and the timing would be better. But maybe that was an easy excuse. Because somehow, here it was, six years later, and Desparre *did* feel like her home. Yet, she hadn't gone out on a single date since those early setups.

Maybe it was pure bad luck, because she'd also never felt a connection to anyone like she'd been feeling with Jax over these past few days. At least, not since her husband.

The thought made her fingers drop away from her mouth and her stomach cramp up. Why did the first man who'd made her think about moving forward have to be one who was also forcing her to face her past?

Spinning away from the glass wall that gave her a view into the bullpen where some of her officers were working, Keara stared through the small window at the back of her office. The view was relaxing, the edge of a dense forest that butted up against this part of town. On the rare occasions that she opened the window, it filled her office with the chirping of birds and occasionally the call of a wolf. Once, she'd spotted a bear off in the distance.

When she'd first walked into this office, knowing it was going to be hers, she'd felt like she could breathe deeply for the first time in a year. Alaska had given her solace, a place to start over and hopefully, to heal.

Now, for the first time, she wondered if her family

was right. Maybe she wasn't here to move on. Maybe she was here to escape the constant reminders that had been everywhere in Houston. The home she'd shared with Juan, their favorite restaurant, the streets they'd once patrolled together. Even the shared friends, the family who meant well but cringed and didn't quite meet her gaze when someone mentioned Juan's name.

Being in Houston, knowing Juan's killer was out there somewhere, walking free while Juan was gone, had filled her with a constant rage on top of the grief. And then there'd been the weight of failure, the knowledge that she—a police officer, a *detective*—hadn't been able to get Juan justice.

Coming here had made it all fade into the background. But it was returning now, that familiar weight that seemed to suffocate her from the inside.

She couldn't run forever. Maybe the bombing wasn't connected to Juan's murder. But whether it was the key or not, regardless of the fact that she had no jurisdiction, she was going to investigate.

The thought made the grief and anger and frustration burning inside her coalesce into something more powerful. Determination.

Keara glanced at the picture she kept framed in a corner of her office, almost hidden behind stacks of paper. Juan stared back at her, serious and proud in his police uniform from when they'd first started dating.

"I promise you," she whispered to that picture, her voice cracking, "this time I'm not giving up. I'm not running away. I'm going to figure out who killed you."

Chapter 9

"Has there been *any* progress in the FBI's investigation? Are we any closer to knowing who did this?"

Justin Peterson's questions were full of frustration, but far less anger than when Jax and Patches had last visited the man. Maybe that was because today the visit was in his home, instead of the hospital.

"Absolutely," Jax said, leaning forward even as Patches continued to do her work.

She'd sat beside Justin as soon as the man led them into his living room. He'd been absently petting her ever since. His three-year-old daughter, Lily, was sprawled on the floor, chatting nonsense to Patches.

Every few minutes Patches would suddenly drop to her belly, full of puppy energy, and Lily would burst into giggles and pet her.

"What is it?" Justin asked, but this time he cracked a

smile as Patches did more of her antics and Lily laughed again.

"I know it seems like a slow process, but doing it the right way now means we won't damage evidence that might help us later. It means that we're checking everything carefully so we get the person responsible. And we will. The FBI has a lot of experience with this kind of crime. And the lead agent managing this case, Agent Nez, has investigated a lot of bombings in his career."

Justin nodded slowly, finally seeming to believe the words Jax had been repeating for five days now. "Someone should pay for this."

His gaze dropped to his leg. He'd pulled up the fabric of his pants on his right side to show Jax before Lily had come into the room. A nasty scar traveled all the way from his ankle to his knee, where doctors had dealt with the large piece of metal that had been lodged there. "It ain't pretty. But at least they saved my leg. At least I'm still here."

Tears filled his eyes that he quickly swiped away as he glanced at his daughter, oblivious as she rolled over and Patches did the same.

A laugh burst free and Justin muttered, "Maybe we need to think about getting a dog."

"Yes, Daddy!" Lily screeched, leaping up and throwing her arms around Patches's neck. "A dog like Patches!"

Woof! Patches jumped to her feet, too.

"Better ask your mom," Justin said and Lily went racing out of the room. "Careful!" Justin called after her.

"We'll continue to be in touch," Jax said, shaking the man's hand as he stood. "I'm glad you're home. I'll keep you updated about the progress. And you can call me if you have questions."

"I appreciate it." A genuine smile lit Justin's face as his daughter screeched from the other room, "Mommy said yes!"

"Good luck," Jax said, then turned to his dog, who was staring in the direction Lily had disappeared. "Come on, Patches."

She followed him out the door and Jax felt his own smile break free. He was helping these victims. Slowly, but surely, they were all starting to move forward. Some were taking smaller steps than others and some had much harder journeys, but they'd all get there.

It was why he'd made the jump to the FBI. He was good at this. Maybe Ben and Anderson were right. Maybe he needed to stick to what he knew best, his own job.

As much as he wanted to help Keara, as much as he wanted to be more directly involved in stopping the person responsible, everything that was emerging from the FBI investigation suggested his and Keara's theories were off base.

There were no other bombs with the symbol. It was possible, though unlikely, that this was the only time the bomber had used the symbol. A bit more likely was that it had only been recovered in this particular bomb. But when Jax had floated that idea with Ben, the agent had seemed unconvinced. More likely, this guy was solely a bomber and the murder in Texas was unrelated. It was what Ben and Anderson believed. They even questioned if the symbols really matched. The loops were so random, they wondered if it was just coincidence, and that Keara, desperate to find connections to the old murders, was seeing what she wanted to see.

And yet… Jax couldn't shake the feeling he'd had

when he'd first seen that symbol, the certainty that it meant something. He couldn't shake the memory of Keara's eyes widening, the way she'd swayed and gone pale, when she'd seen it.

Once he and Patches climbed into his SUV, Jax didn't bother to start the engine. Instead, he pulled out his cell phone and dialed Ben.

"Ben Nez," the agent answered. Even over the phone, he sounded commanding, the tone of someone who'd been an agent for a long time and was comfortable being in control.

"It's Jax. I'm just leaving one of the victim's houses and I have a question."

"A question or information on the case?" Ben asked, a warning tone in his voice, like he knew what was coming.

Ignoring it, Jax pushed forward. He could take the snide comments about being a wannabe agent. What he couldn't take was worrying that he'd kept quiet when speaking up might have made a difference. "I'm just wondering if we have any more details on the bomb. You've got a lot of experience with weapons like this. Does it seem like it's the work of someone who's been doing it a long time? Do you think whoever did this has made bombs before?"

A heavy sigh, meant to be heard, greeted him, followed by a long silence.

Finally, Jax broke it. "This isn't idle curiosity. What do you think?"

"It's hard to say," Ben said, his tone cautious. "The bomb itself wasn't very sophisticated. You can learn how to make something like this on the internet if you know where to look. But the fact that no one noticed anything unusual, that we don't have any cameras that caught anything suspicious, suggests this guy isn't an amateur. Plus, we've been looking hard for a motive, since the most likely reason to target this location is to take out a specific person. So far we haven't come up with anything promising."

"So—"

"You're a great Victim Specialist, Jax," Ben said, cutting him off. "And if there's information you're getting from the victims that could help us figure this out, I want to hear it. If you're asking about this because it's going to somehow help you in your role, then fine. But being an investigator isn't something you do off the side of your desk, no matter what you might have seen on TV."

Jax stiffened. He'd worked side by side with Special Agents and other members of the FBI for four years. He understood all too well how many people—agents, evidence technicians, victim specialists, analysts and more—came together to solve a crime.

"I know I'm not an agent," Jax said, wishing the words didn't feel just a little bit bitter. "And I'm not trying to be one." That much was true. Despite the burnout he was feeling, despite the desire to be more embedded in the investigative side of things, he did love his job. "But this case is different. This case—"

"This isn't the first time you've stepped outside your lines," Ben contradicted. "I don't know if this is how things ran when you were on the Rapid Deployment Team…"

"Not really," Jax admitted. Yes, he'd shared his insights when he could, but he'd often worked with big task forces. And his time at a particular crime scene had been very focused.

Alaska was different. The field office was big, but so was the area they covered. When he'd had psychological insight into a case, the agents had listened. To be fair, that had always included Ben.

Maybe he was stepping over the line with this case. Thinking of his clandestine meeting with Keara just that afternoon, Jax mentally crossed off the *maybe*.

"I'm sorry," Jax said. "You're right. It's just that the symbol is really bothering me in this case."

"We're looking into it," Ben said, but his tone told Jax the truth.

They'd already decided it wasn't important.

"I'm not an agent," Jax said again, sitting up straighter and making Patches stick her nose between the seats.

Absently petting her, Jax insisted, "And I'm not a profiler, either. But my background is in psychology. That means I understand a lot about human motivation and people's desires, especially the ones they can't seem to help. All of my training, all of my experience, is telling me there's something to this symbol."

There was another pause, but this one was shorter. "Fair enough," Ben said. "Do you know what?"

"No. But the fact that you haven't been able to connect it to anything else? The fact that this strange symbol was also near a murder? There's something here."

He'd been trying to deny it, but he couldn't shake the gut feeling he'd had from the beginning. "I need a favor."

"Okay," Ben said, reluctance in his tone, but less hostility.

"Run the symbol through the FBI's database again.

This time do it without the bomb specification. See if that symbol has appeared at the scene of any other type of crime."

"I'll do it," Ben said, "but look, I've been down this kind of rabbit hole before, trying to make connections that aren't there. Be prepared for disappointment."

It had been six long years since she'd been embedded in a case like a detective, sorting through the evidence and clues. But sitting in her relaxing Alaskan home— her escape—with her laptop open to two case files and a mug of coffee that had long since gone cold, a familiar buzz filled Keara.

She loved being a police chief. She liked and respected all of the officers on her force and admired the spirit of the people of Desparre. Moving here had done so much for her mental health. It had made her feel like she was allowed to have a life again, that it wasn't a betrayal to keep living it, without Juan.

For the most part she hadn't really missed being a detective. That role came with too many memories. The surprise party Juan had thrown her when she passed her detective's exam and got promoted. The initial thrill of working a desk in the bullpen close to him. Working as partners had been against policy, since they'd just gotten married when she was promoted. But seeing him across the detectives' area each day had reminded her of their early times together, patrolling.

She'd expected being a detective would bring them closer, feel more like it had at the beginning, when they'd worked together every day. But too quickly, discussions about their cases had started interfering with their relationship. Most of it had been subtle, like the slow deterioration of their romantic dinners into sharing case files over takeout.

Then there'd been the expectations Keara had never seen coming. Being a patrol officer was dangerous, in Juan's opinion. But with Keara in a detective's seat, he'd wanted to try and have kids immediately. While she'd been working late to fit in—being a detective was still a bit of a boys' club—he'd been imagining babies. Toward the end of his life, when Keara thought they had plenty of time to figure it out, they'd started fighting over what they wanted, and when. Now it was all too late.

She minimized the case file for her husband's murder that Fitz had sent her unofficially. It hadn't been easy to go through, though thankfully, Fitz had left out the crime scene photos.

Seven years had dulled some of her grief, taken it from a sharp-edged pain that made it hard to breathe to something duller and more manageable. But she couldn't help wondering if things might have turned out differently if she and Juan hadn't made a pact to stop talking business and focus more on their relationship in those last six months. Would she have seen the threat coming? Would she have been able to prevent it?

"You can't change the past." Keara repeated the words her police-employed psychiatrist had told her seven years ago, when she wasn't ready to hear them. "You can only impact what happens in your future."

Ironic that more and more, the key to moving on seemed like it would involve revisiting her past.

And yet, was it too late? Seven years was a long time in the investigative world. There was a reason those cases were considered cold. A reason they were set aside and detectives' time reallocated to newer cases.

A reason they were rarely reopened, unless some new evidence suddenly came to light.

Rubbing the back of her head, where a headache had started to form, Keara skimmed through Juan's interview with Rodney Brown one more time. The notes were slim, the interview itself a long-shot possibility. No matter how many times Keara reread them, she didn't see anything now that her husband hadn't seen back then. Except...

Keara jerked forward, yanking her laptop closer as an offhand mention describing Rodney's house caught her eye. "Lives with a roommate, not home," Juan had written.

Juan had originally gone to interview Rodney thinking he might have seen something relevant since his car had been photographed near the crime scene the night Celia Harris was killed. Although it was good police work not to rule anyone out as a suspect too quickly, Rodney hadn't been considered one initially. The only reason Juan had left that interview with even mild suspicion was that Rodney had denied driving his car anywhere near the crime scene.

Happening to be near a crime scene wasn't a crime. Still, Juan had thought it was more likely Rodney was just afraid of police after his various assault arrests rather than a legitimate suspect, especially since he had no apparent connection to Celia. While the assault charges and the probable sexual assault told them he wasn't a nice guy, the specifics didn't suggest possible serial killer.

Like hundreds of other people who'd been interviewed in the Celia Harris murder, Rodney Brown had been pushed to the bottom of the list of people who might know something. But what if Juan had been approaching it from the wrong angle?

What if the reason Rodney had so vehemently insisted he hadn't been driving anywhere near the crime scene that night was because he hadn't? What if the roommate had used his car?

A thrill ran through Keara, a jolt of adrenaline she hadn't felt in a long time—the gut feeling that she was onto something with a case.

When Rodney had disappeared, the follow-up interview by Fitz said the house had been cleared out. So that meant the roommate had disappeared, too. Had they left together? Had they been in on Celia's murder together?

Or maybe her earlier theory had been right all along. Maybe the person who'd set the bomb had intentionally used the symbol from Celia's murder to throw suspicion on someone else—his roommate.

If she was right, that triggered a lot of new questions: Who had killed Celia and who had set the bomb? Which of those two had killed her husband, Rodney or his roommate?

And where were they both now?

Chapter 10

Every officer in the Desparre police station turned to stare at Jax as he strode through the station, following Officer Tate Emory to Keara's office.

Jax tried not to feel self-conscious as he juggled two cups of takeout coffee, wondering why he was getting so much attention. He'd been here before; it wasn't like the officers didn't know who he was. Maybe it was the overstuffed bag he had slung over one shoulder, full of FBI case printouts Ben had handed him that morning. Or maybe they could read his newly cautious hope about what those printouts might contain.

As Jax gave subdued nods of greeting to the officers who met his gaze, Patches bounded around him, occasionally darting to a desk for a pat from one of the officers before running back to his side.

"What's going on?" Jax asked Tate softly.

Tate's gaze briefly scanned the room before coming back to him. "Something's up with the chief," he said, then knocked on the door to Keara's office before pushing it open.

From across the station's bullpen, through the glass walls into her office, Keara had merely appeared hard at work. From a distance, he'd assumed her normal professional face was on. It was calm and serious and confident, probably something that had helped her win Desparre's trust when she'd first shown up here, an outsider and young for a police chief job.

Jax had known from her frantic call at seven that morning—when he and Patches had barely been awake—that she was reenergized about the bombing investigation and its possible connection to Juan's death. He should have realized this new information about a roommate she'd discovered would only fuel Keara's desperation.

Up close, he could see the dark circles underneath her eyes that suggested she'd been awake long before she'd called him, maybe that she hadn't gone to bed at all. Jittery energy radiated from her.

As he stepped more fully into the room, she stood and reached for one of the coffees he held. "Is this for me?"

"Yes," he answered.

Woof! Patches circled Keara, tail wagging.

"Easy, Patches," Jax warned her, not wanting his dog to trip Keara.

"She's fine," Keara said, bending down to pet Patches and getting rewarded by a dog kiss across her cheek. Keara laughed, then took a long sip of coffee, closing her eyes like she'd badly needed the caffeine jolt.

Tate gave Jax a raised-eyebrow look that seemed to say "See what I mean?" before he left the office, closing the door behind him.

Jax took a minute to watch Keara while she had her eyes closed, exhaustion and hope battling on her face. All the while, she pet Patches.

His dog's tail wagged, but she glanced back at him, as if she also wondered what was going on with Keara.

What must it be like to have spent seven years knowing someone she loved had been murdered and not being able to do anything about it? What must it be like now, to have this sudden, long-shot hope again?

Dread tightened his chest, knowing he was partly responsible. If they were both wrong, how much worse would it be for Keara?

Her eyes opened, her gaze instantly locking on his like she'd read his thoughts. Instead of making him feel more guilty, the intensity there made his own hope ignite.

What if they were right? What if they could solve her husband's murder? What if she was finally able to get closure and move on with her life? He lived too far away to be a part of it in any meaningful way, but knowing that didn't stop a sudden longing.

She broke eye contact, standing, and her tone was all business when she said, "Let's get to work."

He'd spent the morning like he had almost every other morning since he'd arrived in Luna, talking to victims and their families. Today he'd mostly been returning personal effects. For some of the victims, it was a welcome visit, a sign of moving forward. For others, it was a stark reminder of what, or who, they'd lost.

At lunchtime, when his mind had been ping-ponging

between the idea of Rodney Brown having a roommate and the needs of the bombing victims, Ben had asked to meet. He'd handed over a stack of printouts and told Jax, "This is your theory, so I'm going to let you run with it. It's not protocol and I'm definitely going to be reviewing all of this myself as soon as I get a chance, but I'm expecting you to return the favor. You find something—anything at all—and I want to be your first call. Deal?"

Jax had looked down at the massive stack of printouts, then back at Ben, who'd grinned and said, "Our databases aren't magic. I input the details of the symbol, but with parameters this wide—connected to any crime over the past seven years—it spit out a *lot* of cases across the country. There's a good chance none of them are connected to the bombing or the murder, because the system matches descriptions. And it's all different law enforcement entering them, not just FBI. It's you who has to pull up the actual pictures and do a visual comparison. Still…"

"There's a chance," Jax had said. "It's a deal. I'll call you if I find anything," he'd agreed, although the first thing he'd done when Ben left the room was call Keara and let her know he was coming to the station and needed her help. He knew Ben had thrown the material at him because he still felt doubtful about a connection to the symbol and was more than willing to let Jax do the heavy lifting on that aspect of the case.

"Let's see the cases," she said.

"There are a lot," he warned, pulling out the massive pile of paperwork. "The database spits out all possibilities. It's up to us to wade through them all and narrow it down."

She gave him a one-sided grin and held her coffee cup up like she was making a toast. "Welcome to the life of a detective, Jax. Let's take a look."

As she cleared off some space on her desk and gestured for him to take the seat across from her chair, she asked, "Does the FBI know I'm helping you with this?"

"No." He settled into the seat and set half the stack in front of him, passing her the other half.

Instead of sitting beside him, Patches followed Keara around to her side of the desk.

As Keara dug into her stack of files, Jax couldn't help but stare at her carefully tied-back hair and light, professional makeup. Even the first day he'd met her, dressed down in jeans and a raincoat, she'd looked like someone who was in charge. But the day he'd stopped by her house unannounced…

He smiled at the memory of her hair spilling over her shoulders, the cabernet staining her lips like a funky lipstick. It was a look he doubted many people in Desparre got to see, even on her days off.

"Stop staring and start reading," Keara said, without glancing up.

The smile grew and he held in a laugh. Why couldn't he have met her under different circumstances? Without her husband's unsolved murder hanging over her head like a dark cloud? Without four hundred miles between their homes?

As his smile faded, he asked, "Any luck finding the roommate?"

Her gaze met his, serious and determined. A look that said she would search as long as it took. "No. Assuming Juan was right, this guy wasn't listed on the lease with Rodney. I haven't been able to dig up so much as a name." Her lips tightened as she blew out a heavy breath. "Whoever he is, he's as much of a ghost as Rodney, maybe even more so."

As Jax stared at her, she broke eye contact, lines creasing her forehead. There was a hint of fear underneath her words as she said, "Seven years is a long time. I'm scared I won't be able to track him."

"We can do it," Jax said, resisting the urge to reach his hand out and take hers.

From the other side of the desk, Patches made a slight whining sound, her way of getting attention when she knew someone needed her but wasn't paying attention. From Keara's suddenly surprised look, Patches had also pushed her head into Keara's lap, insisting on being pet.

Some of the lines raking Keara's forehead disappeared as she pet Patches.

He said a silent *thank you* to his dog, then continued, "There is one piece of good news here."

She looked up at him again.

"If he's trying so hard to stay beneath the radar that you're struggling to even find mention of his name, there's probably a reason. We might really be onto our bomber."

"There has to be *something* here," Keara muttered as she set aside yet another case description in her *No* pile.

She and Jax had been sorting through the huge stack of cases he'd brought for almost an hour. In that time, Jax's stack of unrelated cases had grown almost as high as hers. They had a few *Maybe*s, but years spent as an officer, then a detective, then a police chief told Keara none of them were likely to be connected to the bombing, Celia's murder, or Juan's murder.

She'd been so hopeful when Jax had walked into her office, carrying such a big stack of possibilities. After her sleepless night, having Jax to help—along with his calming presence and Patches's cute distraction—had made her feel like answers had to be in sight.

She wasn't so far removed from her time as a detective that she'd forgotten the slog of it all. The hours that felt unending and pointless until one small detail broke open a case. Both Juan's and Celia's cases had remained open for a year, with Houston detectives logging thousands of hours on them, and they still hadn't found that one detail.

Lately, Keara had spent too much time fighting a roller coaster of emotions, rocketing from a certainty she'd finally get closure to the fear that she'd get nowhere and just end up back where she'd been six years ago. Grief-ridden, brokenhearted and stuck.

Back then she'd reacted by finding a tiny job posting across the country, far from anyone she knew. Getting the job had been a surprise; when she'd taken it, her family and friends had all been shocked. Until five days ago, it had felt like a brand-new start.

"We've got a couple of possibilities," Jax reminded her, his dark brown eyes full of determination, like he was trying to lend her strength.

She gave him a shaky smile, both appreciating the effort and not wanting him to see too deeply into her soul. Working with detectives was hard enough—they were trained to see what you weren't telling them. But someone with years of experience as a psychologist and a therapist? The more time she spent with him, the more she wondered if he could tell everything she was thinking.

She redirected her gaze to her stack of cases before Jax could make out the other thing she couldn't help feeling when he was around—attraction.

He was so different from Juan. Half a foot taller, Jax was slower to smile but more likely to have it burst into a full-blown grin when he did. His skin was darker and smoother, his body more lean muscle than Juan's heavier bulk.

But it was more than just the physical differences. Her husband had been hard to win over, suspicious and wary until you proved you could be trusted. Jax seemed to approach everyone like his friend, until proven otherwise. Probably a result of their respective professions.

In other ways, she could see definite similarities. Juan could fill a conversation with lots of small talk so you didn't even realize you'd shared a lot more with him than he had with you. It was a skill that had come in handy as a detective, but frustrated her in the early stages of their relationship. Only once they'd been dating for a few years had he really started opening up to her.

From the little bit she'd asked about Jax's personal life, he hadn't seemed closed off at all. Still, he was good at pulling personal information out of others. It was certainly something that was helping him reach victims. Maybe that was why she'd connected so easily to him.

Was that all this was? Her projecting a connection because she needed someone to help her process the fact that Juan's death had gone unsolved? That she'd *let* it go unsolved, by running across the country instead of staying and trying to figure it out herself?

"No," Jax said and for a minute, Keara wondered if she'd spoken her thoughts out loud.

"What?"

He sighed, ran a hand through his hair that mussed it up just enough to make Keara long to fix it for him. "I thought maybe I'd found something, but I didn't."

He tossed the case summary printout on his *No* pile, then gave her an encouraging smile. "We're onto something. I can feel it." His eyes were already on the next case file as he muttered, "We just have to keep searching."

A smile pulled at her lips despite how discouraged she'd started to feel. For a minute she just watched him, then Patches nudging her leg made her refocus.

Petting the dog with one hand, Keara flipped open a new case file and her heart gave a hard *thump*. "No way," she breathed. She yanked the page closer to her face to scrutinize the scanned picture of a symbol. It looked eerily similar to the one found at the murder, down to the spray paint.

"What is it?"

Jax sounded distracted and Keara shook her paper at him, her excitement growing. "I think I found something. It's…" She shook her head, surprised at the crime. But there was no question that the symbol was the same. "It's an *arson* case. Unsolved, no promising suspects. It's from six years ago, in Oklahoma." She set the paper down. "Maybe that's why the detectives never found Rodney after Juan died. He'd already moved on to Oklahoma."

"Keara." Jax looked up at her, surprise and intensity in his gaze. "I've got something, too."

Her pulse jumped again as she leaned toward him

across the desk, trying to see his case details. "Another fire?"

"No, another murder. Five years ago, in Nebraska."

Excitement filled her, churning in her stomach along with too much coffee. "He was heading north. He was slowly moving toward Alaska."

Jax's gaze met hers again and she saw her excitement reflected there. "Maybe."

"*Maybe?* No, definitely." The buzz she'd felt last night when she'd discovered Rodney had a roommate returned, headier now.

She tossed the case information into her *Yes* pile and kept searching. Over the next half hour, her excitement dimmed slightly, as no new cases looked connected. But then she and Jax found three more in rapid succession, until they had a stack of five with the exact same symbol. The symbol was drawn in different ways, found in different places at the crime scenes, but they had to be connected.

"We're onto him," Jax said, grinning at her over the newly divided stacks of cases.

The dimple just visible on his right cheek as he smiled at her almost made her smile back. Except...

"There's just one problem," Keara told him, dread already balling up in her stomach again.

"What? That we probably haven't found every-thing?" Jax referred to the fact that there was one time gap big enough that they'd agreed there was probably at least one more connected crime. "I'm sure another one will surface eventually."

"Not that," Keara said. "Every single one of these cases is in a different jurisdiction. Hell, every case is in a different *state*."

"Okay, but—"

"Jax, he set off this bomb in Luna, left behind this symbol." Frustration welled up, made her want to take it out at the gym on a punching bag. "This pattern suggests he commits one crime and then leaves. He's probably already gone."

He stared back at her, his grin slowly fading.

Beside her, Patches whined and nudged her leg.

Keara looked down at the dog and gave her a grateful smile, tried to will forward some positive energy. They'd found the criminal's trail, but had it already gone cold here?

Boom!

A sound like thunder directly overhead exploded in her ears, making her flinch and instinctively leap to her feet, her hand already near her weapon.

Through the glass walls of her office, her officers were doing the same, glancing questioningly at one another.

Then the silence following the loud noise was replaced by screaming.

Before Keara made it to her office door, the door into the bullpen opened.

Charlie Quinn, one of her longest-term veterans, appeared, looking pale. Even from a distance, she could read the words on his lips.

"Bomb."

Chapter 11

There was chaos in her police station.

Her officers were all racing for the door, some grabbing weapons from desks and shoving them in holsters, others looking around with panic. The door into the bullpen was open—and probably the door to the station beyond that—so Keara could hear the panicked cacophony outside, too. Screams, crying and a persistent wailing that sent a chill through her entire body.

After yanking open the door to her office, Keara raced into the chaos and yelled, "Wait!"

Her officers stopped moving toward the exit, but their gazes still darted all around. Her veterans seemed filled with anxious determination, ready to find out what was happening and help. Some of the newer officers looked stiff with uncertainty. None of them had ever faced anything like this.

Neither had she.

Dread settled in her gut, her pulse picking up at the worry she wouldn't know how to manage this properly. Houston was a big city, but even there, she'd never been on the scene of a bomb. The closest she'd come was seeing the aftermath of the Luna explosion.

"Right now we don't know anything."

"We know it was a bomb outside, maybe on the street," Charlie interrupted, his voice deeper than usual with tension. "Lorenzo and the Rook are out there."

At his words, everyone started moving again.

"Stop!" Keara demanded. "Listen. We need to be careful. What we don't know is if there are more bombs set. Sam, I need you to stay here and manage the station. Field calls, deal with anyone who comes in off the street and get paramedics on scene. Then call the hospital in Luna and tell them to expect injured. We might need their medevac helicopter. Line it up."

Sam Jennings nodded. He was a five-year veteran who was typically cool under pressure and great at multitasking, especially when it involved tech. But his movements were shaky as he headed toward the front of the station.

"Everyone else, keep your eyes open and stay in contact with each other. Let's go."

As her officers started running for the door, Keara turned back toward her office to ask Jax to inform the FBI.

He met her gaze immediately, and there was worry in his eyes, even as his attention seemed to be half on the phone at his ear. Moving the mouthpiece backward, he called to her, "I'm on with Anderson. The FBI is on the way. They're coming with agents and evidence techs. They'll handle the bigger investigation—they assume it's connected to Luna. They want you to focus on helping the injured and securing the scene."

Keara didn't bother being offended at the FBI instantly calling jurisdiction. They had more experience, more resources. She was happy to focus on the safety of her citizens and let the FBI take the lead. Nodding, Keara delayed a few seconds to take in the calm steadiness of Jax's presence. Then she took a deep breath and raced after her officers.

As soon as she stepped outside, a wisp of smoke wafted toward her, the acrid taste of it filling her mouth and then her lungs. Her eyes watered, partly from the smoke, but mostly from the scene in front of her.

The grassy park down the street from the police station—a popular place for citizens to dog walk or picnic—was now a bomb site. Flames leaped out from a small gazebo at the back of the park, close to the woods. The charred ground around it, a blackened patch where bright blue wild irises had just been starting to bloom, reminded her of the scene at Luna. The set of swings at the center of the park were warped and partially collapsed, one swing completely missing. People were scattered around, some lying on the ground, some hunched over, and others stumbling away.

She'd known some of the victims at the Luna bombing. She knew almost everyone who lived in Desparre.

Keara ran faster. She heard the heavy police station door slam closed and looked back to see Jax hurrying after her. She immediately glanced toward the ground at his side, but he'd left Patches in the station. Probably because of the debris that might be dangerous for her to walk on.

Whipping her gaze back to the park, Keara scanned

the area, trying to take in everything at once. There were people staggering backward, their movements and expressions full of shock. Others seemed frozen. Still others were helping, moving toward the park instead of away from it, risking their own safety for their neighbors. That included her officers.

Whoever had done this was either fearless or making a statement. The park was less than a hundred feet from the police station.

Slowing to a stop as she neared the park, Keara searched for anyone whose reaction seemed out of place. Either too calm or worse, pleased. But everyone appeared shocked and scared. No one was hurrying away from the scene, either.

She glanced at Jax, who'd paused next to her. His expression was serious and troubled, but he still managed to radiate a certain calm. No wonder people gravitated toward him in a crisis.

He shook his head at her and she realized he'd been looking for the same thing, studying people with a psychologist's perspective.

Whoever the bomber was, he was either long gone or one hell of an actor.

"Chief!"

At the tearful tone of Lorenzo, one of her steadiest veterans, Keara's gaze whipped back to the park.

At the edge of the grassy area, near the road, Lorenzo was bent over someone.

The dread in her gut intensified, bubbling up a familiar grief. She didn't need to see the face of the person on the ground to know who it was. The newest and youngest member of her force. Lorenzo's partner, twenty-year-old Nate Dreymond.

Rushing over, Keara dropped to the grass next to Lorenzo.

Nate was prone on the ground, eyes closed and face ashen. There was blood on his head, and his arm was stretched out at an unnatural angle.

"We were heading out for patrol. Someone in the park called us over. I'm not sure who it was or what they wanted." Lorenzo's words were rapid-fire, his voice shaky. "Rook was ahead of me. When the bomb went off, something flew this way and slammed into him. I don't know what it's from, but—" he gestured to a piece of metal, twisted and unidentifiable, and covered in blood "—the force of the blast knocked me down, too." His hand, shaking violently, went to his own head.

When he met her gaze, his focus seemed off, too. "When I could get up, I came over here, but—"

"No," Keara whispered, the image of another man's blood filling her mind. She leaned down, pressing her ear to Nate's chest. She expected to hear nothing, but a weak *thump thump* came through.

"He's in bad shape," Lorenzo finished.

Letting out a long breath, Keara sat up again and barked into her radio, "Sam, get that medevac from the Luna hospital. Nate needs it."

She scanned his prone form, looking for injuries that needed immediate attention. She'd gotten basic training in first aid over the years in Houston. It had been a long time, though, and she frantically ran through the mental checklist she used to know by heart.

She didn't see any way to help him. He was unconscious with a clearly broken arm, but the blood on his head wasn't still flowing.

"Medevac is coming," Sam's strained voice informed her. "They're twenty minutes out."

"Help!"

Keara's head popped up at the cry. She put her hand on Lorenzo's arm and asked, "You okay?"

"Fine," Lorenzo said.

There was no doubt he needed to get checked out by a doctor, but she nodded. "Stay with Nate. Call me if anything changes."

Then she pushed to her feet and hurried across the park to the person calling. The grass felt strange beneath her boots, crunchy where it should have been soft. As she ran, she passed by other Desparre citizens, some simply looking dazed and others clearly injured.

There was a family, fairly new to Desparre, with a six-year-old and a new baby on the way, hugging each other and crying. The owner of Desparre's downtown bar, wrapping his bleeding arm with his own shirt. A loner who lived up the mountain and came into the park every few weeks but still stuck with his own company, sat on the ground, looking dazed. He had a hand to his head and both legs were bleeding, but nothing was gushing.

Keara scanned each of them, but kept moving. None needed immediate attention.

The fire at the gazebo was growing, flames devouring most of it now. The structure was relatively far from other buildings, but it was close enough to the woods to be a concern. She lifted her radio and said, "We need to manage this fire."

"On it," Tate Emory answered and from her peripheral vision, she could see he was also on his cell phone, probably with the tiny fire department. They were located on the edge of Desparre and they served the whole county, including Luna and other neighboring towns. They were also all volunteer and had similar hours as her officers.

"I've got some citizens lined up to bring buckets from the bar while we wait for the fire department," Tate told her. "We should be able to keep this from jumping."

"Good. Radio if you need more help," she instructed, then jammed her radio back into her belt.

At the edge of the gazebo, she discovered who had called for help. Talise Poitra owned the grocery store in downtown Desparre. She was friendly and quick to advise outsiders, which Keara had discovered her first week in town. Talise had celebrated her seventieth birthday last month and hung balloons all over the grocery store. She'd stopped by the police station with cake and told them she insisted the entire town celebrate with her.

Right now the woman with the long gray hair, easy smile and deeply weathered skin from a lifetime in Alaska was holding her leg with one hand and her ear with the other. A deep gash ran the length of her right thigh and blood spurted out at regular intervals.

Swearing, Keara yanked at the sleeve of her police uniform until the arm ripped off. She dropped to her knees and tied the fabric around the top of Talise's leg. But no matter how hard she yanked the knot, blood was still pumping.

"I got it," Jax said, suddenly beside her, his belt in hand. "Brace yourself," he told Talise, then tightened the belt over the fabric.

Talise went pale, her eyes rolling backward as she swayed. But she stiffened before Keara could grab her.

Her hands dropped to the ground, bracing herself, and Keara saw more blood on the woman's right ear.

Fury overlaid the dread she'd been feeling. This was *her* town. These people were *her* responsibility.

She put her hand on Talise's arm, trying to comfort her, even as her gaze met Jax's.

"Two bombs," he said, his tone filled with meaning she didn't understand.

She shook her head and he added, "Two bombs in less than a week. Just one town apart."

The implications sank in fast. The crimes they'd been poring over this afternoon had been filled with differences. The only commonality they'd shared besides the symbol was that the perpetrator hadn't struck again in the same jurisdiction, or even the same state.

"It's not the same person," she breathed.

Chapter 12

The day had gone by in a blur of blood and fire and pained cries. But rushing from one person to the next hadn't been able to fully distract him from the panic.

Over his years on the Rapid Deployment Team, he'd gotten used to mass casualty events. They didn't get any easier, but the fear and panic of his first few scenes hadn't returned in years. Not until today.

Only after most of the victims had been checked by paramedics and Keara was helping put out the last of the fire had he realized why. A flame had sparked, creating a loud *boom* that sounded like a bullet, and his gaze had leaped immediately to Keara.

In that moment it hit him. He was worried about her safety. He was worried about *her*.

Recognizing where the panic was coming from created a different kind of worry, but he'd pushed it aside and spent the rest of the day focusing on the victims.

Jax was exhausted. So was Patches, who'd joined him at the scene as soon as it was clear enough to be safe. The two of them had talked to as many victims as possible. They'd also spent time comforting the Desparre officers, who had never seen anything like this.

For all of his exhaustion, the people around him were even more tired. Ben and Anderson coming in with their FBI team had taken the weight of the investigation off the Desparre PD, but it hadn't taken away the responsibility.

He could see it as he eyed Keara from his peripheral vision, trudging beside him, leaving the bomb site. There was soot smeared across her forehead, someone else's blood on her arms and a furious determination on her face.

As she glanced back at the scene, barely visible in the moonlight, he told her, "There's nothing else you can do there tonight."

Walking between them, Patches nudged Keara with her nose, always sensitive to people's needs.

Keara smiled fondly down at his dog, petting her head as she refocused on their destination: the police station.

Anderson jogged up beside them, shivering even with his FBI jacket zipped all the way up. The agent had come from Los Angeles and even after being in Alaska longer than Jax, he still hadn't acclimated. His normally perfect hair was sticking up in all directions and there were dark craters under his eyes. "We'll be taking another look at that symbol now that we've seen it at a second bomb site."

Jax felt his heart thump harder. "It was on this bomb, too?"

"Not on the bomb. We found it on a tree behind the gazebo. It was carved there, pretty recently, judging by the state of it."

Keara frowned, looking more perplexed than encouraged by the news.

Anderson glanced from Jax to Keara and back again. "Ben said you were combing through other crimes that might have the same symbol. Any luck?"

Jax gave a frustrated shrug. "We thought so, but now I'm not so sure they match. I'll flag them for you guys to look, but..."

"Seems like more than one person is using the same symbol," Anderson finished, not sounding surprised.

Jax glanced at Keara, wanting her take on it, and she gave a discouraged nod.

"This symbol means something we don't understand yet," Anderson said. "You were right about that, Jax. Whatever the meaning, it sounds like it's important to more than one criminal. Maybe it's connected to an organization, possibly some kind of underground group."

"But *what*?" Keara muttered. "The Houston PD researched it seven years ago. *I* researched it this week. None of us came up with anything."

Anderson shrugged, covering a yawn with his hand. "Or it could be more personal. Maybe we have a couple of criminals who were a team once and now they're both taking the symbol to their own crimes."

Keara's troubled gaze met his and he could practically read her thoughts: *If the symbol was from some personal event, how would they ever figure it out?*

Patches nudged her again as they reached the police station and Keara pet her once more before holding open the door.

Jax filed inside with Patches, but Keara stayed there, holding the door open and thanking each of her exhausted officers—and all of the FBI agents, too—as they walked past her.

She was a good chief. It couldn't have been easy for her, being the only woman on the force, being so young for her role and being an outsider, too. But it was obvious her officers respected her. Despite how personally each of them had been touched by today's tragedy, they mustered up weak nods for her in return.

Even the FBI agents, who could sometimes get frustrated with small-town officers who had little experience dealing with major crimes, seemed impressed by Keara and her team.

As Keara finally followed them inside, Sam stood up behind the front desk. "Any news on Nate?"

Keara swept her gaze over her officers, who had all stopped in the entryway of the station to listen. "The hospital is going to update us when there's any change. I'll keep you all informed."

Keara's youngest rookie had been in bad shape when the helicopter had lifted off. So had its other occupant, the grocery store owner who was far stronger than she looked to have held on until the medevac team arrived. Five other people had been taken to the hospital, too, but they'd gone by ambulance, taking the hour ride up and down the mountain to get to Luna. But at least—as of right now—no one had been killed in this bombing.

"We're going to relocate over to Desparre," Ben said, moving to the front of the crowd.

The seasoned agent, who'd lived in Alaska most of his life and managed other scenes where explosives had been set off, was holding up better than most of them.

But even he had cracks in his stoicism, with a tight set to his jaw that suggested this case had him worried.

"There's a hotel just a few miles outside of town," Keara said. "It's called Royal Desparre. It's a nice place, but we don't get many tourists here. They'll have vacancies."

"Thanks," Ben said. "Let's go," he called to the other FBI agents and employees, and then he told Keara, "We'll be back in the morning."

As they trudged out of the station, Jax lagged behind. He didn't want to leave without a chance to talk to Keara alone. He wanted to see how she really felt about the new bombing and what they'd found this afternoon. But it was more than that. He also wanted to be able to talk to her outside her official capacity, away from people who relied on her to set the tone and be a leader. To make sure she was really okay.

"You coming?" Anderson called to him as Keara's officers all started heading out the door, too.

Jax looked at Keara and found her gaze already on him. "I have a pull-out couch," she said, loud enough for Anderson to hear. "In case they won't let Patches stay in the hotel."

Anderson didn't look like he bought her reasoning, but Jax jumped on it. "That would be great. Thanks."

Patches gave her own *woof* of approval.

Keara nodded stiffly at him, then turned away, checking on each of her officers individually. She made sure each one was able to drive home, then waited until they'd all left the station before she finally returned her attention to him.

"How are you holding up?" he asked.

Patches hurried over to her side again, sitting next

to Keara and staring up at her. But it wasn't the look Patches gave when she was trying to help someone; this was his dog becoming attached.

Jax stared at Patches as Keara began to pet his dog, and new anxiety filled him. He was becoming attached to Keara, too. Whenever the end of this case came, he wasn't sure he was going to be ready to stop seeing her every day.

Keara pet Patches for a long moment without answering. Then her troubled gaze met his. "How do you do this, case after case?"

"What do you mean?"

"This." She gestured toward the front door. "How do you come to these scenes, tragedy after tragedy?" Her voice cracked as she continued, "How do you wade into them, again and again, hearing about the worst thing someone has experienced?"

He shrugged, gave her a small smile. "I'm good at it. Patches is good at it."

Woof!

Another smile broke free as he told her, "That's right, Patches." Then he said to Keara, "It's not easy. But knowing that I've helped someone makes it worthwhile. What about *you*?"

She laughed, but it was short and bitter. "The type of crime scene I've probably been called to most often in Desparre is a bar fight. This is way outside of my comfort zone. I didn't experience anything like this, even in Houston."

Jax flashed back to the dangerous situation in the Luna bar the day he'd met her. His arms were still healing from being sliced through with broken bottles when the drunk had yanked him off the bar. He could still feel the panic when he'd jumped into the fray, worried the mob of men was going to overrun Keara at any moment.

"I mean, how do you handle constantly running into danger?"

"It's part of the job. I accepted the danger a long time ago, when I took the oath to become a police officer. But I've been at this career since I was twenty-three. I still get scared on calls sometimes, but I trust my training and I trust my officers to have my back. And I believe in what I do. That's worth the fear."

She frowned, staring at the ground, her hand pausing on Patches's head. Her voice was almost a whisper when she admitted, "It's not the physical danger that really scares me. It's the cases I can't solve. That's what keeps me up at night."

When her gaze met his again, he saw years of pain reflected back at him. "What scares me is the idea that I'll never be able to solve Juan's murder. And that as long as it remains unsolved, I'll never be able to fully move forward myself."

Keara woke up disoriented, a headache pounding at her temples and the smell of smoke lodged in her nostrils. Against her back was a strong, warm body.

In a flash, the night before returned to her. Making the short drive from the police station to her house, every second stretching out as she'd fought to keep her eyes open. Jax in the seat beside her and Patches lightly snoring in the back.

When they'd finally pulled up to her house, she'd barely had the energy to trade the uniform she'd worn to the crime scene for joggers and a long-sleeved T-shirt. She'd leaned over the sink and scrubbed her hands, face and arms, but sleep had sounded more appealing than a shower.

She'd returned to her living room to find Jax already changed into sweatpants and a T-shirt emblazoned with Fidelity. Bravery. Integrity. Apparently, he carried extra clothes everywhere he went.

In that moment, with the weight of the town's expectations and Juan's unsolved case, Jax—half a foot taller than she was with the body of a federal agent and the eyes of a therapist—had seemed like the perfect person to help her shoulder some of it. So when he'd walked over and put his arms around her, she'd sunk into his embrace.

She vaguely recalled him walking her over to the couch and coaxing her to lie down against him. As soon as she'd laid her head on his outstretched arm, the exhaustion had overcome her.

Despite the horror of the day before, despite the gnawing worry about her ability to solve Juan's case so many years later, it was the best she'd slept in years. She glanced at the floor below her, where Patches was just starting to stir, her feet twitching and her eyes opening.

When she met Keara's gaze, her tail started to thump against the wood floor and Keara whispered, "Shhh."

Nerves made her feel clumsy as she slowly slid forward on the couch, carefully lifting the arm draped over her waist. She barely breathed as she tried to slip away from Jax without waking him.

It had been seven long years since she'd woken up with a man's arm draped over her.

She finally took a deep breath as she sat up and Jax didn't move behind her. Carefully setting her feet down so she wouldn't step on Patches, she slid forward, hoping to stand without disturbing him.

"It's morning already?" Jax asked.

His voice was slightly deeper with sleep, and it sent a jolt of awareness through her, even as she cringed at having woken him.

"Yep," she said, her voice too cheery. She stood, heading toward the connected kitchen and resisting the urge to run a hand over her hair, which felt like a tangled mess, the bobby pins half out of her bun. "Coffee?"

Patches leaped up, racing after her, sliding as the planked wood floors of her living room gave way to slicker tile in the kitchen.

Keara couldn't stop the laugh that escaped as Patches ran around her in a circle, tail wagging. She looked more like a puppy than a therapy dog and Keara knew Patches was catching her nervous energy.

"Sounds good," Jax said from the living room.

She could hear him standing, probably stretching, but she didn't glance back. Her neck and face felt warm with the knowledge that he knew exactly why she was trying to busy herself. It didn't take a psychology degree—which he had in multiples—to recognize that she was uncomfortable with what had happened between them last night. The fact that it had been a lot more innocent than the kisses they'd shared a few days ago didn't matter. Spending the night in his embrace had felt more intimate.

As she scooped coffee grinds into the machine, Jax joined her in the kitchen. From her peripheral vision, she saw him lean against her island and watch her.

Before she could get her scrambled brain to come up with small talk—or better yet, a coherent discussion about the investigation—he asked, "What did your family think about you moving across the country to be a police chief?"

"They weren't thrilled." She spun to face him and even knowing where he'd been standing, even though he was still a couple of feet away, it felt too close. His hair was slightly mussed from sleep, making her realize how curly it was, making her want to run her hands through it.

Fisting them at her sides, she continued, "But then, they kept hoping Juan's death would be a wake-up call that I needed to find another profession."

"They worry about you."

"Yeah. I'm an only child, but as my dad likes to joke, with Irish on one side and Italian on the other, we're not a small family. My aunt was a police officer and I was really close to her growing up. She worked a night shift during most of my childhood, and since my parents worked days, she'd pick me up from school every day. She was killed on the job the same year I got my badge."

"I'm sorry."

Keara nodded. The year her aunt had died had been the same time she'd been paired up with Juan. It had been a hugely bittersweet time in her life. She'd wanted to follow in her aunt's footsteps since she was a kid. She'd always imagined them working together someday.

"I've lived here for six years now and they still ask when I'm moving back on a pretty regular basis." She shrugged, even though it frustrated her. "At least it's coming from a place of love."

"What if we solve Juan's case?" Jax stared at her, his gaze so focused that even Patches quieted down.

Her heart jumped at the idea that he still thought it

was possible. Jax wasn't an investigator, but over the past week, she'd discovered he made a great partner. "What do you mean?"

"If we solve it, would you consider moving back to Houston?"

She'd never thought about it. Moving to Alaska had been a concession; her way of admitting that Juan's murder would always remain unsolved.

The Houston PD would probably take her back, if they had an opening. She'd had a good relationship with the officers and chief there. But what had started as a self-imposed exile and escape had become her home.

She shook her head. "I don't think so. I should visit more. I miss my family. But that was a different chapter of my life. Alaska is my future."

Saying the words out loud, she realized how true they were. It freed something inside her, made real happiness seem possible again. And staring at the Victim Specialist in her kitchen made even more seem possible.

Diverting her gaze before he read her thoughts, she spun back to the coffee machine, filled it with water and hit Brew.

When he didn't move, she turned back toward him, bracing her hands on the counter behind her. "This is my town, Jax." She sighed, the responsibilities crashing back around her. "I'm glad the FBI is taking lead in the new investigation. They have a lot more experience than I do. But when they leave, this will still be my home. These people will still be my responsibility. I'm officially involved now, so we don't need to be investigating on the side."

He pushed away from the island, his mouth opening. She cut off the argument she could see coming. "That doesn't mean I want to stop working with you. I don't care what your title is. I want your psychological insight on this. But what we saw in the cases we dug up yesterday? They don't match what's happening here."

He frowned, lines creasing his forehead. "I know."

"If this were one person so savvy and determined to stay off police radar by jumping jurisdictions—hell, jumping *states*—between his crimes, why set off two bombs in less than a week? Most likely, this is still connected to the crimes we dug up *somehow*, if we can figure out that symbol. But right now we have a bigger problem."

Jax nodded. "We're looking at a serial bomber."

"Yeah. And with two bombs in six days, he's probably not finished."

Chapter 13

Jax had a tendency to overanalyze things, but right now he knew exactly what he wanted.

He stared across the Desparre park at Keara, frowning as she talked to Ben and Anderson. As if she sensed his gaze on her, her focus shifted to him briefly. Then her head swung back to the agents.

Patches nudged his leg with her nose a few times and he pet her head.

"Sorry, Patches. You're right. We need to be working."

Although yesterday had been horrific, with people bleeding and crying and the gazebo blazing, the aftermath of the destruction was terrible, too. The once-cheerful white gazebo was now a pile of charred wood, splintered edges reaching into the air. The ground beside it was burned and bloodied. Scattered across the park were discarded personal items that hadn't yet been tagged and collected as evidence. The FBI's Evidence

Response Team members walked among them, gathering anything relevant.

Somehow, it all felt more jarring after the awkward bliss of his morning. While Keara had showered, he'd made scrambled eggs. They'd eaten at her kitchen table and he'd pretended not to notice when she fell for Patches's sad eyes and fed her some under the table.

He'd never dated anyone in law enforcement, despite working so closely with them, despite some mutual interest a few years ago when he'd been in DC. He'd never wanted the constant fear that came along with it. But Keara? His gaze darted to her once more, took in the serious determination in every line of her body. Being with Keara would be worth it.

The four hundred miles between Desparre and Anchorage wasn't ideal, but it suddenly didn't seem impossible.

The bigger hurdle was Keara herself. Her reaction to waking up next to him this morning had been equal parts adorable and frustrating. But even if she was willing to try and pursue something long-distance, would her heart really be in it? Or would she never be able to truly give him a chance while her past was unresolved? Her words at the police station ran through his mind:

What scares me is the idea that I'll never be able to solve Juan's murder. And that as long as it remains unsolved, I'll never be able to fully move forward myself.

As he stared at her, hoping this case would be able to shed light on her husband's murder, would be able to give her that closure, he also hoped he could find a way to breach her walls even if it didn't.

She'd been closed off for years, running away to Alaska but never able to escape her husband's unsolved murder. It probably made her feel like a failure in some ways, and it wouldn't matter how often someone told her that wasn't true. She'd always wonder if she should have done more, if she should have insisted on staying on the case. He didn't need training in psych to guess that. At the very least, he wanted her to find some peace, and maybe it could be with him.

Patches nudged him again, harder this time, and Jax smiled down at her. "I know. Let's do some work."

He angled his arm toward the big tree behind the gazebo, with fresh tape around it marking it as part of the crime scene.

She tilted her head at him, as if questioning why there were no people in the direction he was telling her to go. But she walked that way anyway, periodically glancing back to make sure he was following.

This wasn't part of his job, but he needed to see the symbol himself, needed to evaluate how similar it was to all the others he'd seen in case files yesterday.

The white spruce was charred like the gazebo, strips of wood dangling from the tree. The lower leaves were charred, too, and a few branches had snapped off. But on the side facing away from the gazebo was a familiar set of loops. It wasn't an exact match to the other symbols, but only because they all had some small variation—mostly due to the materials used. This one was neatly carved, suggesting that the person who'd done it was skilled with a knife, and Jax couldn't help but think of the way Keara's husband had been murdered. With one quick slice across the neck.

A chill darted up his arms and Jax shivered, his gaze going to the surrounding forest, dense with trees and places to hide. He didn't have a lot of experience with serial bombers, but it wouldn't surprise him to learn that they liked to stay close, admire their work.

Woof!

Patches's reminder that he needed to get to his own job—and hers—was overlaid by Anderson calling, "Jax!"

The agent was standing across the street from the park, beside a couple Jax remembered from yesterday. When he'd first seen them, they'd had a young girl between them. Now the woman had a hand curved protectively over her stomach, which had just enough of a swell to tell him the reason she'd climbed into an ambulance yesterday, despite looking okay. She'd been checking on her baby.

Jax jogged over, Patches at his heels.

He hadn't had a chance to meet the family yesterday before they'd all taken off, the dad and daughter jumping into their car and following the ambulance out of Desparre. He was surprised to see them back here today.

"Jax is our Victim Specialist and Patches here is a therapy dog," Anderson introduced them. He gestured to the petite Black woman with worried eyes. "This is Imani." Then he motioned to the man beside her, a mountain of a guy whose thick beard and pale skin patchy with anger made him look like someone who could handle Alaska's wild terrain. "And her husband, Wesley."

"Nice to meet you," Jax said. When he noticed Imani eyeing Patches, he added, "She's technically still a puppy. If you want to pet her, she'll love it."

A smile peeked free and Imani reached her hand out toward Patches, who rushed over and sat on her feet.

Wesley pet her, too, keeping his other arm wrapped

protectively around his wife. "We saw you at the park yesterday," Wesley finally said.

Jax nodded, letting the couple lead the conversation, knowing that Anderson had called him over for a reason.

"You were taking to the chief after she helped the officer who was hurt." Wesley and his wife shared a glance full of worry. "Is he okay?"

"He's critical." Jax told them the news Keara had gotten this morning. "But he's a fighter."

"It's our fault," Imani said, her voice tearful. "We called him over and that's when the blast went off."

"That's not your fault," Jax said. Deep down, she knew it. But it often helped victims to hear someone else say it. "But why did you call for him?"

Anderson nodded at him as Imani and Wesley both pet Patches faster, their anxiety suddenly palpable.

"We saw this guy skulking in the woods by the gazebo," Imani said.

Jax's pulse leaped as Anderson leaned in. Had the guy they'd seen been lurking there because he was carving a symbol into the tree behind the gazebo?

"We were here with our daughter," Wesley continued. "We were heading to the swings when we spotted him. It's a park. Why does anyone need to be hiding in the woods? Unless he's there to watch kids. So we called the officers over. We hoped they could talk to the guy or scare him off."

"Who was it?" Anderson asked. "Did you recognize this guy?"

Imani shook her head. "No. We're new to Desparre. We don't know that many people yet. After the blast, he was gone."

"What did he look like?" Anderson asked.

"He was white," Imani said. "In his thirties, probably. Brown hair, I think."

Excitement thrummed along Jax's skin and he suddenly understood how the FBI agents probably felt when they got a promising lead. He'd seen it on their faces before, the sudden thrill of the chase, but he'd never felt it so intensely himself until now.

Rodney Brown had reddish-blond hair, but from a distance it might seem brown. And he was white, would be in his thirties now.

"Anything else you remember?" Anderson pressed. "Height, maybe? Or facial hair?"

Imani shook her head. "No facial hair. But he was pretty tall. Close to my husband's height, I think."

Jax frowned, studying Wesley, who was probably only an inch shorter than Jax's six foot one. Rodney was five foot eight. Then again, the distance between the swing set and the woods was probably twenty feet. If the guy had been skulking close to the trees, maybe that had thrown off her perception, made it hard to get a good look. Plus, a bomb had gone off shortly after she'd seen him.

Then again, maybe it hadn't been Rodney she'd seen. Maybe it was Rodney's elusive roommate.

Keara slipped inside the police station. She checked in quickly with Sam, who was sitting at the front desk again today, then let out a relieved breath when she reached the empty bullpen.

She'd been at the bomb site and talking to members of the community since 7 a.m. Checking the time on her phone confirmed it was now past 3 p.m. She hadn't stopped for lunch and there was only so long the scrambled eggs Jax had cooked that morning could hold her. She didn't have an appetite.

Not after seeing the blood staining her park. Not after talking to the hospital, hearing the words *extremely critical* and *coma* when she'd asked about both Nate and Talise. But her stomach growled and her head pounded, and the coffeepot in the bullpen was calling her name. So was a quick break and a little solitude, before heading back out to talk to more people, find out if anyone had seen something that might help them find the bomber.

After dumping the sludge at the bottom of the pot that someone had brewed early that morning, Keara started a fresh one. Then she leaned against the wall, started to close her eyes.

Just before they drifted shut, she saw the stack of files on her desk through the glass walls of her office. The cases with the symbols.

Technically, they all belonged to the FBI. She probably wasn't even supposed to look at them. She definitely wasn't supposed to have them.

Pushing herself away from the wall, Keara grabbed the coffee carafe and poured everything that had brewed so far into a mug. Then she strode into her office, pushed the door shut and sat at her desk, staring at the stack of *Yes* files she and Jax had been so excited about yesterday.

There were four murders and an arson in those files. Add in the murder of Celia Harris in Houston and the bombs in Luna and Desparre and what did it all mean?

Keara slapped her hand against the desk in frustration, making it sting. Then she took a long sip of her coffee, willing the headache away, and got to work.

First, the murders. Celia Harris had been abducted, left in an alley, her killing brutal, from multiple stab wounds. She'd been a tough victim to grab, a pillar of the community with young kids and a husband at home. The symbol had been spray-painted onto the wall behind where her body was found. That had been seven years ago in Texas.

Skipping over the arson for now, Keara opened up the next murder. Five years ago, in Nebraska. The victim was a nineteen-year-old boy, on his way home from college. He'd disappeared from one side of town, only to show up on the opposite side a day later, with the symbol drawn in permanent marker across his back. He'd been killed in the time in between, from blunt force trauma to the head. He was a popular kid, a basketball star at his college. But he'd also been brought up on two sets of sexual assault charges and was estranged from his parents.

Four years ago, in Iowa. The victim was a middle-aged man, an ex-marathon runner scheduled to speak at the small town's high school track meet. The event was a big deal in the town and when he hadn't shown up, it had caused a huge uproar. His body being found later that night in a cornfield was the biggest crime they'd seen in more than a decade. He'd been shot three times, the symbol drawn thickly in pen on his arm.

Three years ago, in South Dakota. The victim was a popular middle school teacher who'd survived a heart attack the year before. She'd been grabbed and killed within a few hours, but a witness to the kidnapping had only been able to say her killer was a white male. She was strangled, found on a playground with the symbol spray-painted on the slide behind her.

Two years ago, in Montana. The victim was the newly elected mayor of a small town, with deeply polarizing views. He'd been last seen staggering drunk out of a bar. He was found a day later, in his own backyard, dead from a blow to the head. The medical examiner hadn't been able to determine if he'd fallen and cracked his own skull open or if someone had done it for him, but there had been a strange symbol spray-painted on the back of his house.

Keara stared at the glass wall into the bullpen of the station she'd come to call her own. The symbol undeniably connected these cases in some way, but the manner of death was different across all of them, the symbol never exact. It was possible there was a single killer making his way north to Alaska, committing one murder a year. Perhaps there'd been another crime in the gap after Montana and before the two bombs in Alaska, maybe in Canada while he made his way farther north.

Maybe one person had committed the murders and someone else—someone with the same knowledge of the symbol—had set the fire and the bombs.

She flipped open the arson case from Oklahoma six years ago. A brand-new rec center, the pride of the community, had opened the week before. The fire had destroyed half of it and damaged the other half so badly that it would have needed to be razed anyway. The city had never rebuilt it. Behind the rec center, on the brand-new basketball court, the symbol had been spray-painted from one end to the other.

Frowning at the case, Keara downed the last of her coffee and debated getting more. But even though it was calming her headache, her too-empty stomach was protesting. Setting the mug aside, Keara leaned back in her chair.

How similar was setting a fire and setting off bombs? They seemed pretty different to her, both from the practical standpoint of knowing how to do it and from the potential motivations. But maybe the killer was also the arsonist and the bomber had just gotten started.

It didn't feel right. No matter how she arranged the crimes in her mind, it didn't make sense. She couldn't imagine one person killing in so many different ways, with so many different victim types. And she couldn't imagine a pair of killers grabbing victims together, then randomly switching to arson, then later to bombings.

But she wasn't a psychologist. What she needed was Jax's insight.

A brief laugh escaped. Yeah, she wanted Jax's help right now, but that wasn't the only thing she wanted from him. She wished he were sitting across from her to lend his quiet support, too. So she could stare into his dark brown eyes and calm the frustration boiling inside her over all the pieces of this case that didn't quite fit together.

It had been a long time since she'd wanted to work with a man on a case in quite this way. Seven years, to be exact.

Guilt flooded, followed by an image of Juan staring contemplatively at her. The ache of missing him had faded with time, but moving on now would be a betrayal of everything they'd had together.

She was a cop and her husband had been murdered. There couldn't be room for anything else until she'd found the person responsible and made him pay.

Chapter 14

If Jax was home in Anchorage on a Friday night, he'd be having dinner with friends, or maybe talking a couple of the agents into taking him to the shooting range. He'd thought he was mostly finished with the travel when he'd left the Rapid Deployment Team. But Friday night while he was in the middle of a big investigation with a lot of victims who needed him was just another night.

Tonight, though, instead of wanting to grab a quiet dinner and crash, Jax wanted to see Keara. "What do you think, Patches?"

She seemed to know exactly what he was thinking, because her tail started to wag as she stared up at him.

The two of them were on the outskirts of Desparre, back at the diner where he'd met Keara on Monday. Knowing they'd let Patches in had made it an obvious choice for a break. He'd ordered a sandwich. Enough to calm his grumbling stomach, but not so much that he couldn't eat again if Keara was up for dinner. Beside him, Patches was happily chewing the treat the restaurant owner had handed her, ignoring the dog food Jax had brought.

"Spoiled," he told her and she wagged her tail again.

Giving her a quick pat on the head, he dialed Keara, anxious to hear her voice. Although they'd gone to the crime scene together that morning, she'd left way before he had, to canvass the community. He'd spent the day in Desparre, too, but he'd been focused on the victims and families with the biggest emotional need. He and Keara had talked to the same people several times today, but never at the same time.

He missed her.

Her phone rang and rang. Just when he was expecting voice mail to pick up, Keara answered, sounding distracted. "Hello?"

"It's Jax," he told her, although he assumed she knew it from the display on her phone since she'd long since entered his contact information.

He could hear papers shuffling in the pause that followed and then finally she sighed and asked, "Did you speak to Imani and Wesley again today? Did you see the artist's rendering of the person they saw near the woods?"

After Jax had left to talk to more victims—starting with the families of Officer Nate Dreymond and Talise Poitra—Anderson had called in a sketch artist to work with the couple. He'd asked Anderson to send him the picture once it was finished.

"Yeah," he said. "I mean, people change. The picture we have of Rodney Brown is from seven years ago. But—"

"It doesn't look like him," Keara cut him off. "The nose is wrong. The cheekbones are higher. I know Rodney could have started going bald in the past seven years, but the hair seems off, too."

"Sketches aren't perfect," Jax reminded her. "Imani and Wesley weren't that close to the guy and it sounds like he tried to get out of view when he saw them looking at him."

"I know. But the thing is, I spent the afternoon reviewing the cases your system spit out. I know we already agreed the bombings don't seem connected to the earlier crimes, but Jax, I'm not sure any of them are connected."

Jax frowned and set down his sandwich. Since the second bomb had gone off, he'd been thinking they were off base, too. But there was some reason the same symbol was showing up across so many cases. He couldn't imagine a group of killers across the country, all equally skilled at evading police and all committing one crime before going dormant. "It could be a pair," Jax reminded her. "Rodney and his roommate."

"Maybe," Keara agreed, but she didn't sound convinced. "Jax, the thing is, we flagged all of the cases based on the symbols. I even considered sending the symbol to an anthropologist in case it has some kind of ancient significance, but it doesn't seem worth it. It's too rough and random, with nothing to indicate it means anything at all. I mean, you're a trained psychologist, and you haven't seen anything in it to give us a clue to its meaning. I went back and reviewed the details of the cases, too. They're just as…inconsistent. Victimology is all over the place, and the MO is different each time, too. I've never chased down a bomber before and I've never had a serial murder case, either, but nothing I know about them fits what I saw in those case files. If you take the symbol out of it, they don't seem connected at all."

"But we can't take the symbol out of it," Jax reminded her.

She let out a frustrated laugh. "No kidding. But the victims don't fit. Jax, we've got a rec center that was empty and set on fire. The murder victims were a female baker in her thirties who was a pillar of the community, a nineteen-year-old college boy with a couple of sexual assault charges on his record, a fiftyish man who used to run marathons, a popular middle school teacher in her forties and a sixtyish man with a really polarizing platform who was just elected as mayor. Then we've got the bombings, where we haven't identified the target. What ties all of these people together?"

Leaning back against the vinyl seat, Jax contemplated the list Keara had just given him. She was right. They didn't make sense as targets of the same person. They didn't even make sense as targets of two people.

The explosions in Luna and Desparre weren't the first bombings he'd assisted on. And he'd worked with two victims of a serial killer that the FBI had managed to rescue, helping them through the legal process for almost a year. He wasn't a profiler, but he'd learned way more about how serial killers worked during that case than he'd ever wanted to know.

Most serial killers had a specific type. Even when there wasn't specifically a sexual component to the crime itself, many of them were sexually motivated. Such a wide range of victims wasn't unheard of, but it was unusual. And when it happened, there was almost always a specific method of killing that was most important to the killer.

Still, the symbol... It felt almost like a signature to him, a specific thing the killer felt compelled to do, something that marked the crime as theirs. They might be able to change their MO, but a signature would remain.

But was drawing a series of loops on or near the bodies really a compulsive behavior? Or was it being used by a group of criminals, maybe individuals who'd found each other somehow and made a pact to leave behind the symbols to confuse authorities?

Except if that was the case, then why hadn't they seen additional matching crimes in each jurisdiction?

Rubbing his head, Jax admitted, "It doesn't make sense to me. I talked to Ben a bit about it today. He had a quick look at the cases we pulled. He admitted that if we'd found a series of bombs with the symbol, they'd be chasing that lead full-throttle. But across singular killings like this, he thinks it's far less likely to be connected."

"The FBI is still looking into it?" Keara pressed.

"Yeah. But obviously, the bombs are the first priority. Two so close together are a pattern that can't be ignored. And then there's the psychology of a bomber versus a killer."

"Bombers like chaos," Keara said. "They like to create fear and destruction."

"Yeah," Jax agreed. "And a serial killer who murders his victims up close probably isn't going to want to watch from a distance, like with arson or a bomb. It seems like two different personality types to me."

"And unless our murderer is also just determined

to try out every method of killing possible, the single murders in each state don't really seem connected, either," Keara said.

Jax sighed. He'd initiated the call feeling hopeful, almost nervous. He'd been planning to suggest they get dinner and distract themselves from the stress and horror of the case. He'd been hoping dinner might lead to an offer for him and Patches to stay on her couch again, even though he'd confirmed that the Royal Desparre allowed dogs. He didn't expect her to join him on the couch this time, but right now being close to her was enough.

Now he felt exhausted and discouraged. Even Patches, catching his mood, let out a whine and lay on the ground.

"Where do we go from here?" Keara prompted when he didn't speak for a minute.

Jax rubbed his head, pushing aside his sandwich, no longer hungry. "I have no idea." And that was true of more than just the case. Equally frustrating was his inability to help her personally, help her move forward. Without that, there was no chance of this attraction between them going anywhere.

Keara hadn't been back to Texas in over a year. Even then, so many years after her husband's murder, being in Houston had given her anxiety, brought back all of her anger and frustration over Juan's case having gone cold. But maybe it was time to return. The thoughts ran through her mind the next morning as she lay in bed.

Once the bombing was solved, she could take some personal time. If she could convince the Houston PD to reopen the case, if she could work it unofficially, maybe she could finally get some closure.

Seven years was long enough. She needed to be able

to move forward. And for the first time, she wanted to truly move forward, to start living her life fully again.

It wasn't hard to identify the reason. She'd never known a man like Jax Diallo, never connected so quickly to anyone.

He lived on the other side of the state, but that might actually be a good thing. It would keep any relationship from moving too quickly, from getting too serious before she was ready. Because wanting to move forward wasn't the same as wanting to dive headfirst into a serious relationship. Still, she didn't want to say goodbye when the bombings were solved.

She was pretty sure he was interested. Best of all, although he worked for the FBI, he wasn't a law-enforcement officer. He wasn't constantly running into danger. He was helping victims, but he wasn't interacting with the suspects.

Sure, there were no guarantees. Everyone faced some level of risk just walking around in the world. Being a cop for so many years had definitely taught her that. But Jax was a much safer man to love than Juan had ever been.

The unexpected thought made anxiety and guilt bubble up and Keara shoved off her covers, stepped onto the cold wood floor in her bedroom. *Love.* That was an emotion way off in the future, if ever. Right now she had much bigger things to worry about.

Glancing at the clock on her bedside table, Keara groaned. Almost 8 a.m. It might have been Saturday, but she still had a long day ahead of her and she had planned to get an early start.

So much for that plan. Debating whether to jump into a fast shower or just start making phone calls, Keara opted for the phone. She started with the hospital, heart pounding faster as she waited for news on Nate and Talise.

"Both of their conditions are the same," the nurse who finally came on the line told her.

She tried to quell the disappointment. At least they weren't deteriorating. Both had faced serious injuries. Talise had gone through emergency surgery for her leg and Nate had gotten his head stitched up, only for doctors to open it up again a few hours later to release intracranial pressure.

Hanging up with the hospital, Keara sighed and headed to the kitchen. She couldn't stop herself from glancing at the couch where she'd slept—much less fitfully—the night before last. Couldn't stop herself from wishing Jax and Patches were sitting there to greet her again this morning.

When she'd spoken to Jax late last night, he'd been at a diner on the outskirts of Desparre. They'd talked about the case and then he'd had to let her go, to take a call from one of the agents. Even though she'd gone through everything she'd needed to tell him about the cases, she'd half expected him to call back. When she hadn't heard from him, she'd heated up a frozen dinner, done a little kickboxing to combat her frustration, then headed to bed.

As she turned on her coffeepot, Keara pulled up Jax's number. Before she could hit Call, her phone rang. It was a number she didn't recognize.

"Chief Hernandez," she answered.

"This is Ben Nez."

The last of Keara's sleepiness cleared away. Was there a break in the case? "Agent Nez. What's happening?"

"We've been running down all of the victims in the two bombings, trying to nail down a potential target."

From the beginning, she'd heard the FBI theorizing that a specific target was likely, since the bombs could have easily been placed in more populated areas or spots that would have gotten more publicity. Although the bombs had definitely made the news in and around Desparre and Luna, they hadn't been large or spectacular enough to make much of a blip on the national news.

"Any luck?" she asked when he paused.

"Well, I wanted your take on something. We just discovered that one of the people who was killed at the Luna bombing is actually related to a victim in Desparre."

"Who is it?" Keara asked, frowning. The connection was news to her.

"Aiden DeMarco was the victim in Luna. He posted the idea about the soccer game on the chat room, so the bomber would have definitely known he'd be there. He was eighteen, planned to leave Alaska to go to college in California. We looked into him early on, didn't see any reason for him to be targeted, but we could have missed something. His aunt on his mom's side, Gina Metner, was injured in Desparre."

"I know Gina," Keara said. The woman was a transplant from the lower forty-eight. She'd moved up to Alaska to be near her sister and escape from a violent ex. But the ex had since died and Gina had decided she wanted even more solitude than Luna offered, so she'd found herself a home in Desparre. She worked part-time at the library in Luna and part-time at the grocery store with Talise.

"Gina talked about her sister and her nephew, but I

didn't know his name," Keara told Ben. "I didn't realize he'd been killed in the bombing."

"Can you think of anyone with a grudge against Gina?"

"No one living." Keara explained about the violent ex, then added, "Gina and I got to talking a year ago, when she first decided to move to Desparre. She gave me a bit of a rundown on her life. But otherwise, she's pretty quiet. She's got a couple of friends here we can talk to, but I can't imagine her having made a ton of enemies since she moved to Alaska two years ago."

"We spoke to Gina already," Ben said. "She said the same thing. It could be a coincidence." He sighed. "But I was hoping we might have stumbled across the connection we've been trying to find."

"Gina wasn't badly hurt in the bombing," Keara said. "She was leaving the park when the bomb went off. She got checked out since the blast initially impacted her hearing, but she got the all clear to go home the same day. The only thing she needed was a couple of stitches and not even directly from the blast. It was when the explosion knocked her down and she hit the pavement."

"Right. So if the bomber was targeting her and he was nearby, maybe the couple who spotted him and called the police over threw him off. Maybe he was distracted and ducked into the woods to hide, didn't get farther away quickly enough. He wouldn't have wanted to be that close when the bomb went off. Assuming the bomber is the same person Imani and Wesley saw near the tree with the carving on it," Ben added.

"Luna and Desparre are pretty small towns. It's not really surprising that two of the victims would be related."

"Yeah, well, you know what they say about all the bases," Ben said.

Keara mumbled an agreement, trying not to let him hear how disheartened she felt. This kind of investigation was more like a marathon than a sprint. A bomber savvy enough to have set off the bomb in Luna—which hadn't yielded any significant leads more than a week later—probably wasn't going to be easy to find.

"What about the sketch of the suspect?" Keara asked.

She hadn't recognized him. Neither had anyone on her force. That was a little bit surprising if he lived around here, since they were a small town. Then again, Desparre was known for being the sort of place where you could come to disappear. They had a lot of land to get lost in and if you wanted to stay off everyone's radar, there was a whole mountain to hide on. If the bomber was hiding here, it wouldn't be the first time the town had a criminal in their midst.

"We're still showing the sketch around," Ben told her. "So far no one knows this guy."

If the bomber *was* the same person who'd been responsible for the murders and arson in the lower forty-eight, it made sense that no one knew him. He'd be staying far below the radar. But there had been five days between the Luna bombing and the one in her park. It had now been two days since the blast that had been close enough to shake the walls of the Desparre police station.

If he'd gone from a once-a-year, once-a-location killer to a serial bomber, how much time did they have before he struck again?

Chapter 15

When Keara walked into the police station half an hour later, the rest of her department, and most of the FBI agents, were already there. Thankfully, it looked like they were just getting started.

She nodded at her officers, who were all working serious overtime. Since they were a small town, they were constantly on call. But the station was typically closed from 9 p.m. until 9 a.m. In the past two days most of them had been there until midnight.

Then her gaze was drawn to Jax. As soon as she made eye contact, he smiled at her. Patches did him one better, letting out a happy *woof!* and racing across the room, sliding to a slightly uncoordinated stop at her feet.

Keara laughed, grateful for the moment of levity. She wondered if the intelligent therapy dog had done it on purpose. "Hi, Patches."

Patches wagged her tail, staring up expectantly until Keara pet her.

Then Jax was standing beside her, his presence somehow managing to make her more calm and nervous at the same time.

"Today we're hoping to get more information on motive and our potential suspect," Ben announced, his voice carrying over the few conversations and making everyone go quiet.

"Since you know the residents here better than we do, we're hoping to pair agents and officers," Ben said. "The goal is twofold. First, to figure out if anyone knows of a reason one of the victims might have been targeted or anyone who'd want to do them harm. Second, to show them the sketch we got from two of the people on the scene. See if anyone recognizes him."

"What about me and Patches?" Jax piped up.

"We're hoping you can drive back to Luna, talk to Aiden DeMarco's family and see if they have any idea why both their son and his aunt might have been targeted."

Jax nodded, looking unsurprised, and Keara hid her disappointment.

He wasn't an agent. He wouldn't have been paired with her anyway. And if he had been, she would have needed to protest. Although talking to residents wasn't dangerous in theory, it could lead them to a bomber. Hell, they could actually end up knocking on the door of the bomber. Keara didn't know everyone who lived here, especially those who chose to hide on the mountain, who didn't want to be known.

Desparre was a small town only in terms of population. When it came to size—and the distance backup had to travel if you needed them—it was definitely large.

"I've got a list of pairings," Ben continued, "and a stack of printed sketches you can show people. That way, anyone with low vision won't have to squint at your phones. And there's no chance of anyone trying to snatch that phone away from you."

He said the last part like he'd experienced it and Keara raised her eyebrows at Jax, who just shrugged in response.

"Does that work for you, Chief Hernandez?" Ben called across the room.

Everyone's attention swiveled her way and she nodded, appreciating that he wasn't just trying to railroad over her small department. The FBI had more experience, but her officers knew the area and the people better. "The plan makes sense. Everyone stay safe out there. If you get a lead, call it in on the radio before you pursue it. And make sure you stay in contact. I want everyone checking in with regular status updates."

Her officers nodded somberly. Normally, she might have gotten a couple of rolled eyes at that request, but not today.

Policing a small town could get tedious, make you let down your guard. You thought you knew the people, thought you knew the dangers. But out here, where it was common to take calls alone, communication was their best defense. It was something she preached on a regular basis.

"I've got pairings up here," Ben announced, and everyone headed his way.

Keara turned to Jax and lowered her voice. "Did you

talk to Ben and Anderson any more about the other cases and the inconsistencies?"

"Yeah. They're as confused as we are. They think our best chance of figuring out what the symbol means is to follow the other leads right now." Jax's lips pursed. "I still think there has to be a way to use the symbol to find the killer, but I don't know how."

It wasn't his job to know how. His psychological insight was useful, but he'd already stepped into profiler territory by confirming that the symbol was important, that it linked these crimes somehow. Jax wasn't an agent or a detective. It was her job—and Ben's and Anderson's and all of the other agents and officers—to follow the leads and uncover the bomber.

"You should focus on the victims," she told him. "I've seen the difference you and Patches make."

Woof!

Keara smiled and pet Patches more, as Jax stared at her pensively, his expression unreadable.

Had he felt insulted that she didn't think he should run leads? Would he feel the same way if he knew it made her more comfortable pursuing something romantic with him when he was sticking safely on the outskirts of the case?

His lips twitched, like he could read her thoughts.

"Let's get going," Ben said and Keara gave Patches one more pet, nodded goodbye to Jax and hurried over to see who she'd be running leads with today.

"It's you and me," Anderson announced before she reached the more senior agent.

"Great," Keara said. Anderson seemed pretty easygoing and professional. "Where are we headed?"

"Up the mountain. The place most likely for a bomber to be holed up, don't you think?"

"Let's do it," she agreed. She glanced back once more at Jax as she headed out the door and she could have sworn she saw him mouth the words, *Be careful.*

As she led Anderson over to her police SUV—specially equipped to handle Desparre's rough roads and dangerous weather—she wondered if Jax worried about her. She wanted him far away from danger, didn't want to have to fear finding another man she cared for the way she'd found Juan. But she'd understood the dangers with Juan because she faced them herself. What must it be like for Jax, somewhat on the outside, to hear that she was heading into a remote area that would be a good place for a bomber to hide?

Pulling out her phone before she hopped into the car, she sent Jax a quick text:

Let me know how it goes with the victims today. I'll keep you updated, too.

It felt like the sort of thing she'd text if she was actually dating him. Hoping she wasn't making assumptions about plans that weren't reciprocated, she tucked her phone back into her pocket.

Climbing into the driver's seat, she asked Anderson, "Which part of the mountain? You know it's pretty massive, right?"

"We have one of your veterans paired up with one of our longtime agents. They're hitting the far side of the mountain. I thought we'd handle the closer side. We'll do as much as we can today and see what pops."

"Sounds good," Keara agreed as she started up her vehicle.

Some people headed this far north in Alaska just to find a good adventure. But most of the people who landed in Desparre were looking to be left alone. Usually, there was nothing sinister about it. Maybe they were running from a tragedy, like she was. Or maybe they were running from a threat, like Tate Emory was. Sometimes, though, they were hiding because the law was after them or because the vast spaces of Alaska seemed like a great place to stay off law-enforcement radar or hide a victim.

For the first ten minutes of their ride, Anderson was quiet, just texting or watching out the window. Then he slid his phone into his pocket and shifted toward her. "So this symbol…"

She glanced briefly at him, then back at the road. In the spring driving up the mountain wasn't dangerous like it could be in the winter, with the heavy snow and avalanches. But the roads were still narrow, the vehicles here usually large. On a couple of occasions, she'd had to hit the brakes for an animal. Once, it had been a bear.

"What about it?" she asked. "You have a theory?"

"Maybe. I've been thinking through what Jax told me this morning about how different the victimology and MOs in each of the cases has been, even the way the symbol was written. In marker or spray paint or even pen."

"And?" Keara prompted, her hands tensing around the wheel, hoping he had a new idea that would make sense of it all.

"We know savvy criminals learn from each other. What if we've got a group of them on a dark web site, not just trading insight into how to avoid getting caught, but also sharing this symbol?"

"Why?" Keara asked. "You think it's a way to mark their own kills? Keep track and try to outdo each other? But wouldn't using the same symbol defeat the purpose?"

"No," Anderson replied. "I was thinking more like a game, coordinating a single symbol across all these different places and crimes to confuse police."

The tension across the back of Keara's shoulders and neck notched tighter. "That makes sense," she admitted. Not only would it confuse the authorities if they connected the crimes through the symbols, but it also added a cooperative-competitive element that she could imagine appealing to a killer or a bomber. Attention from an eager audience without the risk, since they were all criminals, too.

If Anderson was right, the bomber wasn't committing the other crimes. If the communication was happening in a chat room on a dark web site, then the bomber probably didn't even know who the other people were.

A familiar frustration welled up. Even if they caught the bomber, would it get them any closer to Juan's killer?

Or was her dream of finally solving his cold case just that?

Chapter 16

Talking to Aiden DeMarco's parents had been brutal. All of their dreams for their eldest son had been shattered in a single moment. Jax and Patches had been able to offer them support over the whole day that Jax knew they needed. And he'd managed to gather as much information as he could about what Aiden's parents—who'd been nearby when the bomb went off—had seen. But they had no idea why anyone would target their son or his aunt. Neither did Jax.

Frankly, he didn't think anyone *had* targeted either one.

Halfway through the day Ben had called him after checking in with Anderson. He'd shared the other agent's theory about a group of criminals coordinating on a dark web site. It had Ben excited and the cybercrime unit back in Anchorage pivoting to the theory as a priority.

If they were right, a serial bomber with the knowledge and connections to access a site like that probably wasn't using bombs as a messy way to kill a few specific people. He was way more likely to be an indiscriminate killer more interested in watching the chaos he created.

The fact that they hadn't found other bomb sites with the symbol could have meant his earlier bombs weren't as perfected and the symbol he'd intended to leave behind had been destroyed in the blast. Or evidence had been poorly collected or missed. Either way, this seemed like a practiced criminal.

Someone like that was prepared. He was well hidden, might have even booby-trapped his home in case law enforcement ever figured out his location.

Keara was driving around on top of a secluded mountain, searching for him.

The idea had lodged a ball of fear in his chest that had just gotten worse as the day turned into evening and the sun set, descending the town into darkness.

He'd heard from her again early in the afternoon, letting him know they were at the top of the mountain and hadn't had luck so far, but nothing since then. Jax had resisted calling or texting her, not wanting to distract her at a crucial moment. She was a seasoned law-enforcement officer with more than a decade of experience under her belt, about half of it in a busy city with a much higher crime rate.

Right now, though, making the lengthy drive back from Luna with Patches asleep in the backseat, he'd been alone with his worry for too long. He'd be at the Desparre police station in five minutes, but he wasn't sure if anyone would be there since it was after nine. He knew Ben had gone back to the hotel, but he didn't know whether Anderson and Keara had made it down the mountain yet.

Was this what it would be like if he could talk her into giving a relationship with him a chance? This constant fear about whether she'd make it home? Was that something he'd be able to handle long-term? Because despite the distance between Anchorage and Desparre, if he and Keara started something, he couldn't imagine ever wanting to stop.

"Call Keara," he told his phone.

From the backseat, Patches let out a quiet *woof*, then he heard her sitting up.

It rang twice before Keara picked up. "Hi, Jax."

She sounded happy to hear from him, but he could tell from the exhaustion underneath that the trip hadn't yielded anything promising.

Woof! Patches chimed in loudly.

Keara laughed. "Hi, Patches."

"I take it no one recognized the picture?" Jax asked.

"We had a couple of vague 'he looks sort of familiar, but I don't know where from' kind of answers. But no one had a name and address handy."

"So he might live up on that mountain," Jax said, feeling more encouraged than Keara sounded.

"He might," Keara agreed. "We'll definitely have officers canvassing again tomorrow. The thing is, the mountain is huge. People stake out land and build without permits or actual ownership. It's not like we can stop them if we don't know they're up there. Some of it is pretty far off the beaten path. And if you've got someone willing to venture off the road a ways—which we definitely do—it can be nearly impossible to find them."

"It sounds like the stereotype of Alaska," Jax commented. "That you can just venture off and get your-self completely off the grid, if you're not afraid of the harsh elements."

He'd seen some truth to that when he'd gotten here, but Anchorage was a pretty developed, populated area. Still, he could drive about an hour outside town and find solitude at a glacier if he wanted. He and Patches had done it a half dozen times since moving here and only once had he run into another person.

Compared to Anchorage, Desparre was the wild north.

"Well, sometimes the best thing about a place can also be the worst," Keara said.

He heard her turn signal in the background and the knot in his chest loosened up, knowing she had to be off the mountain to need a turn signal. "Are you going back to the station now?"

"I've already been there. I dropped Anderson off and now I'm almost home. I was just about to call you, actually."

"Oh, yeah?" His long day suddenly seemed less ex-hausting.

"How did the trip to Luna go?"

"Nothing new, really." He sighed, remembering the devastation on the parents' faces, the confusion and grief in every movement of his three younger siblings.

"I guess I'm not surprised." He heard her car door slam, then her voice got more distant, maybe as she juggled the phone and opened the door to her house.

"Me, either, but I was hopeful. The fact that one of the Luna casualties, Aiden DeMarco, was the one who set up the soccer game and then his aunt was also hurt in a bomb? It seemed like maybe there was something to that."

"I don't think this bomber was after a specific—" She broke off on a mumbled curse.

"Keara?"

"Someone's been in my house."

"What?"

"My office doesn't look right."

"What do you mean? Are you sure?"

From the backseat, Patches whined, picking up on his anxiety.

"Yeah, I'm sure."

Her voice was hard and determined and he imagined her pulling her gun from its holster.

Jax punched down on the gas, wishing he was closer to her house. "I'm coming to you. Get out of the house, Keara."

"I'm a police chief, Jax. And I'm already inside. I can handle a walk-through."

"You need backup!"

"I'll call them," she promised, "But I need to go."

"No! Just wait for backup. That has to be proced—"

"*Jax.* It doesn't look like anyone is in here." Her voice had dropped to a whisper and he had to strain to hear her final, "I'll call you when it's all clear."

"No—"

He swore as he realized she'd hung up, then hit the gas harder, taking curves too fast. If a Desparre police officer pulled him over, all the better. Then he'd have backup.

He wasn't an agent. He'd gone to the shooting range with the Anchorage agents enough to be a pretty good shot, but he didn't carry a weapon. That wasn't how

Victim Specialists worked. On some level probably the agents' teasing about him being an "agent wannabe" bothered him because it was true. Some part of him would have loved to get into the nitty gritty of an investigation, follow a trail of clues until an arrest and been the one to slap handcuffs on perpetrators. But he'd never pursued it, knowing the role he had now would ultimately fulfill him more.

At this moment, though, he wished he'd made a different decision. Wished he could be real help to Keara.

"Call Desparre PD," he told his phone as Patches whimpered.

"Desparre Police Department," a tired voice answered. It was familiar, but he wasn't sure which officer had phone duty that night.

"It's Jax Diallo," he blurted. "Someone broke into the chief's house. She needs backup right now."

"What?" The officer's surprise was overridden only by his sudden state of alert. "Okay, we're on it. Do you know details? Is the person still there? Are they armed?"

"I don't know. But *Keara* is there." He couldn't remember ever feeling this helpless.

"I'm sending help now," the officer told him, then hung up.

Jax punched down a bit more on the gas, even though he knew he was approaching dangerous speeds. Then he called Ben.

From the sound of the agent's voice when he answered, Jax had woken him up.

"I need agents at Keara's house. Someone broke in," Jax cut off his greeting.

He didn't bother ending the call as he whipped his vehicle into Keara's drive and slammed it into Park.

From the backseat, Patches slid across the seat and yelped.

"Sorry, Patches," he said, then added, "Stay!" as he jumped out of the SUV and closed the door behind him.

He could hear police sirens in the distance, getting closer, but the house in front of him was mostly dark, only a porch light giving him any real visibility.

It wasn't enough. For a house far from neighbors, set in the woods, it wasn't nearly enough to see if a threat lurked nearby.

Jax glanced back, watching for the police cars. But they weren't close enough yet.

He couldn't wait. He ran around to the back of his vehicle and dug underneath the spare tire, hoping the rental company wanted their renters to be prepared. Relief filled him as he found a big metal hexagon wrench. It wasn't a gun, but it was better than nothing.

He was racing toward the house, holding the wrench too tightly, when Keara stepped out the front door.

"It's empty," she told him, holstering her gun. "Whoever was in here was gone before I got home." The hard fury on her face was only undermined by the vulnerability in her eyes.

His grip on the wrench loosened and he realized his hand hurt from how tightly he'd been gripping it.

Her gaze drifted to the wrench then back up to his face. "You were going to rush in here with nothing but that?" Her lips pursed with what looked like anger, but her forehead crinkled with confusion or concern and she went silent.

He didn't bother to answer, just tried to breathe deeply, encourage his frenzied heartbeat to slow.

From the car, Patches called *Woof! Woof! Woof!*

Keara walked over to Jax, put her hand on his arm and he looped his free arm around her, yanking her against his chest.

Even with the sirens getting louder and louder, there was no way she'd miss his rapid heartbeat; no way she'd misunderstand his fear. But he didn't say anything. Right now as much as he wanted to pursue something more, they were only colleagues. He'd known her for eight days. He had no right to tell her how to manage a crime scene at her own home.

But she whispered against his chest, "I'm sorry I worried you. I should have gone outside and waited for backup."

As if her words had summoned them, a pair of trucks came screeching into her drive, portable sirens blaring.

Jax glanced behind him, letting go of Keara as officers jumped out of their vehicles, weapons ready.

Keara held up a hand. "It's all clear. But someone was in my house."

The officers holstered their weapons as Keara continued, "I don't think anything was taken. It barely looks disturbed. I think whoever was here hoped I wouldn't even realize it. But they definitely went through my office, especially all of my documents."

"Any sign of forced entry?" Charlie Quinn asked. There was exhaustion in the dark circles under his eyes and an invisible weight that seemed to pull his whole face downward, but his voice was focused and clear.

"No." Keara looked troubled as she admitted, "I'm not sure how they got in."

More vehicles raced into the drive and then FBI agents poured out.

Keara looked embarrassed as she said, "I've already cleared the house. It was a break-in, but nothing was taken."

Ben strode toward them, looking purposeful and focused. "You get a lot of break-ins around here?"

She shrugged. "Some."

"Do people know this is the police chief's home?"

She nodded slowly. "I don't advertise it, but this is a small town. So yeah, I'm sure some people have figured it out."

"Ever had any problems here before?"

She shook her head.

Ben nodded briefly at Jax, then asked Keara, "Any chance this is connected to the bombings?"

Jax's calming heartbeat took off again as he stared at Keara, watched her consider it.

"I don't know. But someone was interested in what I had in my office. I don't bring police cases home, except on a laptop, which is in my SUV. My paper files are mostly personal."

Ben nodded. "Just in case this is connected, how do you feel about letting the FBI's evidence techs go through your office?"

Keara nodded slowly. "All of our officers are trained in evidence collection. But in the interest of collaboration, that would be appreciated."

Ben nodded at her, then started calling out orders to the other agents as Keara directed her officers to head home.

Then she turned to Jax, all the vulnerability he'd seen in her eyes earlier gone now and replaced by anger.

"What do you think? Why would the bomber come here? He assumed I'd have case files in my home and it would be an easier target than a downtown police station? You think he hoped to find out what we knew about him?"

Jax stared back at her, all his worry over her home being targeted fading into the background as he remembered the first time he'd seen her at the bomb site. Then the expression on her face when she'd identified that symbol for them. A symbol that, as far as they could find, hadn't appeared on a crime scene in Alaska until the Luna bombing.

"I think we were right from the beginning," he realized. "I think the bomber *is* connected to your husband's murder."

"What? *Why?*"

"I think all of the cases are connected," Jax said, the theory gaining strength in his mind as he said it out loud. "I think we just found the missing motivation."

"What do you mean?" Keara asked.

"I think the missing motivation is *you.*"

Chapter 17

Dread mingled with fury and residual adrenaline as Keara stared at Jax. The excitement in his gaze told her that he thought his new theory was right.

"How could I be the motivation for these bombings?" Keara asked. "I didn't have a close relationship with any of the victims—unless you count the fact that Nate works for me. I wasn't even there when the Luna bomb went off. And if he wanted to target me in Desparre, he could have come out here earlier, planted the bomb at my house."

The thought that the bomber knew where she lived, that he could have been in her house, looking through her personal items, made her home somehow feel less *hers*. The idea that he might have seen her photo album from her wedding sitting on her coffee table, might have flipped idly through the pages, smiled at the memory of killing her husband, made her fists clench.

The bomber coming here to find out if they were onto him made sense. But him setting bombs *because* of her didn't.

When Jax stayed silent, his lips twisted and his pupils rolled slightly upward, like he was still working it out in his mind, she prompted, "You need to explain this theory to me."

Behind her, the other agents had gone quiet, but stepped closer. They were all listening, too, waiting with enough patience that Keara knew they valued Jax's psychological insight as much as she did.

"What if we've stumbled on to a serial killer who isn't interested in a certain victim type or a particular weapon?" Jax asked slowly.

Keara held in her immediate rebuttal: they'd already decided this wasn't a serial killer/bomber *because* there wasn't a common victimology or MO. "Then what's his motivation?"

"He gets off on outwitting police," Jax said, a mix of surprise and certainty in his voice.

"Police in general?" Keara pressed. "So not me specifically?" She didn't like the idea either way, but the thought that a serial killer was somehow focused on her, motivated to kill because of her, was really unsettling.

"Yes," Jax said, his hand reaching out like he was going to take hers, then dropping back to his side. "Sorry. I didn't mean that it was you personally motivating him. I think he's motivated by whoever is working to solve the crime he committed. It's like a game to him—can he keep committing crimes without the police finding him?"

Keara frowned. Behind her, she could hear the agents shifting, like they were impatient and unconvinced, too.

"Every serial killer wants to outwit police," Ben spoke up. "I don't think that's enough of a motivation alone."

"Why not?" Jax countered, crossing his arms over his chest. "You thought a group of criminals were playing games by using the same symbol and laughing at police on a dark web chat room."

"Sure," Anderson said. "But—"

"Hear me out," Jax interrupted. "It could explain why there have been so many different locations. Because he's looking for a new challenge each time, a new police office to test, to see if he can find a worthy opponent."

"Or he's just trying to outrun the investigations by changing jurisdictions," Ben countered. "A lot of serial killers try that."

"Sure," Jax agreed, not looking deterred. "But you didn't think it was a serial criminal responsible for everything, because of all the differences. What about the similarities? How likely is it really that we have six different criminals—murderers, an arsonist and a bomber—all using the same symbol *and* all equally skilled at leaving behind such clean crime scenes? Not to mention, all of them only committing one—or maybe two—crimes before stopping?"

The agents behind her were silent as Jax stared at them with raised eyebrows. Keara thought about each of the case files she'd read, about the total lack of progress in each of those cases. They'd all eventually gone cold, just like her husband's murder.

"Okay," Ben said, sounding like he was reluctantly getting on board with Jax's theory. "Then why bombs now after a series of murders and one arson?"

"Because the weapon isn't the point," Jax said, the excitement in his voice growing.

It set off an excitement in her, too, a hope that they were getting closer to finding the person responsible for all of the crimes. Including Juan's murder.

"When serial killers get away with it, they get bolder, right?" Jax asked, his gaze on Ben.

Keara shifted, so she could see them both.

On Ben's face was interest, the thrill of being on a solid lead that she recognized. The excitement was catching. All the other agents were slowly nodding.

"Usually," Ben agreed.

"Sometimes, they go for bigger challenges, too, right?" Jax leaned in and his familiar cinnamon scent wafted toward her. "They'll try to grab victims who are more high risk for them. They'll spend more time with the victims, leave the body in a more public place, maybe."

"So you think this is just a progression?" Keara asked. "He started with murders, tried an arson—and presumably got more attention with the murders, so returned to them? Then he came here and decided bombs would have a bigger impact, get more of a law-enforcement response?"

Jax nodded. "Yes. And maybe some of this was also him learning what he liked. Maybe initially he figured he'd get more of a thrill from the killing than he did. When he discovered it was actually watching the law-enforcement response—seeing the police scramble to try and find *him*—that became more of his focus."

It made sense in a weird way. Celia Harris's murder almost certainly wasn't the guy's first kill. It was too perfect, too precise, the victim too high risk, the body

dumped in a place too close to public areas. He'd probably started with easier victims, people who were less
likely to be missed, dumping the bodies in places he
hoped they wouldn't be found. The symbol could have
evolved over time, too.

"So if this is all a progression, if it's really about this
guy trying to outwit the police, then what about Juan?"
Keara asked as fury and grief and determination en-
twined inside her. "He got too close to the truth, didn't
he? This guy thought he was outwitting police and then
Juan showed up at his door and the bomber decided he
needed to kill him, didn't he?"

Jax nodded slowly, her own pain reflected in his
eyes. "That's my guess. I think you were onto something all along with Rodney—or, more likely, given that
the sketch we have doesn't match Rodney, his roommate. I think Juan was killed because he got too close
to the truth."

"And the crimes were much bigger than he'd ever
realized," Keara finished.

Keara's gaze was troubled as she demanded, "Do you
think the bomber came here because he knew I worked
here? Because he knows I'm Juan's widow?"

The agents behind her all cringed. It was barely per-
ceptible, because they were all trained and practiced at
hiding emotion. But no doubt they'd all dealt with loved
ones who were afraid of one day getting the dreaded call.

Jax's heart gave a pained kick, but he tried to consider all the angles before he answered. This wasn't his
job. This wasn't his specialty. Yes, he had a lot of training in psychology, a lot of experience working with the
victims this type of criminal left behind. But there were

other professionals out there, profilers who focused on the other side of it: knowing the mind of the criminal.

"I doubt it," he said finally. "But it can't hurt to get a profiler's thoughts on that." He glanced at Ben, who nodded slowly, but didn't seem anxious to get a second opinion.

"If I'm right, then it took him a long time to get to Alaska. If he came here for you, then why stop in so many states along the way? Why take so many years to get here? It seems like it was probably a coincidence."

"He was jumping from one jurisdiction to the next," Anderson said, "changing locations once each case went cold. Unless we just missed some of his crimes, this guy is patient."

Ben nodded. "A year is a long time in between crimes for a serial criminal, if that's really what we've got here."

"Right," Anderson said, sounding excited by Jax's new take on the perpetrator. "But for big investigations like the ones we're talking about, it seems reasonable that police would be actively investigating for a year. Those investigations would slowly ramp down until they were deemed cold and set on the back burner."

"This guy probably wouldn't know exactly when that happened," Ben said. "But once he couldn't see police activity, once the news coverage died down, he moved to a new state, studied a new victim, planned a new crime." He gave Jax an impressed look. "It makes sense. And it explains a lot of things that just wouldn't fit together otherwise. I think you're onto something here, Jax."

It would take a methodical, patient killer. But each of the cases Jax had reviewed with Keara suggested that kind of criminal. Someone who had studied how to avoid leaving forensics behind, who had watched his intended victim beforehand to avoid witnesses, who had scoped out the location he planned to leave the body. Someone who followed the police investigation, followed the officers investigating, without being noticed.

Jax flashed back to the moment he'd been driving to meet Keara and had thought someone was following him. A dark blue truck that had turned another way when Jax started driving erratically. Had it been the bomber, looking for insight on the case? Had he followed Jax in the past, maybe even to Keara's home? Had that been how he knew where she lived?

Guilt flooded, along with a rush of relief that Keara was okay. What if the bomber had been waiting in her house instead of just going through her files? What if he'd been standing in the dark with a knife, ready to do to Keara what he'd done to her husband?

The idea made nausea flood through him and he tried to push it back, tried to keep thinking through his new theory as impartially as he could.

Keara stared back at him, her eyes narrowing as if she could read his emotions.

She probably could. She was a trained investigator, after all. Would it scare her off, the intensity of his feelings for her? How had they gotten so strong, so fast?

"If this guy is following the investigation as closely as you're suggesting, and it is someone who's been here less than two years, then he's been at the scenes," Keara said with certainty. "He's been talking to people. That means someone has seen him. We need to keep circulating that sketch. Has it been shown to all of the victims and anyone else who was near the scenes at the time of the bombings?"

"We've shown it to all of the victims who are able to look at it right now," Anderson said, reminding Jax that there were still two Desparre victims in comas, still three from the Luna bomb who were critical and unresponsive, as well.

"And? No one recognized him?" Keara pressed.

"Some of them said the sketch looked kind of familiar," Ben replied. "But no one could give us a name. Same result as the general canvassing today."

"He's good at blending in," Jax said. "He's got a lot of practice fading into the background."

"This is a small town," Keara said, frustration in her voice. "We notice outsiders. Yeah, we let them have their privacy, but unless they're hiding out on the mountain all day, we see them." She frowned, a ripple of anger rushing over her features. "Of course, I thought that five years ago, too, and we had a kidnapper living among us. People knew him vaguely, but no one seemed to know who he was."

"We'll find this guy," Jax said, hoping he sounded confident. But would they? Why was he still here if it was the same person? "He figured out who you were," Jax breathed, the final pieces that didn't quite fit falling into place in his mind.

"He figured out that I was the chief of police or that I was Juan's widow?" Keara demanded, sounding like she already knew the answer.

"He was probably planning to move on after the Luna bombing like he had with all the other crimes. But you showed up that night," Jax realized. "Or maybe he followed me when I came to Desparre to talk to you about the case." He told Ben about the blue truck and the agent nodded, jotting notes.

"I'm sorry," he told Keara.

She waved a dismissive hand. "We don't know that was him. And if it was, you shook him. Anyway, if he's sticking around because he realized who I was, that gives us more of a chance to bring him down."

"He's breaking pattern now," Ben said, a warning in his voice that Jax felt deeply himself.

"I know," Keara said, glancing at the other agent. "My husband almost caught him. Maybe he's worried I'm just as good."

"With a personality type like this, if he's breaking pattern, he could be fixating on you," Jax said, the worry he felt coming through in his words.

Keara nodded, fury in her own voice. "He can fixate all he wants. I'm fixated now, too."

"Keara." He stepped closer, trying to block out everyone else, everything else, as she tipped her head up slightly, meeting his gaze.

"I think you could be in danger."

Chapter 18

The air felt stuffy and uncomfortable inside Jax's SUV. Or maybe that was just all of Keara's pent-up anger.

She took a deep breath. The anger and grief over her husband's murder had settled over the years, buried deeper where it was less likely to bubble up at any moment and overwhelm her. But right now, knowing the person who had done it was probably here, trying to destroy the new town she'd chosen to call home, had pushed it all to the surface again, as strong as it had ever been.

It wasn't fair to take it out on Jax.

She glanced at him, saw the worry in his tense profile, in the focused gaze that kept jumping between the dark road ahead and his rearview mirror, like he was watching for a tail. It was obvious he felt guilty, thinking he might have led the bomber to her.

"It's not your fault," she told him.

He glanced at her briefly, pensively, then back out the windshield.

"For all we know, this guy found out where I lived by talking up the locals."

"And no one recognized him?" Jax countered.

"Judging by that sketch, he's not exactly a memorable-looking guy." The couple who'd seen him—assuming the person they'd seen *was* the bomber—said he was just shy of six feet, with thinning brown hair. He'd been wearing a shapeless coat, maybe to disguise his build, and sunglasses on a not-so-sunny day. When asked if there was anything memorable about him, Imani had just shrugged and called him "average."

Keara glanced at Patches in the backseat, sound asleep with her head resting on Keara's overnight bag. "This really isn't necessary." She repeated what she'd said back at her house, when everyone else had either headed home or gone inside to gather evidence. When Jax had insisted she come stay at the hotel where it was safer, she'd rolled her eyes and blurted harshly, "Don't be ridiculous."

Ever the therapist, he hadn't taken offense. Probably he'd recognized her misplaced frustration and fury.

Even now he just said calmly, "We agreed you'd be safer at the hotel. Plus, Patches will love the company."

Woof! she chimed in from the backseat.

Keara twisted to look at the Labrador retriever and couldn't stop her smile. The puppy had been wound up an hour ago, jumping over the seat in Jax's SUV where she'd been shut inside, barking and trying to get someone to let her out. As soon as Keara had given in—and given herself a welcome distraction while federal agents combed through her office, looking for evidence—she'd nudged repeatedly at Keara, like she was mad it had taken so long. Then she'd lain down at Keara's feet and promptly fallen asleep.

She'd been asleep for most of the ride from Keara's house toward the Royal Desparre Hotel, too. But apparently saying Patches's name woke her instantly.

"Can't argue with that, can you?" Jax asked, giving her a tense smile as he pulled into the hotel parking lot.

As he put the SUV in Park and shifted to face her, focusing those compelling deep brown eyes entirely on her, Keara resisted the urge to fidget. She was a police chief. She didn't fidget.

"Jax, look, I don't mean to be rude, but let's be honest here. You're not law enforcement. You can't protect me."

He shrugged, only a brief flicker of offense in his eyes. "Well, then it's a good thing this hotel is full of FBI agents, isn't it?"

"Then what's the point of me staying with you instead of just getting my own room?"

Woof! Woof! Woof! Patches seemed to argue from the backseat.

"If I'm right, then this guy has gotten away with it for at least seven years, Keara," Jax said, sounding tired as he retread the argument they'd already had at her house.

It was an argument he'd won, since she was here, with her bag packed with her uniform for tomorrow and her work laptop. She'd left her personal vehicle in front of her house, hoping it would seem occupied if the killer decided to return.

Still, the idea that she was leaving the house empty, making it easy for him to go back through it if he wanted, made her antsy. She'd finally agreed to come with Jax when he suggested that if she didn't want to stay with him, she should bunk with one of her officers. The idea of staying with Jax was making her nervous, the attraction between them palpable in the air. But asking one of her officers to lend her their couch felt too close to admitting she wasn't up for being their leader. And that was something she'd never do.

"You know I'm armed," she said once more as he opened the door and started to climb out. "Maybe you don't know this—I'm a damn good shot."

He leaned down, met her gaze with his own less patient one. "Your husband carried a gun, too, right? And this could be the same asshole who killed him, only now he's got seven more years of practice."

Jax held her gaze for a long moment, surely seeing the horror and grief rush across her face at the low blow. Then he stood and shut the door behind him, before opening up the back for Patches.

His dog stared at Keara for a long moment, offered up a *woof!* then climbed out, too.

Keara sat motionless in the SUV, imagining the beautiful sunny day she'd found Juan dead in their backyard. He'd been caught completely by surprise, even when the killer had slipped up right behind him to slit his throat.

Swallowing back the surge of tears that threatened, Keara reached into the back to grab her overnight bag. Then she followed Jax silently into the hotel.

Jax opened his eyes to find Keara staring at him.

She immediately redirected her gaze, sipping a cup of coffee he'd somehow slept through her brewing. She'd gotten dressed while he was sleeping, too, changing out of the joggers and long T-shirt she'd put on before climbing into the second bed. Now she was wearing her uniform, with the four-star emblem on her collar designating her role as chief of police.

He tore his gaze away from her still-loose hair and makeup-free face to check on Patches. When his dog had realized Keara was staying last night, she'd run in circles for a minute, then leaped onto the bed with Keara and slept at her feet.

His dog was still at the end of the bed, her front paws dangling off the edge. When she saw him looking at her, her tail thumped the bed.

He grinned. He couldn't believe someone had tossed her out. It was hard not to smile when you saw her. "Hi, Patches."

Throwing off his covers, Jax climbed out of bed and asked, "How did you sleep, Keara?"

He'd zonked out. He wasn't sure how, with the woman he was falling for only a few feet away from him, but it had been a long, stressful day. Apparently, it had caught up to him.

But right now he felt refreshed, reenergized and determined. And the woman he was falling for was still only a few feet away.

Her eyes widened as he stepped closer and she set her coffee down, her mouth moving like she was getting ready to speak.

When he stepped closer still, into her personal space, she surprised him by looping her arms around his neck. "I slept fine. Not quite as well as I did on my couch, though." He could feel her heart rate pick up as she stared at him, giving him a small, sassy grin.

He flashed back to the feel of her spooned against him on her couch and couldn't help but smile back. He wanted to stay in this moment, savor the feeling of being with Keara as if they were a long-established couple and not a pair of colleagues who'd barely known each other more than a week. But her lips were too close to him, her gaze broadcasting a mix of uncertainty and desire.

As he slowly bent his head closer, one of her hands slid into his hair and the other stroked along the back of his neck, making all of the nerve endings there fire to life. He pressed his lips softly to hers as she sank into him. The gentle meeting of their lips sent sparks through him, but he kept his kiss slow, wanting to linger in the moment.

She tasted like coffee with cream and sugar. She smelled faintly of the lavender soap in the hotel bathroom. She felt exactly right in his arms, like she belonged there.

Too soon, she was pulling back, her gaze serious, despite the passion that still lingered. "Sorry I was hard to deal with yesterday."

He laughed, surprised at the admission. "Thanks for letting me win the argument."

A grin burst on her face, her own laugh soft and short, and somehow, in that moment, he knew. However many dangers she faced because of her job, he still wanted to be with her.

Pulling free of his embrace, she told him, "I may not have known you long, Jax, but I'm figuring you out. And I didn't want you and Patches trying to stand guard at my house." She picked up her brush, started to pull her hair up into its customary work bun. "Much as I appreciate it," she added.

He watched her a minute longer, gave her an easy smile when she glanced questioningly at him. It wasn't time to talk about anything serious. He knew she wasn't ready. But maybe if they could resolve this case, that would change.

Mentally shifting into work mode, he said, "If we assume the killer was planning to stick to pattern and leave after he set the bomb in Luna, that means most likely he spotted you at the scene at some point. Do you think he could have recognized you from Houston?"

Keara froze, one hand holding up all of her long hair, the other holding her brush. Then she continued working it into a bun, her voice steady but underlaid with anger as she replied, "It seems unlikely, but I guess it's possible. More likely he heard my name and recognized that. Then he might have started digging up details on me. There was a picture of me in the paper back in Houston from Juan's funeral. I'm sure that would come up if you dug enough."

"So either he heard someone at the scene say your name or he talked to people, asked who you were," Jax continued, thinking out loud.

"Probably," Keara agreed, jamming bobby pins into her hair and then slapping her hands on her hips. "What are you thinking, Jax?"

At her insistent tone, Patches jumped off the bed, ran to her side and plopped down at her feet, staring up at him, too.

Jax couldn't help another laugh. "Okay, Patches. I'll get to the point." He redirected his attention to Keara. "I'm the one you've had the most contact with from the team in Luna. Maybe the killer followed me, maybe not. But we know he's been paying attention to you. We can assume he knows who I am."

Keara's eyes narrowed. "And…"

"We also know he didn't get any information about the status of the investigation when he broke into your house."

"Assuming this whole theory is right and it was the killer who broke in, then that's true," Keara agreed. "I don't have any information about the bombings—or the killings or arson—at my home."

"So he's still looking for information."

"And you have an idea," Keara said.

"He might have already seen the sketch of himself, so I'm sure he's being careful. Maybe he's tried to change his appearance. But if he's still here, he'll want to find out the status of the case. Who better to get it from than the guy who's been giving *you* information?"

"Okay," Keara said slowly, her narrowed eyes telling him she didn't like where this was headed.

"What if I go back to the scene in Desparre? The FBI has finished processing it, but I've seen residents there every day, leaving signs and stuffed animals for Nate and Talise, looking for information. They all know Patches and I are here to help the victims and the community. We can stick around, let people know we're there for anyone who's struggling to process this, to share what we can about how the investigation is going."

"You hope he'll hear about it and come talk to you," Keara said, her expression telling him she liked this less and less with every word.

"Yes." He stared back at her, trying to project confidence, even though it felt like a long shot. But a long shot was better than nothing.

She started to shake her head and he cut her off. "It's daytime, so there are going to be plenty of people around. He's not going to set off a bomb in the same spot twice."

When she scowled even more at that, he insisted, "Hitting twice in the same state is already a departure for him. Yes, he's been getting away with his crimes for a long time. But that's because he's smart and he's patient. This is a pretty low-risk thing for me to do. It's not really even that far from what I'd normally be doing right now. But maybe it will work. You and some of the agents can set up at a distance and watch. What do you think?"

She sighed and gave him a reluctant-looking nod. "Let's call Ben and get his opinion."

As Jax headed to the bathroom to get changed, he heard her on the phone with the FBI agent. She talked through his idea impartially and fully, even though he knew she would have preferred not to have him involved. But when he stepped out of the bathroom, ready for the day in his standard dark dress pants and a button-up shirt with an FBI jacket over it to let citizens know who he was, she nodded.

"We're on."

Twenty minutes later he was standing next to the temporary short fence that had been erected around the crime scene to keep anyone from hurting themselves before the damage could be repaired. As he looked around the empty scene, Jax wondered if his plan was a mistake.

Three days after the bomb had gone off in Desparre's downtown, people were starting to get back to normal. Instead of congregating near the stash of signs, candles and teddy bears that had been piled high with messages for the dead and wounded in both Desparre and Luna, residents were giving it a wide berth today. Their gazes darted his way briefly, pausing with grief and fear, before they resumed their business. Apparently, they'd hit the point where they hoped to move on, try to forget while they waited for good news on the victims and the suspect's capture.

Jax sighed and knelt next to Patches, who looked as dejected as he felt. She whined a little and he scratched behind her ears.

"I know, Patches. You want to work."

Her tail thumped lightly at the word as she stared up at him, then glanced toward the part of Desparre with all of the shops, with all of the people. It was Sunday morning and in the distance, he could see people in dress clothes starting to stream toward the church down the street from the police station.

His gaze shifted from the far end of town with the church, to a little bit closer, at the police station. From an attic Jax wouldn't have guessed existed in the police building, Keara, Ben and Anderson were watching him through binoculars. So far there was nothing for them to see.

"We'll give it another half hour here, then go find people to talk to," he promised Patches.

Her tail wagged and he grinned at her.

Then dirt sprayed up from the road in front of him, pebbles stinging his legs as a distant *boom* sounded.

For a second he was confused, even as Patches started frantically barking, already standing.

Then the sound registered. Someone had just taken a shot at him. But from where?

Panic followed, tensing his whole body as he glanced

around frantically, looking for the shooter, looking for a safe place to go.

Then there was another *boom* like a firecracker going off and a metallic screech as the bullet hit the small fence behind him.

"Run, Patches!" Jax yelled, angling his arm toward downtown. Toward the police station.

She barked, staring up at him, waiting for him, and he took off, too.

He ran as hard as he could, Patches keeping pace at his side, even as he wished for her to outrun him, to get to safety faster.

He was pretty sure the person shooting at him was using a rifle. Which meant either they weren't a great shot or they were playing with him, forcing him to run for his life even though they could end it at any time.

Chapter 19

"Wait!"

Ben's voice echoed behind her as Keara leaped down from the attic in the police station, skipping the entire ladder and landing hard on the floor below.

Pain jolted up from her legs, making her teeth slam together, but she ignored it the same way she ignored Ben. She'd agreed to Jax's plan to try and fool the man who'd killed her husband and now he and Patches were in danger.

She couldn't survive losing another man she loved.

The unexpected thought made grief and dread clamp down hard, almost doubling her over. It was too soon. Way too soon.

"Keara!" Ben yelled. "Get someone up here with a long rifle!"

"Okay," she gasped at him, but she didn't even need

to yell the order, because Tate Emory and Charlie Quinn were already rushing toward her, both holding rifles.

They didn't know where the shooter was, but they knew his target.

Maybe she'd make a better one.

There was no time to grab a bulletproof vest, so Keara just straightened and kicked into gear again, running for the front of the station. She blew past her officers, warning them, "Active shooter! Gear up before you come out!" Then she raced outside.

Yanking her pistol from its holster, she ran into the center of the street. Near the church, residents were looking around in confusion and she yelled at them, "Get inside!" Then she spun the other way, toward the park.

Jax and Patches were still running toward her, but there hadn't been any more shots fired. If the killer was smart, he was already trying to disappear. Even with a rifle, there was only so long he could hold off police. They were too close.

They could get him. She could get him.

The thought fueled her, added fury to her fear and determination to her strides, lengthening them even as she kept her gun ready. She'd been one of the best shots in the Houston PD back in the day and she still kept up her practice. If she saw the shooter, he was finished.

As Jax met her gaze, he waved his arm, made a motion at her that clearly meant "turn back."

"Move!" she barked at him as she got close and he started to slow, like he was planning to grab her arm and try to turn her.

His gaze lingered on her, his head pivoting to watch even as he followed her orders and kept going, Patches keeping pace with him.

Then he was behind her and her focus sharpened, her gaze sweeping the empty street in front of her. The killer couldn't be far.

She kept pushing, legs and arms burning as she ran hard toward the park. Her lungs ached, too, out of practice at this kind of running, especially with the chilly Alaskan air sending an icy blast down her throat with every breath. Where would a shooter have the best angle?

As she drew alongside the park, she realized. Down the side street that bisected Main Street, ending just past the park. He'd be able to see Jax, but Jax would be unlikely to see him because the woods continued that way, offering plenty of places to hide.

Boom!

Keara instinctively cringed, even as she dodged left and then right. It wasn't a rifle this time, but the sound of a pistol firing. As she rounded the corner onto the side street, nearly skidding off her feet, she saw him.

About Jax's height, wearing dark green—a good choice to blend into a forest—he was running hard, too. And there was a dark blue truck parked on the street ahead.

She could yell out a warning, shoot him when he inevitably spun and fired at her. Or she could tackle him, bring him in. Force him to admit all the things he'd done, force him to serve time the way he deserved.

Keara hunched inward, pushed her strides as long as she could, as he slid to a stop alongside his truck, stopping himself by grabbing the side mirror.

Then he was spinning toward her, aiming his gun again.

Keara dove for the ground, twisting as she flew through

the air, trying to get her own gun up as another gunshot blasted. She slammed into the hard-packed earth with a grunt that stole all of her air and made her vision momentarily fuzzy.

Then he was in the truck, the tires spitting dirt as she lined up her pistol and fired. She heard the *ping* of her bullet hitting the truck, but it wasn't enough.

The truck careened around the corner and out of sight.

Jax's heartbeat refused to slow.

He'd been back at the hotel for half an hour, but his body was still amped up, the adrenaline overload not subsiding. He wasn't sure it would until Keara walked through that door and he could see for himself that she was okay.

Kneeling on the floor, he wrapped his arms around Patches's neck, hugging her.

She whined a little, pushed her head up into the crook of his neck. She'd seen a lot of terrible things during her six months as a therapy dog—and she'd definitely had a rough start in life. But she'd never been in danger while she'd worked for the FBI.

Fury and guilt mixed as he stroked the soft fur on her back, whispered, "We're okay, Patches. Keara is okay, too."

She whined again at Keara's name and he knew she had to be wishing for the same thing he was.

As he'd reached the safety of the Desparre police station, a small group of officers had poured outside, wearing bulletproof vests over their uniforms and helmets on their heads. They'd looked serious and nervous, but moved confidently in pairs toward the threat.

Not long afterward, Ben and Anderson had climbed down from the Desparre Police Department's rarely used attic, frowning and shaking their heads. "He got away," Ben had told him. Then he must have seen Jax's panic, because he'd added, "Keara is okay. We're putting out an APB on the truck. Dark blue, like you said."

Now, back in the hotel room where he'd been escorted by a pair of police officers and told to "stay put," Jax wondered: If he'd done something differently when he'd seen that truck, would they have already caught the bomber?

Pushing aside the frustration, he continued to pet Patches until her presence calmed his raging heart. She seemed to relax, too, and she pulled her head off his shoulder to glance at the door.

"I know, Patches. You want Keara."

Her tail wagged and new nerves filled him. Keara hadn't been hurt chasing down the killer, and hopefully they'd get lucky and catch him quickly with the APB. But then he and Patches would be leaving.

He'd been putting off telling her how he felt, putting off telling her that he wanted to pursue a relationship, despite the challenges. He'd been waiting for the right time, hoping this case would end with her getting closure on her husband's murder and make it easier for her to move on. But there was never going to be a perfect time to talk, not even if that happened.

He needed to act.

As if on cue, there was a knock at the door and Patches leaped to her feet, giving an excited bark as her tail whipped back and forth. A reaction like that could only mean one thing: Keara was here.

His heart rate picked up again as he looked through the peephole to confirm it before letting her in.

Keara looked formidable, despite torn sleeves and the dirt covering her once-crisp uniform, despite the strands of hair pulled loose from her bun, and the smear of dirt across one cheek. Determination blazed in her eyes and there was a hard set to her expression that said it didn't matter how far the bomber ran, she was going to find him.

He stood staring at her, watching her gaze run over him like she was reassuring herself he wasn't injured, as Patches ran in circles around her.

Finally a shaky smile broke and she bent down to pet Patches, before standing and moving closer to him. Close enough to touch, but the intimidating, focused expression was still in her eyes, mixed suddenly with a fear he knew he'd caused.

"Are you okay?" she asked, her voice barely above a whisper.

"We're fine," he reassured her. "I'm not sure he actually wanted to hit us."

She blew out a heavy breath that he felt across his face. "We lost him." She shook her head, and her hard mask broke, showing all the frustration underneath. "The FBI is working with my officers to find him, and we've coordinated with all the surrounding towns to be on the lookout for him or his truck. I got a partial plate, which will help, but…"

She sighed again, ran a hand through her hair that just pulled out more pieces of her bun. "We found the rifle, too, and we're running it for prints. The bastard was wearing gloves, but there's a good chance he loaded it without them, so hopefully we'll get a hit there."

"We'll get him," Jax said, discovering it was easy to inject his voice with confidence. This killer was savvy and he'd gotten away with it for a long time. But the Anchorage agents were very good and very dedicated. And Keara? Jax knew this was the most important case of her life. She wasn't going to rest until she found him. And he'd bet on her over anyone else.

It was something he needed her to know. "Keara—"

"Shh." She put a finger to his lips, then stepped closer. She blinked and the last of the frustration and angry determination faded, leaving behind residual fear and need.

"Are *you* okay?" he asked as he settled his hands on her hips, desperate to pull her to him, desperate to hold her until the threat was gone. But he needed to hear her say it.

"I'm okay now." She pushed his hands aside, unstrapped her holster and set it up on top of his TV. Then she looped her arms around his neck, pushed up on her tiptoes and fused her lips to his.

It was nothing like the kiss they'd shared this morning. Instead of going slow, her grip tightened as soon as his lips started to move against hers. Her tongue breached the seam of his mouth and she moaned, sending his pulse skyrocketing.

Gripping her hips again, harder this time, he pulled her closer until there was no space between them. She was a perfect mix of lean muscle and feminine curves, and her tongue was dancing around the inside of his mouth in a way that made his eyes roll back in his head.

Her kisses were fast and frantic, and Jax met her pace, learning the curves along her body with his hands as she looped a leg around his hip.

Then she pulled back slightly, breathing heavily, her eyelids at half-mast as she panted, "I can't stay long, Jax. I have to get back out there."

As she was leaning back in, he whispered, "We have all the time we want, Keara. Anchorage and Desparre are only a jumper flight apart." His lips sought hers again, desperate for another feel of her before she went off chasing a killer.

But she pulled away, her hands dropping from around his neck and her leg returning to the floor.

When he opened his eyes, she was still breathing hard, but the desire in her gaze was fading. She nodded, stepping out of his embrace so quickly he almost stumbled, and he tried to figure out what was happening.

"You're right," she said. "And those jumper flights happen every day. The killer has obviously targeted you, Jax, and I don't want it to happen again. You need to get on one as soon as possible. You and Patches should go home."

He stared back at her, his own passion cooling as understanding dawned. Keara wasn't here right now because the overwhelming relief that he was okay had made her realize she wanted something more serious.

She was here to say goodbye.

Chapter 20

Patches whined and glanced from Jax to the closed hotel door.

"I know," he said softly, petting her. The look Keara had given them as she'd grabbed her overnight bag and paused at the door, before shutting it softly behind her, was lodged in his brain. It had been full of regret and sorrow. But it had also been full of finality.

She believed he'd follow her advice. She believed she was never going to see them again.

It had been hours since she'd left and he hadn't heard from her since. He knew she was out there somewhere, searching for the bomber. She'd thrown herself into danger while she asked him to run away from it. For the FBI's part, they didn't like that he'd been targeted, either. Ben had called to check in on him. The agent hadn't suggested that he go home, but he'd sounded discouraged as he advised Jax to stay inside.

Jax had agreed, but asked for a favor in return. When Ben had originally run the symbol through the FBI database, they'd focused on the past seven years, since Celia's murder. But today Jax had asked Ben to run the symbol for a ten-year stretch about thirty years ago.

After Keara had left, he'd needed something else to focus on. Sitting in the quiet of his hotel room with no victims to help and nothing else to do made it too easy to think about the expression on Keara's face as she'd walked out the door. He wasn't about to give up hope of changing her mind.

Still, it was one thing to wish for this case to be solved, for her husband's murder to be solved. For Keara to get closure. He believed in her. She was dogged and a damn good investigator. Maybe it wouldn't happen quickly, but he believed she'd find the person responsible.

But after what happened this morning, he wasn't sure closure would be enough to make her move on. At least not with him.

His job wasn't usually dangerous. Still, he enjoyed using his knowledge of psychology to help investigations. If the opportunity arose again, he didn't want to turn it down. Even if he was willing to promise that, maybe Keara just couldn't bring herself to ever date someone connected to law enforcement again.

He understood it. He'd seen the details from her husband's case file. The murder had been gruesome. He couldn't imagine finding someone he loved that way. He definitely empathized with her need never to lose anyone violently again.

It was why she'd backed away from him. And it wasn't a fear he was sure he could breach, no matter how hard he tried.

Patches whined, nudging his leg, and Jax nodded at her. "You're right. I need to focus."

She slid to the floor, looking dejected, and he wondered if she understood exactly what was happening with Keara, if she was just as upset over it.

Giving her one last pet, he clicked to the next result in the files Ben had sent over. Thirty years ago the FBI's system to compare unsolved crimes was newer. There were fewer entries, so fewer possibilities to go through. But maybe he'd get lucky.

Because the thing he'd realized as he'd tried to find a way to distract himself from Keara's departure was that he'd been right from the very beginning. The symbol meant something. And if it was being used by a single criminal, it was probably connected to that person's childhood.

Working with the victims of a serial killer last year had been brutal. It had taught him that human beings were capable of far worse atrocities than he'd ever seen before up close. It had also taught him that many of the perpetrators came from violence themselves. Instead of learning empathy from it, they'd sought it out, tried to inflict pain on others.

Maybe the bomber was the same. Maybe the symbol came from a traumatic incident in his childhood and he was now marking his own crimes with it. Maybe...

Jax sighed and set aside one more case, wondering if he was wasting time. Even if he was right, the symbol could have been overlooked or never entered in the FBI's voluntary database.

Then his pulse spiked as he flipped to the next case. Here was the symbol he'd seen at two bomb sites, staring back at him from a twenty-nine-year-old case. A murder that had happened in Texas, not far from Houston.

He read fast as Patches sat up, scooting closer and resting her head on his leg. Although the FBI database was meant for unsolved cases, the police in this case had known exactly who the killer was. They just couldn't find him.

Arthur Margrove had been known around the community as a violent man. Prone to picking fights with anyone—including his wife—he'd been arrested repeatedly for assault. He'd served multiple short sentences in jail, but never learned his lesson. After being fired from yet another job, he'd returned to his job site, broken in and smashed everything he could find. Then he'd gone home and murdered his wife.

Today Arthur would be in his sixties. He wasn't the bomber.

But Jax tapped the computer screen, his fingers marking the information he'd been searching for all afternoon and into the early evening. Arthur Margrove had a son.

Todd Margrove had been five years old at the time of the murder. He'd been standing beside his mother's body when police came looking for Arthur, covered in her blood, probably from trying to help her. Both of them were underneath a bloody symbol drawn on the wall. A symbol that had now been replicated across the country.

Jax grabbed his phone and dialed Keara's number. Frustration gnawed when the call went to voice mail, and he left a tense message:

"Call me back, Keara. I know who the bomber is."

Keara glanced at the readout on her phone as she drove down the mountain. Jax was calling.

She gripped the wheel tighter as she debated whether to answer. She'd spent the day running leads with her officers, the fury and frustration in her chest building and building until it felt ready to burst.

Nothing was panning out. Thinking about what had happened with Jax in the morning just added fear to the mix.

Whatever Jax wanted now, it wasn't to tell her he'd gone home; she knew that much. She hadn't spoken to him since she'd left his hotel room that morning, but she had talked to the FBI agents, suggesting they get him a flight. Ben had raised his eyebrows at her and told her Jax understood the threat and was staying off the streets. The FBI didn't believe he was in real danger. They thought if the bomber wanted him dead, he wouldn't have missed.

They thought today's shooting was a message. The bomber knew what they were doing and he wasn't falling for it.

He was having fun with them, because after all, if Jax was right, this was what he wanted anyway. A strong opponent to chase him, the thrill of getting away despite their best efforts.

It wasn't going to happen. Not this time.

They might not have prints to give them a name, since the rifle had come up empty. But they had a partial license plate. They had a sketch.

Her phone stopped ringing as Keara rounded another bend, riding the brakes because this stretch of road was steep. She'd gone up to the top of the mountain to talk to the loner who'd been at the scene of the Desparre bombing. He'd called the station and implied he might have seen the person in the sketch. He'd asked for her personally, and because he was a recluse who'd opened up to her in the past, she'd agreed.

Charlie Quinn and his FBI partner had spoken to him yesterday and reported back that he was crotchety and uncooperative, but didn't have any useful information. It seemed unlikely he'd have something new today, but she had to check. Plus, it gave her some time to herself.

But when she'd arrived, no matter how many ways she asked, the information he'd claimed to have didn't surface. Instead, he'd spent the entire discussion digging for details on the case. Maybe it was because he'd suffered some minor injuries, cuts to his legs that had required stitches. Or maybe he was just one of those guys who got off on crime scene details.

He wasn't the bomber. In his late fifties, in poor health and bad shape, not only did he not fit the description, but he'd lived in Desparre too long.

Still, Keara's radar was up. As soon as she'd returned to her SUV, she'd called the station to update them, let them know she was heading back in.

The whole thing had been a waste of time. Peering up at the sky through her windshield, she scowled at the fading light filtering through the towering trees. Pretty soon it would be dark. Her officers had been working a lot of overtime in the past four days. The shooting downtown today meant they'd needed to spend as much time reassuring the public and keeping a visible presence there as running leads.

The more time that passed from when the bomber had shown up in the park, the farther he could run. Yes, he'd found a police department—and a group of federal agents—to try and outwit. But he hadn't made it so many years without being caught by being stupid. Maybe the shots at Jax had been his parting ones. His way of telling them they'd gotten as close as they ever would. His own form of goodbye, before he showed up in some other state, committed some other crime.

Rounding another corner, Keara's SUV jolted as it ran over something in the road. The back of her vehicle did the same and then the tires started making a rhythmic *thump thump thump.*

Flat tires.

What the hell had she hit?

Glancing around her at the darkening woods, Keara put her SUV in Park and pulled her gun as she stepped out of the vehicle.

Scanning the area and seeing nothing unusual, she walked to the back of her vehicle. There was a plank of wood driven through with upward facing nails directly behind her back wheels.

Adrenaline rushed through her, all her senses on alert as she lifted her weapon. She spun around just as something flew toward her head.

Keara ducked, trying to center her weapon at the figure that had rushed out of the woods, but the slab of wood still made contact with the top of her head.

Pain exploded in her skull, bringing tears to her eyes. Her feet came out from underneath her and her arm slammed down on the edge of the board of nails, making her lose her grip on the gun. It skidded away from her, out of reach.

Then the man she'd seen only from a distance that morning was filling her vision, a smile on his face. The bomber, murderer, arsonist. The man who'd shot at Jax. The man who'd killed Juan.

He wavered in her sight, her vision blurry from the hit to the head, her lungs screaming from the hard landing. Fighting the urge to throw up, ignoring the burning pain in her arm, Keara shoved herself upward, launching at him.

But he moved fast, swinging that slab of wood again.

Even though she threw up her arm to block it, the wood still made contact with the side of her head.

She hit the ground again, head throbbing, nausea welling up hard.

Then she was moving, her head bumping over every uneven piece of ground, into the woods.

Her vision went in and out, as dizziness threatened to overtake her, threatened to suck her into unconsciousness. Panic erupted, flooding her system with terror, but keeping her awake. She was weak from the blows to her head, too dizzy to stand. Too dizzy to fight.

He left her for a moment and she swallowed the nausea, tried to move, but her body wouldn't cooperate. Then the bushes in front of her were moving and she blinked, trying to right her swaying vision, until she realized it wasn't bushes she was seeing.

They were camouflage, broken branches strategically covering the truck he'd hidden just off the road. He planned to put her in that truck, to take her somewhere else.

It wasn't a quick death he planned for her, but probably a painful one.

Keara rolled onto her belly, biting down on her cry of pain as her vision swung one way and then back again and her head throbbed violently. *Where was her gun?*

Too soon it didn't matter because she was being lifted, thrown over his shoulder with frightening ease. He carried her around to the back of the truck where a metal gun box was propped open.

Keara kicked, raking her fingernails over the backs

of his arms, still coherent enough to think like the cop she was. To get his DNA on her.

He yelped and swore and then he was swinging her fast enough to make her nausea overwhelming, make her vomit on the ground beneath him. Soon the ground disappeared altogether and she was being stuffed into the empty gun box.

She shoved upward, trying to escape, but he'd dropped her into the box awkwardly, making it hard to move. The multiple blows to the head and the new wave of dizziness slowed her down, too. The lid closed, leaving her in darkness.

As she heard him move away from her, she took deep breaths to reduce her panic, then slammed against the metal lid, trying to open it. The lid buckled slightly, but held. Then the truck started to move, taking her away with Juan's killer.

Chapter 21

"Have you heard from Keara?" Jax asked Ben over the phone, trying not to give in to worry. He'd called the agent after Keara hadn't picked up, and told him the same news he'd given Keara's voice mail.

"No. She's on her way back from talking to someone up the mountain. She got a weird vibe from it, though. Said she'd stay in touch on her way down." There was a pause and Jax imagined Ben frowning at his watch. "If I don't hear from her in the next ten minutes, I'll give her a call."

Could she have followed a trail right to the bomber's home? Or maybe he'd followed her up there, ambushed her on her way back?

Jax only halfway paid attention as Ben went on about what a great find Jax had made and said he'd start running the name Todd Margrove immediately. Then he asked if Jax thought it was Rodney's elusive roommate from back in Texas. From the way he asked, Jax had a feeling he'd repeated the question a few times.

"Yeah, maybe. Look, let me call you back, okay?" He hung up without waiting for an answer, dread forming in his gut.

Maybe he was overreacting because he'd been shot at that morning, but he suddenly couldn't stop picturing Keara in trouble. "Come on, Patches. Let's go for a drive."

Woof! She leaped to her feet, danced around him even as she didn't get the usual laugh out of him.

He moved faster the closer he got to his SUV, scanning the semidarkened parking lot. He opened the back door and Patches jumped in, then Jax got behind the wheel.

"Hold on, Patches," he told her, driving faster than was legal as he whipped out of the parking lot and headed for the mountain. It was closer from here than the police station and he couldn't wait the ten minutes for Ben to follow up with Keara, then call back and tell Jax he was overreacting.

He could hear Patches sliding around a bit in the backseat as he rushed toward the base of the mountain, where the main road led up to the best place in Desparre to hide out. But were there other roads off it? He had no idea.

"Sorry, Patches," he told her, wondering if he should have left her in the hotel room. But most likely he *was* overreacting. And if he caught up to Keara coming down the mountain, maybe she'd be more open to talking with an adorable dog begging for her attention, too.

"Almost there," he muttered a few minutes later as the road that led off the mountain came into sight.

Before he reached it, a dark blue truck sped away, making a turn in the opposite direction Jax was coming from.

It was *the* truck.

Jax's pulse picked up as he instinctively punched down harder on the gas. Had Keara run into the bomber on the mountain? Had he hurt her? Was she still up there?

Yanking his phone out of his pocket, he told it, "Call Ben Nez!"

As he reached the base of the mountain, Jax's gaze pivoted from the road that went up the mountain to the street heading out of Desparre that the blue truck had taken. Should he go search for Keara up the mountain? Or follow the bomber?

He clenched his teeth, panicked at the thought of making the wrong choice. *Go after the bomber.* It was Keara's voice in his head. He could imagine her insisting she could take care of herself, to keep the bomber in sight and get the police and FBI on him now.

"Ben here. What is it, Jax?"

The way Ben said his name, the stress in his voice, told Jax he'd repeated himself again.

"I found the bomber. Coming down off the mountain in that same truck. He's heading out of town. I'm following him." Jax's voice sped up as he made his decision. He passed the road up the mountain, hoping he'd made the right choice.

"*What?* Jax, where are you exactly?" Ben asked.

Jax gave him the road, then demanded, "Did you hear back from Keara?"

There was a pause that made dread drop to Jax's stomach, then Ben admitted, "She's not answering her phone. Anderson and I were just about to head up the mountain."

"Should I turn around?" Jax demanded, trying not to panic. Maybe Keara couldn't answer because the roads were dark. He'd heard agents the other day complaining about how narrow they were, how the sudden drop-offs alongside the road in places were startling. Maybe she didn't want to dig her phone out of her pocket and be distracted from driving.

"No," Ben insisted. "Stay on the bomber. Just make sure you stay at a distance. You don't want this guy spotting you, okay? Just stick behind him and keep giving us updates. We're on our way."

"No," Jax insisted. "Send someone else. You need to go find Keara."

"Jax, if Keara's in trouble, it's probably connected to that truck," Ben said, his tone darkly serious, noises in the background suggesting he was already heading for his vehicle. "But we'll send officers up the mountain just in case. We're coming to you. Just be safe. The road you're on leads out of Desparre. It eventually goes into a neighboring town so small they don't even have their own police department. What they do have is a lot of secluded, wooded areas where a bomber might hide. One of Keara's officers was just talking about it earlier today as a place where the bomber could be if he wasn't in Desparre or Luna."

"Okay," Jax agreed, only half listening as he focused on the road ahead. It was empty except for him and the blue truck. He didn't want to get too close and tip the bomber off that he was being followed. He also didn't want to lag too far behind, have the guy take a sudden turn and disappear before Jax could catch up.

"This guy is a killer, Jax," Ben stressed, as if Jax needed the reminder.

He knew all too well what the bomber had done to Keara's husband, what he'd done to Keara's life.

"If you think he's spotted you, turn around. Give us his last coordinates and we'll be right behind him," Ben insisted. "Don't risk your life. You're not an agent. You're not trained for this. Do you hear me? You do *not* want to end up alone with this guy."

"Okay," Jax agreed, not sure if he meant it. Where was Keara? Why hadn't she called him back? Why hadn't she answered Ben's calls?

"Shit," he swore as the truck suddenly sped up, whipping off the road and onto a bisecting trail into the woods.

Jax hit the gas, and as he headed farther away from town, Ben's voice came through a burst of static. "Jax! Did you hear me? Don't engage!"

From the backseat, Patches yelped as she slid across the seat.

"Hang on, Patches," he said, slowing as he reached the turn the blue truck had taken. He eased off the gas entirely, until his SUV was just creeping forward, until he could crane his head and stare down the road.

Boom!

Jax punched the gas again as the gunshot blasted, and his SUV raced forward. Hopefully, they'd pass the road before the bomber could hit them. Hopefully, the bomber wouldn't follow, but would use that opportunity to keep going.

Patches yelped again as Jax gripped the wheel hard, ducking his head low, hoping neither of them would be a visible target.

But as they passed the trail, the truck was still stopped, the brake lights lit up. A hand disappeared back inside the driver's side window, and the truck started up again as if the driver was going to take this chance to get away.

He had a brief instant of relief. Then the gun box in the back of the truck popped open and Keara partially emerged from it.

Keara gasped in the cool night air as she finally got the lid free. She pushed herself upward, desperate to get out of the box that had felt like a too-small coffin.

Ironically, it had been the truck slamming to a stop after taking that nausea-inducing turn that had given her the right angle, just enough leverage, to shove open the box. Now she ducked low again as the unmistakable sound of a bullet pierced the air.

Was he shooting at her?

As quickly as the thought entered her head, she realized it was wrong. The bomber was shooting at Jax, who was amazingly behind them. His SUV had been racing past the trail where they were stopped, but then his eyes widened in the window, his expression caught in the glow from the bomber's brake lights.

Jamming the box lid fully upward, Keara pushed unsteadily to her feet, ready to leap out and race for Jax's SUV.

Then the bomber hit the gas.

Her upper body went flying forward, wrenching her mostly out of the box and into the truck bed. The metal lid of the box slammed against her calves, but she barely felt the pain over the jolt to the rest of her body as she

landed hard, then slid toward the edge where the back
of the truck bed had popped open.

Catching herself before she slid right out, Keara
grabbed the edge, holding on. Her fingers sliced open
on the metal as she held on hard, as she tried to angle
her legs to brace herself against the side. She eyed the
ground below, moving rapidly enough to intensify her
dizziness. They were going too fast. She'd missed her
chance to jump.

Then Jax's SUV backed up and spun wildly onto the
road, chasing them.

The truck jerked to the side and Keara lost her grip
on the edge as she flew sideways across the truck bed.
She slammed into the side of it, grabbing the edge there
as her body spun and her legs dangled off the vehicle,
hanging in midair. Head pounding, she scrambled to
get fully back on the truck as it swerved again and the
boom of a bullet fired.

Maneuvering onto her knees, she peered into the
front of the truck, where the bomber leaned out the
window, slowing slightly as he fired backward at Jax.

Gritting her teeth, Keara pulled herself slowly, painfully, up the truck bed, smearing blood in her wake.
Could she get to the left side, near the front of the truck
bed? Could she reach the bomber's hand, yank the gun
free? Shooting him while she was in the bed of his moving truck wasn't her best plan, but it didn't seem like
her worst option, either.

The truck sped up again and Keara's knees slid out
from underneath her. She swore as she slammed against
the truck bed again, and her arms were yanked hard as
she kept her grip on the side. Ignoring the sharp ache

in her arms and shoulders, Keara kept dragging herself forward.

She glanced back and saw Jax gaining. She wanted to tell him to get off this trail, get himself out of danger, but she was also grateful for the backup, grateful that she wasn't completely alone with a practiced killer.

Taking deep breaths to try to ease the pounding in her head and the throbbing across her entire body, Keara grabbed the front of the gun box. Painfully, far slower than she would have liked, she moved on her knees across the front of the truck bed, pulling herself with her bloodied hands.

When she was halfway there, the bomber twisted to look at her. His eyes inches from hers through the glass startled her, almost made her lose her grip.

There was a darkness in his gaze Keara had never seen before in over a decade of policing, a fury to his scowl that said he was going to make her pay for daring to go up against him.

Keara glared right back, refusing to show him any fear. Today this ended. And it wouldn't be with her painful death. It would be with his arrest.

Lurching sideways, Keara made it to the left side of the truck. Adrenaline or determination was helping her vision even out, pushing the pounding in her head to the background. Now that he knew she'd gotten free of the gun box, would he hold his pistol out the window again? Would he be expecting her to make a grab for it and not take the risk? Or would he focus it on her?

Glancing behind her, she saw Jax. He was gaining on them, close enough now that she could make out the grim determination on his face.

Then the bomber hit the gas again, hard.

Keara swore as her knees came out from under her once more and she banged into the edge of the gun box headfirst, slicing a cut across her forehead. Holding on tighter to the side, she scrambled, trying to wedge her legs against the front and side of the truck. No way could she let go at such a high speed, with the way he kept wrenching the wheel back and forth slightly. No way could she make a grab for his gun if he tried to fire at Jax again.

But from the corner of her eye, she saw Jax getting closer. He was almost on top of them now, gesturing for her to do…what? Try to jump onto the front of his SUV? She shook her head at him, knowing that was a move made for movies, and would probably be deadly at this speed.

Then the bomber slammed on the brakes and Keara's grip came loose from the truck edge. She was thrown against the front of the truck and the gun box, but barely felt the pain as she twisted toward Jax, and the SUV still racing for her.

He was going to hit the truck. At that speed, with that much force, it would probably kill her.

She took a deep breath and tried not to show any fear as she stared back at the man she'd somehow fallen for in such a short time.

It felt like everything was moving in slow motion as his eyes went huge, then his jaw clamped down.

The SUV wrenched sideways as Jax must have yanked the wheel hard. The right wheels came off the ground and for a terrifying moment, she thought he was going to flip it. Then the SUV came back down again and he must have hit the brakes. But not hard enough, because the front of the SUV slammed into one of the trees lining the trail and the whole front of the vehicle crumpled inward.

"No!" Keara screamed as the bomber hit the gas again, and she went flying to the back of the truck.

She grabbed hold before she was tossed over the edge, her hands shaking with the desire to let go, let momentum carry her. But if the fall didn't kill her, the bomber would surely get out and finish the job while she was incapacitated or out cold.

Praying that Jax had survived the crash, Keara stared at the SUV, hoping to see him climb out. But all she could see was smoke billowing from the front of the vehicle, and then too soon, the bomber turned off onto another trail.

Trying to push Jax to the back of her mind, Keara scanned the truck bed, searching for something she could use as a weapon. But there was nothing here. The gun box had been empty, too. But it was old, dented from her twisting inside it and slamming her boots into the lid. Could she rip it off? It wasn't much, but it was better than nothing.

Before she could even start to pull herself back to the front of the truck, the bomber slowed and then came to a stop.

Shoving herself to her feet, Keara glanced over the top of the truck at a tiny cabin, tucked deep into the woods. Swearing, she leaped off the truck, ready to make a run for it.

Too fast, she heard the truck door open behind her and the bomber snapped, "Do it and I shoot you in the back."

A small part of her, knowing it was probably the least painful way to go, wanted to do it anyway. But that wasn't her. She was a fighter, right to the end.

Gritting her teeth, she turned toward him.

He laughed, surprise evident in the sound. "That was a rougher ride than I thought, wasn't it?"

Ignoring the jibe, she tried to throw him off guard, give him a reason to think she was still a worthy opponent, not worth killing yet. "So where's Rodney Brown? Is this all your doing or are you two working together?"

He let out another sound, somewhere between a laugh and a grunt, and his gun lowered to his side. "Rodney has been dead for seven years."

Surprise jolted through her as he continued, "I borrowed his car when I killed Celia Harris. You know I did that, right?" He nodded, a slight smile forming. "I didn't expect anyone to come looking for the car. Rodney was belligerent with the cop, of course, and I couldn't take any chances."

Pain and anger filled her, overriding her physical pain as he spoke of her husband.

His smile grew, as if he could see it. "Rodney has been dead since the day that cop—your husband, right?—came to the house. I dumped his body in the ocean. Then I tracked down the cop and slit his throat."

Keara felt herself sway at the words, felt a familiar, incapacitating grief rip through her as the bomber shrugged and added, "And then I moved on."

He lifted his gun again as she tried to breathe through the pain. "And I'll tell you, you've been a lot of fun, but it's getting a bit dicey for me here. I think it's time for me to move on again."

Chapter 22

Something was burning.

Jax groaned and lifted his head off the steering wheel, not sure if he'd blacked out or if he'd just hit his head when he'd slammed his SUV into the tree, trying to avoid smashing into Keara.

Keara!

Opening his eyes, he saw nothing but white. The airbag had deployed. He groaned again as he twisted his head, peering around it out the side window. The truck was gone.

Woof!

Jax whipped around in his seat, and his chest and shoulder screamed in protest. "Patches! Are you okay?"

She whimpered and he cursed himself for having brought her along.

"I'm sorry, Patches. I'm coming." He tried to smash the airbag out of his way and the movement sent a tearing pain through his left arm. Cursing, he unhooked his belt and twisted, ignoring the way his shoulder screamed as he slid out from behind the airbag.

Peering into the backseat, he saw his dog on the floor. She stood when he met her gaze, her tail wagging slowly, pointing downward.

"Are you okay, Patches?" He reached back with his right hand, letting his left arm hang limply. Had it been wrenched out of the socket in the crash? He wasn't sure.

When he pet Patches, she leaned closer, stretching her head between the seats and licking his face.

His gaze ran over her, searching for injuries, but she looked okay. Then she leaped up, putting her front paws between the seats, and relief filled him. If she could move like that, she probably hadn't broken anything.

Resting his head on hers for a second, Jax tried to take deep breaths. It hurt his chest a little, but he was pretty sure it was the way he was twisted, pain radiating from his shoulder.

Then the hint of smoke hit him again and he spun forward, peering out the front. There was a lot of smoke coming out of his vehicle, but he didn't see fire.

The whole front of the vehicle was smashed in. Would it still drive?

He turned the key, giving it a try even though it seemed pointless. It didn't even make a noise.

Swearing, he slid over to the passenger side and opened the door. He half fell, half climbed out of the SUV and then Patches was outside next to him, having leaped over the seats.

How far had the bomber taken Keara? And where was his backup? Had they driven right past this trail, sticking to the road Jax had given Ben on the phone?

Jax stuck his head back into the SUV, fumbling around for his phone, which had been in the center console. When he finally found it underneath the passenger seat, he discovered the screen was smashed. He tried turning it on anyway, but nothing happened.

"Damn it!" Heaving out a sigh, Jax glanced back toward the road he'd followed the bomber down, the road that presumably his backup would be rushing to. Then he looked the other way, in the direction the bomber had probably taken off.

How far had he gone? Jax could see another trail bisecting this one up ahead, but the trail he was on continued as far as he could see, too. The sun was very low in the sky now, casting pinks, oranges and yellows over the tops of the trees. He wasn't sure where he was or where exactly this trail led. But it was going to be completely dark soon and one thing he did know: they were far from help.

Woof! Patches ran down the trail slightly, then glanced back at him, barking again.

"You want to find Keara?"

Woof!

Jax nodded. Hurrying to the back of his SUV, he grabbed the tire iron that had been useless the last time he'd pulled it out. But it was the closest thing he had to a weapon. Not much use against a gun, but better than nothing.

Then he jogged after Patches, breathing through the pain that rattled in his head each time he put his foot down, and the sharp ache that kept searing through his left arm.

She stayed ahead of him, glancing back periodically

to make sure he was following. When she reached the connected trail, she turned onto it without hesitation.

Jax followed, his heart thumping harder from adrenaline and pain, but also fear of what was up ahead. Was Keara here? Was he already too late to help her?

He jogged forward a few more steps, caught up to where Patches had stopped to stare back at him. And then he saw it. A driveway with a dark blue truck in it. Behind that, a small wood cabin.

Putting his finger to his lips, he knelt beside Patches and whispered, "Shhh." He glanced at the drive again, searching for any sign of Keara or the bomber, but he didn't see either one.

Hugging his good arm around Patches, he kissed the top of her head, then stood. Angling his arm back the way they'd come, he told her, "Go back to the car, Patches. Wait there."

She glanced behind her, then stared up at him, confusion in her soft brown eyes.

"I need you to go back to the car," he repeated, knowing she understood the word. Eventually, Ben and Anderson would find his vehicle, even if they needed to contact the rental company and run a trace on it. If Jax was dead by then, he knew the agents would find Patches a good home.

"I love you, Patches. You're such a good girl," he told her, trying not to let his voice crack.

She sat down and he shook his head, angling his hand again.

"Go, Patches," he said, then turned away from her, creeping toward the cabin. He knew she didn't want to do it, but she *was* a good girl. She'd go and at least she'd be safe.

Taking deep breaths, Jax tried to block everything out: fear for Patches, fear for himself, fear for Keara. He tried to just focus on his surroundings as he crept up to the cabin.

They were inside. They had to be.

Praying that Keara was still alive, Jax slunk up to the edge of the cabin. The windows at the front were totally covered, so he slid along the side of the house, searching for a view inside, some idea of what he was getting himself into.

Feeling hyperattuned to every sound, Jax cringed as dead leaves from last fall crunched lightly under his feet. The edges of fir trees brushed against him as he crept alongside the cabin. His adrenaline was pumping hard, but he felt focused. He gripped the wrench harder, hoping he'd be able to use it.

Then he came up to another window, with a small space where the curtain hadn't been fully shut. Inside the cabin the bomber was standing with his back partially to Jax, a gun held loosely at his side. Across from him, Keara was swaying on her feet, blood on her forehead and her uniform, a dark bruise across her cheek. But she was alive. And she looked fighting mad.

Relief and fury mingled, and Jax picked up his pace, slipping around to the back of the house. There was a door here.

Jax tested the handle and it turned under his hand. Heart pounding, he eased the door open and slid inside.

The bomber didn't turn. If Keara saw him, she gave no indication of it.

Taking light, careful steps, Jax moved forward. His breath was shallow as he tried not to make a sound, as he lifted the wrench, got it in position to smash it down across the back of the bomber's head.

One more step...

The bomber spun toward him, gun lifting fast, a smile rushing over his face. "Welcome to the party."

Jax was here.

Keara tried not to look past the bomber as he stared at her, snarling the way he'd been doing for the past few minutes. She'd thought he was going to shoot her on the driveway, but then a distant noise had made him frown and usher her inside.

Since then he'd bragged about paying off the loner on top of the mountain, laughed at the police response to his Desparre bomb. He'd done it all with a slight smile hovering on the corner of his lips, like he was hoping she'd rush him. Hoping to infuriate her before he shot her.

She'd gritted her teeth and stared back at him with as unaffected a look as she could manage. But she'd known he was just working himself up to something she couldn't withstand. He was working himself up to Juan's murder. Maybe to Jax's, too, if he hadn't made it out of that SUV.

But now Jax was here. Alive and somehow in this cabin.

Just as he raised a big metal wrench over his head and Keara thought it was all about to end, the bomber spun and told Jax, "Welcome to the party."

Keara wouldn't have dared trying to rush the bomber when he was that close to Jax, the gun pointed. But he spun back to keep them both in his eye line quickly.

The bomber shook his head, said to Jax in a mock-sad tone, "And here I let you live at the park." But he couldn't seem to stop a smile from breaking.

Jax slowly lowered the wrench, dropped it to the floor with a *clang* that made Keara flinch.

"If you killed me, then how would I be able to rue how much smarter you are than me?" Jax asked, his tone and expression even.

The bomber's eyes narrowed, like he wasn't sure if Jax was mocking him. Then he shrugged and said, "Like I told Keara, you've given me some fun here. I like a challenge. But the heat is getting a little too close. It's about time for me to move on. And I'm afraid you can't come with me."

"Where to next, Todd?" Jax asked.

Keara's attention jolted from Jax to the bomber, who visibly jerked.

Then he gave a forced smile. "You're better than I thought you were. How'd you get my name?"

"An old case," Jax said and the bomber's eyes narrowed as he shifted more to face Jax, his gun lowering slightly as he took his attention mostly off Keara.

Her breath stalled. She had no idea how Jax had come up with Todd's name, with details of his past. But if Jax could keep Todd talking, keep his attention, maybe she could rush him. She wasn't at full strength—not even close—but she had rage and desperation on her side. She would *not* watch another man she loved die.

"How old?" Todd asked, his voice squeaking slightly.

"Twenty-nine years old," Jax replied evenly, his gaze never shifting to her. "Committed by your father."

Todd scoffed. "He was no *father.*"

"Then why use his symbol?" Jax asked. "Why repurpose it as your own?"

Todd grinned slowly, and the evil there made a shiver race over Keara's skin.

"That might have been his kill, but it's always been my symbol."

"You smeared your mother's blood on the wall?" Jax asked, surprise in his voice that told Keara he hadn't found all of the answers. "Why?"

Todd scowled, shook his head. Something in his expression told Keara even he wasn't sure of the answer. "Does it matter? That's my symbol."

"And what about the man who killed your mother? It didn't bother you that people thought it was his symbol?" Jax asked.

Keara slid forward, one tiny millimeter at a time, holding her breath, trying not to listen too closely to the horrible tale of Todd's childhood. She needed to get close enough to launch herself at him and she needed him to be distracted enough that she'd land before he could lift his gun and fire. But she had to be completely focused.

"I dealt with him. Right before I killed Celia Harris," Todd said, his head tipping up, pride and hate in his words.

Jax nodded slowly, not looking afraid. "It gave you the courage to try a riskier kill."

Todd scowled again. "I didn't need courage, but yeah, I went for someone people would actually miss." He shrugged, then gave a broad grin that told Keara she needed to move soon. "And then I discovered how much *fun* it was to fool the police."

He started to turn back toward her and she knew: this might be her only chance.

But he was twisting too fast, his gun lifting again.

She wouldn't make it. But she had to try.

Keara launched herself off the ground even as Jax's "Keara, no!" rang out and Todd's smile shifted into a sinister smirk.

A familiar *woof! woof! woof!* came from behind Jax and a blur of brown and black fur raced through the doorway.

Todd's smirk slipped as he twisted back in the other direction.

Then Keara landed hard, roping her arms around Todd, trapping him beneath her as they hit the ground. The force of it reverberated through her body as she focused on his gun hand. Ignoring the searing pain in her own hands, the slippery blood making it hard to hold on, she gripped his middle fingers and twisted them backward.

He yelped and lost his grip on the gun.

Keara shoved it away from him as she leveraged herself into a crouched position over him, yanking his arms up behind his back like she was going to cuff him.

Before she could, he rolled, shoving her off him.

Then he was pushing himself off the ground.

"I wouldn't do that," Jax said, his voice low and deadly.

Keara glanced up.

Jax stood with his feet braced apart like he was on a firing range, the pistol in one hand as the other arm dangled strangely at his side. Patches stood beside him, her teeth bared in a way Keara had never seen.

Todd lowered himself back down and then the room erupted in noise as the front door crashed inward and Ben and Anderson rushed inside.

"You're under arrest," Ben yelled, weapon directed

at Todd as Anderson yanked Todd's hands up behind his back and cuffed him.

Jax lowered the pistol he held and gave Keara a shaky smile.

It was over.

Epilogue

A week later Keara stood in front of her officers in the Desparre Police Department, trying not to choke up. "It's been an honor working with all of you for the past six years," she told them.

They stared back at her, giving each other uncertain looks, not having expected this speech on her first day back in the office.

She'd spent the past week at home recuperating. Although the most concerning of her injuries had been the repeated hits she'd taken to her head, everything had looked normal on all the tests. It was the small puncture wounds across her arm from the nail board, her sliced-open hands from hanging on to the edge of the truck and the split on her forehead requiring stitches that had actually kept her away longest.

"Desparre has truly become a home to me," she continued, wanting to get it all out before she became over-emotional. "It's going to be hard to leave."

"You're leaving?" Nate Dreymond asked, surprise and disappointment in his tone.

He wasn't officially back on duty yet and wouldn't be for a few weeks, at least. But ever since he'd been released from the hospital, he'd come in each day to see his colleagues.

Talise, too, had woken from her coma. She was still in the hospital, but doctors expected her to make a full recovery.

The town was moving forward. With Todd Margrove behind bars and expected never to be free again, it was going to help everyone heal. Including her.

"It's time," she told them, even though she'd never expected to be leaving the place that had given her so much after Juan died. It had given her a reason to live again, a purpose to help her move on. And it had led her to Jax.

She glanced behind her, where Jax and Patches stood in the doorway. Patches was fidgeting, more full of puppy energy than Keara was used to, her tail thumping whenever Keara glanced her way. Jax was more subdued, his arm still in a sling, the sympathy in his gaze lending her strength.

He knew this wasn't easy for her. But she'd come back to Desparre someday, to see the people and the place that had changed her life.

"Where are you going?" The way Tate's gaze shifted briefly to Jax when he asked it, he probably already knew.

"I'm moving to Anchorage. I'm going to be a detective again."

She'd officially had her interview over the phone two days ago, gotten the call that they wanted her yesterday. It probably hadn't hurt that a longtime agent of the FBI had contacted them and said they'd be crazy not to hire her.

The officers glanced at each other again, and she could feel the mix of emotions in the room: still some confusion and sadness, but they were happy for her, too.

Technically, being a detective was a step down. And moving across the state, to a place where she barely knew anyone, was definitely a sacrifice.

It was also fast. Fast enough that it scared her a little. If she was being honest with herself, it scared her a lot.

She'd known Juan for more than a year before they started dating, had been with him for nearly three years before they got married. But she'd only spent a year as his wife before losing him.

She didn't want to waste any time with Jax, didn't want to look back and have regrets. Not everyone got a second chance like this and she wasn't going to let it go because she was afraid.

She hadn't wanted to fall for him. Hell, she hadn't wanted to fall for anyone, especially not someone who was remotely in harm's way. And despite Jax's official title, he was too good at psychoanalysis to stay completely removed from the investigative side of things. He would never be one hundred percent safe.

Then again, no one was.

"Congratulations," Charlie said, his voice booming over the silence that had fallen.

Then all of her officers were chiming in, offering her congratulatory handshakes and hugs.

Twenty minutes later she walked to the door, giving the room one last, long look. She wasn't officially leaving for a few weeks. She was going to help find her replacement, so she wouldn't leave the town she loved in a lurch. But today felt like goodbye.

As she reached him, Jax took her hand and she smiled at him. Today also felt like a new beginning.

Woof! Patches said and Keara laughed, bending down to pet her. Then she stood and took Jax's hand again.

"Are you sure this is what you want?" Jax asked as they stepped outside into the brilliant sunshine. "You know I'm willing to do any amount of jumper flights. Patches and I can try to be here every weekend if you want to stay."

He gestured at the police station where she'd spent so many of her waking hours in the past six years. "I know these people have become like family to you."

Keara squeezed his hand tighter. "I've loved being a chief. And you're right, I'm going to really miss everyone in Desparre. But being a detective is in my blood."

She let out a cleansing breath. "After Juan's murder went cold, I didn't want to do it anymore. Every part of being a detective was just a reminder that he didn't have any justice. But I'm ready now."

She stared up at him, knowing he could probably read her nervousness in her smile. "I want to do it near you. If you don't think it's too soon."

"Too soon?" He laughed. "I was ready to profess my love a week ago."

She felt herself jerk slightly, at the surprise of his words, at the fear they evoked inside her. But she pushed the fear down. There were no guarantees in life, but Jax had faced down a murderer for her. They'd both come out of it alive. And for as long as they both had left, she wanted to be with him.

A grin burst free, the fear suddenly overrun by an absolute certainty that she was doing the right thing. "I love you, too, Jax."

Woof!

Keara laughed, the sound louder and more gleeful than expected, as she bent to scratch Patches's ears. "I love you, too, Patches."

As she stood again, still holding tight to Jax's hand, he tugged her toward the park. Work was already well underway to return it to its previous state.

Keara took a deep breath of the crisp, clean Alaskan air and glanced around at Desparre's downtown. People were walking around, smiling and laughing, unafraid.

Then she turned back to Jax, the last of her fear fading into the background. She was ready to live that way, too.

She was ready to forge a new future, with him and Patches.

* * * * *

K-9 HIDEOUT

I love writing strong heroines.
This book is dedicated to a few of the strong women
in my life: my mom, my aunt Andy, my sisters
Kathryn and Caroline, and my sister-in-law, Lamia.

Acknowledgments

Huge thanks to the team at Harlequin,
who has helped me bring fifteen books to readers!
This book is better for the beta read by
Caroline Heiter and the online #BatSignal
writing sessions with Tyler Anne Snell, Regan Black,
Janie Crouch, Louise Dawn and Nichole Severn.

Chapter 1

Desparre, Alaska, was so far off the grid, it wasn't even listed on most maps. But after two years of running and hiding, Desparre made Sabrina Jones feel safe again.

She didn't know quite when it had happened, but slowly, the ever-present anxiety in her chest had eased. The need to relentlessly scan her surroundings every morning when she woke, every time she left the house, had faded, too. She didn't remember exactly when the nightmares had stopped, but it had been over a month since she'd jerked upright in the middle of the night, sweating and certain someone was about to kill her like they'd killed Dylan.

Sabrina walked to the back of the tiny cabin she'd rented six months ago, one more hiding place in a series of endless, out-of-the-way spots. Except this one felt different.

Opening the sliding-glass door, she stepped outside onto the raised deck and immediately shivered. Even in July, Desparre rarely reached above seventy degrees. In the mornings, it was closer to fifty. But it didn't matter. Not when she could stand here and listen to the birds chirping in the distance and breathe in the crisp, fresh air so different from the exhaust-filled city air she'd inhaled most of her life.

The thick woods behind her cabin seemed to stretch forever, and the isolation had given her the kind of peace none of the other small towns she'd found over the years could match. No one lived within a mile of her in any direction. The unpaved driveway leading up to the cabin was long, the cabin itself well hidden in the woods unless you knew it was there. It was several miles from downtown, and she heard cars passing by periodically, but she rarely saw them.

Here, finally, it felt like she was really alone, no possibility of anyone watching her from a distance, plotting and planning.

After a year and a half of living in run-down motels and fearing each morning as much as she feared putting her head on her pillow at night, she'd desperately needed a change. She hadn't expected to end up here. She'd driven north for days, finally stopping because heavy snowfall had made traveling farther impossible. And for the past six months, she'd stayed. There was something magical about Desparre.

It was far from the kind of place anyone who'd known her as a sun-loving city girl would have expected her to end up. Far from anywhere she would have expected to ever call home.

But damn, did she love it. If she had to spend the

rest of her life in solitude, this was where she wanted to do it.

Tipping her head back, she closed her eyes and let the crisp, cool Alaskan air refresh her. With a smile, she pulled out her phone to check the time. Although she had nowhere to be, she wanted to run into town early, then get back to do some work.

As soon as she saw the date on her phone display, her smile dropped under the force of her shock. Today marked exactly two years since she'd left New York City. Two years since she'd left behind everything and everyone she knew. Two years of missed birthdays and holidays. Two years of not being able to talk to her mother or her brother, not being able to see her friends.

A familiar ache welled up, one that only Alaska had been able to keep somewhat at bay.

When she'd said goodbye to New York, she'd expected—hoped—to be home long before now. The police couldn't guarantee they could protect her, but they were hunting for her stalker. She'd believed it was only a matter of time. But with her in hiding, new leads had probably dried up fast.

An image of her mom and her brother back in New York City looking at the calendar together popped into her mind. Her mom would be frowning, a tightness to her jaw that Sabrina had seen in her childhood. Her brother would try to comfort her, try to hide his own anxiety. But they would both be wondering where Sabrina was, wondering if she was okay. Wondering if she was still alive.

She tried to suppress the instant mix of anger and sadness. She'd explained to her family what the PI she'd hired had told her: disappearing was the only way to ensure her safety—and theirs. She wouldn't be able to contact them, and she couldn't tell them where she was going.

They'd fought her on it, but it hadn't mattered. She wasn't going to let anyone else die because of her.

Tucking her phone back into the pocket of her pajama pants, Sabrina stared into the woods, hoping to regain the peace she'd felt only moments ago. But tears pricked her eyes, and today even the woods couldn't ease the tension between her shoulders.

Six months was longer than she'd stayed in one location since she'd gone into hiding. Three months ago, she'd actually started venturing out for more than just essentials. This tiny little town had given her back something she hadn't felt in a long time. Something she hadn't felt since that very first contact from her stalker.

Despite all the solitude, she felt less alone than she had in almost two years.

She'd actually made friends here. Sure, they didn't know her real last name, and in her normal life, she would have called this level of familiarity simple acquaintances. But with two years of loneliness, two years of running whenever she saw a shadow out of place, it felt like real progress. It almost felt like a real life again.

Guilt surged at the very idea that she could just move on with her life, in any small way. Now, the three months of memories she'd built with Dylan felt so distant, so short. She'd been naive to invite him into her life with a stalker following her, leaving her his twisted version of love notes. It wasn't that she hadn't been taking the threat seriously; it was just that she'd thought the threat was only against her.

But on a brilliantly bright Saturday afternoon when

she'd gone to meet Dylan's family for the first time at their lake house, Dylan had been late. She'd been annoyed until police had shown up to tell his family why.

He had died simply because he'd dated her. It was something she'd carried with her ever since.

Before Dylan was killed, police had been taking the letters seriously, but compared to the other crimes they were investigating, it was low priority. When Dylan had been shot inside his own home and then the letter arrived, telling her not to be sad because Dylan had been standing in the way of her true happiness, the police response had been much more intense.

A month later, though, they'd been at her door, their discouraged, too-serious expressions telling her everything she needed to know. With fingerprints and some DNA left behind at the scene of the crime, they were sure they'd get Dylan's killer eventually. But he wasn't in the system, so they couldn't match the forensic evidence to a name. In the meantime, he'd continued to contact her, somehow slipping past the cameras police had installed, and once, slipping a note into her purse on her way home from work.

Dylan's murder showed that her stalker was escalating, police had told her. She was in real danger, quite possibly his next target. They were committed to keeping her safe, committed to stopping the person who'd killed the man she had only just begun to call her boyfriend.

But they couldn't provide twenty-four-hour protection. And she hadn't been willing to risk anyone else she loved.

Sighing, Sabrina stepped back inside, all the healing powers of the Alaskan wilderness no longer working. The PI who'd helped her create a fake name and then disappear had set up a system, a place for her to check safely for updates. The investigator would post a specific message on her website if the stalker was ever caught.

In two years, there had been no updates. But no one else had been hurt because of her, either. If she had to spend the rest of her life running, at least she'd finally found somewhere she could imagine having even a fraction of the life she'd left behind.

If the years in between had taught her anything, it was that living like this could break your will, break your heart if you let it. Her stalker had taken the life she'd built, but he wasn't going to steal all of her happiness.

"Buck up, Sabrina," she told herself, then squared her shoulders to face the day. By the time she'd gotten dressed and was headed for the door, ready to run into town for some groceries, she felt almost normal. She was even smiling at the thought of trading small talk with the owner, Talise, who'd lived in Alaska all of her seventy years and always had good stories.

Then she opened the door, and the whole world spun in front of her. All the oxygen seemed to disappear as she gripped the doorframe to keep herself upright.

There was a single white card on her doorstep. On it, the same angled, spidery font she'd come to dread back in New York. The same bright red ink that reminded her of blood even more since Dylan's death.

The message was simple, exactly what she would have expected if she hadn't started to believe she'd finally outrun her stalker.

I've missed you.

Chapter 2

Her first instinct was to run. As far as she could, as fast as she could. Just like she'd done countless times over the past two years.

Instead, she put on latex gloves and picked up the card carefully by the corner, even though she knew it was wiped clean. Her stalker had left prints and a small amount of DNA at the scene of Dylan's murder but never on her notes. She sealed it in a plastic bag and then ran to her truck, almost tripping as she glanced around for any sign of him—a man she'd never seen but who'd somehow tracked her almost four thousand miles.

Then she was driving, white-knuckled, eyes danger-ously focused on her rearview mirror, toward down-town Desparre. The roads were unpaved, and the rough winters didn't do them any favors. The rusted old truck she'd gotten at a steal when she'd crossed into Alaska

six months ago jolted her with every uneven patch of
road. Her head started to throb from her clenched jaw,
shooting pain up the side of her head with each bump.
But she couldn't seem to unclench it.

No one was behind her.

Of course, she'd been assuming that for six months.
And yet, somehow, her stalker had found her.

Tears of frustration welled up, and she blinked away
the moisture, refusing to give him more power over her
than he already had. If he could find her here—a place
that felt like the end of the earth—was anywhere truly
safe? Was running the wrong move?

It was time to find out.

As she steered her truck down the incline onto Main
Street, right into the center of what passed as a downtown in Desparre, she ignored the cheerful laughter
coming from the little park. A few months ago, a bomb
had gone off in that park, shattering her illusion that
Desparre was one of the most peaceful places she'd
ever lived.

But people here were resilient, and they'd rebuilt the
gazebo that had been destroyed. The scorched earth
was now covered with green grass and blue irises, and
the metal butterfly benches she'd admired when she'd
first driven into town but had been blown to bits in the
blast had been replaced with new ones. Residents who
thrived through dangerously cold winters, who knew
how to avoid the avalanches that could slide off the side
of the mountain, had flocked back to the park as if the
bombing had never happened.

She needed some of that Desparre resilience right
now.

Parking the truck, Sabrina took a deep breath and

glanced around the small downtown, looking for anyone who seemed unusually fixated on her.

The downtown was tiny, with a post office, clothing store, bar, drugstore, grocery store and church lining the unpaved street. To someone who'd grown up in the big city, it looked like one of those fake towns where tourists came to see reenactments of miners showing off their pans of gold.

None of the people walking around, soaking in the sun as if it were ninety degrees instead of fifty-five, showed any interest in her. From three months of coming into town, she recognized many of them as long-time residents.

That was the thing about Desparre. It wasn't New York City. It was much bigger in terms of land size, but population density was minuscule in comparison. Yes, people came here to hide, many of them running from their own tragedies or threats. Some even running from the law. But most of them had lived here a long time. Most of them knew each other. They might wholeheartedly embrace a *Live and let live* attitude where they allowed everyone to keep their secrets—something she'd greatly appreciated when she arrived—but they still recognized the outsiders.

Maybe, just maybe, they could do what the New York City cops had been unable to accomplish. Identify her stalker and end her nightmare for good.

Glancing around one last time, Sabrina strode up to the other building located downtown, the police station.

Nerves churned in her stomach as she pulled open the door, wondering if she was being watched even now. Wondering if involving the police again would make her stalker more violent.

The front of the station was a small area mostly taken up by a desk where a young officer sat. His reddish-blond hair looked vaguely familiar, and she remembered he was the officer who'd been hurt in the bomb blast. Maybe he was still healing and had pulled desk duty in the meantime.

He looked up when she walked in, his expression a mix of boredom and friendliness. "Can I help you?"

"Y-yes," she stuttered, trying not to lose her nerve. "I-I'm being stalked." She held up the bagged note as he stood, his brow furrowed.

Then the door opened behind her, and a white-and-black dog bounded toward her.

"Sitka, sit."

The commanding voice, underlain with humor, made Sabrina's gaze jump from the dog up to the man coming in behind her. Nerves immediately followed.

Officer Tate Emory. She'd seen him around town over the past six months and been immediately drawn to him. She'd even talked to him a few times. Back in her old life, the six-foot-tall man in the police uniform with the angular cheekbones and the dark, serious eyes would have had her flirting hard. Here, she'd stammered her way through their brief conversations, her gaze mostly on the floor, hoping she'd be unmemorable.

That was what her stalker had reduced her to. Hoping no one noticed her. Hoping she could slip through life silently, until what? He finally caught up to her and killed her and no one even knew to look for her body?

Shaking off the morose thought, Sabrina glanced at the dog she'd never seen before, who had followed instructions to sit—right at her feet.

Tate shook his head at the dog. "She's still a puppy.

She finished her K-9 training, but sometimes she needs to be reminded about her manners."

At the words, Sitka glanced back at her owner and wagged her tail.

Tate's smile at his dog faded as his gaze locked on the paper Sabrina was still holding up. Then, his attention was entirely focused on her. "Is someone harassing you?"

She nodded, then blurted, "Stalking. For two years." She almost succeeded in keeping her voice steady as she added, "He's found me again."

Tate walked past her, using a key card to open the door marked *Police Only.*

"I've got this, Nate," he told the other officer.

Then he looked at her again, his gaze projecting confidence. "Come on back with me, Sabrina. Let's talk through what's going on, okay? We take care of each other here. We'll take care of you, too."

As she followed him, Sitka sticking close to her side, something fluttered in her chest, something that felt suspiciously like hope.

This was *not* how he'd hoped to strike up a conversation with Sabrina Jones.

Tate Emory had seen her around town for the past half year, usually on the outskirts of Desparre. But to his frustration, it was always when he was in uniform, on the job. He'd struck up a few short-lived conversations with her, but he kept hoping to run into her when he was off duty. He'd wanted to get to know her a little more, maybe even ask her out.

Right now, though, seeing the fear in her green eyes,

he just wanted to help. Holding open the door to the back of the station, he ushered her through.

His newly certified K-9 police dog, Sitka, followed. She was seventy-five pounds of Alaskan Malamute, a funny mix of puppy energy and police-dog intensity. He'd been petitioning the department—and his previous chief—for a K-9 practically since the day he'd joined the force five and a half years ago. The last thing Chief Hernandez had done before leaving Desparre was grant approval.

Now, after two months of training, his shelter-dog adoptee was a full-fledged police dog. He smiled down at her as she stayed in Sabrina's footsteps like the woman's protection detail.

"This way," he told Sabrina, leading her through the mostly empty bullpen toward the glass-encased office at the back where the chief worked.

When he knocked on the door, the new police chief, Brice Griffith, called out, "Come on in."

Chief Griffith was seven years older than Tate's thirty-one, with fourteen years of experience in police work back in Vancouver. He'd made the jump to Alaska with his young daughter in tow when the town's old chief had decided to follow her new boyfriend to Anchorage and return to detective work.

So far, Chief Griffith seemed like a fair boss. He was personable enough, though like most of the people in this town, he'd definitely come to Desparre to outrun something.

Not that Tate could throw stones. If the chief knew Tate's true history, he'd probably be fired on the spot.

"What's up?" Chief Griffith asked, standing as Sabrina followed Tate into the room.

"This is Sabrina Jones," Tate said, noting the surprise on her face that he remembered her full name. "She's being targeted by a stalker."

The chief frowned. "Take a seat," he told Sabrina, then added to Tate, "Close the door."

Tate did as he was told, then sat in the chair next to Sabrina. Sitka settled in the space between them, her ears perked as she glanced from Sabrina to Tate.

"This was left on my doorstep today," Sabrina said, handing the note to the chief.

The chief read it, then stared at Sabrina. "This isn't the first time you've been contacted by this person, I take it?"

"No. He followed me from New York." She took a shaky, visible breath. "I've been running for two years. I thought I'd lost him here."

Two years? Tate stared at her, wondering how he hadn't realized sooner she was trying to escape a threat.

He should have. Every time he'd spoken to her, she'd directed most of her responses to her feet. He'd thought she was shy, maybe even nervous because the attraction he felt for her was reciprocated. But the truth was that she'd been afraid of anyone taking too great an interest in her.

Had he gotten so comfortable here that he'd forgotten what it had been like in the beginning? Gotten to accept this life so much that he'd completely let his old one go?

The idea made an old ache start up in his chest.

Even though his previous chief had known his history, had helped him come on board with his faked background and fake last name, he'd spent a long time thinking he'd made a mistake. That staying in police

work would be a way for the people who'd tried to kill
him once to find him again.

He should have recognized that same fear in Sabrina,
should have found a way to help her sooner. Some police officer he was.

Chief Griffith's eyes narrowed at him like he could
see Tate's internal struggle, like he suspected Tate
wasn't quite who he said he was. Then his attention
was fully on Sabrina. "Tell us about this stalker."

She shifted forward in her seat, her hands gripping
the arms of her chair as her wavy, blond hair fell over
her shoulder, obscuring part of her face. "It started two
and a half years ago. I began getting notes on my doorstep." She nodded in the direction of the note the chief
had placed on his desk. "They all looked like that, with
the red text and the creepy messages. The first one just
said *I've been watching you.* They were always short,
usually things like *One day, we'll be together* or *You
must know how much I love you.*"

She shuddered a little, glancing at Tate and then back
at the chief. "The first one spooked me, and my friends
convinced me to call the police. Initially, they took my
report but didn't seem that interested. But when this
guy kept writing, they said they could officially call it
a stalking case. Still, it didn't feel like much was happening until—"

Her head tilted toward her lap, her hair falling over
her face even more until Tate couldn't see her expression at all. "I started dating someone."

Dread sank to his gut, suspecting where this was
going before she continued. "Three months later, he
was shot in his home. Then my stalker left me a note
saying *Don't be sad. He was just in our way.*"

"That's when you ran," the chief said, sympathy in his voice and an expression on his face that told Tate he was familiar with that kind of pain.

The expression was gone too fast for Tate to figure out what it meant. Next to him, Sabrina swiped at her face quickly, like she hoped no one would notice.

Her head lifted again, and she squared her shoulders, nodding. "Yes. I hired a PI to help me disappear. I spent a year and a half running from one tiny town to the next, trying to stay below the radar. I never got another note, but sometimes I'd just start feeling…jumpy. So, I'd go somewhere else, get a different car, leave anything unimportant behind. Then I arrived here."

A smile trembled on her lips. "I've been in Desparre for six months. I've felt more normal than I had in a long time. I thought… I really thought I'd finally escaped. Then I got this letter. I considered running, but…" Her knuckles whitened around the edges of the chair, her jaw clenching. She turned toward Tate, pleading and hope in her gaze. "I want this to end."

The new chief had been here for a few months. Most of that time, Tate had been doing K-9 training with Sitka. But he'd still felt constantly on edge, worrying Chief Griffith would notice something off in his doctored personnel file and realize Tate wasn't who he said he was. He'd feared that the life he'd built for himself here could be destroyed at any moment. He'd worried about a threat to his life, too, but he was a trained police officer. He was armed and relatively dangerous if provoked.

What must it feel like to be a civilian with no training? What must it feel like to be completely alone, being chased by a threat that hadn't even been fully identified?

Not waiting for the chief's assessment, Tate said, "Desparre isn't New York. We have resources we can put on this."

He kept his gaze fully on Sabrina, wanting her to see in his expression how committed he was to helping her, but from the corner of his eye he could see the chief's raised eyebrows. Still, Chief Griffith didn't contradict him.

The fear in Sabrina's eyes started to shift, turning into tentative hope.

"We're going to find this guy," Tate promised. "It's time to stop running and let us make a stand for you. We're going to get you your life back."

Chapter 3

Sabrina Jones had chosen a good place to hide.

Desparre was a big town in terms of geography. It stretched from wooded patches with houses hidden among the trees through small commercial areas and across half a mountain. Besides the tiny downtown, they had other, more out-of-the-way spots to get supplies if you really wanted to stay unseen.

Tate had grown up on the other side of Alaska, in a coastal town that was much bigger and busier than Desparre but still boasted that wide-open-spaces Alaskan charm. But he'd lived in Boston for so many years that when he'd moved to Desparre, the expansive spaces without people had felt as foreign as the big city had initially seemed.

Still, he'd never hidden away in the woods or up in the mountains, like so many people did who came here running from something. He'd been confident in the backstory that had been created for him, confident that Alaska was too far for anyone to even think about searching for him. But the threat against him was one of revenge, not an obsessed wannabe-lover.

The fact that Sabrina's stalker hadn't given up after two years, hadn't found someone else to fixate on, was worrisome. His department back in Boston had handled a couple of stalker cases. They'd tried but been unable to keep either of those stalkers locked up, and he'd felt frustrated for the targets who'd continued to live in fear.

Tate frowned as he opened the back of his modified police SUV for Sitka to jump in. The department didn't have the money for a true K-9 vehicle; they'd barely been able to cover his and Sitka's K-9 training.

But all he'd really needed was the official approval. He'd been happy to shell out the money for Sitka's special stab-and bulletproof vest, happy to pay out of pocket for her vet bills and food. She was his partner, but she was also his pet. Every night after their shift was over, she came home with him. If all went as planned, eight years from now, she'd retire and just be his dog.

His puppy's tail wagged as she leaped into the vehicle. She knew it meant they were going to work.

He glanced back at her as he climbed into the driver's seat. "How about we practice your tracking today?"

Her tail thumped harder, and she gave an enthusiastic *woof!*

Grinning, Tate put his SUV in gear. But his smile faded fast as he thought about the message Sabrina had found. Being such a small town, they used the state's forensic lab for big, complicated jobs, but all of the local officers knew how to do basic work, like dusting for fingerprints. The note left on Sabrina's doorstep had none.

Maybe her stalker had left something else behind, like his scent.

Heading out of downtown, Tate turned onto one of the dirt roads that passed as a highway around here. Sabrina's address wasn't in the most remote part of Desparre, but she'd definitely picked a spot where people weren't likely to know she lived there unless she told them. Or unless someone spotted her elsewhere and followed her home.

Once they did that, the location was much less appealing. It was too far for neighbors to hear a cry for help, too secluded for anyone else to see a threat.

Gripping the wheel tighter, Tate wondered if they were doing enough. Based on what Sabrina had said about the investigation back home, there wasn't much to go on there, especially since NYPD had determined it was someone on the very outskirts of her life. Still, she'd been cagey with the details, flat out refusing to give them her boyfriend's name or the names of the investigating detectives back in New York. She'd asked them not to contact the police department there, insisting that her family's safety would be compromised if they learned where she was.

She'd looked so panicked that they'd finally agreed. The fact was that if the NYPD had gone two and a half years without being able to identify her stalker, even after he became a murderer, the leads in New York were slim. For now, it made more sense to concentrate on new arrivals to Desparre, people who might have tracked Sabrina here. After Sabrina had left the station looking a lot more confident and hopeful than when she'd walked in, he and the chief had finished mapping out a plan to keep her safe. They'd already given her an emergency-alert button that connected directly to the station. They had scheduled police drive-bys of her house multiple times a day, with scattered times to prevent her stalker from seeing a pattern. Sabrina was supposed to call them if she had the slightest concern, wanted a police escort somewhere or just wanted someone to do a walk-through of her home.

Hopefully, they'd spot the guy before he could get close again. But Tate and the chief had agreed they needed to get more proactive rather than just hoping her stalker made a mistake.

So today, he and Sitka would get a chance to test out their training.

As he pulled into Sabrina's long dirt driveway, Tate glanced around. There wasn't much to see besides trees. Someone passing by on the street wouldn't spot the cabin without binoculars or very keen eyesight. To drop the note on the doorstep, her stalker had probably left his vehicle on the road and crept through the trees. Otherwise, Sabrina could have seen him coming.

When Tate put the SUV in Park, the curtain moved on the front window, and Sabrina's face appeared in the crack. He hopped out of his vehicle and waved at her, then let Sitka out, too.

Sabrina stepped outside, scanning the woods before her gaze settled on him.

"Sitka and I are going to try a little tracking work," he told her.

She looked surprised, probably having expected he was doing a check-in. Her gaze went to Sitka, whose tail wagged at the attention.

"She's a tracker dog?"

"Actually, she's a dual-purpose dog." He rubbed her

head, the thick coat perfect for Alaska, even if Malamutes weren't usually used as police dogs. "She specializes in both patrol and tracking."

"Patrol?" Sabrina smiled, humor in her eyes that had been missing every other time they'd spoken. "Does she write speeding tickets with those big paws?"

Tate smiled back at her, wishing he'd realized something was wrong one of the dozens of times he'd chatted her up around town and reached out to her sooner. "Close. She's my partner. So, if I need to chase someone down, she can help me. Or she can clear a building or provide security. She's trained to bark and detain, too. That's pretty much exactly what it sounds like. She finds someone and keeps them from running so I can come in and cuff them."

"Can I pet her, or is that off-limits when she's on duty?"

"Go ahead." Although he didn't let civilians pet Sitka while she was actively tracking or doing a specific patrol task, she was great with people. Letting the people in Desparre pet her also made them comfortable having her on the force, something which was brand-new for the town.

She was off leash now because they weren't downtown, but at the chief's request, Tate had been using a leash in town while people got used to her. He hoped she'd bring good press and pave the way for expanding their K-9 team in the future.

Sabrina smiled at Sitka as she rubbed the dog's ears.

Sitka's head tilted up like she was enjoying the attention, and her tail thumped.

When he'd gone to the shelter, he'd been hoping to find a young German Shepherd or Malinois, both typical breeds for police work. But as soon as the little Alaskan Malamute had seen him, she'd dropped her chest to the ground, backside still in the air, tail wagging, and barked. She'd wanted to play. And he'd been totally charmed.

The shelter hadn't known anything about her background, other than that she was obviously a Malamute and not afraid of people. She'd been found alongside a highway, way too thin but anxious to please.

Although he'd been approved to become a K-9 officer back in Boston before the attempt on his life, he'd never actually gotten a dog or gone through training. He'd done research on traits that made good police dogs, but ultimately he'd known that whether or not Sitka would make a good partner would only be determined once they started training.

Still, his mind had been made up the moment she'd demanded his attention. He had to take her home.

After some initial hurdles with her energy level and distractibility, she'd received high scores in all of her certifications. But now was the real test.

She'd only been patrolling with him for a few weeks, not enough time in a place as low in crime as Desparre to really test out her skills. And so far, there'd been no reason for her to do any tracking in real conditions.

Tate could happily stand around half the day, chatting with Sabrina while she pet Sitka, but he was on duty. "You can watch from inside if you want. We're just going to see if Sitka picks anything up here."

The smile that had stayed on her face the whole time she pet Sitka faded, replaced by wariness at the reminder of her stalker. "Okay. Thank you."

Tate watched her walk inside, heard the loud *click*

of the dead bolt turning and then said to Sitka, "Let's see where this guy came from."

Most likely, they wouldn't get much. But knowing which side of the street the stalker had parked on might indicate whether he'd come from the direction of town or somewhere more secluded. Tate was betting on the latter, betting that her stalker had chosen an out-of-the-way cabin, too.

Directing Sitka onto Sabrina's porch, he told his dog, "Scent, Sitka!"

She sniffed the air briefly, then her nose went to the ground, and she barked at Sabrina's door.

"Another one. Scent again," he told her, knowing she'd just alerted on Sabrina, since the woman had been on the porch most recently. Hopefully, the stalker's scent was still here, too.

If it was, Sitka should be able to find and follow it. Compared to the paltry five million scent receptors in the noses of humans, dogs had two hundred and twenty-five million.

Sitka's nose went back in the air, then down to the ground, sniffing around for a minute. Then she walked off the porch, nose still down. She headed straight into the woods off the side of Sabrina's porch like he'd expected. But instead of bounding toward the street, she ran around the side of the house.

Had the stalker crept around Sabrina's home, maybe peered in her windows? The idea made his fists clench, but it shouldn't have surprised him.

Instead of circling the cabin, Sitka raced into the woods, away from Sabrina's house.

Frowning, Tate ran after Sitka. He glanced back

once, saw the big sliding-glass door at the back of the cabin, Sabrina's face peering out at them.

Then he was hurrying after Sitka again. She was definitely tracking a scent. Her nose came up a few times, as she slowed and sniffed the air, before dropping down again.

As they moved away, the woods got more dense. It wasn't long before he glanced back, and even knowing where the cabin was, he couldn't see it.

He couldn't imagine a stalker finding a random road somewhere else alongside these woods and then trekking through the trees for miles to leave a note on Sabrina's doorstep. But Sitka seemed certain, her tail wagging as she ran, because K-9s were trained to think of their police tasks like games. She kept a pace that was hard to match.

Then a noise up ahead put Tate on instant alert. A rustling, like someone was there. Had the stalker stuck around this long?

His hand dropped to the grip of his gun in his duty belt even as he continued to scan the woods ahead of Sitka.

She'd slowed, the fur on her back rising. The fact that she hadn't shifted slightly and raced toward the noise meant it wasn't the same person who'd left the scent she was tracking.

Tate swore as a shape materialized from behind the tree. A black, furry shape, a solid twenty pounds lighter than Sitka, followed by another.

His pulse spiked, and he tried to keep the panic out of his voice as he called, "Sitka, come! Back up, girl."

She backed toward him, her movements slow and

controlled, like she was backing away from a suspect so he could take over.

Only this time, she was backing away from a pair of baby bears. The question was, where was the mom?

Then there was more rustling, and Tate saw her. A cinnamon-colored black bear lumbering after her cubs. Her head swiveled in his direction, then Sitka's, as her babies continued to run perpendicular to his dog.

"Sitka, slow, girl," Tate said softly, hoping the bear wouldn't see either of them as a threat. The bear might have weighed about the same as he did and was probably only a foot shorter if she stood, but he was no match for her strength-to-weight ratio. And his pistol was no match for a furious mom protecting her cubs.

Sitka's movements became even slower, but she kept backing toward him, showing no fear even as the bear got up on her hind legs, still watching them.

Then the bear dropped back down, and Tate held his breath, wishing he'd brought the bear horn he kept in the back of his vehicle. He reached for his pepper spray with one hand and got ready to shout and try to seem as large as possible if she rushed them.

He let the breath out slowly as she followed her cubs instead, but his pulse didn't return to normal until she was out of sight and Sitka had backed up against him.

"Good girl," he whispered, stroking her head as her tail wagged.

She looked up at him, then back in the direction she'd been tracking, ready to keep working.

But Tate didn't want to risk running into the bear again. They usually weren't dangerous if you were smart, but he didn't want to startle a mom with cubs. He had no idea how far these woods went before they led to a road. "We'll look at some maps instead," he told Sitka.

Her talents were unproven in the real world, and Tate knew his boss would question whether the stalker had actually trekked so far through the woods, not giving himself easy access to a getaway vehicle if Sabrina or someone else had spotted him. But Tate trusted Sitka.

He glanced around, seeing nothing but woods in all directions. If Sabrina's stalker was confident enough to sneak up on her house through a mile or more of woods, he was more skilled than a typical city boy. Or maybe he hadn't just recently found Sabrina. Maybe he'd been right behind her all along and only today decided to make himself known.

But if he'd been in Alaska for six months like Sabrina, what had changed to make him announce himself? And what did that mean for Sabrina's safety?

Chapter 4

"He came through the woods."

Sabrina stared at Tate, a sick feeling in her stomach. "Through the woods?" Had her stalker seen her in the mornings when she stood outside on her deck, enjoying nature, sometimes in her pajamas? How close had he gotten without her ever suspecting anyone was there?

She resisted the urge to reach up and touch the alert button that was hanging on a thin chain around her neck. There was comfort in knowing Tate and the rest of the Desparre PD were on the other side of it.

"Yeah, I know it's strange," Tate said, misinterpreting her surprise. "I'm not sure where he came from, because we ran into a bear."

"A *bear*?" She glanced from him to Sitka, relieved that they both looked fine, then realized she'd basically been parroting his words since he'd returned to the house after trying to track her stalker.

Flushing, she stepped back a little and did something she hadn't done in two years. "You want to come in?"

The words felt foreign on her lips, and she realized just how much had been stolen from her. Even the little things, like feeling comfortable enough to trust anyone in her home, had become a thing of her past.

Not anymore. She stared at Tate, watching a debate play on his face. He was on duty. But he wanted to come inside.

She hadn't been imagining that the attraction she'd felt in the brief moments they'd spoken over the past six months was reciprocated. A zing of excitement darted through her, lodging in her chest and quickening her breathing.

"Can you tell me more about the tracking?" she asked, hoping it would make his decision easier if it was connected to his work.

"Sure." He wiped his boots on the mat, and Sabrina held in a smile.

She wouldn't have cared if he'd brought in all the mud in the forest. Despite the nerves suddenly dancing in her stomach, this was the most normal she'd felt in a long time.

"Come on inside, Sitka," she told his dog, and the Alaskan Malamute glanced at her owner.

When Tate nodded, Sitka bounded inside, danced a circle in the tiny entryway and then sat.

Laughing, Sabrina asked, "How come I've never met Sitka before?"

Tate stepped inside, closing the door behind him and throwing the dead bolt for her.

The loud sound made her jerk, her nerves doubling at having a man she'd admired from afar for six months crowding her entryway. He was tall and lean, but whether it was the six inches of height he had on her, the fact that there was obvious power in his frame despite his lack of bulky muscle or just his nearness, the space suddenly felt much smaller.

"I only got Sitka a few months ago," Tate answered, either not noticing or pretending not to see her discomfort. "The two of us have mostly been down in Fairbanks for the past two months getting our training."

No wonder she'd seen him so infrequently lately, even though she'd gone to town more often, hoping to run into him.

"What was that like?" she asked, tilting her head back so she could see his face better.

"A lot of work." He grinned, and the expression softened the sharp lines of his face, made him seem even more approachable.

It eased her nerves but only increased her awareness of how little space was between them.

For six months, every time she'd seen this man, she'd wished she dared risk asking him out. Now he was in her home.

Taking a step back, she gestured for him to follow, then headed into her combined kitchen and living area. The big sliding-glass door, nestled between two equally large windows, showcased a gorgeous view into the forest. This had always been her favorite spot in the house. But now, as she peered into the dense woods, she wondered if the solitude that had always made her feel so safe and alone had just been camouflage. She wondered how often someone else had been staring back at her unseen.

"He's not out there now," Tate said.

When she glanced at him, there was sympathy on his face, and anger, too, like he was as upset about the invasion of her privacy as she was. "If he was, Sitka would have found him?"

At the mention of her name, the dog hurried over to stand between her and Tate, tail wagging.

Tate reached out and stroked Sitka's head. "Yes. The guy trekked a long way to get here."

"I wish *he'd* run into the bear," Sabrina muttered, earning a brief laugh from Tate. Then, she awkwardly gestured to the couch facing the view. "Have a seat. Do you want something to drink or—"

"No, I'm fine." Tate settled on one side of the couch, giving her plenty of space. Sitka followed, lying beside the sofa.

Sabrina sat on the opposite end of the couch, twisting slightly to face him. He looked at ease in her home, and she wondered if being a police officer brought that level of calm confidence or it was just his natural personality.

She was the opposite, usually filled with a jittery energy, a need to be active or creative. Sitting still had always been a challenge. As she stared at him, he watched her quietly, and she wondered if he could tell that she wanted to jump right back up and move. She wondered if he could tell just how much nervous excitement filled her at his nearness.

"How does it work, the tracking?" she blurted, partly because she was curious and partly to fill the silence.

"Whenever you move, you leave a scent behind. So, on your porch, Sitka actually scented on you first. She followed the scent to your front door." He laughed, then continued. "Then she found the second scent, presumably the stalker. She sniffs the air to locate a scent and then puts her nose to the ground. Dogs can track scents for long distances, through water, through all kinds of weather conditions. It's pretty amazing, actually."

Sabrina looked at the Alaskan Malamute, who had enough of a gangly puppy look that she couldn't have yet been quite full-grown. "Very impressive."

As if she knew she'd just been complimented, Sitka's tail wagged.

"Did you grow up with dogs? Is that why you wanted to be a K-9 officer?"

"I *didn't* grow up with dogs, which is probably why I wanted to be one," Tate said, leaning back against her couch, shifting to more fully face her.

Suddenly, despite his uniform, despite the reason he was here, it felt more like a first date than an update on the investigation. Not just that, but it felt like a *good* first date, the kind that would ultimately lead to a second date.

"I always wanted a dog. When I saw Sitka in the shelter, she was just so—" he grinned at her, his expression full of affection "—energetic and goofy."

Her tail wagged again, and he added, "She was also smart and eager to please, which helped her in training."

Then Tate's expression got more serious. "What about you? Did you have a dog? Who's waiting for you back home?"

"I didn't have any pets, mostly because I lived in a fifth-floor walk-up in New York City. But I guess it was a good thing, since running with a pet would have been harder and might have been a way to track me. I'm close to my mom and brother, though. They're both back in New York. I haven't dared to contact either one, and I miss them every day. The PI who helped me said it was safer to cut all contact on my end unless there was an emergency."

Tate frowned slightly, sympathy on his face, but instead of turning it into a discussion about her stalker like she'd feared he might, he said, "I haven't seen my family in a while, either. I can imagine how much you must miss yours."

She nodded, trying not to dwell on the memory of the last time she'd seen them both, when they'd fought her so hard on her decision to go into hiding. Now, after all the sacrifices she'd made, her stalker was still right behind her.

Shaking off the frustration, she focused on the fact that she had Tate here. After two years of trying to keep everyone at a certain distance, she deserved at least one normal conversation. One semi-*truthful* conversation. She hadn't told him her real last to protect her family's safety, but this was the closest she'd felt to normal in more than two years. She could actually be herself and not have to watch every word, worrying she might accidentally let something slip about who she really was, why she was here.

And talking to Tate was easy, comfortable. Despite her hyperawareness of him, she'd gladly just sit and chat with him all day.

"Have you always lived in Desparre?"

He looked surprised by the conversation turn. "No. But my mom's family is part Tlingit, and they've been in Alaska forever. My dad's family has a long-running charter business, so they've been here a long time, too. My parents divorced when I was young, and I was an only child, so I was shuttled back and forth a lot. We lived in a bigger town than this, but it was still small enough to run into one parent while I was with the other. They get along okay now, but in those early years, not so much."

"Where in Alaska did you grow up? I got here and pretty much headed straight north until I was snowed in. But I've heard some parts of Alaska actually get a real summer." She grinned, because the locals always seemed silently amused by anyone who wasn't native to Desparre and was bundled up when the locals were wearing shorts.

"I…" Tate frowned, shook his head slightly. "My family is from here originally, but I actually grew up in the Midwest. I moved to Desparre five and a half years ago."

She stared at him, wondering why his words were suddenly so stiff, his gaze averted like he wasn't giving her the full story. But why would he lie about where he'd grown up?

She'd probably just become unpracticed at getting-to-know-you conversations. But if she was truly going to stop running, if the Desparre PD was going to help her make a stand here, then maybe all the things she thought she'd never have again were actually possible. That meant she needed to figure out how to talk to a man like Tate Emory again.

After what had happened to Dylan, she'd vowed never to date again, never to put anyone else in danger. But now, staring at Tate, seeing how dedicated he was to helping her, seeing her interest reflected back in his gaze, everything seemed possible again.

What had he been thinking?

Tate had managed to spend five and a half years

without telling anyone—not even his old partner, Peter—the real details of his past. Half an hour with Sabrina at her house yesterday, and the words had just come out of his mouth, without him even realizing his mistake until she'd asked which Alaskan city he'd lived in as a child.

Hopefully, his awkward attempt at correcting his mistake hadn't been an obvious lie.

Tate had spent most of his morning patrol going over the conversation in his mind, trying to figure out if he'd just blown his own cover. He didn't think so. Despite having been on the run for two years, Sabrina seemed to take his word at face value. It made him feel worse about needing to lie to her.

No wonder he hadn't entered into many deep friendships, let alone any relationships, since he'd come here. It wasn't in his nature to lie to people.

He missed having someone who knew the truth about him. Even though he and Chief Hernandez had rarely talked about his real past, knowing that someone here was aware of his secret had made him feel less alone.

It had also given him a stronger sense of security. Chief Keara Hernandez had let him go through the police academy as if he really was a rookie, then brought him onto the force. She could face legal repercussions if the truth ever came out, but she'd done it as a favor to an old family friend who worked for Witness Protection. That family friend also knew Tate's family. The man had agreed to help him hide outside official channels. That favor had allowed Tate to return to a career he loved, let him return to a state he loved.

Yes, he was more than a thousand miles from his childhood home, from his family. But the beauty he'd taken for granted as a kid made him feel closer to them now, even if he couldn't see them. It made him feel one step closer to who he really was.

Chief Griffith had no idea he wasn't actually Tate Emory, security guard from the Midwest who'd moved to Desparre for a change of pace and a chance to fulfill a lifelong dream of becoming an officer. Tate had no idea what the new chief would do if he found out.

As he parked his SUV outside the police station, ready to spend some time in downtown after a morning patrolling the outskirts, Tate vowed not to be so careless again. He wasn't sure what about Sabrina Jones made him so unguarded, but he needed to be especially vigilant around her. Just because she was being honest about her past didn't mean he could do the same.

As if thinking about her had made her appear, Tate spotted Sabrina walking out of the grocery store. She had one small bag in her hand and was glancing around anxiously.

"Come on, Sitka." He hopped out of the vehicle and put on her leash. "Let's go say hello."

Woof!

His dog's enthusiastic reply caught Sabrina's attention. As soon as she met his gaze, her shoulders relaxed, and she smiled. It was a real smile, not the nervous, hesitant kind she'd given him over the past few months. A smile born of the belief that she knew him, that she could trust him.

It made guilt bubble up, and Tate tried to suppress it. She might not really know him, but she *could* trust him.

He headed toward her, and she met him halfway, immediately bending to pet Sitka. "How has your day been?" She peered up at him from where she'd crouched down. "Did Sitka help you write a lot of speeding tickets today?"

He grinned back at her. "Nah. She was in a good mood. She just handed out warnings."

Woof! Sitka's tail thumped, and she glanced back and forth between them, as if she knew she was the subject of conversation.

"What about you? How are you doing?"

When Sabrina stood again, she was smiling, too, looking far less worried than when he'd spotted her. "I'm just trying to live my life like normal." She shrugged. "Well, as normal as it gets these days." She lowered her voice, glancing around again, even though the closest person was across the street. "I don't suppose you've made any progress at figuring out who's doing this?"

Tate shook his head, expecting disappointment, but she didn't seem surprised. After two years of running, her expectations were probably pretty low. "Just keep being careful. The chief and I talked through strategy yesterday after you left the station. I know you're worried about us contacting New York, but we'd like to dig into your history to see if fresh eyes make anything pop."

She immediately tensed. "My cousin's wife works at the station. You contact them and she'll find out and it will get back to my mom and my brother. Then they'll come here. And after what happened before…"

Tate held up his hands, understanding her fear for her family. "Okay. Most likely, we'll find him by looking at people here. So, if anything seems unusual or anyone gives you a weird feeling, let us know. There's nothing too small for us to check out."

She gave him another smile, but this one was shaky. "Thanks."

"Why don't you drop your groceries in your car and walk with me and Sitka? We were going to the park, to let some more people meet her."

"Okay."

There was happiness in her voice, and as he walked with her to her rusted old truck, he tried not to let it ignite a similar thrill in him. She was a citizen who needed his help. Yes, he'd been considering asking her out for months—something he hadn't done any of since he'd gone into hiding himself—but things had changed. He couldn't be distracted by her, not when he needed to be thinking about her safety.

Still, he couldn't keep his gaze from lingering on the way the sunshine created golden highlights in her hair, the way it emphasized the smoothness of her ivory skin. Couldn't keep his mind from traveling down an imaginary road where she wasn't living in fear and he didn't have to keep his real identity a secret.

She dropped off the groceries, and then they headed toward the park, Sitka tugging slightly on the leash and giving him glances as if to ask *Why am I wearing this?* In that moment, it felt like he was off duty. It felt like he was just enjoying the company of a woman he liked and a dog who'd given him family here.

From across the street, Yura Begay gave him a nod. The gruff former Marine and lifelong Alaskan resident owned a check-cashing place on the outskirts of Desparre. He was known to be rude, but ever since Tate had gotten Sitka, he'd been warming up. Tate hoped it was a sign of how the rest of the town would respond.

It was the middle of the day, and the sun felt fantastic after the brutal winter, but it had been raining half an hour ago, so there were only a handful of people besides Yura downtown. Still, there were a group of kids in the park, parents chatting on the benches nearby. Hopefully it would give Sitka a chance to charm some more people and Sabrina a chance to relax. One thing he could be relatively confident in: if her stalker had tracked her across the country over the past two years, he was pretty unlikely to be chasing her with a wife and kid in tow.

The closer they got to the park, the slower Sabrina's steps became.

"Do you know anyone here?" Maybe he could introduce her to some of them while he was introducing them to Sitka.

She shrugged. "Some. I've been trying to talk to people more, but it feels insincere when all the typical questions you ask someone you've just met are things I have to lie about."

The same guilt filled him, the desire to share his secret with her, to trust someone enough to be truly honest. But it was a selfish wish, one that could put her in danger. So, he kept quiet and just continued walking.

As they reached the park, Sitka whined, tugging on her leash like she wanted to cross the street.

Tate frowned, pulling her back as he glanced around, trying to figure out what had caught her attention. He didn't see anything. Then again, despite two months of intense training, Sitka was still a year-old puppy. And walking with Sabrina probably felt more like off duty to Sitka, as well.

"Come on, Sitka. You'll like talking to the kids."

She glanced at him, whined and tugged once more, then gave in.

As he stepped onto the grass, a shout from the far side of the park commanded his attention.

"He's going to fall! Help! Help!"

The group of parents who'd been talking and laughing near the benches jumped up as one and raced toward the gazebo, where a boy of about seven had somehow managed to get on the roof. Now he was dangling off it.

"Stay here," he told Sitka. Because she'd been acting unusual, he looped her leash quickly around the edge of the bench, knotting it to keep her in place.

Then he raced toward the gazebo, passing the group of parents just as the kid's grip slipped and he slid farther, hanging only by fingertips now.

Pushing his strides as hard as he could, Tate suddenly felt like he was back in Boston, chasing a suspect down a city street. But the speed he had now, after two months of chasing Sitka around practice obstacles and trails, made his Boston days seem slow.

He reached the gazebo just as the boy lost his grip with a pained cry.

Skidding to a stop underneath him, Tate braced himself as he threw his arms out.

The boy landed awkwardly, smacking Tate in the face and sliding half out of his grasp. But Tate broke his fall and was able to set him on his feet without injury.

"Thank you, thank you, thank you," said a man who had to be the boy's father.

The boy had been fairly calm but burst into tears as his dad scooped him up.

Tate's heart rate slowed as the other parents reached them, clapping him on the back and hugging their own kids even as they admonished them not to climb the gazebo.

He smiled and accepted the accolades. He was turning back toward Sabrina and Sitka when Sabrina's shocked scream burst through the relieved voices. Sitka's panicked yelp followed.

A big green truck was rolling backward and at a slight angle down Main Street, rapidly picking up speed. It was headed right for Sitka.

His dog was straining against her leash, but he'd tethered her too well to the bench.

Tate started running again, pushing himself as hard as he could, but he was too far away. He'd never be able to get back to her in time, let alone unhook her.

Dread, guilt and anger slammed through him like a punch to the chest, then doubled as Sabrina raced in front of the truck to help his dog. He was about to lose them both. And there was nothing he could do to stop it.

Chapter 5

Panic intensified as Tate ran faster, his frantic strides still not good enough. The truck was speeding up, the incline working against him.

Sabrina dropped into an awkward squat and worked at the leash, struggling with it as Sitka whined and pulled, probably yanking the knot even tighter.

The truck hit the grass, no difference in height from the unpaved street to slow it, and Tate's whole body jerked in response, not wanting to see Sabrina get hit. Not wanting to see Sitka get hit.

Then suddenly Sabrina shifted, unhooking the leash from Sitka's collar instead.

Sitka scampered backward, away from the oncoming vehicle.

Sabrina twisted, throwing herself to the side. She landed hard on the grass as the truck zoomed past, plowing into the bench.

The metal bench crumpled under the truck's bumper, screeching enough to raise goose bumps on Tate's arms. As the bench collapsed and split, the truck kept going, then got snagged on the twisted pieces of metal. The truck made a sputtering sound, and then the engine cut out.

"You okay?" Tate panted as he slid to a stop beside Sabrina, his gaze searching for Sitka, too.

Behind him came the gasps and shouts of worry from the group of parents and kids, but Tate ignored them as he dropped to his knees next to Sabrina.

She rolled over and pushed up on her elbows, her arms shaking. There were grass stains streaking the front of her T-shirt and dirt on her face. "Did Sitka get out of the way?"

Woof!

His dog came running around the back of the truck. She didn't stop until she'd bumped him, knocking him off his knees and onto his butt.

"I'm sorry about the leash," he told her, burying his head in her fur for a moment, relief relaxing the tightness in his chest as he saw that she hadn't been hurt.

Then he lifted his gaze to the truck, stalled and silent. When he'd seen it moving toward Sitka, it had appeared empty. As if someone had forgotten to put on their parking brake. But was it really that simple?

Dread built up again. The truck hadn't been aimed at Sabrina. But it had been close enough to her. Could her stalker have sent it down the street?

From what he knew about stalkers, it seemed unlikely. After two years of chasing her, why would he try to kill her in such an impersonal way? Usually, when stalkers got violent, they did it up close, with a gun or a knife.

Still, he swept his gaze over the area where the truck had come from. No one was there.

Pushing himself to his feet, Tate scanned the rest of the park. All he saw were the parents and kids, looking horrified.

Sitka pivoted away from him, moving to Sabrina, and gave her a sloppy kiss across the side of her face.

Sabrina laughed, petting her. "You're welcome."

Tate held out a hand for Sabrina. "Are you okay? Do you want to have a doctor look at you?"

She put her hand in his. It was a little shaky, but there was a power in her grip as she helped him pull her up.

"No doctor. I'm fine, just a little freaked out." She glanced up Main Street, where the truck had come from. "What happened? Do you think this was an accident? Or..."

Reluctantly, Tate let go of her hand as the rest of the people in the park surrounded them.

"What happened?" The dad of the kid who'd fallen from the gazebo put a hand on Sabrina's shoulder, looking worried as he clutched the boy with his other hand.

A woman bouncing a crying baby leaned closer to Sabrina, too. "Are you okay?"

"Look at the bench!" someone else exclaimed.

"Who would be so careless?"

The cacophony of voices faded into the background as Tate stepped closer to the vehicle and peered through the window. The truck was set right between Reverse and Park, the key fob in the center console. A freak accident? He'd seen it before with these old trucks, where the owner thought it was in Park, but it was actually partway to Reverse. When he glanced up Main Street, he saw no one. No panicked owner racing for the park, horrified and ashamed. But maybe they'd walked away and the truck hadn't rolled backward immediately?

Still, he couldn't take any chances, especially not when Sabrina had been nearby, when they knew her stalker was here. He stepped farther away from the crowd and pulled out his radio. Speaking quietly, he said, "A truck just plowed into a bench in the park. No one was inside the vehicle, but Sabrina Jones almost got hit." Stepping behind the truck, he read off the license-plate number, dreading the potential news that it was a rental, maybe something that would come back to a fake name.

There was surprise in Officer Nate Dreymond's voice as he replied a minute later. "That vehicle belongs to Talise Poitra."

The seventy-year-old owner of the grocery store. She'd been injured pretty severely in the bombing, even been briefly in a coma. Maybe she wasn't back to a hundred percent yet.

Tate relaxed slightly as he glanced at Sabrina, who was hunched inward as she nodded and assured the townspeople that she wasn't hurt. Beside her, Sitka's tail was wagging as everyone took turns petting her.

"I'll walk over to the store and talk to her," Nate said. "I'll radio you once I have an update."

"Thanks." Tucking the radio back into his duty belt, Tate slipped through the crowd up to Sabrina and Sitka. "Why don't you come with me to the station, where you can clean up, and we'll take a statement?"

She nodded, looking grateful for the excuse to move away from the crowd.

"What happened?" Maria Peterson asked, clutching her three-year-old daughter tightly. A few months ago, when the park had been bombed, her husband had been injured.

"Probably just an accident," Tate said. "But we're going to investigate and make sure. Did anyone notice someone by the truck before it started moving?"

The group shook their heads and shrugged, glancing at each other, but Tate wasn't surprised. They'd all been too focused on the kid on the gazebo roof.

If this *hadn't been* an accident, someone had waited for the perfect moment.

Tate led Sabrina back toward the police station. His gaze swept the area as they walked, looking for anyone who seemed out of place, who seemed too interested in Sabrina. But besides a blonde woman facing away from him as she took pictures of the stalled truck and ruined bench, all he saw was Yura Begay.

The ex-Marine called out, "Everyone all right?"

"Yeah. Just a runaway truck," Tate replied.

"You think that's all it was?" Sabrina asked.

When he glanced at her, she was biting down on her lip, her brows furrowed. Guilt was all over her face as she ran her hand down Sitka's back.

"I hope so. But no matter what, this isn't your fault. I'm the one who tied Sitka to the bench."

"Hey, Tate?" Nate's voice crackled over the radio. "I've got an update."

"Go," Tate replied, glancing at Sabrina.

"Talise said she had her keys in her purse and that she'd put the parking brake on. She parked up past the park because she wanted the exercise. Said she's still trying to get back up to speed after the bombing."

"Is she sure about the keys?" Tate asked. "Because there was a key fob in the truck."

"I asked her to check. When she went to grab her purse from behind the counter to show me, it was open and her fob was missing. She thinks someone grabbed it sometime in the past hour."

Tate felt his jaw tensing as Sabrina went pale. But was Talise right about someone taking her keys? Or had she just forgotten them in her truck? "She have any idea who?"

"No. There are no cameras in her store. She says she was in the back for a while, dealing with inventory. Normally, she brings her purse with her back there, but this time she forgot. She said the bell over the door rang a few times, but she figured people would call out if they needed her to ring them up. No one did, and it was empty when she came back up front. She said it could have been anyone. But obviously if she's right, this person knew which vehicle belonged to Talise."

"Thanks," Tate said.

"It was my stalker." Sabrina's voice was barely above a whisper. "He was trying to kill Sitka."

Her stalker hadn't been trying to kill her. Not this time.

No, Sabrina felt it in her gut. If he wanted to kill her, he'd do it up close, and she'd know exactly who he was before she died. He hadn't been after her today.

It was worse than that. He'd been trying to kill Sitka. Maybe because he'd seen Sitka trying to track him from her house. Or maybe because she'd been walking with Tate, because the stalker had seen her invite Tate into her home yesterday.

She hadn't even kissed Tate. She hadn't gone on a

real date with him. But somehow, her stalker had known she wanted to.

He was punishing her for it by sending a message:

I'm watching. I can get to you—or someone you care about—anytime I want. Just like Dylan.

Shivering as she yanked the curtains closed on her back windows, shutting out the view of the sun sinking below the trees, Sabrina tried to stay calm. It had been hours since one of the officers had driven her home, then done a walk-through of her house before leaving.

Police still weren't sure if the truck backing up had been a targeted attack or just a freak accident. Still, they'd promised to investigate under the assumption that her stalker could have been involved. They might have been uncertain, but she wasn't. Her stalker was here, he'd made contact, and now he was back to threatening anyone who dared to enter her life.

She hadn't heard any updates. Despite the short amount of time she'd known Tate, she knew if they'd found anything, he would have told her.

She should have run the moment she'd spotted the new note on her doorstep. It didn't matter that her stalker kept finding her. She'd let herself become too invested in her life here, too invested in the life she *could* have. And she'd let herself forget how high the stakes were.

Sabrina glanced around the little cabin. It was barely eight hundred square feet, but it was cozy and the rent shockingly cheap.

Here, for the first time since she'd left New York City and her growing career in fashion design, she was doing something she loved again. No more waitressing jobs in dingy diners. No more constantly scanning the customers, searching for a face that was vaguely familiar, that might belong to a man who wouldn't leave her alone. No more endless tension between her shoulder blades, always on high alert for harassment or an attack from someone who knew she didn't want to attract attention, who knew she probably wouldn't risk going to the police.

In Desparre, she'd dared to start designing jewelry. It was what she'd always wanted to do, but back in the city, general accessories, like belts, scarves and sunglasses, were as close as she'd come. Here, she'd used an e-commerce site, made up a name with no connection to her and given it a shot. The first sale had been thrilling. As it continued to grow, she'd started to believe this could be her future.

Would she be able to do it somewhere else so easily? With Alaska's history of gold rushes, big and small, getting the raw materials had been easier than she'd expected. The cabin's tiny second bedroom had been perfect to set up a small workspace. And the view out her back windows was endlessly inspiring.

The sharp set of raps on her door made Sabrina jump. Her hand darted immediately to the alert button around her neck, but she didn't press it. Would her stalker really knock?

He'd knocked at Dylan's house.

Or at least that's what police assumed, that Dylan had opened the door to his killer, because there'd been no sign of forced entry.

The thought refused to go away as she moved slowly toward the door, heart thumping way too fast. But Dylan hadn't had any reason to suspect the person at his door was a threat. She'd mentioned the stalker, but she hadn't gone into details. She hadn't told him to be careful. Even knowing there'd been no reason for her to think he'd be in danger, the same guilt rushed forward, stinging her eyes with old tears.

Blinking them clear, she glanced around for a weapon. Making a quick detour into the kitchen, she grabbed the cast-iron pan the owner had left behind. She hefted it to shoulder height as she approached the door. It was solid and thick, tough to open even when it wasn't locked tight with a dead bolt, and especially now when her hands still shook.

Leaning in, she peered through the peephole.

It was a woman. A blonde with perfectly smoothed hair and a lot of makeup by Desparre standards, but not far from what Sabrina was used to in New York City at a club or at the design studio.

Sabrina had no idea who she was, but she lowered the pan as she leaned back. It seemed unlikely that her stalker was a woman, and equally unlikely he'd be able to convince one to help him. As the heavy pan came down, it banged the door, and she cringed.

"Hello?" the woman called when Sabrina didn't open the door.

She frowned, wondering what the woman wanted. Not that it really mattered. She wasn't about to open up for anyone right now.

When another minute went by and Sabrina continued to ignore the raps at the door, the woman called out, "My name is Ariel Clemson. I'm a reporter for the *Desparre Daily*."

There was a long pause, as if she thought that would be enticement enough, then she added, "I saw what happened at the park earlier, and I'm hoping to do a story about it." Another pause, then a hint of frustration underneath her hopeful pitch. "You know, *Local Woman Bravely Rescues Police K-9?*"

Sabrina's heart gave a small kick of anxiety. The idea of any exposure, even in the small-town newspaper, was a bad idea. There was no telling how it might get shared or who might ultimately see it. Yes, her stalker had found her, but her family hadn't. With her stalker nearby, she didn't want them to have any idea where she was.

"If you change your mind, give me a call," Ariel said through the door, and then a business card slid underneath.

Sabrina stayed quiet, still pretending not to be home, even though the reporter clearly knew she was, until the car backed out of her driveway.

Then she turned back into the cabin that had started to feel like a real home. She took one last look at the closed shades obscuring the view she loved, and headed into her bedroom to start packing.

Chapter 6

Was there anywhere on earth that her stalker couldn't track her?

Sabrina had been so careful when she'd come here, leaving her last hideout in Washington in the middle of the night when there'd been almost no one on the roads. She'd kept a close eye on her rearview mirror for hours, not stopping until she was well into Canada. There was no way he'd been behind her. Was there?

If he hadn't physically followed her, how had he found her here? She'd stopped all contact with friends and family, not even daring to send them letters from the road in case he was watching their mailboxes, waiting to intercept them. She'd stopped shopping at any of the places she used to love, even online. She'd quit her favorite exercise program that let her join in virtual sessions. She'd stopped working in fashion design, only recently making the jump to jewelry—still design, but a different field. She'd stopped using her social-media accounts entirely.

When the PI had first suggested she leave town, when she'd detailed the extent of the changes she wanted Sabrina to make to her life, giving up hobbies and activities that could be a way to locate her, it had all sounded excessive. It had all seemed unnecessary. Now she wondered if she'd missed something, some small piece of her former life that had given her stalker a way to locate her.

She had no idea what it was. But if he'd found her all the way in no-stoplights-in-downtown, snow-you-in-un-til-spring Desparre, was there anywhere she'd be safe?

Hefting a bag full of her jewelry supplies, Sabrina peered through the peephole at her truck, ready in the drive. Last night, after she'd made the decision to leave, she'd packed everything and then stared, frustrated and tense, out into the darkness. She'd been afraid to go outside. Afraid her stalker was waiting in the woods, ready to ambush her.

This was worse than any of the other tiny towns she'd stopped in over the past two years. All the other times she'd run, she'd done it because she'd gotten jumpy, started seeing every shadow as a possible threat. But she'd never received a note until Desparre.

She'd gotten too comfortable here. She'd actually started to believe she could have some semblance of a life.

Now she was back to where she'd been two years ago. Scared and alone.

It didn't matter. All that mattered was her life, and the lives of the people she cared about. It was what the PI had drilled into her when she'd told Sabrina all the things she'd have to give up if she wanted to stay safe. Back then, even knowing how real the threat was, she'd burst into tears more than once in the days leading up to her planned disappearance, hoping the police would pull out a miracle and catch him.

After all this time, she thought she'd become more hardened. But at least now that she'd made the decision to leave, she knew she could do it.

She could go back to jumping from one town to the next, one state to the next. She could go back to the tedious waitressing jobs, the sleazy hotels. She could go back to being totally alone.

Pushing an image of Tate from her mind, Sabrina willed away the fear and the frustration as she yanked open the door and scanned the area. Then she hurried to her truck, pepper spray clutched in her free hand. She dropped the bag inside, scanned the woods and hurried back to the cabin.

She hadn't run with so many belongings since she'd first slipped out of New York, in the middle of the night. Back then, she'd done it with the help of the investigator, who'd made sure she wasn't followed.

In the time since then, she'd purged more and more of the things she'd once thought she couldn't live without. Small pieces of her past that had started to feel like too much baggage or that she could get a little money for in a pawnshop.

Was it even worth bringing her jewelry supplies? Probably not, since she doubted she'd be able to continue finding the things she needed to keep up her small online business. But maybe she could sell the last of it along the way. The past few years had shown her how expensive it could get to stay invisible.

Any reputable place wanted multiple forms of ID and a credit check to rent to you. Sabrina had a fake ID and the PI had made a fake credit history to go with it. But the woman had warned her that it was always safer not to rely on it. If someone dug deep enough, they'd figure out it wasn't real. Then she'd be in legal trouble herself.

Using her real ID or her real name meant someone could run a real credit check on her. She had no idea what resources her stalker had, but if he'd managed to get a hold of her social security number, he could track her from a simple credit check. She wasn't willing to take that risk, either.

So, she'd stuck to cheap motels that didn't care who she was. She'd stuck to sleazy employers who were happy to pay her cash under the table as long as they could pay her below minimum wage.

Only in Desparre had she dared to rent. She'd stopped in the grocery store downtown, and Talise had immediately noticed a scared, exhausted outsider and tried to help. She'd introduced her to the only other person buying groceries at 8 p.m., an elderly man who was going to stay with his daughter in southern Alaska, probably indefinitely. He wasn't ready to give up his cabin, but he was willing to rent it cheaply. If she was willing to pay for each new month several weeks in advance, he wasn't interested in anything more than her word.

She'd felt guilty for taking him up on it, even knowing she'd never leave him in the lurch. Now she wrote his name on an envelope and stuffed enough for next month's rent in it, hoping he wasn't relying on the income. Eventually, Tate would figure out she'd gone, and word would get to Talise, who'd pass it on to the owner.

Lifting onto her shoulder her second and final bag,

one filled with her clothes and a framed picture of her mom and brother, Sabrina glanced around the cabin one last time. Then she set the emergency button the police had given her on the table in the front hall. There was a lot she'd miss about Desparre, but she couldn't stay.

It was one thing to risk her own life to put an end to her running, to regain an existence beyond simple survival. She wouldn't risk Tate's.

She liked him, probably too much for the short time she'd known him. Yes, he was an armed police officer, but her stalker had already proven how dangerous he could be. No one had seen him slipping into Talise's truck on the street, shifting it partway to Reverse and then disappearing into the woods. What if, next time, he stood in those woods and used the gun he'd taken into Dylan's home? What if he aimed it at Tate and the officer never saw the threat coming?

She refused to be responsible for anyone else's death.

It was time to go.

Tate jerked upright in bed, slick with sweat, his heart pounding as though he was still trapped in his nightmare.

It had plagued him all night, waking him on and off and making him sleep later than usual. As he'd thrashed around in bed, he'd kept Sitka up, too. Periodically, she'd stood up in her dog bed in the corner and whined.

He'd reassure her, try to shake off the memories, then feel himself being sucked right back into the same nightmare of that fateful morning run five and a half years ago. He'd been jogging, pushing his body hard as his mind went over and over the payoff he'd witnessed, as he stressed over the upcoming arrests. Or at least those he'd assumed would be arrested. Not just a crime lord, but also three fellow cops. Officers he'd respected, officers he'd worked with, officers who'd once come to his aid.

Then the past and present had blended. In his dream, Sabrina had jogged up next to him, distracted him with her shy smile and the far-off look in her eyes. When the gunfire had started, he'd raced off the path and into the woods, trying to make himself a difficult target, just as he'd done back then. Knowing he was probably going to die, the same certainty he'd felt back in Boston. But in his nightmare, he'd been pulling a confused and terrified Sabrina with him, and instead of a group of cops trying to corner them, her stalker had stepped out of the woods in front of them.

He'd been huge, just a dark shadow among the trees, except for a wide, evil smile. Tate had lunged for Sabrina, trying to flatten her to the ground, but before he could reach her, he'd woken.

Over and over throughout the night, the same nightmare had plagued him.

Was it a premonition? The subconscious knowledge that he couldn't fully protect her?

Stalkers and abusers were some of the hardest threats to eliminate. The law got murky, precedent not always favoring the victims, and that personality type—a man so obsessed with controlling a woman that he couldn't let go—was often willing to give up his whole life just to hurt her.

The chance that it was just driver error that had sent the vehicle racing down the street yesterday was strong. There'd been no prints besides Talise's in the car, no cameras on the street to confirm if someone else had gotten inside. So even if Tate could figure out who the stalker was, even if he *had* been responsible, Tate couldn't prove the guy had done anything with the truck.

Whether or not he'd set the vehicle in motion, Sabrina's stalker was here. He was watching her. Was Tate risking Sabrina's life even more by convincing her to stay?

The worry gnawed at him as he kicked off his covers, then stepped out of his shorts and into the shower. The heat and steam relaxed him in a way that nothing else except a good hard run could do. Five minutes later, dressed in civilian clothes since it was his day off, Tate opened the back door for Sitka.

His small house was located on the outskirts of downtown. He'd dared to buy the home, to set down roots here, because the family friend who'd created his fake name and backstory worked for Witness Protection. He hadn't created Tate's pseudonym officially. But if anyone knew how to do it right, it was a man who'd spent two decades doing it professionally.

In the years since Tate had returned to Alaska, he'd struggled with bouts of frustration and depression, especially from not being able to see his family. He could only contact them periodically, through a complicated system that would protect his safety and theirs. He'd left behind all the friends he'd made in Boston, with no notice to anyone that he was leaving. And he'd had to start over in the Desparre PD, going through the police academy a second time, pretending to be a true rookie.

But he'd taken for granted that he was safe here in Desparre.

Sure, he'd become even more cautious, but he'd been

a police officer for two years in Boston, patrolling the streets during the late-night shift. Boston's crime rate was a lot higher than Desparre's. So being safety-conscious was already a way of life. His ability to be attuned to danger was probably what had saved his life five years ago.

He'd had his moments of paranoia and fear since then, but nothing like the constant terror chasing Sabrina. She was convinced yesterday's attack had been meant for Sitka, a warning that her stalker could get to her anytime, that she shouldn't let anyone close to her.

Tate's hands fisted at how well her stalker had succeeded. He'd forced Sabrina to leave everyone she loved behind, to stay all alone for two long years. From the way she'd reacted when people had tried to talk to her in the park, he could see that she hadn't let anyone truly get close to her since leaving.

It was a common tactic of scum like domestic abusers, so why not stalkers, too? Make the target of their obsession feel vulnerable and completely alone. Make them feel that if they dared to try and get help, things would only get worse. And not just for the target but for anyone she reached out to for help or companionship.

Sabrina was going to run again.

It hit him with a certainty that stole the breath from his lungs. "Sitka," he wheezed.

His dog came running across the yard, nudging him with her nose like she knew something was wrong.

"Come on," he said, hurrying back through the house and out the front door to his truck.

She raced beside him, her head pivoted slightly toward him like she was worried. She knew this wasn't a typical work mission.

"We need to stop Sabrina from running," he told her as he opened the door for her and she hopped into the truck, then leaped over to the passenger side.

His heart thundered as he silently berated himself for not recognizing what his subconscious had been trying to tell him all night. Was he already too late?

He took the roads fast, jaw clenched and his breathing too rapid, like he was headed to a distress call knowing before he arrived that all he'd be able to do was clean up the mess. If she'd already left, he had no idea how to even begin to search for her.

Based on what she'd told him about leaving New York, she'd done everything right. How the hell was her stalker still tracking her?

After what had almost happened to Sitka, she was unlikely to reach out to police again for help. She'd just keep hoping to outrun her stalker, to simply survive. But if he could track her here, how would she ever lose him? Eventually, a stalker this obsessed wouldn't be content with simply watching and leaving notes. Eventually, he'd try to make her his own. And when that inevitably failed, he'd kill her.

A sharp pain sliced through Tate's chest, and he hit the gas harder, making Sitka give a sharp bark as she hunkered low on the seat.

"Sorry, Sitka." She was used to fast driving in the police SUV, but that was better designed for her than the front seat of his truck.

He raced up the dirt road leading to Sabrina's house, and then his heart gave a little kick when he spotted tail-lights in her drive. Sabrina? Or someone else?

He didn't slow until he'd swung into the driveway, effectively blocking whoever was in that vehicle from escaping. Then, he hit the brakes hard, apologizing to Sitka as she yelped and righted herself again.

The brake lights on the old truck in the drive flashed and then stayed lit for a long moment, until the car turned off and Sabrina stepped out.

She crossed her arms over her chest, glancing repeatedly at the woods as she approached. When he rolled down the window, she demanded, "What are you doing?"

"What are *you* doing?" he shot back. "We agreed that the Desparre PD would help you, Sabrina. No more running. So why are you sneaking away without even a goodbye?"

As the angry words burst from his mouth, he realized how much the idea hurt. They barely knew each other, but he'd felt an instant connection. He admired her strength and determination, the way she was willing to make sacrifices to keep the people she loved safe. He liked the way her eyes lit up when she gave him a real smile, the silly jokes she made about Sitka patrolling. He liked *her* and the idea of her not being in Desparre just felt wrong.

She frowned back at him, then her gaze darted briefly to Sitka, before returning to his. "It's one thing for me to make a stand and try to put an end to what's happening to me. I've lived with this threat for a long time, and I'm willing to take that risk to get my life back. And believe me, I want the help. But this is my fight. And now it seems like he's targeted Sitka. I'm not going to let anyone else get hurt because of me."

"We're trained for this," he insisted, trying to push his personal feelings to the background. "This threat is never going to just go away. We have to stop it."

She seemed to pale at his words, but her jaw clamped down, and she shook her head again.

Turning off his engine, he stepped out beside her. Before he could shut the door, Sitka was out, too, sitting next to Sabrina and looking up at her as if to say *I'm off duty. Pet me, please.*

A ghost of a smile flitted across Sabrina's face as she complied.

"Sabrina."

When she met his gaze again, fear and determination there, he said, "You don't want to spend your life running from this threat. I'm not going to let you do that. We're going to eliminate it."

He tried to infuse his words with certainty. It was his duty to protect her, to help her feel safe again, so she could finally regain her life fully, something he'd probably never have himself.

He couldn't stop himself from reaching out and taking her hand in his, couldn't help himself from wanting to step a little closer, to wrap his arms around her.

Duty was only part of it, he realized. He was falling for Sabrina Jones...if that was even her real name. He didn't want to lose her.

She stared up at him, warring emotions on her face, until finally she nodded. "Okay, I'll stay. Just promise me that you're all going to be careful. If this guy turns his focus on you and Sitka and you can't find him, I want you to be honest with me. I want you to tell me, so I can make my own decision about whether to stay or go."

He nodded, not breaking eye contact. "I promise."

But he knew it wasn't a promise he could keep. This wasn't a fight he was letting her take on alone anymore.

One way or another, they were going to end this here.

Chapter 7

"Are you sure about this?" Sabrina asked as she let him into her cabin.

In response, he picked up the emergency button she'd left on the front-hall table and slipped it over her head.

She tried not to visibly react as his hands skimmed her neck, lifting her hair out of the way so the thin chain could lie underneath. But even after he removed his hands, his touch lingered, making her neck tingle.

The scent of sandalwood—his aftershave maybe—drifted toward her, intoxicating. This close, she saw how purely deep brown his eyes were, no variation to distract from the intensity of his gaze. Her breath caught, and the tingling in her neck spread down her arms and across her back.

His gaze lingered on hers, and the desire she felt was reflected back at her, beneath a layer of anxiety and concern. The corners of his lips tipped up slightly, making her want to step forward, lean into him and see what happened.

Then Sitka stepped between them, tail wagging, and broke the spell.

Sabrina laughed, releasing some of the tension both from the situation and her proximity to Tate. She leaned down and pet Sitka, giving her pulse a chance to calm.

Then she straightened and asked, "If you're sure this is the right move, how do we find him? And are you sure you should even be here right now?" Her gaze dropped to Sitka, then rose to Tate. "I'm pretty sure he targeted Sitka because he saw you here."

Because he thinks you could be important to me, Sabrina didn't add. *The problem is, he could be right.*

A pair of vertical grooves appeared between Tate's eyebrows, marring his perfectly smooth skin. He nodded slowly. "I still think this could have been a badly timed accident. But if it wasn't, then yeah, that makes sense. Anyone who might be an ally to you, anyone who might be a friend, he sees as a threat. Competition."

Competition. Sabrina couldn't help her indignant snort, but it quickly turned into a familiar angry frustration. She'd spent two years as the object of some man's unrequited obsession, and he thought it was his right to destroy everything in her life so he could have her for himself.

"I know," Tate said softly, as if he could read her mind. "It's unfair."

Unfair was too simple a word for this. It was more than just unfair that she'd been forced to give up seeing her family and friends again, possibly for the rest of her life. That she had to take low-key jobs so she could stay below the radar. That she never felt truly safe, all because some man she might never have even spoken to thought his right to want her was greater than her right to live the life she wanted.

"Tell me," Tate said softly, compassion in his eyes. "Tell me what you're thinking."

"I just…" She sighed, looked away. She'd grown up with a strong single mom who'd worked hard to raise her and her younger brother. A mom who'd never sugarcoated the dangers women faced in the world or the inequities. Still, she'd always felt loved, supported, protected, *safe*.

Until her stalker had shown up. He was someone she might have smiled at once politely. Someone she might have had a brief conversation with at a kiosk or never spoken to at all. Someone who lived in the shadows because he was too much of a coward to tell her who he really was.

She didn't realize she'd clenched her hands into tight fists until Tate's hands were over hers, loosening them. Shifting her gaze back to him, she pulled her hands free and missed the contact immediately. "Police in New York said my stalker probably wasn't anyone identifiable in my life. They think he was somewhere on the outskirts, that I might not even recognize him at all when—if—they finally figured out who it was. But *he* has some kind of fantasy where he's essential in my life, and *I* have to live with that."

Breathing through the tears that wanted to rush forward, Sabrina said bitterly, "I can't even use my real name."

"Your name isn't Sabrina?" Tate asked softly, not sounding particularly surprised.

"It is Sabrina." The way he said her name made her suddenly glad she'd only changed her last name. She'd done it because the PI thought keeping the same first name would be easier to remember and respond to. Over the years, she'd had moments where it had felt like the only thing left in her life that was still *her*. "But it's not Jones."

His eyes narrowed slightly, and she could see him debating whether to ask what her real last name was.

"Don't," she told him. "It's better if you don't know."

He continued to stare back at her, like he might argue, until Sitka stood, spun in a quick circle and barked.

Sabrina laughed, and a grin broke out on Tate's face. "You're right, Sitka," he told her. "Maybe we should go sit down."

Realizing she'd kept him standing in the entryway a long time, Sabrina felt her cheeks heat. She turned into the house, leading him toward the living room where they'd sat before. Even though she was all packed up to disappear, the house looked mostly the same.

Seeing how small an impact she'd had on the space in the six months she'd lived here was slightly depressing, but it was less depressing than the series of dingy hotels she'd called home before this.

Glancing around as he chose the same side of the couch he'd sat on before, Tate asked, "You want me to help you bring your stuff back in?"

Shaking her head, Sabrina sank onto the other side of the couch. Her gaze was immediately drawn into the woods. But the view that had inspired so much of her creativity now made her shiver. Was her stalker outside right this moment, seeing that his attack hadn't scared away Tate and Sitka? Was he already planning a new way to permanently remove them from her life?

Anxiety bubbled up, the certainty that she'd made a mistake letting Tate block her in. "I—"

"Don't," Tate said.

Woof! Sitka contributed, either picking up on Tate's tone or stating her own agreement. She pushed her way between Tate and the coffee table and sat in the space between them, her brown eyes intent on Sabrina.

"I feel selfish staying," she admitted softly.

"That's ridiculous." He shifted on the couch, one knee up so he was facing her. "I'm a police officer. Believe me, I've faced worse threats."

He said it like he was speaking about something specific. Sabrina couldn't help the shiver that went through her, imagining him in danger. But in law enforcement, it was part of the job.

When he'd first promised to help her get free of this threat, she'd immediately seen all the possibilities open up in her life again—possibilities like asking him on a date. But she was wrung out from two years of impending danger. How would she handle being in a relationship with a man who went to work each day anticipating danger?

"Running forever isn't the worst thing," Sabrina told him. Having police show up at Dylan's family's lake house, hearing the news that he'd been shot inside his home and then getting the note a few days later? That was the worst thing.

"No," he agreed. "But that's not your fate, Sabrina. So let's talk through some things, see if we can figure out how he found you here."

She couldn't stop herself from glancing out the window again, into the vast woods. She didn't think she'd ever see them the same way again.

"You said you haven't spoken to your family in two years, so I assume you've had no contact with anyone else, either, right? Not even this PI who helped you disappear?"

She shook her head. "No. I check her website every once in a while, to see if the New York police caught my stalker. She's supposed to leave a coded message there if it happens. In the first few months, I checked it a lot. Now I look once every month or two." Was there some way to look at her site and see where people accessed it from? "You don't think he's somehow tracking me from that, do you?"

"No. What about jobs, hobbies?"

Sabrina sighed, shook her head. "The PI I hired was good. And expensive. She worked with a skip tracer to help me disappear. What it boiled down to was basically that I needed to change everything about my life to stay safe."

Something flickered in his eyes at her words, something more than sympathy.

"Back in New York, I was a fashion designer. Accessories," she added, when he looked surprised. "Here, I've been selling jewelry I make over an e-commerce site. It's the closest I've come to normal, but it's a pretty different field."

"What did you do in all the places you lived in between?"

"Waitressing. I picked cheap diners or places near highways that were open all night and catered to truckers. Places that didn't want an employment check or actual ID."

His lips tightened into an angry line. "Places where they could pay you under the table in cash, which means they didn't bother giving you a living wage."

"Yeah," she agreed. "But I could manage on the money." Anxiety twisted in her belly, remembering what had made that year and a half before Desparre so unbearable. "It was the other threats."

The anger on Tate's face shifted into a deeper fury. "From the people working at these places? Because they saw you as part of a vulnerable population, someone with no real ID who wouldn't dare go to the police about anything illegal?"

"Sometimes," she agreed, because at almost every place she'd worked, dodging someone's hands as she served food had started to feel normal. "Sometimes it was the customers, because these places weren't exactly in the safest areas. And I'd take any shift I could get, which usually meant nights."

Her mouth suddenly went dry, thinking of all those nights rushing to her crappy car after a shift, usually in a parking lot where they didn't care about safety lighting. More than once, she'd used pepper spray on a customer who'd tried to corner her, even one who'd tried to drag her into his long-haul truck.

That had been one of the scariest moments of her life, second only to the moment she'd realized Dylan's death was because of her. She'd been exhausted after a long shift and fitting the key in the twenty-year-old junker she'd been driving in Iowa when goose bumps had erupted across her neck. She'd already had her pepper spray out because she'd learned the hard way that she needed it. As she'd spun around, lifting that spray, fear had exploded. The guy was huge, well over six feet and at least twice her weight. It might not have all been muscle, but it didn't matter. She'd barely started to depress the trigger on her pepper spray before he swatted the canister away like he was swatting a fly.

She'd choked on the fumes, but he'd just coughed and slapped a hand over her mouth, as if there was anyone around to hear her scream or care if they had. His other arm had yanked her flush against him, shoving her face into his sweat-stained T-shirt. It had been hard to breathe as he'd dragged her, ignoring the fists she'd slammed into his arms and the one solid kick she'd gotten to his knee, like he barely felt them.

He'd loosened his grip slightly to open the door of his truck, and she'd wrenched herself away, simultaneously flinging a desperate punch. She'd gotten lucky as he'd twisted back toward her and her punch had landed right on his prominent Adam's apple. He'd gagged and she'd run.

She'd gotten in her car and raced out of that town, out of Iowa. She'd never had such a close call again, but it had been a tough reminder: her stalker wasn't the only threat out there.

"I've been careful," she told Tate, trying to shake off the remnants of that memory. "He shouldn't have been able to track me here. I've changed cars. I've lived in eight different states before coming to Alaska."

Frustration bubbled up, stronger than it had been in a long time, because she'd actually started to hope again. "So how the hell did he find me here?"

Tate ran up the hill outside Desparre's downtown at a punishing pace, let the steady rhythm of his pounding feet calm his fury.

Sabrina had almost left. If he'd been seconds later, she'd have been gone, and he wouldn't have been able to find her.

The idea hurt a lot more than it should have and Tate tried not to focus on why. Because right now, his feelings for her didn't matter. Only her safety did.

Gritting his teeth, he pushed himself harder, his chest heaving as he finally crested the hill. He was alone, having dropped Sitka off at home after they'd left Sabrina's cabin. Sitka liked to run with him, but when he was in this kind of mood, he never brought her along. There was no reason to punish her for his bad mood.

Bending over, Tate rested his palms on his knees as his heart rate slowed. Then he straightened and peered over the edge of the hill. If downtown Desparre was sleepy, the outskirts were damn near comatose. There were lots of places to get lost in nature. A boon for locals who knew the area and the safety precautions. Not so great for unprepared tourists looking for adventure. Or for a cop who'd been ambushed on a quiet trail.

These days, though, he didn't constantly scan his surroundings on his run. The impulse was still there, but he tried to resist. It was a slippery slope from appropriate caution to paranoia.

When Sabrina had shared some of her experience, he'd wanted to open up about his own. He'd wanted to tell her he knew exactly what it was like to have someone come after you. Sure, the reasons and methods were different. The outcome, too. But the terror of that moment in the park would never fully go away. The nightmare he'd had last night was rare, but the fear was always in the back of his mind.

One of the officers who'd tried to kill him was in

prison. The moron had actually used his police-issued weapon to shoot Tate, so when the bullet had been dug out of Tate's arm, that had cinched Officer Jim Bellows's fate. But the other two had gotten off. Not enough evidence, the jury had ruled. Not enough evidence that they'd participated in the payoff, and not enough evidence that they'd participated in the attempt on Tate's life.

Tate had only seen Jim in the park. But Jim wasn't the only officer there, Tate was sure. Jim must have brought his two closest friends on the force, Paul Martin and Kevin Fricker. Tate had seen all three take the payoff, but financial forensics had only found a large deposit to Jim Bellows.

It was no surprise that the other two had used throw-away weapons or that they'd hidden the money better. Jim had always been a liability, constantly on the verge of an Internal Affairs investigation for one reason or another. Usually his inability to curb his drinking, since he'd shown up intoxicated at work a few times.

Kevin and Paul were smarter, more cautious. It had turned out they were just as crooked.

Still, Kevin and Paul had managed to stay on the force, at least for a time. But Tate's accusations had stained their reputations, as well as his own. The rest of the officers hadn't known who to believe, or who to trust. Eventually, Kevin and Paul had left—and so had Tate.

The court had decided Kevin and Paul hadn't been involved. The feds decided they weren't an ongoing threat. But Tate knew otherwise. The last thing Kevin had whispered as he'd walked past Tate on his final day at the police station had been "Jim was my best friend, and you destroyed his life. Watch your back. One day, we might just destroy yours."

Tate hadn't bothered to tell the FBI about the threat. The case had been closed. And a vague threat wasn't enough to reopen anything.

Instead, he'd contacted an old family friend and asked what it would take to disappear. Until that moment, he'd expected to stay in Boston. Even though the other officers hadn't gone to jail, the fact that he'd accused them would make them immediate suspects if any harm came to him. But the look in Kevin's eyes had told Tate he wasn't the only one in danger.

Now, staring down into the town he'd grown to love so much, the town that sometimes made him wonder why he'd ever left Alaska in the first place, Tate wished he'd seen it coming. Some of the signs were there, but until he'd stumbled onto the three cops taking a payoff, he never would have guessed it was happening.

Before the incident, Jim Bellows had seemed like a time bomb. Kevin and Paul had seemed more even-keeled, more professional. They were partners and had actually come to Tate's aid on a dangerous call once. Still, he'd always seen something volatile in them, something vague that made him intuitively understand why they'd befriended Jim.

One of the lieutenants used to call Paul *Napoleon* because he made up for being five foot six by lifting weights until he resembled a tank. The officer had always loved to intimidate with his size. Kevin, who looked a solid decade younger than his thirty-nine years, used the fact that he *wasn't* particularly intimidating—even at six foot four—to get close to someone. Then he'd bring the hurt.

Both tactics were fine, in the appropriate situation. But Tate preferred to stick to tactics that didn't have an undercurrent of bullying.

He hadn't destroyed their careers fully. Both had gone on to other departments in other cities. But he doubted he'd happened to catch them taking their first payoff. What he probably *had* destroyed was their illegal-income source. And that day, Tate had known they'd never forgive him for that. Or for putting Jim behind bars.

So, when his family friend had said he could do unofficially for Tate what he'd done for years for federal witnesses—only to a lesser degree, giving Tate some contact with his family—he'd jumped on it. Better to start over than to constantly live in fear. Especially if that fear was for more than just himself.

In the years since, he'd kept tabs on Kevin and Paul, expecting one day their illegal activities would catch up to them. But they were both still police officers, both still a potential threat. He'd finally accepted that this was his life now and allowed himself to embrace it.

He would probably never go home again. But he was going to make sure that wasn't Sabrina's fate.

Chapter 8

Someone was staring at her.

Sabrina's breathing became shallow as the certainty washed over her. She glanced around the little downtown, trying to be subtle but feeling obvious as her gaze lingered on any man she didn't recognize as a longtime Desparre resident.

Maybe she just sensed the police watching her.

Tate had told her that the police wanted her to act normal, try to get out and engage with people. She was supposed to notify them whenever she went anywhere, so they could watch from a distance. They figured that's what her stalker was doing, so they would look for anyone paying her too much attention.

As she glanced around, Officer Lorenzo Riera nodded briefly at her. It evened out her breathing, made her shoulders relax from where they'd crept up her neck. If she couldn't have Tate watching over her—she knew he was off duty today—having the serious veteran officer keep watch was a close second.

Walking from where she'd parked near the grocery store toward the park felt strange today. She'd done this walk many times, but somehow, even after doing it just once with Tate and Sitka, it felt unnatural not to have them at her side.

Every step felt stiff, and the swing of her arms that was meant to look casual seemed awkward. No matter how many times she told herself not to make it obvious she was watching for someone, she couldn't stop herself from scanning the area.

A tall man with dark hair and a terrible mustache stood up the hill, near a vehicle that was parked close to where Talise's truck had been yesterday. He met her gaze and gave her a brief nod the same way Officer Riera had done. But this man wasn't a cop.

She didn't know him. The way he immediately averted his gaze after that nod made her shoulders tense up again. Was the bad mustache a disguise? She didn't recognize him from around town, but then again, she didn't know everyone.

Her gaze went back to the officer, to see if he'd noticed, but his expression was even. He didn't even seem to be paying attention to her as he meandered across the street, stopping to chat with people along the way.

She tried to will Officer Riera to look her way as the mustached man got into a light-colored sedan, but the officer still wasn't watching. So, she picked up her pace, hoping to get a license-plate number. As the vehicle pulled onto the street quickly enough to make the tires squeal, she saw that the plate was caked over with mud.

Frustrated, she glanced back at the officer again.

This time, he looked in her general direction, his gaze sweeping over and past her. As he continued walking, he shook his head.

Did that mean he knew the man? Was she being paranoid? Seeing every man as a threat now?

She reached for her phone to text the officer, to make sure he'd seen what she had.

"Sabrina!"

She jumped at the sound of her name, almost dropping her phone as her hand jerked automatically toward her purse, where she still kept a canister of pepper spray.

When her gaze swung toward the park, she saw Lora Perkins and Adam Lassiter waving. Lora was frowning, like she knew something was wrong, and Adam seemed like he was faking enthusiasm at seeing her.

After Talise, they were some of the people she knew best in Desparre. So, she tucked her phone away and pasted on a smile she could feel quivering as she walked toward them.

"Are you okay?" Lora asked, putting a hand on her arm when she reached them. "We heard about the truck almost hitting you yesterday."

Sabrina nodded. "Yeah. The police think it was a freak accident." It was what they'd said to tell anyone who asked about it, just in case her stalker had been responsible. They wanted him to feel like he'd gotten away with it, so he'd be more confident continuing to follow her. Talise had been asked to play along, pretend she couldn't believe she'd forgotten to engage her parking brake. Police hadn't given her specifics on why, just that they thought the ploy would help draw out the person responsible.

Lora's frown deepened, the perfectly smooth, pale

skin on her forehead furrowing as if she could tell Sabrina was lying.

Lora was only a few years older than Sabrina, but from the moment they'd met, she'd mothered Sabrina. She'd even commented on it once, laughingly telling Sabrina she knew she was doing it, but that she couldn't help it. She'd grown up in the mountains of Desparre, with drug-addicted parents and three younger siblings who needed to be fed and cared for. They were all adults now, all successful and married and living far away from the town where they'd grown up. While Lora claimed she couldn't bring herself to have kids and spend the rest of her life the way she'd spent her childhood—looking after others—she couldn't seem to stop herself from doing it with everyone she met.

"Are you sure?" Adam asked.

Sabrina's gaze shifted to him. He, too, was a few years older than her. He was newer to Desparre than she was and knew even fewer people. He probably never would have spoken to her or anyone else if Lora hadn't pressured him to do it. Once you befriended Lora, it was hard to say no to her good-natured attempts to help.

He didn't seem particularly suspicious of her lie, but it was hard to tell beneath the look of despair and grief that was always on his face. His wife had died a few months earlier, and he'd left behind their home on the other side of Alaska for some peace and quiet here.

She shrugged, trying to sound flippant. "Yeah, what else would it be? It was scary, but trust me, Talise will never forget to put her parking brake on again!"

Adam nodded, his gaze drifting to the other side of the park, where a group of kids were playing. But Lora still looked suspicious.

Sabrina averted her gaze, and her attention caught on a man standing by the park gazebo. He was lowering his phone like he'd had it up to take a picture, and his gaze locked on hers, lingering for a moment before he turned and walked out of the park.

Her breath caught. Something about his build and his walk was familiar. From seeing him around town? Or from back in New York?

"Sabrina." Lora squeezed her arm. "Are you sure you're okay? You seem really spooked."

Ripping her gaze away and hoping Officer Riera was paying attention, Sabrina tried for a smile. Because it shook way too much to be believable, she admitted, "I guess yesterday scared me more than I realized. I keep thinking a car is going to come at me out of nowhere."

She tried for a laugh and was amazed when it came out self-deprecating but real. "I think I'm going to head home and relax for a while."

"That's probably a good idea," Lora said.

"Let us know if you need anything," Adam added.

The look on his face—like he'd finally lifted out of his own grief enough to see something around him was wrong—told her this wasn't working at all.

She needed to get it together. Because the best way to find her stalker was to give him a chance to watch her. And give the police a chance to spot him doing it.

The way things were going, she was more likely to alert him to the fact that police were watching. And if he knew that, would he leave? And leave her in a perpetual state of limbo?

Or would he make one last bold move and kill *her* this time?

* * *

Tate stared at the picture of Dylan Westwood on his computer screen. This was Sabrina's old boyfriend. It had to be.

Leaning back in his chair in the second bedroom he used as a home office, Tate studied the man Sabrina had been dating two years ago. He'd woken early to do some digging into Sabrina's life, but he only had another hour and a half until he needed to be at work.

The photo someone had chosen to accompany Dylan's obituary showed him grinning, amusement clear in his dark blue eyes. According to the obit, the twenty-eight-year-old marketing associate at a record label had been survived by both parents and four younger siblings.

Tate had found the obituary from cross-referencing an article about Dylan's murder from New York two years ago. He'd found *that* article by searching for information about a murder in that time frame that mentioned a stalker. Dylan had been shot in his own home and the story said police believed his girlfriend's stalker had murdered him. They were asking anyone who had information to come forward.

Sabrina Jones's real name was Sabrina Reilly.

Tate tried the name out on his lips. Something about it matched her more than Jones. But Jones was a smart choice for going on the run, since it was one of the most popular last names in the US. If she ever ran into trouble with her fake ID, it might have been easily explained away as a mix-up with some other Sabrina Jones.

Pulling up a couple of social-media sites, Tate typed in *Sabrina Reilly* and searched through the possible matches. He found her on the third site. Her account was set to private, but there were certain things he could still see, including her profile picture, which told him he'd found the right Sabrina. In the picture, her head was thrown back, and she was laughing. Her hair was shorter, still with those natural waves. Her dress was more trendy, less practical than what she wore in Alaska. But mostly, she looked the same—minus the haunted look in her eyes.

Scrolling through the posts that weren't hidden from view, including pictures she'd been tagged in—all from over two years ago—Tate searched for anything or anyone that seemed out of place. But all of the comments seemed to be from friends, and even meticulously cross-checking each of the people who'd liked her photos didn't reveal anything that stood out as odd.

So, he went deeper, checking each of the friends in those photos, until he found a few who had their profiles set to public. He dug into their older pictures, too, looking for anywhere Sabrina was not tagged or in the background, searching for anyone who commented or liked too many of them. Still nothing.

With a frustrated sigh, he kept going, finding other people with the last name Reilly, until he came across one who had to be her older brother. Conor Reilly. He was a stockbroker with a long-term girlfriend and a love of baseball. Two years ago, his posts had suddenly become public. On some of his early posts, there were multiple comments asking about his sister, all of which he'd ignored.

Tate dug into each of the people who'd asked about her, but none seemed likely to be her stalker. They all seemed far too embedded in the Reillys' lives. And Tate agreed with the New York police: the person stalking

Sabrina had to be on the outskirts of her life. If he was too close to her, she would have noticed that he paid her too much attention or that he acted extra awkward, nervous, angry or overly emotional around her.

Leaning back in his chair, Tate frowned at the screen. He felt a hint of guilt at digging into Sabrina's personal life without her permission, but if this led to a promising lead, it would be worth it. He'd learned early as a cop that people put way more of themselves online than they realized. And a lot more of it was discoverable by strangers than they probably wanted.

The missing piece he needed might still be here, somewhere, tangled in a web of loose social connections. He'd keep picking at it when he could, but for now, it confirmed what the Desparre PD had decided from the outset: the key to finding Sabrina's stalker would be tracking him here. Not trying to dig him out of her past.

Woof!

Startled, Tate glanced over and realized Sitka was standing in the doorway. "What is it, Sitka?"

She took a step forward and barked again.

Tate frowned at her, knowing she wanted his attention but not sure why. He glanced at his watch, realizing that he'd lost track of time while he'd been searching. He needed to hurry and get ready for work. Jumping to his feet, he said, "Thanks, Sitka." Then he heard the sound of a car engine starting up.

She hadn't been trying to tell him they were running late for work. She'd been alerting him that someone was here.

Hurrying down the stairs, Tate peered through his peephole out to his drive. The area around his house was partly obscured by woods, but he didn't see anyone.

The car was gone. Except... He squinted at his front stoop, where something had been left.

Sabrina's stalker had obviously identified him and Sitka as allies of Sabrina. Even if he'd figured out where Tate lived, would he dare to come here?

Thinking of the description of Dylan's death from one of the articles about the unsolved murder, Tate ran upstairs, where he kept his gun locked up. Less than a minute later, he was back downstairs, phrases from the article floating through his brain.

...shot in his own home...house ransacked...only suspect is an unidentified person stalking his girlfriend.

Compared to the fingerprint-free notes the stalker left Sabrina, Dylan's murder seemed uncontrolled, full of rage.

"Sitka, move over here," Tate instructed, pointing back toward his kitchen, away from the front door.

She followed his instructions, backing quickly into the kitchen. But she was looking at him like she didn't understand. They weren't working; they were at home. Home was safe and fun.

He didn't think anyone was out there, but he didn't want to take any chances if the stalker had left some kind of explosive device or wanted to lure him closer.

Peering through the door once more, Tate tried to identify the object, but it was right up against the door, mostly out of view. Instead of opening his front door, he told Sitka, "Stay," then ran around to his attached garage at the side and slipped out that way. He didn't see anyone skulking near his house, but then, he'd heard a vehicle drive away. So most likely, the person had dropped something at the door, then run.

Locking the door leading out of his garage behind

him so no one could slip inside while he was investigating, Tate did one more sweep of the area. Then, gun raised, he crept toward the front of his house. He forced his breathing to stay deep and even, the way he would on a run. Years as a police officer helped prevent his senses from dimming into a dangerous tunnel as he scanned his surroundings. Not having a partner at his side made him extra aware of every twig breaking beneath his feet, telegraphing exactly where he was and where he was going.

When he reached the front of his house, he blew out a surprised breath. The item leaning against his front door was a newspaper. Still not putting his weapon away, he moved closer, studying it carefully as he approached. It wasn't a copy of some New York paper like he might have expected if Sabrina's stalker wanted to send him a message, but the *Desparre Daily*.

As he reached the porch, he was sure it wasn't rigged. There was just a sticky note on it that read, *Thought you'd enjoy this!* It was signed by Ariel Clemson, a local reporter he'd helped out once.

Tucking his gun into the waistband of his pajama pants, Tate picked it up and unrolled it. His heart gave a hard thump as he read the headline: *Woman Rescues Police K-9 from Runaway Truck.*

He swore as he stared at the picture underneath the headline. The photo was grainy, taken from way down the street at an awkward angle, but there was Sabrina frantically trying to free Sitka as the truck barreled toward them. And in the background there was Tate racing to help.

Dread sank from his chest, settling low in his gut. The *Desparre Daily* was a tiny local paper, with such low distribution that they were constantly in danger of folding. But they had an online presence.

Were the officers who wanted revenge on him actively searching for him the way he'd been searching for Sabrina's stalker? Would they find this photo and consequently find him?

He flashed back to the warning from his friend who handled Witness Protection relocations: "If we think someone has been exposed, we don't wait and hope. We get them out and start over somewhere else. New name, new backstory and no contact with their last life. I recommend you follow the same protocol."

The dread he felt expanded outward. After promising Sabrina that he'd help her get her life back, would he have to desert her to save his own life?

Chapter 9

As he came back inside his house, Tate was swearing enough to make Sitka stare up at him with concern.

He dropped to his knees in front of her and rested his head on top of hers. Although he'd adopted her and covered her everyday costs, the Desparre PD had paid thousands of dollars for their K-9 training. If he had to leave, they'd probably expect to keep her.

"What am I going to do, Sitka?" he asked softly.

She whined in response, then gave him a sloppy kiss across his chin.

The idea of leaving her behind made his chest tighten painfully. But if he took her with him, would the Desparre PD search for them? Since the safest option would be to leave without any notice or explanation, they probably would. He'd be a lot easier to track with an Alaskan Malamute at his side. Plus, if he was in danger, bringing her along would put her in danger, too.

She might be better off staying here, being placed with another officer. But Tate wasn't sure if anyone else at the station would want to become a K-9 handler. Even if they did, he doubted the station could afford more training. That meant Sitka might be paired with someone who didn't know what they were doing, who inadvertently put her in danger anyway.

He swore again, the anxiety in his gut and chest expanding as his head started to throb. Maybe he'd been a fool to get so comfortable here, to make connections that he'd ultimately have to leave. Maybe Sabrina had the right idea, trying not to get close to anyone.

Squeezing his eyes shut, Tate continued resting his head on Sitka's until she let out another whine. Knowing he was worrying her, Tate lifted his head and stroked her fur until it helped relax him enough to think clearly.

Maybe his old police chief would have an idea. Although he and Keara Hernandez had rarely talked about his past, there had been comfort in knowing he *could* go to her if the burden of his past started to impact his present.

He grabbed his cell phone off the kitchen table, then cringed as he glanced at the time while he made the call. He'd have to hurry if he wanted to be on time for work. But should he even go?

When Keara answered, Tate replied, "Hi, Keara." He cringed at the anxiety in his voice.

"What's going on?"

Trust his old police chief to get right to the point. She'd always been that way, and he was happy to see that trading in her job as police chief in tiny Desparre for a detective job in Anchorage hadn't changed her.

"I think I might have been exposed." He told her about the article.

There was a slight pause, then she asked, "How clear are you in this picture? How much detail does it give about you?"

"I'm in the background. The image is a little blurry, but my face is recognizable. And I'm named in the article—by my fake name, of course. The focus is on Sabrina and how she rescued Sitka. It's a feel-good kind of story."

"Sitka? Really? That's what you named your pup?" Keara demanded to know.

"Yeah."

"Well, I was about to say that the risk was minuscule, but that just increased it a little."

"Because someone searching for the name Tate Donnoly—" his real name "—might think to search with Sitka, Alaska," Tate realized.

"Exactly," Keara affirmed.

He'd chosen the dog's name because it had felt like a way to hold on to some small piece of his past, the place where he'd spent his childhood. It had felt like an inside joke no one knew but him. Now it just seemed reckless.

"Did your old colleagues know you grew up there?"

"I didn't talk to those guys much. But it probably wouldn't be hard to figure out if they asked around."

Keara sighed. "It's still probably a low risk level. I'm sure these guys know you disappeared. How likely would it be for you to get another job as a police officer under an assumed name? But if you want to feel totally safe…"

"I know. But I have a life here."

"I'm sorry I'm not there to help," Keara said.

Tate smiled. "I'm not. I can tell you're enjoying being a detective again. Plus, being in Anchorage must be better than a long-distance relationship." Her boyfriend, Jax, was a Victim Specialist for the FBI in Anchorage.

"Well, there's that," Keara said, and the tone of her voice told him what was coming before she announced, "We got engaged last weekend."

"Congratulations, Keara. That's great." He tried to sound enthusiastic, because he *was* happy for her. If anyone deserved it, it was his old chief, who'd come to Alaska to escape memories of her husband's murder. But he couldn't help the tinge of jealousy that came with it. Would he ever be in a place where he'd feel safe enough to let someone in his life that way?

"Look," Keara said, her voice back to serious. "It's pretty unlikely those officers would dig this article up. But there's no guarantee. If it was me, I'd be cautiously patient. But, Tate, you need to get ready to run. I can try to help you. Jax isn't an investigator, but maybe he can talk to his colleagues at the FBI, help you disappear."

"No," Tate said. Right now, he was using a name illegally. He was acting as a police officer under a false name, too, and if it ever came out that Keara had known it, he wouldn't be the only one facing legal action. "If I need to disappear again, I'll do it alone."

There was another pause, and Tate knew that even though Keara would risk her own life to help him, she had to be relieved he wouldn't ask her to do it. "Keep me informed, if you can."

"I will."

"And, Tate? Watch your back, okay?"

"Yeah," he agreed, saying goodbye. He hoped it wasn't the last time he'd talk to her.

He hoped this newspaper article wasn't the beginning of the end of his time as Tate Emory.

Sabrina stared at the headline of the *Desparre Daily* that Adam Lassiter handed her when she ran into him later that afternoon at the grocery store, dread clenching her chest.

"You're a hero," Adam said, looking surprised that she wasn't excited. "You rescued a K-9."

She offered a wan smile, then glanced at the article. It was written by Ariel Clemson, the woman who'd shown up on her doorstep the other day. Apparently, she'd decided she didn't need Sabrina's input to tell the story.

As she stared at the slightly blurry photo, she remembered a woman standing off in the distance that day, snapping pictures after Sabrina had jumped out of the way of the truck. At the time, she'd thought the woman had simply been a gawker. She'd turned her head, hoping the images wouldn't be plastered on social media.

Looking at Adam, she asked, "How many people get this paper?"

He shrugged, reminding her that he hadn't lived here all that long. "I have no idea. I doubt very many. I mean, I came to Desparre because I figured I was more likely to run into a moose than another person most days." He flushed, then added, "Not that I mind talking to you. I just—"

"I understand," Sabrina said softly. She hadn't shared with anyone that she'd come here after losing a boyfriend to violence, but she'd been tempted to share a sanitized version with Adam because he was clearly so lost since his wife's death a few months earlier.

"Yeah." Adam looked away, probably thinking

she was just trying to be supportive. "Well, anyway, I thought you might want the paper. I already bought it." He hefted his bags of groceries, then nodded goodbye.

After he was gone, Sabrina read the article more closely. It was heavy on drama, a firsthand report of watching the vehicle slide out of control. It detailed Sabrina's "heroic" determination to free the town's new police K-9, a dog Ariel described as "a town treasure."

Sabrina's amusement faded as she got to the section that described the incident as "suspicious," saying police were investigating the possibility that it had been targeted. Ariel hadn't mentioned *who* police thought the attack had targeted, however.

"Sabrina!"

Her head jerked up at the sound of her name, and she tried to smile as Lora hurried toward her.

"I see you read the paper!"

"Yeah." Sabrina folded it into her purse to look at more closely later. "How many people see this paper?"

Lora laughed, a rich, hearty sound that sounded like it belonged to a much bigger woman than the barely five-foot-tall Lora. "I never took you for a fame hound! Sorry to say, not very many. I think our population is *maybe* five hundred. And that's including all the recluses up the mountain who avoid everyone and I doubt are keeping up with local news. But it is online."

Online. Of course it was. Sabrina gritted her teeth to keep from swearing.

"What's wrong? You don't like the fame?" Realization washed over Lora's face, and she lowered her voice. "You're running from something, aren't you, honey? I should have realized. So many of the people in this town are."

She put a hand on Sabrina's upper arm and squeezed lightly. "Don't worry. The *Desparre Daily* website is poorly run. It goes down at least once a month, and you'd really have to search hard to find it. Besides, I'm guessing *Sabrina Jones* isn't your real name?"

Sabrina shrugged, not wanting to lie to one of the few people she'd dared to call a friend since going on the run. But she wasn't about to tell her the truth, either.

Lora squeezed her arm again. "This is a pretty remote spot. Someone would have to be *really* determined to track you down here."

Sabrina mustered up another smile, and this one must have been more convincing, because Lora smiled.

Patting her arm once more, she said, "Try not to worry. No one's going to use that tiny little article to track you down."

Sabrina hoped it was true. Because her stalker might have already found her, but he wasn't the only one she wanted to stay hidden from.

Her family loved her. They hadn't wanted her to go. She'd bet a lot of money that both Conor and her mom searched for her still. And she didn't want them to find her, didn't want them to be in any danger like Dylan. If they did, it would defeat most of the purpose of her leaving.

Glancing up as a young officer whose name she couldn't remember entered the grocery store and gave her a subtle nod, Sabrina hoped the Desparre PD found her stalker soon. Because no matter how small the risk of exposure was with this article, she wasn't willing to take chances with her family's safety.

It was definitely time to figure out a contingency plan.

Chapter 10

A day after her picture had shown up in the paper, people were still yelling out, "Great job!" and "Thanks for saving our K-9!" when she walked around. But the newspaper's online site had been down most of the day, and she hoped it would stay that way. Hoped the only people who'd ever hear about her supposed heroics were Desparre locals.

She'd acted on instinct that day in the park, and she'd do it again. But she could do without the attention.

Stepping out of her old truck, she couldn't help but glance around for the man who'd put her in the paper. Whoever he was, he wasn't obviously staring. Hopefully today they'd identify him.

She walked into the police station and Officer Nate Dreymond rose from the front desk and opened the door to let her into the area marked *Police Only*.

"Good luck," he told her.

"Thanks," she said as she walked through and immediately spotted Tate and Sitka.

Tate smiled at her, a soft smile that somehow managed to be perfectly professional but still completely directed at her.

It made her pulse pick up, and her feet followed suit. When she reached his side across the open-concept space a minute later, he asked, "What's it like being a local hero?" But something in his eyes told her the newspaper article bothered him as much as it did her.

"You saw that?"

Woof! Sitka contributed.

The dog's tail thumped the floor when Sabrina looked at her, and Sabrina grinned and pet her.

"The reporter left a copy on my doorstep. I forgot that she lived near me. I helped her when she thought someone was sneaking around her house last year and mentioned that I lived close in case she was in trouble. Apparently, she remembered."

Sabrina felt a brief, ridiculous spurt of jealousy that she pushed aside. "So you think we can find this guy today?" She heard the hopeful note in her voice and realized that it felt different than it had in a long time.

The fact that the stalker hadn't left her a note or tried anything else since he'd sent that truck speeding toward them three days ago made her wonder if he'd noticed that police were always around and he'd fled. For once, she prayed he hadn't, prayed he'd stick around long enough to get caught.

"I'm ready to look at those pictures."

Tate had called her that morning, letting her know the officers who'd been watching over her the past couple of days while she walked around town had managed to get pictures of men who might be paying too much attention. She'd been shocked; she hadn't noticed any of the officers taking pictures. But then she'd felt a surge of hope. Maybe she'd recognize someone. Maybe this two-year-long nightmare would actually have an end.

"Let's do it, then," Tate said, leading her into a conference room with a long table where the chief of police was waiting.

Sitka followed, too, pushing past her to stand next to Tate at the far end of the table.

The police chief stood. "How are you feeling, Sabrina?"

She gave a smile. "Hopeful."

Chief Griffith smiled back at her. "Me, too. My officers got a lot of pictures." At the look she must have given him, he laughed and said, "Don't worry. We didn't notice tons of people watching you. But someone skilled who has practice stalking gets good at blending in, at appearing like he's *not* watching you. We took pictures of anyone around you."

"Oh." She heard the surprise in her voice. Police in New York had tried hard to locate and catch her stalker. She knew they had. But this was a whole different level.

The same hope sparked again, a little stronger this time, as she took a seat where the chief indicated. On the table in front of her was a folder.

"Take a look at the pictures in there," Chief Griffith said. "We printed them out and blew them up to make it easier. Take as much time as you want. You don't need to be certain. If you think you recognize anyone from New York or if you've seen anyone in places you wouldn't expect—near your house or around you more than once—let us know. It might just be that we're a small town, but we'd rather check it out. Even if you're just getting a weird vibe from someone, point him out. Okay?"

She nodded, opening the folder as Tate sat next to her and Sitka pushed her way between the chairs to sit beside her, too.

Sabrina smiled at her and paused to pet the sweet dog. "Thanks, Sitka," she whispered. It might have been her imagination, but it felt like the dog knew she was nervous and was trying to support her.

Then she started flipping through the photos. She stopped periodically to study some more closely, but she didn't remember any of the people in them hanging around her in Desparre. And she definitely didn't remember any of them from New York.

She paused on an image from two days ago, when she'd been heading toward the park. One of the photos had captured the man she'd seen standing beside a car parked right near where Talise's had been before it came racing toward Sitka. Even in the photo, the way he was looking toward her made her shiver. Just like it had when she'd first seen it, his mustache seemed out of place on his face, as if it was some kind of disguise. She pointed at him and looked over at Tate, then Chief Griffith.

Tate shook his head. "That's Shawn. I don't remember his last name, but he lives one town over, in Luna, and has for at least four years. He comes into Desparre pretty regularly. He's kind of antisocial, but there's no way he was stalking you in New York two years ago."

Her shoulders dropped. Was this all for nothing?

She flipped to the next photo, and her anxiety

sparked again as she looked past herself, Lora and Adam talking, to a guy in the background watching them from near the gazebo. "What about this guy? I thought he might have taken a picture of me that day."

Tate frowned at the photo, leaning closer and giving her a whiff of the same sandalwood scent she'd noticed the day he'd come to her house to stop her from leaving Desparre. It was a scent she'd started to associate entirely with him, a scent that made her want to breathe more deeply.

"I don't know this guy." He looked behind him. "Chief?"

Sabrina passed the picture over and then watched as the police chief studied it carefully and finally shook his head. "No. And it does look like he might be trying to hide. I'll check with the other officers and see if anyone else recognizes him."

Was this him? Hope started to build again, with whiplash intensity, and Sabrina met Tate's gaze, knowing that hope was reflected in her eyes.

As he gazed back at her, the rest of the room, the chief, the pictures all seemed to fade into the background. All she could focus on was Tate, on the sharp angles of his face and the fullness of his lips. On the way his dark hair swept over his forehead and the hypnotizing deep brown of his eyes. Her breathing went shallow as a familiar spark ignited inside her, one she'd been feeling more and more often when she was around him. The way his gaze seemed to intensify on her said he felt it, too.

But if the man in the picture *was* her stalker and they could finally end this threat, she'd be leaving. Trying to begin a long-distance relationship all the way from

New York while she was trying to reintegrate into her old life wasn't practical, even if Tate was interested. If they finally found her stalker, she'd never get the chance to see if her growing interest in Tate could have become something.

"Does anyone recognize this man?" Tate asked, holding up the photo Sabrina had identified earlier. She'd gone home, and Tate had felt a sudden pull to go with her, to stay beside her, but he had hours of work left today.

The few other officers inside the police station stopped their work and came to look.

Veteran officer Charlie Quinn, a gruff guy who looked a lot older than his forty-two years, squinted at it for a long moment, then finally shook his head. "He looks vaguely familiar, but I don't know him. If he's a local, he must not come around town much."

It was a problem they'd run into before in investigations. Desparre was a small town in terms of population, but large when it came to acreage. So, while locals tended to recognize each other, if someone wanted to hide, they definitely could. In fact, one of Tate's earliest cases on the Desparre PD had involved a couple of kidnappers who'd hidden out in the mountains for years without anyone realizing.

Charlie's partner, Max Becker, pushed his way through. "Let me see."

Max was a few years older than Tate and had been on the force a few years longer. He was brash and seemed to think there was no space in a professional setting for friendships, but he got the job done.

He stared at the picture for less time than Charlie had, then shook his head, too. "Nah, I don't know him."

"Nate?" Tate called into the front of the station.

The youngest officer on the force, who'd recently turned twenty, hurried into the bullpen.

"You recognize this guy?" Tate asked hopefully. Nate might have been relatively new to the force, but he'd lived in Desparre all his life.

Nate's lips pursed as he leaned close to the photo, making Max snicker. "Try not to go cross-eyed."

Ignoring him, Nate hedged. "Maybe. He does look a little familiar, but I don't think he's local." Straightening, he asked, "You think this is Sabrina's stalker?"

"Maybe. Any idea when you might have first seen him?"

Nate frowned, creating lines across his pale, freckled forehead. "Not that long ago, actually. Maybe a month or two?"

"You ready to go?" Lorenzo Riera called to Nate as he came into the bullpen.

"Give me a few minutes," Nate said. "I need to find Sam to cover the front desk." He left the bullpen as Lorenzo strode quickly toward Tate.

"What are you all looking at?"

Tate showed Lorenzo the photo and pointed to the guy in the background, skulking near the gazebo. "You know him?"

"This guy?" Lorenzo snorted. "Yeah."

Tate's interest perked at the derision in Lorenzo's voice. "How? Who is he?"

"I don't know his name. But about a month and a half ago, I was at the park with my two youngest kids.

You know Julie Waterman? Paul and Frannie's oldest? She's about to start her first year of college, I think."

Tate nodded. The Watermans had moved to Desparre long before he'd arrived, looking for a different lifestyle than they'd had back in Tulsa.

"Well, like most of the locals, she knows I'm a cop. She came over and told me this guy was creeping her out. Said he'd been watching her all afternoon."

Tate frowned. Was that why Sabrina hadn't gotten a note until recently? Because her stalker had been busy fixating on someone else for a while? It seemed odd that he'd track her all the way to Alaska and then get distracted, but maybe a month and a half ago, he'd known Sabrina was in Desparre but hadn't located her yet. Or maybe he was the kind of creep who always harassed women.

"So I went over to talk to him," Lorenzo continued. "I wasn't on duty, but I let him know I was a cop, tried to get his info. He acted like he didn't have ID on him and gave me a name I looked up later, but it was fake. Claimed he wasn't following anyone, but he was definitely aggravated. He left the park, but a few days later, I spotted him in his truck. I followed him just to see what he was up to, and he headed into the mountain. I lost him there, but I suspect he lives up that way."

"We need to find this guy, see how long he's been in town," Tate said. "See if he's ever lived in New York."

"You really think he's Sabrina's stalker?"

"Maybe. You see him watching Sabrina in this picture. She thinks he took a picture of her, too."

Lorenzo nodded, squinting at the picture again. "Could be he's just a garden-variety jerk and he comes to the park to stare at the women."

"Maybe," Tate agreed. "But he's the best lead we've got right now."

Tate was always careful not to get too excited about leads that could be coincidence because they could blind you to other options. But something about the way the guy was looking at Sabrina made all of Tate's protective instincts flare to life. His gut was telling him this was the guy.

Now they just needed to find him.

"Hey, Tate!" Nate said, rushing back into the room, wearing a big grin. "Guess what?"

Lorenzo smiled at his rookie partner, obviously amused at his enthusiasm.

"What?" Tate asked, a bad feeling forming that he couldn't explain.

"You and Sitka are famous."

The bad feeling turned into dread. "Why?"

Nate's brow furrowed. "What, you don't want to be famous? You're the only one. Anyway, the local story that Ariel Clemson wrote got picked up by national news!"

From what seemed like far away, Tate heard Lorenzo asking, "You okay, man?"

He couldn't seem to get it together enough to answer. Not only his first name but a picture of him was splashed across the national news.

He needed to drive home, take off his uniform and leave town now.

As the thought formed, his cell phone rang. He glanced at the screen. Keara.

No doubt she'd seen the story, too. There shouldn't be any hesitation now. He needed to go.

But he loved the life he'd built in Desparre. And even though the other officers were committed to Sabrina, he'd made her a promise. Besides, against all his instincts, he'd started to fall for her.

Tucking the phone back into his pocket and ignoring what he knew would be Keara's advice to run, Tate prayed the wrong people wouldn't see the story.

Because he needed to stay long enough to help Sabrina.

Chapter 11

It had been two days since the small heartwarming story Ariel Clemson had penned for the *Desparre Daily* had gone national. Two days without anyone showing up and trying to kill Tate. Two days without him receiving any death threats.

Maybe he'd gotten lucky.

The day after the story was picked up nationally, it was bumped out of the spotlight by a multistate manhunt for a group of escaped convicts. That story was still hogging the media's attention, enough so that Ariel approached him as he and Sitka walked downtown.

She had a pout firmly in place as she said, "I thought that story was going to be my big break."

"You'll get there," he assured her. He tried to appear sympathetic, though all he felt was relief that the story had been buried. Ariel didn't seem to notice that his concern was fake. She also didn't seem to notice that he couldn't stop his gaze from wandering away from her to study everyone around them. To see if he recognized someone from his past.

She shrugged and muttered, "I hope so," and then finally headed off, leaving him and Sitka alone.

With her gone, Tate gave in to his desire to scan his surroundings again. The woods up ahead, where Sabrina's stalker might have disappeared after sending Talise's car racing toward Sitka, in particular kept grabbing his attention. Probably because of the way he'd been ambushed on a trail near the woods back in Boston.

Escaping that attempt on his life had been a result of his quick thinking and quick action. But it had also been partly luck. He couldn't help but wonder when his luck was going to run out.

In the news picture he was in the background, he reminded himself. Sabrina and Sitka had been the focus. Plus, the story didn't have his real last name. Even if Kevin and Paul were searching for him, how likely was it that they'd have set up alerts for just his first name? And he doubted they regularly read feel-good stories.

Still, as his cell phone rang yet again, it amped up Tate's anxiety even more. He felt guilty about not returning Keara's calls, but he didn't want to pick up while he was on patrol.

Sitka tilted her head, watching him as she strode alongside him. Her steady attention told him she knew something was wrong.

"It will all work out," he told her, hoping he was right. Every time he thought about leaving Desparre, the same no-win choice kept haunting him: Did he bring Sitka or did he leave her behind?

As if she could read his thoughts, she whined, high-pitched and sustained, until he pet her.

"I'm just trying to do the best thing for you," he said softly. Stroking her fur calmed his heart rate and seemed to relax her, too.

Ever since the incident with Talise's truck, he'd stopped using a leash with her in town. She didn't need one anyway, and if any locals had been wary of her before, Ariel's story seemed to have given them all a soft spot for their new police K-9.

Straightening, he headed for the park. He was hoping his luck would hold and he'd see the guy who Sabrina had identified in the photo, since it seemed he liked to hang out there. So far, police hadn't been able to positively identify him. Even quietly asking longtime locals hadn't yielded any results beyond "He looks familiar" or "He might live up the mountain" or "I think he moved here in the past couple of months."

When Tate reached the park, a group of kids ran over from the swings and started petting Sitka. His dog promptly sat, wagged her tail and tipped her head back, tongue lolling.

Tate held in a smile and resisted the urge to explain to the kids that he and Sitka were on duty. His dog was wearing her thick collar that identified her as a police K-9, but she wasn't wearing the dark vest that immediately screamed *Dog at Work*.

"How old is she?" one of the kids asked.

"Sitka is a year old," he told them. "She's an Alaskan Malamute. Did you know that this kind of dog got its start as an arctic sled dog?"

"Oh, cool," one of the other kids said.

"And feel her fur," he advised as Sitka's tail thumped harder, making the youngest of the kids laugh. "It's a double coat, and it's actually waterproof."

From the benches, several of their parents watched with amusement as Tate shared details about how Sitka worked as a police K-9.

"She can even find people who get lost," Tate continued, "by tracking them with her nose. It—"

Movement at the edge of his line of vision caught his attention, and Tate did a double take as he spotted the man from the picture, back behind the gazebo. When his gaze met Tate's, he slid his phone into his pocket and ran toward the street.

"Sitka, come on!" Tate called, as he pivoted and raced after the man.

Behind him, he could hear the parents calling their kids to get them out of Sitka's way.

Tate didn't wait for Sitka to break free of the kids. He just gritted his teeth and ran onto the street, determined not to let the guy escape.

Instead of taking a sharp turn into the woods as Tate had expected, the guy ran down a perpendicular street.

"Police!" Tate yelled after him. "Stop!"

The guy glanced back, giving Tate a better look at a scowling, scared expression and a lot more muscle than had been evident in the photo. Since that picture had been taken, the guy had grown a short beard, as if he knew someone was looking for him.

Instead of heeding the directive, he ran even faster, and Tate swore at the speed such a muscle-bound guy should have had trouble achieving.

Yanking his radio off his duty belt, Tate panted, "I

spotted the guy from the photo. He just took off on foot down Fleming Street. I'm in pursuit."

"Backup is on the way," Officer Sam Jennings returned immediately.

Behind him, the familiar sound of Sitka's footsteps were gaining, but Tate didn't slow to wait for her.

Ahead of him, the guy made a quick turn around the corner onto a street that housed nothing but a big, deserted warehouse. It was an eyesore in Desparre's otherwise nicely kept downtown, and it seemed like a strange spot to try and hide. Unless maybe he'd left a vehicle this way?

Tate pushed himself harder, pivoting onto the street fast.

He realized his mistake before he'd finished rounding the blind corner. But it was already too late.

The guy had stopped, hidden up against the massive warehouse. He stepped forward just as Tate turned into view, lifted a huge, tattooed arm and clotheslined Tate.

Tate's feet went out from under him, and then he slammed into the dirt and pebbled ground. The impact stole his breath, and his vision went black.

Chapter 12

Tate fought his way out of the darkness, blinking his vision clear only to see the guy's massive fist heading toward his face.

Swallowing back nausea, Tate tried to roll out of the way.

Before he could, Sitka flew around the corner and leaped on the guy at a speed that dropped him to the ground.

As he flailed, yelled and swung those fists at Sitka's unprotected back, she bit down on his arm and shook her head.

He screamed louder and curled inward, then his feet rose like he was readying to kick her.

Shoving himself to a partly raised position, Tate pivoted and then knelt on top of the guy's legs, trapping them in place. "Let go, Sitka!" When Sitka dropped the guy's arm, Tate fought to flip him to his stomach.

The guy bucked and yanked an arm free, raising it to take a swing.

Then Sitka stepped closer and let out a deep growl.

The guy froze, panic in his suddenly wide eyes, and Tate didn't waste any time. He yanked the guy over until his face was pressed against the dirt road and wrenched his arms up behind him. As Tate snapped on the cuffs, he asked, "Sitka, you okay?"

Woof!

It was part of her training to take down a suspect this way, but until now, she'd only done it in practice. At the training facility, the trainers, wearing protective gear, had shaken their arms and lifted her off the ground, teaching her to hang on through anything. They made loud noises next to her ears, lightly hit her back, and still she'd held tight.

Even though Tate had been proud of her, he'd hated seeing her get yanked around. Today had been worse. But judging by the tail wagging as she stood beside him, alert and ready to jump in again, she really was okay.

As his adrenaline calmed, Tate heard pounding feet heading toward them. "Back here!" he called.

"You good?" Officer Riera yelled back.

"All good!"

Lorenzo and Nate rounded the corner. The veteran was breathing hard as he leaned over and asked the guy, "You have anything on you that can stick me? Any needles or a knife?"

The guy on the ground forced his head to the side so he could look up at the five-foot-six Latino with muscles that rivaled his. He scowled, then shook his head.

"Rook?" Lorenzo used the nickname for the partner who hadn't been a true rookie in several months, since he'd marked a year on the force. "You want to check him?"

Lorenzo helped Tate pull the guy to his feet, and they watched as Nate patted him down. A minute later, he handed Tate a wallet and a cell phone.

Scowling at the guy who might have gotten his weapon if Sitka hadn't leaped in at the right moment, Tate opened the wallet and pulled out a driver's license. "Mario McKeever." His scowl deepened as he saw the state. "From New York."

"Let's get him processed," Lorenzo suggested, taking the guy by the crook of the arm as if he worried Tate would start an interrogation out in the street.

This was Sabrina's stalker. A good four inches shorter than Tate's six feet, with flexing biceps that suggested he spent a lot of time at the gym, he wore a snarl that made him look even more intimidating. His face wasn't all that memorable, with small features partly hidden by a thick layer of scruff. Still, now that Tate had a better view than the grainy picture they'd taken in the park, he knew for sure. He didn't recognize Mario from the social-media images he'd been poring over. How far on the outskirts of Sabrina's life had he been?

As Lorenzo and Tate led the suspect around the corner and toward the police station, with Nate and Sitka trailing slightly behind, Tate tried to keep his mouth shut. It was something he was good at; more than once, his old chief had asked him to stand in the room or help out with an interrogation of a challenging suspect because Tate wouldn't lose his cool.

But right now, thinking of the fear on Sabrina's face as she'd been trying to slip away at dawn, he couldn't help himself. "Why can't you just *leave her alone?*"

"Tate," Lorenzo warned.

Tate took a deep breath, then clamped his jaw shut.

Mario looked back and forth between them, then snapped, "I don't know what you're talking about, man. I ran because you and your attack dog started chasing me for no reason. You let me go now and I won't sue you. Look at my arm!"

He tried to pull it forward, but between the cuffs and Lorenzo's grip, he couldn't. He didn't need to move it for Tate to see the damage. Mario's forearm was bleeding, the bite wounds obvious.

Instead of telling him that Sitka wouldn't have knocked him down if he hadn't been a threat, Tate followed protocol this time and didn't engage. He managed to keep his silence all the way back to the station, where the new police chief was waiting.

"Let's get him fingerprinted," Chief Griffith said.

Mario jerked back so quickly that Tate and the chief shared a look as Lorenzo yanked him forward again. The guy had a record.

"I need a doctor," Mario insisted, his eyes wide as he kept trying to pull away from Lorenzo.

"No problem," the chief said calmly. "We're going to get you some first aid right now, and then we'll take you to the hospital."

Tate ground his teeth together, trying to hold in his frustration. It was protocol. And with the guy in custody, Sabrina was out of danger. But he wanted more answers now—like how Mario had managed to track her all the way from New York.

The guy relaxed as another officer came in, snapped on a pair of gloves and wrapped up the wound. Then the chief took Mario's arm, pulling him farther into the station.

"What are you doing?" Mario demanded. "I've got rights! I want to see a doctor."

"And we're taking you to one," the chief replied. "But first we're going to have to get your prints."

Mario planted his feet, and his muscles bulged as he resisted the chief's tugs.

Showing a lot more calm than Tate felt, the chief just smiled and nodded at Officer Max Becker, who grinned and came over with the portable fingerprint system, pressing the suspect's thumb against it before he knew what was happening.

"Hey!" Mario yelled, yanking his hand away.

"Got it," Max said, backing away from Mario's swinging arms.

Mario's snarl returned, and every officer in the front of the station tensed at once, ready to react to an attack.

His gaze swept them, then he seemed to realize he was outmanned, and his head fell forward. The chief pulled him toward processing.

"Mario McKeever," Max announced. "We've got two stalking charges within the past decade. Resulted in a short stint in jail and a couple of restraining orders. And—" Max snorted as he looked back at Mario "—the reason he ran. He's wanted in a sexual-assault case back in New York."

"From when?" Tate asked.

"Four months ago."

"And then he came here," Tate said. "Lucky coincidence, or did he already know Sabrina was here?"

Mario twisted in the chief's grip. "I don't know a Sabrina. And I ran because I was framed."

He continued to protest as the chief frowned and called to Lorenzo. "Can you and Nate manage the hospital transport?"

"Sure," Lorenzo said, and the chief turned to Tate.

"Step outside with me."

As soon as they were out the door, Tate insisted, "I can go along. I'll be careful what I ask."

"Tate, it's not him," the chief said.

"What do you mean?"

"This isn't Sabrina's stalker."

"Come on," Tate insisted. "He was taking pictures of her. He's got a history of stalking. And he's from New York!"

"Coincidences, but not proof. This guy has a known stalking problem, and Sabrina isn't the only woman here he's taken pictures of." Before Tate could continue arguing, the chief said, "He's in the national database. He's wanted in New York. That means he would have popped for police in the murder of Dylan Westwood. But he didn't."

Tate swore under his breath. The chief was right. It was someone else's prints that had shown up in Sabrina's boyfriend's house. Someone without a record.

Was he wrong? Was Mario just a general creep and not specifically the creep harassing Sabrina?

What about the New York connection? He must have come here within the past few months—and then Sabrina's stalker had suddenly restarted contact. Was it all coincidence?

"Maybe Mario hired someone to make the hit on Westwood. Or maybe the murder wasn't actually committed by her stalker," Tate said. "Maybe he just capitalized on it, sent that note to Sabrina to make her think he had more power than he actually did."

The chief nodded slowly. "Yeah, both of those things are possible. We'll question Mario thoroughly. In the meantime, you and Sitka should take the rest of the day. Fill out your incident report and then head home. Take a break and get your head clear. We'll update you."

Tate shook his head, shocked that the chief thought he wasn't fit to be working. "Chief—"

"You're too invested. And while I'm not worried about you crossing a line, I also know Lorenzo and Nate can get the job done. I'll be watching the interrogation, too. But you were knocked to the ground today, and technically, you need to get checked out. I'll trust you to handle that. But I don't want you back on duty for twenty-four hours. Rest, have a doctor look at you, and I'll update you. Okay?"

Frowning, Tate nodded. It *was* protocol, especially since the world had gone black on him when he hit the ground. The chief didn't know that, but he was being cautious.

Even though Tate wanted to be the one questioning Mario, the closest hospital was one town over. That meant going up and down a mountain, an hour each way. And that didn't include time spent being checked out by a doctor.

That was time Tate could use to return to Sabrina's social media, see if he could find Mario McKeever somewhere on the platforms.

"Okay," he agreed.

The chief's eyes narrowed slightly at his ready agreement, but he didn't say anything as Tate opened the door to the station and called Sitka.

She came bounding out, and he led her to his personal vehicle. As he opened the door for her, she looked up at him questioningly, as if to ask *Why aren't we staying at work?*

"We have some things to do at home," he told her, as Lorenzo and Nate exited the police station and pulled Mario toward their police vehicle.

The criminal's eyes met his briefly, and then he scowled and looked away.

If this guy was Sabrina's stalker, Tate vowed to find the connection before Mario was back at the station for his interrogation.

But two hours later, as Tate checked the time yet again and Sitka whined at his feet, he had nothing. He'd been following every thread he could find from Sabrina's social media, through her brother, through friends and even friends of friends. He'd blown images up threefold, staring into the background, searching for Mario's unremarkable face or his nasty sneer.

How much time did he have left before Lorenzo and Nate brought Mario back to the station for questioning? Finding a link between Mario and Sabrina that they could show the suspect early in the process was likely to be far more effective than if they did it later, after he'd lawyered up and some of the initial shock of being caught had faded.

Rubbing a hand over his head, which was throbbing from two hours of staring at his computer screen and the bump to the back of his head earlier, Tate clicked back to one of Sabrina's friends who posted the most publicly available pictures. She and Sabrina didn't appear to be especially close, but he'd found Sabrina in the background of several of her older pictures. Maybe he needed to go back even further. Maybe Mario had fixated on her long before he'd started writing to her.

He opened a photo from three years ago on the woman's feed and found Sabrina, laughing in the background. The lighting was crap, the surroundings some dimly lit bar. She was surrounded by a couple of people he recognized from hours of looking through feeds as work colleagues. Beyond that were more people who seemed to be part of the same crowd.

His shoulders dropped. It had seemed like a real long shot, but he was still disappointed that none of them were Mario McKeever.

Then his pulse shot up, and he leaned in close to the screen as a familiar face in the background caught his attention.

Beside him, Sitka got to her feet, whining as she caught his mood.

"No way," he muttered, blowing the picture up. It got grainier as the size increased, but he wasn't wrong. The guy standing two rows behind Sabrina—maybe part of the group, maybe not—had his gaze solidly fixed on her.

It wasn't Mario McKeever. It was worse.

It was a man Sabrina trusted, one of the few people in Desparre she seemed to consider a friend. It was a man who'd been in the forefront of the photo in the park with Mario. He'd been talking to Sabrina, completely overlooked as a threat because he'd supposedly moved here after his wife had died.

It was Adam Lassiter.

Chapter 13

"Adam." Sabrina heard the surprise in her own voice as she opened the door to her cabin.

Her friend was standing on the front stoop slightly hunched forward, hands shoved in his pockets. "Hey, Sabrina. I'm sorry to stop by unannounced, but I…" He blew out a breath, then gave a self-conscious smile. "I just needed a friend, and since you lived kind of nearby…"

Sabrina glanced around at the vast expanse of woods surrounding her cabin, the enclosure that had felt like a protective barrier when she'd first arrived. Now it felt like a place for a stalker to hide. Even standing in her open doorway felt too exposed.

She hadn't invited anyone except Tate and Sitka inside in two long years. Adam might be her friend, but the idea of letting anyone too close still made anxiety knot her stomach.

"I should have called," Adam said, stepping back. "It's just—I didn't have your number. But Lora told me where you lived, and I was passing near here, so I thought maybe… I'm sorry."

Her gaze snapped back up to him. They didn't really have the sort of friendship where you just showed up unannounced. She wasn't even sure how Lora had known where she lived to be able to tell him, but it didn't really surprise her that she knew it. Lora seemed to know everything about everyone.

As her attention refocused on Adam instead of the vast expanses where someone could be hiding behind him, she realized he looked worse than usual. There were deep circles under his eyes, as if he hadn't been sleeping. A downward tilt to his mouth as if he'd been frowning all day.

"I'm sorry," she told Adam, trying to shake off her unease. She almost hadn't opened the door, even after seeing through the peephole that it was just him. "It's been a tough week."

"For me, too." His words were soft as his gaze lifted from the ground back up to her. "Today would have been my wife's birthday." He took another step backward, shaking his head, his back and shoulders sloped inward. "I was going to go for a walk, clear my head. And then I realized I didn't want to be all alone. But it's an imposition. I'm sorry. I—"

"No," Sabrina cut him off as guilt bubbled up that she'd made him feel like he couldn't reach out to her.

In the few months she'd tried to venture out more, Adam and Lora had made her feel like she could have friends here. Even if she couldn't tell them the truth about who she was, she'd always thought Adam had sensed she'd also experienced a recent loss. It was in the way his gaze sometimes cut to her when he mentioned his grief, as if he expected her to share her own loss.

She never had. She'd been tempted once or twice to talk about it, to be vague enough that she wouldn't get tripped up on her real past. But something had always stopped her, a voice in the back of her head that sounded like the PI saying not to take any risks she might regret. Not to give in to the desire for connection at the expense of safety.

So right now, instead of inviting him inside, she grabbed her keys off the table in her entryway and stepped outside. Her fingers fluttered briefly up to the emergency button hidden underneath her T-shirt as she locked the door behind her. Then she mustered up a smile and said, "Lead the way."

An answering smile trembled on his face, but it didn't quite reach his eyes. "Thanks."

He walked down her drive, out to the dirt road. Then, instead of heading toward town, he moved in the other direction, where the woods started slowly thinning out as the road tilted upward. "There's a great view about a mile from here. A good place to clear your head," he said, keeping a brisk pace.

He was about four inches taller than her and Sabrina had to increase her pace to keep up with his long strides. She struggled with the appropriate thing to say, but words evaded her. She had no idea how his wife had passed, but she was pretty sure he was only a few years older than her, in his early to midthirties. Young to have lost a spouse.

He was probably here because he thought she knew that same kind of grief. But although the horror of

Dylan's death would probably always be with her, it was different. They'd only been dating for three months before he was murdered. It had been the beginning of something, but where it would lead she'd never know. She couldn't begin to guess the grief he was experiencing.

He kept hurrying along, slightly ahead of her, and unease pricked as he moved off the road and onto a path with a steeper incline. Her thoughts went immediately to the bear and cubs Tate and Sitka had run into behind her house.

"Adam?" she huffed. She'd been in good shape back in New York, often choosing a long walk instead of public transportation. But since going into hiding, she'd been afraid to go running alone. She always felt safer behind the locked door of a vehicle or a hotel room.

He glanced back at her, slowing slightly. "Sorry. I hike a lot."

"No, it's not that. There are bears in the woods."

He laughed, although it sounded a little forced. "Nah. I've come this way plenty of times. We'll be fine. Trust me, the view will be worth it. You wouldn't think so, but there's a big drop-off this way. It's an amazing place to look out onto the valley below. You just can't get too close to the edge." He laughed again, a little chortle that sounded like he was trying too hard to be cheerful for her sake. "And anyway, I have bear spray." He patted the pocket of his cargo pants as he kept moving up the path.

Sabrina hesitated, glancing back down the empty road, then into the forest. The trees were thinner here than by her house, but that didn't mean it wasn't a great place for bears to wander.

Up ahead, Adam was still pressing forward, not realizing she wasn't right behind him. Since they'd left her house, he hadn't said a word about his wife. Maybe he'd just needed silent, understanding company. Or maybe he wanted to wait until they reached this peaceful view he'd mentioned. But something about the way he'd shown up and then just plowed forward was making discomfort creep in.

Was she being paranoid? Adam was her friend. One of her only friends.

But she'd learned a long time ago that her stalker wasn't the only threat. That sometimes, danger came in the guise of a friend. Like the coworker who'd walked her out to her car, joking about women sticking together, then nodded at someone hiding in the shadows. That guy had rushed for her, only charging the other way when one of the cooks happened to pop open the back door for a smoke. She'd left that place behind like so many others, but she thought she'd carried the lesson with her.

Sabrina's hand reached for the alert button without conscious intent.

Then, Adam glanced back and called, "Come on!"

At some point, she had to be able to trust her own judgment again. At some point, her life couldn't be all about fear.

She lowered her hand, hurrying to catch up.

Yes, her stalker was here. But so was Tate, who'd dedicated himself to helping her, who represented a possibility even greater. So were Adam and Lora, people who'd befriended her despite how closed off she was. Who'd given her a chance when they could have walked away. Maybe she needed to do the same.

The path Adam had chosen was thin, not enough

room for them to walk side by side even if she could keep up with his pace. The edges of wispy pine trees brushed her arms as she alternated between walking and a semijog. Her breath came in uneven puffs that reminded her how long it had been since she'd felt comfortable going anywhere. The reminder made anger knot in her chest, but it also made the view that appeared as they crested the hill more spectacular.

Adam was right. It was like the forest suddenly dropped away. Way down below was a green valley, spotted with trees. In the middle, she could see a group of animals.

Stepping up beside him at the edge, she glanced briefly his way, feeling a smile break free. An image of his expression, strangely pensive, flickered in the edge of her vision as she moved a little closer to the edge, straining to see. "Moose?"

"Yeah."

His voice was closer than she'd expected, and as she twisted toward him in surprise, she felt something shove against her back, right under her shoulder blade.

Her arms jolted up, a desperate attempt at regaining her balance as her stomach dropped and the valley below seemed to reach up toward her.

Then Adam's arm clamped around her biceps, and he yanked her backward.

Breathing hard, Sabrina stared at him, then glanced behind her. Had she imagined a push? Had something fallen from a tree?

Her arm twitched under his grasp, fear squirming in her belly.

Letting go, Adam stepped slightly away. "Sorry. Did I scare you? You looked like you were slipping. I didn't mean to grab you so hard. I thought you were going to fall."

"No, that's—" The spot beneath her shoulder blade prickled with the feel of that phantom force. Had she imagined it? Had she just slipped?

She glanced down at the loose pebbles where she'd been standing, then back up at Adam.

There was something different in his eyes, hurt that she'd misinterpreted his help. Before she could say anything, he took another step backward.

"Maybe we should head back," he suggested. He didn't wait for her to answer, just moved away from her, down the path.

With one last glance around, Sabrina hurried after him.

Chapter 14

"Sabrina, damn it, call me back!"

Tate hung up the phone and grabbed his keys. "Come on, Sitka."

She leaped to her feet, tail wagging as she chased him down the stairs and out to the truck.

His mood was decidedly less jolly, a dread in his gut that no amount of telling himself he was overreacting would calm. He'd called Sabrina three times in a row before leaving a voice mail. He had no idea how close she kept her cell phone. Maybe she was in the shower, perfectly fine but unable to hear the ringing. Or maybe she was in town, chatting away with Talise in the grocery store, her phone tucked in her pocket, ringing unheard underneath Talise's nonstop stories.

"Let's just check," he muttered, opening the door for Sitka, then hopping up into the cab beside her. Then they were taking a route that had become familiar over the past week, out to Sabrina's cabin.

As he drove, his gaze swept the narrow road, bracketed by beautiful old trees, seeing it all in a new way. Sabrina's cabin was too isolated. Even with an alert button connecting her directly to the police, he'd seen firsthand what the vast distances out here could mean when responding to an emergency call.

He clenched the wheel tighter, pressing down on the gas as Sitka hunched low in the passenger seat. He should have insisted that Sabrina move into town and stay at the hotel until they'd found her stalker. Better yet, he should have offered her his pullout couch and convinced his colleagues to trade off shifts at his house watching her.

It was impractical. Impossible to sustain. But right now, knowing that Adam Lassiter had once lived in New York City, had once been photographed staring at Sabrina from afar, made panic and guilt tense his entire body.

They'd known he was close. They'd known he was escalating.

But they'd never suspected it was someone Sabrina trusted, someone she called a friend. What if they'd miscalculated how much time they had to stop him before Sabrina paid the price?

Sitka whined, catching his anxiety, and Tate gave her a quick pet meant to reassure. She just whined again, softer, as she hunched lower on the seat.

When he finally pulled up to the cabin, he released a deep, relieved breath. Sabrina's car was in the drive. She was home. Even though he'd gotten the impression she'd never let anyone inside besides him, he was happy not to see any other vehicle in the drive.

Parking behind her, he stepped out, then turned back to whistle for Sitka.

She was already leaping out of the truck and bounding toward the front door.

Tate slammed the truck door and hurried after her. Then he knocked on Sabrina's door loudly, calling out, "Sabrina? It's Tate. Are you home? I need to talk to you."

There was no answer.

Unease settled in his chest, and his hand dropped automatically to where he normally kept his duty belt and his weapon. But he'd run out of the house so quickly, he hadn't even thought about snapping it back on.

Stepping off the porch, he followed the same path along the side of her house that Sitka had taken when she'd tracked a scent. Instead of moving into the woods, he crept along the edge of Sabrina's house.

Sitka kept pace with him. Her nose nudged his leg hard every few steps, like she was demanding an answer about what they were doing.

"We're looking for Sabrina," he told her softly. If someone was inside with her, preventing her from answering, they'd know Tate was here. But he didn't want to advertise his location.

He was probably being paranoid, and she was simply wearing headphones or had a dead battery in her cell phone. But he couldn't take any chances.

Knowing how safety-conscious she was, he didn't expect to find an open window, but he hoped to at least find one that would give him a view inside. The curtains were all down, but on the far side of the cabin, he discovered one of the windows was old. It would be easy to pop the lock.

If she was inside dancing around the cabin with music blasting in a pair of headphones, he'd apologize profusely and replace the window. If not… Gritting his teeth, Tate wrenched the window upward and sideways at the same time, and it slipped free of the old locking mechanism.

Pushing it open, he moved the curtain aside and peered into a bathroom. "Stay," he told Sitka as he hauled himself inside. If he needed her, she could leap through that window easily.

He landed awkwardly on the other side, with a lot more noise than he'd hoped to make. Pushing himself to a partially upright position, he peered around the corner. Seeing no one, he eased into the connected bedroom.

It looked like the rest of the cabin, with functional, comfortable furniture. There wasn't a lot of Sabrina's personality on display, except for a pile of colorful drawings pinned to the wall above the dresser and pictures of her mom and brother on the side table.

Moving forward, he did a slow and careful check of the second bedroom, then moved into the open kitchen and living area. She wasn't here.

Confusion turned quickly into dread as he saw her phone on the kitchen table. Tapping the button to check that it wasn't dead, he saw notifications of all his missed calls, but nothing else evident without unlocking it.

Why was her car here if she wasn't? He couldn't imagine her walking into town, but where else would she go? Still, if she was in trouble, why was there no sign of a struggle and no alert from her emergency button?

Grabbing Sabrina's sweatshirt from where it lay draped over the couch, Tate hurried to the front door and let himself outside. Sitka was standing beside him before he'd closed the door behind him. "Time to track," he told her.

Her tail wagged as he held out Sabrina's shirt and let her sniff it. Then her nose dropped to the ground, and she pivoted toward the driveway.

Tate felt a hint of relief as she led him down the drive instead of into the woods, but it faded just as fast. Where had she gone? And had she gone alone?

When Sitka turned right instead of left at the end of the drive, heading away from downtown instead of toward it, his anxiety increased. Then his dog let out a happy bark and started running.

Tate's gaze jolted to the right, where Sabrina was emerging from the woods far down the road. Stifling a curse of equal parts frustration and relief, Tate ran after Sitka.

"Sitka," Sabrina exclaimed, jogging until she met his dog in the middle of the road. She knelt in front of Sitka, wrapping her arms around the dog's neck in a brief hug that told Tate something had spooked her.

Tate skidded to a stop beside them, scanning the woods as his heart thudded too fast and anger knotted in his chest at how overemotional he'd gotten. He'd been so worried that he'd left his weapon behind. Now how much of a barrier would he be against a threat?

"What's going on?" He wrapped his arm around Sabrina's upper arm, pulling her upright.

She flinched, pulling her arm free and rubbing it.

His gaze met hers, even more troubled because he

hadn't grabbed her *that* hard. "What are you doing wandering around the woods alone? I've been calling you."

"I—I'm sorry. I went for a walk with Adam and—"

"Adam?" His pulse skyrocketed as he scanned the woods again. He didn't see the man anywhere. Had Sabrina managed to escape from him? Or had they gotten lucky and Adam had just been trying to see how close he could get to Sabrina?

Or was Tate wrong entirely, and it was merely a bizarre coincidence? He'd learned in past cases that you couldn't get too focused on one suspect at the expense of others. Mario McKeever might not have killed Sabrina's boyfriend himself, but that didn't mean he hadn't hired someone to do it. It didn't mean he hadn't been stalking her and simply taken advantage of someone else's crime to scare her.

Sabrina crossed her arms over her chest, and she glanced around the woods, shivering. "What's going on?"

Obviously sensing her distress, Sitka leaned against her. His dog didn't always recognize her own size, and she must have leaned hard, because Sabrina stumbled slightly before dropping her arms and absently petting Sitka.

"Where is Adam now?"

Sabrina shook her head, gesturing vaguely behind her. "I don't know. I wanted to come back, and he said he wanted to keep walking. He turned back into the woods when we got close to the road, and I kept going."

Tate lowered his voice. "So he could be nearby?" Not waiting for Sabrina's answer, he put his hand on her back, ushering her forward. "Let's go to your place. Now."

"Tate, what—"

"*Now*, Sabrina."

She started to run, and Tate gave Sitka a nod. His dog raced up beside her, and Tate followed slightly behind, his gaze pivoting all around, even though he knew most likely if Adam was still around, he was behind them.

His heart didn't stop racing until they were back in Sabrina's house and he'd checked all the rooms again, locked the door and braced the wooden handle of her mop in the bathroom window. Then he called the station and gave them an update, requesting backup and an extra weapon.

After hanging up, he met Sabrina in the living room. She stood in the center of the room, anxiety on her face as she stroked Sitka's head.

"What's happening?" she whispered.

"What did Adam say when he showed up?" Tate demanded. "You took his car out to the woods? Where did he leave it?"

"I…" She frowned, shook her head. "He said it would have been his wife's birthday. She died a few months ago. He wanted company. He said there was a great view out in the woods, and he was right. It was beautiful. We went for a walk. He—"

"You went for a walk? What about his vehicle?"

"I—I don't know. I guess I didn't think about it when he showed up, but I didn't see a vehicle. Maybe he walked here? He said he lived nearby. Or…" She frowned again. "Maybe he said he happened to be nearby. He said Lora told him where I lived, and he just didn't want to be alone today."

"And then what?" Tate asked, knowing his rapid-fire questions without answers were making her more nervous. But none of this made much sense. If Adam had gotten Sabrina alone, why hadn't he made a move to grab her? If his goal was to harm her, why not now? Or maybe he'd come to Alaska, realized he could start over as her friend and woo her long-term, with her never being the wiser that he'd once stalked her and killed her boyfriend.

"Then I followed him up that road awhile, and into the woods. He took me to this beautiful drop-off and…" Her lips twisted, her forehead creasing with confusion. "I'm not sure what happened. I thought someone pushed me, but then Adam grabbed me and kept me from falling. I looked down, and there were a lot of loose rocks, so maybe I just slipped? Or something fell from a tree?"

"Or Adam pushed you, then saved you," Tate said grimly.

"Why would he do that?" Sabrina demanded, crossing her arms over her chest again. She seemed to fold inward, visibly shrinking as Sitka whined, glancing back and forth between them.

"I found him in a picture with you that one of your coworkers took back in New York. I think he might be your stalker."

"But—" fear mingled with the confusion on Sabrina's face "—he's new to Desparre, and he's always lived in Alaska. His wife died a few months ago. He—"

"How do you know that's true?" Tate asked.

"I… I guess I don't. But Lora told me a lot of it. She introduced me. She's known Adam longer than I have. She's the one who told him where I lived."

"Okay." Tate nodded. "You have Lora's number?"

"Yeah." Sabrina spun and grabbed her phone off the kitchen table. She paused, her gaze darting back to him, probably as she noticed all his missed calls. Then she tapped her phone and handed it to him.

She had Lora's number pulled up. He hit Send and waited only briefly before Lora answered cheerfully, "Sabrina! How are you?"

"This is Officer Tate Emory. I—"

"Oh, no! Is Sabrina okay?"

"Yes. I'm sorry, Lora. She's fine. Look, I need to ask you some things in confidence, okay?" When she hesitantly agreed, he asked, "How long have you known Adam Lassiter?"

"Adam?" There was surprise in her voice. "Um, I guess about three months, since he moved here."

"Where did he move from? Did you know his late wife? Or have you seen pictures of her?"

"He lived in Fairbanks most of his life. He said his wife died about a month before he moved to Desparre. He wanted to get away from the constant reminders of her. I'm sorry, but what's going on? Why do you want to know about Adam?"

"What did he say when he asked for Sabrina's address?"

"He never asked me for Sabrina's address. I don't even know where she lives."

A curse lodged in Tate's throat as his own phone rang. "Lora, I'll get back to you, okay? But keep this conversation between us. And one more thing. Do you know where Adam lives?"

"Kind of. If you take the main road out of town north for a while, he's in the woods. A little cabin. I don't know the exact location."

The dread building in his gut amplified. "Thanks, Lora."

"Why did she tell him my address?" Sabrina asked as Tate hung up her phone and answered his own.

"She didn't," Tate told her. "But Adam lives somewhere out this way." Lifting his phone to his ear, Tate said, "Emory. What's going on?"

"We're coming up on Sabrina's place," Charlie Quinn answered. "You'll hear us in two minutes."

"Thanks. We also need to get someone on finding Adam's address. According to one of Sabrina's friends, he lives out this way somewhere."

"Yeah, that's my other update," Charlie said, his tone telling Tate before he finished speaking that it wasn't good news. "We can't find any information on an Adam Lassiter who fits his description. Not in Desparre and, as far as Max could tell with a quick search, not in Alaska."

Tate's gaze darted to Sabrina, who was watching him wide-eyed and wary. "It's not his real name."

"Probably not," Charlie agreed. "And without his real name…"

Charlie didn't continue, but he didn't have to. If Adam got any hint that police were here, if he'd been watching from the woods as Tate ran up to Sabrina, Adam might hide.

Without a real name, how would they be able to track him?

Chapter 15

Two hours later, Sabrina sat at Tate's desk in the bull-pen of the Desparre police station. Blown up to two hundred percent on the computer screen in front of her was a picture taken by a coworker back in New York almost three years ago. A good three months before she'd received the first letter from her stalker.

In the picture, she was smiling and laughing. She wanted to reach out and touch the screen, try to re-capture that level of happiness. There was no cloud of fear hanging over her then, no paranoia. Three years wasn't that long ago, and yet, that feeling seemed so out of reach now.

Behind her, maybe loosely a part of the group she was with, maybe not, was someone who sure looked like Adam Lassiter. The picture was grainy enough that she couldn't be positive. If it was really Adam, he'd lost about fifty pounds, replacing it with lean muscle.

He'd also cut his hair close to the scalp, making it seem lighter than it did in the photo. He even dressed differently now, in a lot of cargo pants and T-shirts, rather than the striped button-down from the photo.

Maybe it was just wishful thinking to believe it might not be the same person. She'd talked to Adam, laughed with Adam. She'd walked blithely into the woods with him alone. She'd almost invited him into her house.

All her earlier feelings of determination to move forward, to trust her own judgment again and stop jumping at shadows, fell away. What was left was a sadness that seemed to hollow her out.

Tate's hand closed over her forearm, and when she glanced at him, there was sympathy in his gaze.

She eased her arm away and turned to face him. The other officers were occupied on their computers trying to dig up more information about Adam, yet she kept her voice soft, so much so that he leaned closer. Ever since they'd gotten to the station, she'd been holding in her question about how he'd found Adam in an old picture. There was only one way she could imagine. "How did you figure out my last name?"

Guilt crossed over his face, quickly enough that she wasn't sure if she'd imagined it. "I looked for information on a murder in New York City from two years ago where news stories mentioned a stalker."

She nodded and turned back to the computer, saying nothing. The most basic information about why she was running, and it had given away more details about herself than she'd wanted to share.

"I'm sorry," he said, maneuvering so he was in her line of sight, as Sitka whined at her side.

She didn't respond to either of them, just continued

to stare at the image. How had she been so wrong? "Do you think Adam was trying to push me off that cliff? Then he changed his mind and grabbed me?"

"I doubt it," Tate said, but his tone told her what he thought was worse.

Reluctantly, she refocused her gaze on him.

"I think both were intentional from the start. He gave you a push *so* he could save you. Create a sense of obligation, make you feel grateful to him. More trusting."

She snorted, not quite meeting Tate's gaze. "It didn't work. I thought I'd offended him, which I figured was why he wanted to keep going on his own."

Tate nodded. "Maybe that's what happened. His plan backfired, and he decided to continue playing the long game."

Her hands tightened into fists, and she knew her anger wasn't all about Adam. Yes, Tate digging into her background had probably found her stalker. But he'd still betrayed her trust. "It's not a game. It's my *life*."

Tate took hold of the arms of her chair and turned her to face him. He knelt in front of her, and Sitka scooted over, forcing her head onto his knee, her puppy eyes staring up at Sabrina.

The expression on Sitka's face threatened to soften her. Before Tate could speak, she said, "I understand why you dug up information on me. It worked, so I guess I have no right to be mad. But—"

"You have every right to be mad," Tate said. "I should have told you. You've given up so many pieces of your identity to try to feel safe, and I broke your trust. That's another way to make you feel unsafe, and I'm sorry."

Lifting her gaze to his, she saw sincerity, even regret,

in his eyes. How had he known exactly what she was feeling? He spoke as if he really did understand. But it was more than that. She'd chosen to trust him in a way she hadn't trusted anyone else in a long time. And he'd still gone behind her back.

She'd been by herself for two years. But she'd never felt more alone than she did right now.

Tate cringed, as if he could read her thoughts. Then he fit his hand around hers and whispered, "I really am sorry, Sabrina. You're... I care about you. All I want to do is help you."

She glanced from his hand, which felt so comforting on hers, even though he was part of the reason she hurt right now. She wished they were anywhere but at the police station, with his chief watching across the room. Pulling her hand free, she scooted her chair slightly backward, away from him.

Sitka let out another low whine, and Sabrina forced a lightness to her voice she didn't feel. "It's okay, Sitka." She pet the dog until her tail thumped, then told Tate, "I forgive you. Let's figure out..."

She trailed off as the image of Adam caught the corner of her eye. Seeing it from this angle sparked a memory, brought the image she hadn't really remembered into focus. She'd been out for a coworker's birthday, at a bar that was too loud. The bar had been stuffy, the night too hot, the drinks flowing too freely. After a few hours, she'd started to feel more comfortable, have more fun.

The woman in the forefront of the picture with her—Jessamyn, who'd later become a good friend— had sensed her discomfort, grabbed her arm and taken her around the bar, introducing her to everyone, even people Jessamyn didn't know. And a group of guys who were friends of one of Jessamyn's friends.

"I think I remember him," she breathed, as more of the evening solidified in her mind.

Each of the guys had given their names, and some of them had provided other random information about themselves, like their job or hobbies. Her gaze had floated over each of them quickly. She remembered laughing through most of the introductions, partly because she'd been a little tipsy and partly because she'd been having fun.

She hadn't spoken to Adam again that night, that much she was sure. After being introduced to the group, she'd set down her beer and gotten onto the dance floor with Jessamyn. She hadn't left it until a few hours later, when she'd hopped into a cab and gone home.

"What do you remember?" Tate asked, making her refocus on him.

She let out an ironic laugh. "Periphery of my life is no joke. The most conversation we had was a quick introduction. I told him my name, he said his, and I was off to the dance floor. I never saw him again."

"Are you sure?"

"Pretty sure."

Tate nodded. "I don't suppose you remember his name?"

"You really don't think it's Adam Lassiter?"

"Well, we haven't found any property in his name, nor have we found any Adam Lassiter that matches his description. So, I'm thinking it's not his real name."

"I don't remember. All those guys were a blur, just a quick hello and on to the next person. It was a party.

I was new to my job and made friends with coworkers that night. That's mostly what I remember."

"It's okay," Tate told her. "We'll dig it up."

"Tate."

Sabrina looked up, and Tate stood as the chief reached his desk.

"Chief. What is it?"

Chief Griffith nodded at her. "Sabrina." Then he looked at them both as he said, "I spoke to your friend Lora. We asked her to call Adam, but he's not answering."

"He should show up in town eventually, though, right?" Sabrina asked. Or had he been close behind her when she'd trekked back toward the road and discovered Tate and Sitka waiting for her? Had he realized his identity was blown and already disappeared?

The way the chief's lips tightened made dread settle in her stomach even before he replied. "When you were giving me a rundown of what happened with Adam in the woods, Officer Emory here was drawing a map for two of our other officers. He detailed exactly where Sitka went through the woods when she was tracking from your house last week."

"Did they find anything?"

The chief glanced at Tate again, and something unspoken seemed to pass between them, something that made Tate's expression tighten, too. "We found a cabin. It's old, and the bank foreclosed on it last year when the guy who owned it passed away. It's been sitting empty ever since, at least as far as anyone knew."

"Adam was squatting there?" Tate asked, fury on his face. "Where is this place?"

The chief nodded. "We think so. We found evidence

that someone has been there recently, including some clothes, food and pinholes in the wall like something had been posted there. It looks like it was cleared out in a hurry."

Tate swore as the chief fixed his attention entirely on her.

Sabrina stiffened as he continued. "This cabin would take a while to get to on the road from your place, but if you go directly through the woods, it's about a mile away, a straight shot. You probably never even knew anyone was back there."

The dread intensified, a familiar feeling from her early days of running, constantly feeling like her stalker was right behind her. She thought it had just been paranoia, but had he been there all along?

Six days after Adam had cleared out of the cabin behind hers, there was no sign of him.

Sabrina had spent the time alternating between extreme emotions. One day, she'd be certain a police officer would knock on the door to the hotel room where they'd stuck her and announce that it was all over and she could go home to the family she hadn't dared to contact in two years. The next day, she'd be sure this would continue forever and she'd be forced to make a new impossible choice: go back to running and assume Adam was right behind her in every new town or stay here and wait for the police to run out of resources to waste on her. Wait for him to come after her.

Most likely the story Adam had told about living in Alaska all his life, about having recently lost a wife, were all lies to make her feel comfortable letting him get close. It had been brilliant. Especially befriending

Lora before he'd ever approached her. Getting the story secondhand that he was a widower mourning the too-recent loss of his wife had immediately ruled him out in her mind as her stalker.

The fact that he'd appeared in a picture with her in New York suggested he'd actually lived there, at least for some amount of time. If he'd grown up in the city like her, there had to be only so long he could hide out in the treacherous Alaskan wilderness before the locals tracked him down.

But they hadn't found him yet.

Meanwhile, she was going stir-crazy in the ridiculously opulent room in Desparre's only hotel, the luxury Royal Desparre. When she'd nervously asked about the cost, Tate had said it was being taken care of and insisted it was safer than being in the middle of nowhere. She still had her alert button and the owners—who doubled as management—knew to call the police if they spotted Adam. Tate checked in several times a day, usually by phone, but he and Sitka also stopped by every night.

Still, she spent most of her days alone. Since she couldn't contact anyone and there were only so many hours she could spend making jewelry, especially with her creativity having taken a dive, she was bored. Having too many hours to think was making her more anxious.

So, when there was a knock on her door, she was up and reaching for the lock before her mind caught up and she checked the peephole. A grin burst free, and a familiar anticipation settled in her stomach when she saw Tate standing on the other side, looking serious in his uniform but holding a pizza box.

He didn't usually finish up at the station and make his way over to her hotel until almost eight, so she'd gotten used to waiting for dinner. They'd never made plans to eat together each night, but he kept showing up until it felt like a standing date. Only the fact that he wore his uniform and always updated her on their progress reminded her each day that it wasn't really a date. Reminded her that nothing she felt for Tate could be permanent.

She still hadn't fully forgiven him for digging into her past without her permission, for not telling her when he'd learned her real name and searched her brother's social media. But he'd done it to help her. And it had worked. The more time she spent with him, the less she wanted to think about the mistakes in the past. The more she wanted to entertain a future that somehow had him in it.

It wasn't meant to be. But she could pretend.

Flinging open the door, she asked, "How did you know I needed some pizza?"

Woof! Sitka walked forward, butting Sabrina hard enough with her nose to knock her back a step.

As Tate reminded his dog to relax, Sabrina laughed and leaned down to pet her. "I think she wants pizza, too."

Woof!

Grinning, Tate followed his dog into the room, closing and locking the door behind him like always.

Sabrina couldn't help the flutter of nerves that erupted in her stomach. They seemed to be increasing in intensity each evening she spent with him. Since updates on the case only took so long—especially since there'd been nothing to report on Adam, and the guy they'd arrested last week still wasn't talking—their conversations had been getting more personal.

He'd already dug through her life on his own, so she'd decided she might as well tell him the truth about everything. The decision had been freeing.

And, she had to admit as he set the pizza box on the table by the window, the man looked good in his dark blue police uniform. She'd been attracted to him from the start, admired the thick dark brows that added even more intensity to his angular face and fixated on the full lips that drew her attention. But she'd always found that she grew more physically attracted to a man when she was emotionally attracted to him, too. Every day she spent with Tate, that attraction increased.

He turned back toward her, and from the way he went still, she knew her feelings were broadcasted across her face.

Ducking her head on the pretext of petting Sitka, Sabrina cursed her pale skin, which felt like it was on fire.

When she finally had her blush under control, she lifted her head again and found that Tate had crossed the room without her hearing him.

With Sitka sitting between them, he stood in front of her, his gaze locked on hers, a matching desire in his deep brown eyes.

She swayed forward, leaning over Sitka, without even consciously planning to do it.

He leaned toward her, captured her hands in his, and the touch sent sparks over her skin and up her arms.

Her lips tingled in anticipation, and as she moistened them with her tongue, his gaze darted there.

His voice sounded slightly strangled as he told her, "I have news."

News? Her brain struggled to focus on anything other than the heat in his eyes and the closeness of his lips. "About the investigation?"

"Yeah."

She stared at him, trying to decide what to pursue, until he finally gave her a half grin and leaned slightly away.

He kept hold of her hands, though, his fingers stroking lightly against her knuckles a distraction. "Mario McKeever still isn't talking. But we've been able to confirm his whereabouts two years ago. He's from New York, but he hasn't lived there in almost four years. And when you were getting notes, he was living in South Carolina and having regular run-ins with the law. No arrests, but the local police definitely knew his name."

"Okay," she said, her brain still processing everything more slowly. But she didn't want to pull her hands away, break the connection he'd initiated. "We were already pretty sure it was Adam, so that's not much news, right?"

"No. But I thought you'd want to know." He paused again, and she could see the fight in his eyes as his gaze drifted back to her lips. "There is one other thing. Since it's been almost a week with no sign of Adam, Chief Griffith suggested a plan to lure him back into the open. Stop waiting on his timetable and take back some control."

"Okay." Now, this was an idea Sabrina could get behind. She was tempted to lick her lips again, just to see if it would break Tate's concentration, but she resisted as his gaze lifted back to hers.

"Adam's MO has been to go after anyone who might be a source of support, right? I mean, he came after me and Sitka after presumably seeing me stop by your house. And of course, there's Dylan."

Sabrina nodded, the memory of the police showing up at Dylan's family's lake house with the news of his death erasing all desire. "Yes."

"So, the chief thinks we should use that to our advantage. Get him angry enough to come after someone again."

Sabrina frowned at him. "Who? How? I don't want to put anyone at risk. I don't really have any friends here except Lora and—"

"You have me," Tate said, his tone firm. "We're going to make sure Adam takes the bait so we can take him down. The chief doesn't want it to look like I'm a friend, a source of support. He wants us to publicly play out a romance and get Adam to take his shot."

Chapter 16

Tate held Sabrina's hand loosely in his own as he walked in downtown Desparre. Her long delicate fingers, slightly calloused from making jewelry, felt so right in his. There was a smile on his face he didn't need to fake or force, but it didn't mean he'd lost sight of the dangers.

The bench straight ahead, still crumpled and destroyed from the truck Sabrina's stalker might have sent after Sitka, was a stark reminder. So were the woods beyond that, which looked too much like the forest in Boston he'd darted into to escape his fellow officers' gunfire.

The desire to constantly swivel his head, keep an eye on his surroundings, was hard to ignore. But Tate trusted the Desparre officers he'd worked with for the past five and a half years. This wasn't Boston. Besides, both he and Sabrina wore bulletproof vests beneath their lightweight jackets.

He was a little overheated walking in the sunshine. Or maybe it was just from his proximity to Sabrina.

Except for the weight of that vest and the knowledge that his colleagues were hiding nearby and watching his every move, everything about this felt right. A natural progression of the attraction he'd felt from the moment he'd met Sabrina. Getting to know her more over the past week had only intensified those feelings.

He glanced at her, taking in things he'd noticed the first time he'd seen her: the way the sun cast a golden sheen over her wavy hair, the natural elegance of her face, the depths of her green eyes. But also seeing new things now that she'd truly let him in: the way her lips tightened at the corners when she was stressed. The flush that rose easily to her cheeks when she was flustered or embarrassed. The way her gaze was always moving, taking everything in and strategizing. For someone who made a living in creative arts, she was analytical enough to run through police strategy with him. And successfully evade a stalker for two years on her own.

A swell of pride filled him, even though he had no right to it. Without conscious intent, he squeezed her hand, and she looked his way.

Her smile was equal parts shy uncertainty and knowing amusement. But it was probably hard to miss the effect she had on him. Even his chief had picked up on it, used it as the basis to suggest this pretense.

"Sabrina!" From one of the intact benches near the park, Lora had spotted them. She came running and Tate took a deep breath.

They were about to discover if their ruse was working.

He hadn't been thrilled about telling Lora their suspicions about Adam, but after his call to her, it had seemed like the best approach. She'd promised to keep it to herself and although she was often in everyone's business, she was trustworthy. Still, he and the chief had agreed it was best not to give her any more detail than they had to, including the truth about his and Sabrina's supposed relationship.

Lora slowed slightly as she approached, her gaze dropping speculatively to Sabrina's and Tate's linked hands before she threw her arms around Sabrina's neck.

Sabrina was knocked back a step by the force of it, and Tate dropped her hand. While she was distracted, he glanced around.

Nothing seemed out of the ordinary. Just another day in downtown Desparre. There were more people out than usual because of the brilliant sunshine, but not so many that Adam would be able to hide in a crowd.

Then again, he knew his fellow officers were close, and he didn't see them. The sliver of anxiety he'd felt since they stepped outside grew, and he wished for Sitka's comforting presence. His K-9 partner was back at his house, since Tate was pretending to be off work. He'd initially argued to bring her, but the chief had overruled him, saying he didn't want to provide a reason for a group of kids to surround Sitka and distract them.

"I'm so sorry," Lora exclaimed, squeezing Sabrina's hand and looking upset. "I had no idea... I believed Adam when he said he'd grown up in Alaska. He knew so much about the state. And his wife—"

"Don't worry," Sabrina interrupted, her smile almost reaching her eyes. "We're not completely sure it was him, but whoever it was, the police seem to have scared him off. And the upside of it all…"

She took Tate's hand again, and he stepped closer, returning the soft smile she gave him.

"I met Tate," she concluded, an upward lilt to her voice that made the whole thing sound even more real.

He wished it was.

He'd shared things with Sabrina he hadn't shared with anyone in a long time. Pieces of his life that he'd been purposely evasive about with colleagues, even those people he called his friends. But after a week of dinners in her hotel room, there'd been only so long they could discuss the investigation, only so many awkward attempts at chitchat before she'd dived in with real questions. He'd looked into parts of her life without her consent, so he figured he owed her some truths, too, even if he couldn't give her all the details.

She was the only person here who knew how badly he missed talking to his parents, their respective partners, and even his mom's boyfriend's kids, who were younger than him and he hadn't grown up with but were all nice. She didn't understand his vague excuses for not having seen them in over five years, but the rest of it had been true. She understood because she missed her family, too.

Their connection went deeper than their shared experience—especially since she didn't even know they shared one. As he watched her smile and tell Lora the story about how they'd started dating, he wished he'd asked Sabrina out the first time he'd met her. Their relationship still would have had an expiration date, but at least it would have been real.

The ache that filled him at that moment must have

shown on his face, because Lora shifted her attention to him. As he attempted a smile to cover up whatever she'd seen, she let out a surprised laugh.

"You know, the first time Sabrina admitted she thought you were cute, I told her to go for it. But I thought you were too much of a loner to ever get involved."

Her assessment of him stung a bit, but it was hard to focus on that part. He grinned at Sabrina, couldn't help himself from nudging her the way he might if he was actually dating her. "You thought I was cute, huh?"

She flushed an even deeper red, but instead of mumbling something vague like he'd expected, she countered, "Yep. But it was Sitka who pushed you over the edge and got you a date."

A surprised laugh escaped. "Figures. Everyone always tells me she's the better-looking one in the partnership."

Lora laughed at that, then gave Sabrina another hug. "I should let you two enjoy your date." She glanced from Sabrina to him and back again. "I'm happy for you, Sabrina. You deserve this." Then she leaned in and hugged Tate. "I think you do, too, Tate."

As she walked away, Tate glanced at Sabrina again. She was smiling at him, amusement and something that looked like longing on her face.

The longer he stared into her eyes, the more the amusement dropped away until she swayed slightly forward.

He felt himself lean toward her instinctively and then forced himself to straighten, squeeze her hand and tug her forward again. He made his voice overly cheerful, overly loud. "Want to walk around the park?"

It was a reminder to himself as much as her that most of the Desparre police department was watching them right now. As much as he wanted to kiss her, he didn't want to do it in front of an audience. And he didn't want to do it when it wasn't real.

At least if Adam was watching, he should have no doubt that they were a couple.

Sabrina blinked a few times, the desire there fading away until she gave him a tentative smile. "Sure."

As they continued down the street, regret welled up. Regret that he hadn't given in to the moment and kissed her. Regret that he couldn't tell her the full truth about who he was. But even more than that, regret that their time was limited.

Because once they arrested her stalker, she'd be leaving. And he couldn't follow. New York was too close to Boston to ever be safe for him.

After two full days of flaunting her supposed relationship with Tate all over town, Sabrina was exhausted. And Adam—if he was still here—hadn't taken the bait.

Still, as she walked beside Tate around the cute set of shops outside downtown, hyperaware of the feel of his hand in hers, she didn't care if Adam took a week to make his move. The outdoor shopping center, a quirky assortment of stores that seemed to have holiday lights on the roofs year-round, was normally one of her favorite spots. But she couldn't focus on them with Tate beside her.

If she squinted a little, she could make their surroundings go blurry and just keep Tate in focus. If only there were a way to do that with her life. Make all the challenges drop away and just be here with him for real.

For the first time in two years, it felt like someone actually *knew* her again. Sharing more and more about herself with him each night seemed right. Even if she'd met him back in New York, surrounded by plenty of friends and family, she would have wanted him in her life.

"What made you decide to become a cop?" The words popped out of her mouth without her even realizing she'd been thinking them. But it was something she'd wondered about since the moment that truck had raced toward Sitka, and again later, when she'd heard Tate had been knocked off his feet chasing Mario McKeever.

He seemed surprised by the question, but then his steps slowed slightly, something she'd come to recognize he did when he got serious.

"I told you my parents divorced when I was young." When she nodded, he continued. "I wouldn't say it was an ugly divorce, not compared to the things I've seen as a cop. But as a seven-year-old, it felt scary. It seemed like all they did was argue, and I was always in the middle. They shared custody, which in the long run, I'm glad about. But at the time, it felt like as soon as I got settled in one house, I was shuttled to the other."

"I'm sorry," Sabrina said when he paused, his lips pursed, his forehead creasing. "My dad took off when I was five. Totally different thing, because he spent most of my childhood chasing after the next new thing—usually his next girlfriend or his next car. He reappears every few years, wanting to reestablish a relationship. Even as an adult, it's disorienting. And honestly, I saw him occasionally, but I'm not that interested. It's not much of a bond when it's all on one person's terms."

He squeezed her hand. "I'm glad you had your mom and brother. And I'm glad you'll get back to them soon."

His words sent a pang through her—a desperate longing to see her family mixed with dread at the thought of leaving him behind.

Maybe he saw how conflicted she suddenly felt, because he cleared his throat and started walking again. She hadn't even realized they'd stopped.

"So, dealing with my parents' divorce made me angry, frustrated." His lips tilted downward as he added, "Lonely. And just adrift. My dad had already moved across town, into a different school district. Then mom couldn't afford our old house by herself. She moved closer to my dad, thinking it would be easier. But it meant I also had to change schools, and I started getting bullied."

Sabrina put her free hand against his arm. "That's a lot to deal with all at once. I'm sorry you went through that."

He gave her a quick smile that seemed to say *Don't worry*. It was so typically Tate that she couldn't help but smile back. The smile faded as he looked forward again, kept talking. How had she gotten to know what all of his smiles meant? How had it happened so quickly?

She'd known him for just over two weeks. They weren't even *actually* dating, and already, she felt more connected to him than she had with Dylan after three months.

The thought made guilt rush through her. She tried to push it back, to just focus on this moment, on this man. Even if it wasn't real, it was the best thing she'd had in her life in years.

"I started getting into fights, too." At the surprised

glance she shot him, he laughed. "I know. It's out of character. It was then, too. My parents didn't know what to do with me. Then one day I was walking home from school, and a group of kids started beating up on me."

Sabrina gasped, and he squeezed her hand again.

"I was ten then, I think. Three years of struggling at school and at home and letting my anger get the best of me. A police officer stopped his car, sirens flashing. All those kids took off *fast*. I wasn't in any shape to go anywhere, so the cop gave me a ride home. He talked to me about channeling anger the right way, about making the right choices even when the people around me are making the wrong ones. It made an impression."

Sabrina tried to imagine a younger Tate, angry and hurting. She pictured him at ten, his light brown skin covered in bruises, his deep brown eyes—always so intuitive and kind—filled with cynicism and frustration. "Did you stay in touch with him?"

"It wasn't *that* big a town. Even if I hadn't wanted to, he would have found me." Tate laughed. "He retired a couple of years ago down to Florida." The fondness in his tone faded to something wishful. "I haven't talked to him in a while."

"Maybe you should call him," Sabrina suggested, wishing the solutions were so simple for the people she missed.

He paused, regret flitting across his face before he smiled down at her. "Yeah, I should."

She stared back at him, wondering if there was any way to turn what they had into something real. If he could stay connected with his friend in Florida, he could do the same for her in New York. Maybe he'd want to visit, let her show him around. Could they build a relationship from that long a distance?

Then again, did it make any sense to let someone like Tate go over something as simple as geography?

Her pulse picked up as he continued to stare at her, as if he was trying to read her mind. But wondering if he'd ever leave Alaska if they got serious was getting ridiculously ahead of herself. They'd never broached the idea of dating for real. They'd never even *kissed*.

His gaze darted to her lips.

Could he read her mind? A smile trembled on her lips, and each breath came faster as it occurred to her. What better way to see how Tate felt about her? And as an added bonus, maybe it would finally give Adam the incentive he needed to take the bait.

Before she lost her courage, Sabrina fisted her free hand in Tate's T-shirt, pulling him downward and swiveling him toward her all at once. She grinned at the surprise that flashed in his eyes, followed immediately by a dark intensity that told her he wanted to kiss her, too.

Dropping his T-shirt, she pulled her other hand free from his and slid both of her hands slowly up his arms, holding his gaze. His eyelids dropped and his muscles flexed under her fingers, emboldening her. She kept going, leaning up on her tiptoes as she slipped her hands beneath the sleeves of his shirt. She vaguely registered the feel of puckered, uneven skin beneath her left hand, and then his lips were pressed against hers.

They were soft, even fuller than she'd realized. Electricity buzzed over her skin as he brushed his lips against hers, once, twice, before sliding his tongue across the seam of her mouth.

She sank against him, gripping his shoulders as his

hands clamped onto her hips and raised her up more. Opening her mouth, she invited him in, flicking her tongue against his as her body flushed at the feel of him against her.

Then, too quickly, he was setting her away from him, his hands on her biceps, the apology in his eyes not hiding the desire. "Maybe we should do this without an audience," he suggested, his voice huskier than usual.

A smile broke free, echoing the hope bursting in her chest. He shared her feelings. She could see it in his gaze, feel it in his touch.

Maybe she wasn't a fool to think about a future with him. Maybe, thanks to him, she could finally *have* a future.

Before she could voice any of the things she was thinking, he frowned and dug into his pocket. Then, he was holding his phone out for her to read a text message from Chief Griffith.

I don't know if Adam left or if he's just not taking the bait with so many people around.

Sabrina glanced around the sparsely populated shops. She could see Officer Nate Dreymond in plainclothes pretending to window-shop down the street, a couple arguing about their weekend coming out of the shop next to them, and a handful of people wandering in and out of stores. It was less busy than the park where Adam had set Talise's truck on Sitka. Then again, maybe he was worried the police were watching. Maybe he suspected it was a trap. She glanced down at the rest of the text.

We have a new plan. Something that will look like an easier mark for Adam. You and Sabrina pretend to go away on a romantic weekend together.

Chapter 17

"His real name is Adam Locklay," Tate announced as Sabrina opened the door to her hotel room.

He paused to hand her the tea and muffin he'd picked up for her in the hotel's restaurant, taking in her hair, which seemed more wavy and untamed than usual. From the sleepy way she blinked at him, she hadn't been awake long. He paused to take in a fresh-from-sleep Sabrina as she seemed to register what he'd said.

"What?" Her voice was barely above a whisper as Sitka pushed past him and sat at Sabrina's feet, wagging her tail.

Sabrina's eyes were wide enough to momentarily distract him with their various shades of green, shifting from emerald to moss. The scent of the tea he'd bought her wafted toward him, along with the faint smell of vanilla. Her shampoo or lotion? Whatever it was, it was as distracting as the rest of her.

Closing the door behind him, he asked, "Does the name mean something to you?"

"No. How did you figure it out?"

"By spending a lot of time on social media. Using that picture I found, we identified other people in the background close to Adam and dug into their social media until we finally got to a picture where he was tagged. With his real name, we could dig up a lot more about him, too."

As Sitka gave a short whine, Sabrina smiled briefly at his dog, absently petting her. "I can't believe I finally have a real name to put to these years of notes and…" She lifted her hand, palm up, as if she couldn't sum up all of the horror of her past two and a half years.

He slid his hand underneath her upturned palm and she flipped it over to entwine their hands. "A name is the first step. We're on *his* tail now. It's a matter of time before we catch up to him."

"I hope so." She glanced down at their linked hands, then up at him, and he could see the questions in her eyes.

Questions about that kiss they'd shared yesterday. About his suggestion that they hit pause until they were alone again.

They were alone *now*.

Nerves tightened his chest, and anticipation quickened his breathing. She'd always seemed shy, so despite the heated looks she'd been giving him, he'd been shocked when she'd grabbed him and kissed him yesterday. And damn, she really could kiss.

His gaze dropped to her lips, and her tongue darted out to wet them, making him sway forward. But he caught himself before he pulled her to him.

He hadn't come here to finish something he never should have let her start. He'd come to talk about the status of their search for Adam and their plan to finally lure him out of hiding and end the threat against Sabrina for good.

Letting go of her hand, he stepped around her and set his take-out coffee on the table, giving himself a chance to refocus. He leaned against the wall, putting a little space between them. "Adam Locklay moved out to New York for college and stuck around. He's got a history of stalking."

Sabrina set her tea and muffin on the table beside her bed, moving toward him.

Sitka stuck close to Sabrina's side, her tail wagging. His dog stared up at Sabrina happily, the way she did with him at home, when she was relaxed and off duty. She was going to miss Sabrina as much as he was.

"He's done this to other women?"

She sounded furious on their behalf, and it made him like her even more. She'd spent two and a half years afraid for herself, afraid for the people she loved because of Adam, and here she was, mad that he'd dared to make anyone else feel that way.

"Yeah." He tried not to get distracted by her approach, by thoughts of how little time he might have left to spend with her. "But as far as we can tell, never like this. In the past, he stalked women he knew. Two ex-girlfriends and one coworker, who all went to the police. Two of them ended up with restraining orders against him, and one called the police multiple times because of incidents, usually him stopping by unwanted and refusing to leave."

"Any violence?" Sabrina asked, her tone hesitant,

like she was afraid to hear who else he'd killed chasing the objects of his obsession.

"None that I could find. He escalated with you."

"Aren't I lucky," she muttered darkly.

The only one who was lucky in any of this was him. If Adam hadn't stalked her, then Tate never would have met her. She would have gone on with her life in New York, gone on dating Dylan Westwood, maybe even married him.

Even the idea of never having the chance to know her put an uncomfortable tightness in Tate's chest that made it hard to take a full breath. But he wished Adam had never set eyes on her, wished Sabrina had never known this terror.

When he didn't immediately answer, she stepped a little closer, sending another waft of vanilla his way, and asked, "Have you been able to track his movements? Has he been behind me this whole time?"

"I don't think so. We don't know how he found you, but there's evidence he was still in New York five months ago. He works as an independent software developer, and he's able to work from home, so it's possible he's been traveling and returning to New York. But given what you've told me about all the places you've been, I have to think he found you here and then followed."

Her shoulders jerked, and she let out a huff. "Of all the places I've hidden, this one is the most remote. The place I felt most safe. The place that felt most like *home*."

Something pensive crossed her face, some emotion he tried to latch onto but couldn't quite read.

It wasn't fair to her not to keep his distance. But he couldn't seem to stop himself from moving a little closer. "This *is* your home, at least right now. It's your town. And we look out for each other here. We're going to find him. It just…" He frowned, trying to figure out the best way to tell her, then decided straightforward was the best approach. She'd managed the threat alone for two years. She could handle his other news.

"It just might take a little longer than we'd hoped. Which is why I think the plan the chief mentioned yesterday is a good one. If you're okay with it, we're getting things prepped right now. In two days, it will be set up."

Sabrina stared at him a minute, like she wasn't sure which part of that to question first. Finally, she asked, "Why will it take longer?"

"We assumed Adam's stories about living in Alaska were all lies." When shock and compassion crossed Sabrina's face, Tate rushed on. "And they were. He was never married. You don't need to feel sorry for his loss. We suspect he made it up as a way to connect with you, to get you to talk about your own loss."

Grief and fury flashed across Sabrina's face in rapid succession, and Tate felt an answering pang of sympathy. Adam had killed someone she cared about and then tried to connect with her by pretending a similar loss.

Sabrina clamped a hand against her stomach. "He was hoping I'd talk to him about Dylan's death, never knowing he'd actually caused it? That's even sicker than the notes."

"I know. I'm sorry."

Lines creased Sabrina's forehead as she wrapped her arms around her middle, seeming to sink inward. "I'm glad I never did."

But he could hear it in her words. She'd thought about it, thought Adam was someone who'd understand her loss.

Cursing inwardly, Tate readied himself to give her

more bad news. "He never lived here, either. The thing is, he was probably able to convince someone like Lora who *did* grow up here, and in the mountains, no less, because the wilderness isn't foreign to him. He grew up in Michigan's upper peninsula, with parents who were known to have some survivalist mentality."

"He understood how to hide here," Sabrina summarized. "That explains why he was so comfortable trekking through the woods to spy on me."

"Yes," Tate confirmed. He took another step closer, until all he'd need to do was reach out and take her hands in his, pull her to him and hold her until the worry and betrayal left her face. He wanted to, especially when his movement made heat spark in her gaze again.

He wanted to forget all of his good intentions of remaining professional, helping her reclaim her life without making it even harder to say goodbye. He wanted to feel her lips on his again, wanted to run his hands through her hair and walk her to the bed that was way too close. Instead, he fisted his hands at his side.

From the way Sitka's gaze moved from him to Sabrina, he couldn't even fool his dog.

The last of the anger left her face as her lips twitched with sudden amusement. "So you want to go away with me for the weekend, then." Her tone was teasing, but her gaze was serious as she moved close, slid her hands up his arms. The soft glide of her fingertips and the mix of nerves and desire in her eyes weakened his resolve.

Her fingers stalled on the edges of the scar hidden by the sleeve of his T-shirt. "What happened here?"

"A danger of the job," he answered, a semitruth because he didn't want to outright lie to her. "Gunshot wound." At her gasp, he added, "It was a long time ago. And it just skimmed me."

Summoning his willpower, he took a step back, watching the confusion in her eyes as he said, "I don't want you to worry. You're not going to be in danger. We have two days to set this up right. This is going to be a trap for Adam."

She bit the edge of her lip, then whispered, "I'm not worried. I feel safe with you."

Her words sent a rush through him even before she moved forward again. This time, she was less hesitant, giving him a shaky smile before she pressed her hands against his chest.

His arms twitched at the contact, and her smile grew more confident as she leaned into him, replacing her hands with the length of her body. "I think it will work."

It took him a minute to take his focus off the feel of her pressed against him and understand her words. "I think so, too." Adam was less likely to be able to resist if he and Sabrina were supposedly alone.

"And once he's no longer a threat—" she slid her arms around his waist and leaned back slightly to stare up at him "—I was hoping you and I could try this for real."

His mouth went dry, and for an instant, he couldn't breathe. The desire to nod and press his lips against hers was overwhelming, but how could he make a promise he couldn't keep? Even though there was no indication Kevin or Paul had found him as a result of the news article, he'd planned to leave town as soon as he'd eliminated the threat of her stalker. Even if he decided it was safe enough to stay in Alaska, what would he say when she inevitably wanted him to come see her in New York? What if he got too close to Boston again and the threats against him became a danger to her?

"I can't," he said, his voice a scratchy whisper.

She flushed deep red and backed out of his arms as Sitka whimpered and nudged up against her, eyeing Tate like he'd just become the enemy.

"I'm sorry. I want to. You have no idea…" He took a deep breath, trying to be as honest as he could. "But Desparre is a long way from New York City."

She nodded, ducking her head as she backed farther away.

An ache settled in his gut, for hurting her, for saying no when he so desperately wanted to say yes. But it wasn't right. He'd come to care about her too much to hurt her. In the long run, pursuing a relationship with Sabrina could make her the target of someone new. The threat against him might never end.

"I promised to give you your life back." He stepped closer, tipping her chin up with his hand even as he longed to pull her back into his arms. "I won't stop until I do it. But that means leaving everything in Alaska behind. Including me."

Nerves churned in Sabrina's stomach as she waited for Tate to come to her hotel room and pick her up for their supposed romantic weekend away together.

Three days ago, when she'd kissed him in the street, their pretending had felt so natural, so *real*. When he'd said he wanted to continue what she'd started in private, she thought he felt all the same things she did. So when he'd shown up the next morning and insisted long-distance would never work, it had been a shock. Embarrassing. And devastating.

Yet, he'd kept coming to see her the next two evenings, bringing dinner and smiling at her like nothing had happened. She'd tried to smile back, act as unaffected as he appeared, but *that* pretending had left her exhausted and depressed.

At least he'd continued to bring Sitka with him. The sweet dog definitely sensed something was wrong, and she'd spent a lot of the visits at Sabrina's feet, her head perched on Sabrina's knees. She would miss Sitka when she left, too.

Despite everything, she still believed their plan could work. Adam had gone after Dylan the day she was meeting his family for the first time. Back then, she'd thought it was a terrible coincidence. But now, knowing how closely he could have been watching her in her cabin? Remembering how he'd managed to slip a note into her purse even after the police had been on high alert trying to find him back in New York? He'd probably known.

She'd been about to take a serious step in a relationship, and he'd stopped it. Given how much she and Tate had been spreading news about their intended getaway to a secluded cabin, she had to believe he'd repeat that pattern.

Her nerves intensified, shifted into fear that made her breathing way too fast. "Relax," she told herself. Tate was a trained police officer. And they wouldn't be alone. Much of the Desparre PD would be hidden nearby, ready to take Adam down.

It would work. It had to work. Because Tate was right. It was time for her to go home.

Acute homesickness swept through her, pricking her eyes with tears. Without conscious thought, she moved toward her phone. She'd never dared to go onto social media, hadn't wanted to sign into an account that might leave some kind of trail. But if Tate had been able to see details about her brother...

Pulling up Conor's social-media account without signing in, she realized he'd made a lot of his posts public. Her stockbroker brother, who lived by numbers and rules and always warned her about keeping her personal information locked up, had purposely left pieces of his life open to the world.

As she scrolled through, so fast the pictures and posts were nothing more than quick glimpses, she realized he'd done it two years ago. A way for her to stay connected with them, no matter how far she ran. And she'd never known, never even thought to check, because she'd been focused on pure survival.

Conor's face blurred, and she swiped at the tears that had welled in her eyes as she scrolled back to the top of his feed. His latest post, dated yesterday, showed him beaming beside Jie, his longtime girlfriend. Jie was grinning, one hand held up to the camera, showing off a sparkling diamond.

They'd gotten engaged. Finally. They'd met in college, dated ever since. In the year or two before Sabrina had run, she could tell Jie was starting to get frustrated. They'd been together a long time. She wanted to get married and have kids. Conor was dragging his feet.

Sabrina got it. Their dad had taken off when she was five and Conor was seven. While she and Conor had watched their mom struggle to make ends meet, to try to fill the void their father had left, their dad had jumped from one woman to the next, carefree. He'd appeared every few months, or sometimes every few years, and dropped off presents, wanted to take them out. It hadn't really put Sabrina off the idea of marriage, but from a young age, Conor had vowed never to wed.

Jie was so good for her brother. Sabrina had been worried he would lose her if he didn't make that commitment. Now the leap of faith had happened. And she'd missed it. Still, a bittersweet smile pulled her lips at the happiness radiating from that picture.

Maybe she'd make it back to New York for the wedding. The idea buoyed her, took away some of the pain of seeing all she'd missed. She scrolled more, seeing birthdays and holidays. More happiness, but she could see it on everyone's faces that they missed her as much as she missed them.

Then she found a picture of Conor and her mom from a few weeks earlier, smiling in Central Park, and a sharp pain clamped back down on her chest. She ran her finger over the side of her mom's face, seeing new lines at the corners of her mouth and across her forehead. She looked like she'd experienced way too much sadness in the past two years. Conor, too, looked older, more weary.

Sabrina had done this to them by leaving. If she had to go back and make the same decision now, she'd do it again. But she was tired of being forced to choose safety over happiness.

There was a familiar knock at the door, a particular beat she recognized as Tate's, followed by Sitka's enthusiastic *woof!*

Closing the browser on her phone, she stood and took a deep breath.

It was long past time she made a stand for herself and reclaimed the life she'd left behind.

Chapter 18

"Hi," Sabrina breathed, feeling a flush creep up her neck and cheeks at the shy, uncertain tone of her voice. Clearing her throat, she opened the hotel door wider.

Sitka rushed inside at the invitation, running around Sabrina in a circle that made her laugh.

Tate smiled, something hesitant in his gaze, but he couldn't seem to help a laugh at his dog's antics. "She's a pro at work, but get her off duty and she's a big goofball."

Woof! Sitka glanced back at him briefly, then returned her attention to Sabrina.

"You know you are," Tate teased his dog as Sabrina leaned down to pet Sitka and hide her face behind a curtain of hair.

This was the Tate she wanted to know better. The Tate who teased his dog, who made her feel safe and excited at the same time. Even knowing that today was all for show, it was too easy to imagine a version of this that was real. The idea of going on an actual romantic weekend away with him made her pulse pick up again.

Her attraction wasn't one-sided, that much she knew for sure. But Tate was too practical and realistic, probably the result of being a police officer—or maybe why he'd become one. She, on the other hand, had always indulged her creative, fanciful impulses. It was how she'd ended up in fashion design and now, finally, jewelry-making. More than once, those impulses had led her to take a chance on the wrong relationship. But until Adam had forced his way into her life, she'd lived without fear.

She hadn't been irresponsible. Her mom had drilled into her from a young age the need to be diligent about safety. But she'd refused to let her dad's leaving color the way she looked at relationships just like she'd refused to let her mom's overprotectiveness and caution send her into a safe, staid career instead of the uncertain field of creative arts that she loved.

After six months of notes and then Dylan's murder, she'd lost too much of that freedom to fear. Tate made her want to toss aside caution, toss aside her own pride and go after what she wanted, no matter the obstacles.

Sitka gave a sudden wet slosh of her tongue over Sabrina's cheek, as if she knew what Sabrina was thinking and was on board. Laughing, Sabrina wiped away the dampness, pet Sitka once more, then stood.

It was still awkward, with Tate standing there, looking way too tempting in black pants and a T-shirt that didn't hide the lean muscles underneath. At least some of her embarrassment had faded, and her face no longer felt like it was on fire.

She'd kissed him. He'd ultimately rejected her. But that didn't mean she had to give up.

The idea brought a slow smile to her face, and he swayed backward slightly, as if he'd felt the sudden force of her determination. Still, he gave her a smile in return, then asked loudly, "You ready to go?"

Then she realized something. Usually, he closed and locked the door as soon as he arrived. Today, it was wide open. She didn't see anyone in the hallway behind him, but that didn't mean Adam wasn't somewhere nearby.

Shoving back a surge of fear, she nodded and grabbed her duffel bag, packed with enough clothes and toiletries for the weekend. Hopefully, Adam would take the bait early and not make her and Tate play out a whole weekend of this awkward farce with all of Tate's colleagues watching. If he didn't, maybe she should take advantage of it, see if she could change Tate's mind.

The idea gained traction as he reached over and took her bag, slinging it easily over his shoulder. Then he took her hand in his and pulled her toward the door.

She sidled closer to him, the way she'd do if they were really dating, and he shot her a quick glance, full of surprise and heat, before calling, "Come on, Sitka."

The dog raced after them, sticking close to Sabrina as they took the elevator down to the lobby. Even where no one could see them, Tate kept his hold on her hand. But his gaze was focused on the closed door.

She could see his reflection in the shiny metal, the stern set of his jaw, the stiffness of his posture, the seriousness in his gaze. But his fingers slid back and forth over her knuckles, a soothing caress she wasn't sure he was aware he was giving.

As the numbers on the elevator readout counted

down, Sabrina tilted her head and rested it against Tate's arm. She breathed in his familiar sandalwood scent and closed her eyes, trying to mentally prepare for the weekend ahead.

The idea of spending any romantic time with Tate— even if it was pretend—made her pulse quicken. But it couldn't eliminate the building fear.

Adam was still out there, still obsessed with her and presumably still willing to kill anyone who got in his way.

Her hand clenched reflexively in Tate's as the elevator dinged and came to a stop.

"You okay?" Tate whispered as the doors slid open.

"Yes." She opened her eyes and took a deep breath, leading him through the lobby. "Let's do this."

"Hang on a second," he said, tugging on her hand just as they stepped outside. With a sudden grin, he pulled a cap from his back pocket, showed her the logo for a police K-9 training facility. "I got us a nice, secluded cabin where you'll be able to see the mountains and water, and even a glacier. But this is still Alaska, not New York City." He settled the cap on her head, then nodded. "Now you fit in."

She gave him a perplexed smile, glancing down at her simple jeans and top. Okay, yes, her jeans were slim and showed off her figure, and her top was a piece she'd found at one of the quirky shops in Desparre, flowy and lacy and the same green as her eyes. She'd swiped on some lipstick and a couple of coats of mascara before he arrived. But she wasn't exactly decked out for a party in the city.

Instead of asking about it, she turned toward his truck, parked out front. She itched to glance around, reassure herself that other police officers were keeping watch, but she resisted. If Adam was nearby, she didn't want to tip him off.

Before she could get more than a step, Tate was tugging on her hand again, pulling her back to him. "I'm glad we're doing this," he told her, his voice dropping to a husky whisper.

His eyes locked on hers as he threaded his free hand through her hair, then cupped the base of her neck. The feel of his fingers made her nerve endings spark to life, sending zings of electricity through her body.

He dipped his head slowly, the intensity in his eyes telling her he wanted to kiss her, even if the location said this was all for show. To prove to Adam it was real, to goad him into making his move.

Looping her free hand around his neck, she rose up on her tiptoes to meet him. Surprise flashed briefly in his eyes, followed by desire, and then his lips settled softly against hers.

He tasted faintly of coffee underneath mint toothpaste. The scent of sandalwood she'd started to crave when he wasn't around filled her senses as she closed her eyes and gave in to his kiss. Gave in to the intoxicating feel of his body pressed against hers, the way she could rest all of her weight on him and he'd hold steady. Gave in to all of the emotions she'd been trying to deny.

He paused for half a second, and then his hand slipped free of hers to clamp onto her hip, to haul her higher onto her tiptoes against him. His fingers flexed there, kneading into her hip as he nipped at her lips with his mouth and tongue. Then his tongue slid between her lips, sending sparks down to her toes.

She hung on tighter, linking her hands at the back of

his neck as she urged him with the slide of her tongue to go faster. She felt frantic, desperate to get closer to him, as all of the dreams she'd started to envision of a future with him swept over her. Maybe those dreams were possible. Or maybe this was her one chance to create a memory with him.

Either way, she wasn't going to waste it. She tried to slow down, to memorize the imprint of his body against hers, the slight rasp of his chin as his mouth claimed hers over and over.

Too soon, he eased back, and she dropped down to her feet, tugging on her shirt where it had ridden up slightly. He stared at her, a mix of surprise and uncertainty in his gaze, until Sitka made them both jump with a sudden *woof!*

"You're right," Tate said, shifting his gaze to the dog and breaking the spell. "We should get going. You don't mind Sitka joining us for our romantic weekend, do you?"

He looked at her again, and even though his gaze was more controlled, his emotions veiled again, he let out a heavy breath that told her he wasn't as composed as he was pretending.

She gave him a knowing smile. "Of course not." Threading her hand through his, she said, loudly enough to be overheard, "I'm ready."

He blinked at her again, his forehead creasing as if he wasn't sure if he should be reading into her words or not.

Letting him wonder, she tugged on his hand as Sitka trotted along beside her toward the truck.

He held open the door for her, then warned, "It's a

little tight in the cab for three. I'm sorry about that. I've never needed to fit an extra person in here with us."

He'd only had Sitka a few months. But the way he said it made it sound like he'd never taken another woman on a romantic getaway like this—at least not while he'd had this truck. Maybe she was reading into it, but the idea made her smile.

The dog leaped into the truck, settling into the middle and taking up some of Sabrina's seat, too.

Sabrina stepped up after her, settling her hand on Sitka's back as Tate closed her door and went around to the driver's side.

On top of everything else, he was a gentleman. Of course, maybe that was part of the problem. Part of the reason he was so determined to do what was right and practical by not jumping into anything when they were trying to make it safe for her to leave.

How could she change his mind? The distance from Desparre to New York City was no joke. And this town could easily snow you in through winter. But she didn't care. She wanted to try.

Maybe Adam would wait, give her at least part of the weekend to show Tate that the bond they'd developed was worth the effort, worth the challenges. But when the truck came to a stop ten minutes later, she realized she wasn't sure how.

Glancing around with surprise, she took in the cute house with the big front porch in the woods. It was much closer than she'd expected. Then the garage door in front of them opened, and Sabrina realized they weren't at the vacation spot he'd mentioned at all but his house.

She turned toward him, questions forming, as he turned off the truck and shut the garage door behind him.

Then the door leading to his house opened, and a woman stepped into the garage. She had wavy blond hair and wore a cap identical to the one Tate had slid onto Sabrina's head. She was even wearing the same jeans and green blouse—the outfit she'd shown Tate two days ago when he'd asked what she planned to wear. Until this moment, she'd never really wondered why he'd asked.

Realization about what was happening hit at the same time as the knowledge that she wouldn't get a chance to convince Tate of anything. Because she wasn't going on the romantic getaway with him at all.

Tate was doing the right thing. He knew he was.

Still, as he glanced across the truck at the rookie police officer from nearby Luna—on loan because she looked enough like Sabrina to pass for her—dread clamped down and refused to leave. He gave her a forced smile, trying to reassure her. "There are officers already in place around the cabin. We'll be fine."

"I'm not worried," she said, an echo of the words Sabrina had told him earlier, her face strategically hidden behind an open map.

Unlike Sabrina, Officer Angie Hallen didn't quite sound like she meant them.

He'd been a rookie once, on foot patrol back in Boston, with a veteran officer whose training method was to toss you into the fray and hope you came out in one piece. He remembered the adrenaline and the nerves all too well. Time and experience calmed both, but if you were smart, they never fully dulled, because losing your edge on the job could cost your life.

"I appreciate you agreeing to do this," he told her.

Angie didn't know the Desparre officers, and although she'd been briefed on the threat, she didn't have a history with him, didn't know what kind of officer he was.

Then again, he knew all too well that sometimes even people you knew and trusted could become a threat.

Angie nodded stiffly, and Sitka, maybe noticing her nerves, or maybe just missing Sabrina, let out a whine.

"We'll be there soon," he told his dog.

The romantic getaway spot was well-known among Desparre locals and would be easy for Adam to figure out. It was on the far southern border of Desparre, an hour away from downtown. People who weren't used to the area tended to be shocked when they suddenly came out of the woods and upon another, smaller mountain, this one edged with water and a small glacier.

Sabrina would have loved it. The thought popped into his mind and wouldn't leave, along with an image of the look in her eyes when she'd fallen into his arms and taken his kiss to a whole other level. But the look on her face when she realized she wasn't coming with him? That one stung. He'd seen a hint of betrayal, along with regret. The same regret he was feeling now.

Her kisses had held more than simple passion. There had been a promise in them, a glimpse of what he could have if he gave in to what they both wanted.

There was an ache in his chest just thinking about what he was giving up. But he needed to find a way to just be happy they were going to get her life back. Because as he glanced once more at Angie, tensing as their cabin came into view, he felt it in his gut. Adam was going to take the bait.

Even though it meant saying goodbye to Sabrina, Tate couldn't help feeling a sharp anticipation at the idea of snapping a pair of handcuffs on Adam and throwing him behind bars for good.

He pulled into the drive of the cabin he'd rented, far from the others scattered along the glacier's edge. Officers Riera and Dreymond had already picked up the key for him, letting the owners know to stay away. So now all he had to do was grab his and Sabrina's bags from the back of his truck. Then he tucked Angie into the crook of his arm, her face hidden against his chest, and hustled her into the cabin. With one sharp whistle, Sitka raced in after them.

Shutting and locking the door behind him, Tate did a quick check of the cabin, confirming it was empty and secure and that all the shades were drawn. "We're good," he told Angie as he returned to the main room.

She nodded and tucked her pistol back into the waistband at the back of her jeans. "Good. Let's check in with your backup."

"Our backup," he reminded her, grabbing his cell phone from his bag. He sent a quick text to Lorenzo Riera, and the response came back almost immediately.

We've got you. Stay alert.

"They're in place," Tate told Angie. "Now let's hope Adam makes his move quickly."

He settled onto the couch across from the front door, which gave him good visibility into the bedroom and the window access there. Then, he raised his eyebrow at Angie as she stood by the door, knowing that even though he wanted a fast resolution, this kind of operation was often a waiting game.

"I'm good here," she told him.

An hour later, she pulled a chair next to the couch and sat stiffly in it. An hour after that, she started pacing. Ten hours after that, she was slouched on the other side of the couch. By then, Tate was ready to do the same. But he also knew the darkness was Adam's friend, a time when he might feel safer sneaking up on the woman he'd been stalking and her new police-officer boyfriend.

So, when his cell phone rang, he grabbed it fast. "Talk to me," he told Lorenzo, hoping the veteran officer had already wrestled Adam to the ground and slapped cuffs on him.

"It's... We're—" The sound of gunshots made Angie jerk beside him just as Tate realized it wasn't Lorenzo, hiding in the woods with most of the Desparre officers.

It was Charlie Quinn, who was back at Tate's house, keeping Sabrina safe.

He leaped to his feet as Charlie's garbled voice filled the room again, too high-pitched with pain. "Sabrina... Get her—"

Then, another gunshot fired, and the line went dead.

Chapter 19

Sabrina sat in the living room in Tate's house, with the shades drawn and one lone light on, frustrated and worried and anxious for news.

According to officers Charlie Quinn and Max Becker, she hadn't been given the full details of the plan because they were need-to-know, and it was better if she really planned for a trip in case anyone was watching. Tate had never intended to take her on a weekend away, even a pretend one.

Pushing aside her frustration, Sabrina stood from the couch where she'd been sitting for over an hour, with nothing to entertain her but her thoughts.

Charlie wanted her to keep the television off since the house was supposed to appear empty and he didn't want to take any chances—a decision that had made Max roll his eyes and mutter something about "BS protection detail." But Charlie was the veteran so he'd won.

The two officers had been flipping through magazines in between walking around the small house and checking all the entry points. Sabrina had turned down the offers for their leftover police magazines and just waited.

After the way she and Tate had announced their plans all over town for the past few days, then flaunted that kiss in front of the hotel, she'd expected Adam to strike fast. As the time went by, she worried she might be here for days. And Tate had taken her weekend bag with him.

If she had to be here without him, she wanted to go upstairs and explore the rest of his house, see if it matched the easy comfort of the first floor. Tate had told her a lot about himself in the past few days, but he hadn't invited her into his home. Knowing it was probably the only chance she'd have to see it, she was tempted to explore. Instead, she walked over to the curtained windows.

"Please don't touch those," Charlie said, without looking up from his magazine.

"I was just—"

"If Adam followed you from the hotel to here and *didn't* fall for our ruse, we don't want to confirm anything."

He must have sensed her sudden apprehension, because he looked up and gave her a kind smile. "Don't worry. That's unlikely. But it's why we're here. And it's why we're keeping the shades down and most of the lights off. Just in case. Until we hear from Tate."

"I'm going to check in again," Max said, heading into the other room.

Sabrina strained to hear the conversation, but only the low rumble of Max's voice reached her.

When Max returned, all he said was, "No action."

She got the same update every hour for the rest of the day, until it got dark enough outside that even Charlie had given up on his magazines and was scrolling on his phone, periodically sighing.

"Maybe he's too smart to fall for this," Max suggested from the opposite side of the couch, where he'd settled an hour ago and had looked half-asleep ever since. "Or maybe he's moved on entirely, left Desparre and decided to find himself someone new to stalk."

Charlie scowled at his partner, then suggested to Sabrina, "Why don't you go upstairs? I saw a full bookshelf in Tate's second bedroom. I'm sure he wouldn't mind."

She debated only a few seconds, then hurried up the stairs. Lining the hallway were framed prints that looked like various nature scenes from Alaska. When she stepped closer to one, she saw it was labeled *Sitka, Alaska*. Wondering if he'd ever been there, if he'd loved the place enough to name his dog after it, she continued into the first room on the right.

Tate clearly used the room as his home office. There was a laptop open on a small desk against one wall, a pair of comfortable-looking chairs on another, and a bookshelf in between, overflowing with paperbacks. Smiling, Sabrina stepped closer, studying the titles in the light coming in from the hallway.

Tate had an affinity for historical nonfiction and spy novels. He also had a whole section devoted to K-9 training. Even though he'd stuffed the shelves, he hadn't put anything on top of the bookshelf. She could picture her romance novels lining that space.

A wistful smile twitched, then dropped away, leaving behind an ache in her chest she didn't think would leave anytime soon.

The sudden boom from downstairs made her jump. Was that a gunshot?

For a brief moment, she felt paralyzed. Then she eased to the edge of the room, peering into the hallway. Should she go downstairs, look for Charlie and Max and stick close to them?

Boom! Boom! Boom!

A scream punctuated the final blast, and Sabrina raced into motion, scanning the room for something she could use as a weapon. Her heartbeat thundered in her ears, dimming the noise around her, but she still heard another anguished scream, followed by footsteps pounding up the stairs.

Spinning in a circle, Sabrina desperately looked for anything that might do some damage. But there was nothing except books and a laptop.

Hide! her mind screamed at her. Racing for the closet, Sabrina had just yanked open the door when a hand clamped on her shoulder.

A scream lodged in her throat, choking her, as she spun around, lifting her fists to fight back. But it wasn't Adam. It was Max, with smears of blood across his cheeks and a look of horror in his eyes.

"Charlie?" she managed to ask, but he either didn't hear her or couldn't answer as he hustled her to the doorway, peeked out, then shoved her through it and across the hall into the bathroom.

"Get in. Lock the door." When she hesitated, wondering what he would do, he gave her a push. *"Now!"*

Shutting the door behind her, Sabrina fumbled with the lock, her hands shaking violently on the simple push mechanism. Someone could break through it easily.

Boom!

Sabrina shrieked at the gunshot, louder now, closer, and instinctively dropped to her knees in the dark bathroom.

Then the whole house seemed to fill with gunshots, and the sounds seemed to be all around her. She slapped her hands over her ears, blinking to try and see in the darkened room. Vague shapes took form—the bathtub, the toilet, a vanity—and she launched herself at the medicine cabinet.

She knocked her hand through it, searching for something useful, in the process dumping half the contents out. Then her hands closed around a straight razor. But what good would it do against a gun?

As another blast and then a loud thump sounded from right outside the bathroom, Sabrina dropped the razor and grabbed the lid off the toilet tank. Standing just past the edge of where the door would open, she hefted it, ready to swing, even as she prayed Max would knock and tell her the threat was gone.

Instead, the door smashed inward with a loud thud, making Sabrina jump. It bounced against the wall, and then a hand caught it.

Sabrina lurched forward, raising the porcelain lid with shaky arms, hoping Adam would pause long enough at seeing her to let her get a swing in before he fired.

But it wasn't Adam who entered. It was someone

shorter, but much more muscular. Someone decked out in dark fatigues, a ski mask over his face and a pistol in his hand.

In her surprise, she hesitated, and then his fist flew toward her, smashing into her face before she could jerk out of the way. The lid flew out of her hands, shattering as it hit the ground. She fell hard after it, the sight of Max's prone, bloodied form wavering at the edge of her vision before the world went dark.

Chapter 20

"What's going on?" Tate barked into the phone, sliding Sitka's vest on as Angie took the roads at dangerous speeds.

She was handling his vehicle like a pro, instead of a rookie who'd probably only done tactical driving at police academy.

"We're heading there now," Chief Griffith replied. "I don't have any updates. You know most of the officers were with you." His voice was dark and filled with self-blame as he said, "I didn't see this move coming."

Neither had Tate. In fact, Tate had thought this was the best way to keep Sabrina far away from any danger.

"Have Charlie or Max checked in?" If they had, the chief already would have told him, but Tate couldn't stop himself from asking the question. "Do we know if Sabrina is okay?"

"I don't know anything right now," the chief told him patiently. "Sam and I are on our way to your place. We closed up the station. I'll update you as soon as I can."

He hung up without another word, and Tate looked at Angie.

She didn't even glance his way, just hit the gas harder as Tate put his arms around Sitka to keep her from sliding around the truck. Then, mostly one-handed, he slid his own vest over his T-shirt, thankful that Angie had had the foresight to put hers on while he was trying to call Charlie back at the cabin.

Two other vehicles kept pace behind them, filled with the rest of the Desparre PD officers who'd been at the cabin to provide backup to him instead of watching Sabrina.

Frustration and anger built inside him until they burst out in a single curse.

"It's not your fault," Angie said, her voice high-pitched enough that he knew her outward calm was a facade. "This guy's a software engineer. Yeah, he's killed before, but I saw the report before I agreed to help. That murder was sloppy. He was going against a civilian, a marketing specialist with no reason to think he was in danger, not a pair of experienced officers."

How the hell had Adam gotten the jump on Charlie and Max?

Off the job, Tate was neutral on both of them. Max was the kind of guy who loved the power of the job, who didn't fraternize much with his fellow officers and wouldn't stick his neck out if you were in trouble with the brass. Charlie was a longtime veteran with strict ideas about who belonged on the force—and that hadn't included Tate's former partner, because Peter was hard of hearing. Still, if you were in danger on the job, both men would be there in an instant. In fact, they'd both risked their lives for him in the past. He respected them as officers.

He'd trusted them to watch over Sabrina without question. Even now, having heard the sheer amount of firepower Adam must have brought to the scene, Tate wasn't sure how Adam had gotten past both men.

Maybe he hadn't. The hope that refused to die was foolish, he knew. But he hung on to it as tightly as he could. Because ultimately, Adam's target wasn't Charlie or Max. It was Sabrina.

Stalkers who got to this level of obsession often killed their targets and anyone who stood in their way. But sometimes, they'd go a different route—abduction, assault.

Tate closed his eyes, wishing he didn't need to pray for the second choice. But at least she'd still be alive. At least he'd still have a chance to find her.

"We're close," Angie announced, and Tate opened his eyes, realizing he'd had them closed awhile, praying for Sabrina, Charlie and Max.

"All right," Tate said. "Let's—" He frowned as his phone buzzed with a text from the chief at the same time that an ambulance rounded the corner, coming from the direction of his house, sirens blaring.

They'd gotten help fast. The nearest hospital was an hour away, so they'd probably also gotten lucky, with medics happening to be nearby. It meant someone was still able to be saved. But who?

Tate's pulse rocketed as he opened the chief's text, hands shaking. But all it said was Scene is contained.

"Shit," Tate breathed. It was bad if the chief wasn't

giving him news over text. The screen on his phone went blurry as tears flooded his vision. He blinked, swiping a hand over his eyes, and told himself it didn't mean Sabrina was dead.

It didn't mean all the impossible dreams he'd had about a real future with her were forever gone. It didn't mean the promises he'd made to her about getting her life back had been lies.

"We're here," Angie announced, slamming his truck to a stop and making Sitka yelp. "You good?"

"Yeah," Tate said, his hoarse voice marking him a liar. But even if the scene was contained, he still had a job to do. Justice to mete out.

Taking a deep breath, he tried to shove his fear and grief as deep as he could. Because being unfocused right now could get someone killed.

He stepped out of the truck, and Sitka leaped out beside him, moving one pace ahead of him as if she was trying to protect him from what he was about to see.

His house looked okay from the outside, except for the trail of blood leading down his front steps. His breath caught at the sight, then lodged painfully in his chest, and Tate faltered.

Before he could get moving again, the chief stepped outside. There was blood on his arms beneath the rolled-up sleeves of his uniform, and exhaustion and grief on his face.

As other vehicles slammed to a stop behind him and his fellow officers crowded around him to hear the news about their own, Tate stared at the chief. The air felt too heavy, too thick to get a solid breath, and his house wavered in front of him.

"Charlie was just rushed to the hospital," the chief said. "Max died at the scene."

A collective gasp behind him registered as the words hit Tate like a punch to the gut. No, he hadn't been personal friends with Max, but the man had put his life on the line for Sabrina. He was only a few years older than Tate, with a wife and two young sons at home.

"Sabrina is missing."

Tate blinked, trying to focus. Sabrina wasn't dead.

"There were at least two gunmen here today," the chief continued. "As Charlie was being loaded into the ambulance, he said they were wearing all black, looked like tactical gear. And black ski masks."

Tate swayed violently on his feet, an image in his mind of two masked men emerging from the trail parallel to him on a run five and a half years ago. Someone's hand—Angie's?—slapped his back and kept him upright as the chief demanded, "Talk to me, Emory. Could Adam have an accomplice?"

"It's not Adam," Tate breathed, a million regrets filling his mind.

He should have left Desparre the moment that news story had gone national, if not before then, when it had first been printed. He should have left Sabrina in the capable care of his fellow officers. Instead, he'd been selfish and stayed. That mistake had probably just cost Sabrina her life.

But not in a quick burst of gunfire like it might have happened if this were Adam. No, the officers who'd tried to kill him back in Boston were out for blood. His blood. And if they couldn't have it, they'd settle for making someone he loved suffer.

Chapter 21

Sabrina's head throbbed violently, shooting pain through her eyes as she tried to open them. Her mouth was cotton dry, and her hands and feet felt swollen and heavy.

She tried to move, tried to open her eyes. Panic flooded when she couldn't seem to do either, and her heart pounded frantically, almost painfully. Fear sent adrenaline shooting through her system, along with a realization of the last thing she'd seen.

Officer Max Becker lying in a pool of blood outside the bathroom door. A masked man standing over her, wielding a pistol. Then, the world had shifted and disappeared.

Was she still in Tate's house? Had the gunman left her for dead?

Swallowing back the sudden nausea, Sabrina forced her eyes open. The world in front of her swayed as it finally emerged from darkness.

She was lying awkwardly on her side on the floor. She definitely wasn't in Tate's bathroom or hallway but lying on dusty concrete. The world around her was dim, and she didn't think it was just her vision. The light seemed to be coming from certain areas only, the rest of the space in darkness. She could make out the wall across from her. It was concrete, too.

Where the hell was she?

Did Tate's house have a basement? Could she be down there? Or had the man taken her from Tate's house?

As she tried to push herself upright, her hands and feet caught, refusing to separate. The panic intensified, bringing tears to her eyes. She was bound at her wrists and ankles, tight enough that her hands and feet were partially asleep. Movement sent pins and needles pricking her nerve endings.

"She's awake."

The hard, emotionless statement made Sabrina jerk, searching for the source.

Booted feet stepped into view and she twisted, straining to see the face above her.

It wasn't covered by a mask anymore, yet she still didn't recognize him. Somehow, her abductor looked much taller than he had in Tate's bathroom. Lankier, too, with pale skin and reddish-blond hair. As he leaned toward her, she saw light blue eyes that didn't match her memory of hazel eyes behind the mask. He smirked at her and stood straight again as she tried to get her mouth to work.

"Whhhoare you?" she slurred.

"Get the camera," he called, and it took Sabrina a minute to realize he wasn't alone.

Another set of boots moved toward her, and as she

twisted to look up at the person wearing them, she saw the hazel eyes from Tate's house. The man who'd knocked her out.

He was shorter than the first one by a solid nine inches, but he made up for it in bulk. His dark hair was sheared short, and his nose looked like it had been broken, probably more than once.

Hired guns Adam had found? It seemed more likely than him having made friends in Alaska who were willing to abduct someone for him.

The muscle-bound guy dragged a tripod across from her and set an old-fashioned video camera on it.

Dread dropped to her stomach as her fear multiplied and tears rushed to her eyes. What were they planning to do to her that they wanted to record?

Instinctively, she fought the bonds at her wrists and ankles, even though it just caused more pain.

The lanky one let out a harsh laugh and muttered, "No need. We'll take these off for you." The tone was so dark, it sent new fear through her.

"Who are you?" she managed, blinking until her vision cleared. "Why are you doing this?" Her voice came out stronger than she'd expected, sounded less afraid.

If Adam had sent them, why? Was he too much of a coward to hurt her himself?

"You picked the wrong man to shack up with," the lanky one said.

His accent registered as Bostonian, and Sabrina frowned, trying to understand. Did they think she'd *wanted* Adam to chase after her?

The bulky one snorted. "She doesn't get it," he told his friend.

His accent was also distinctly Boston. But none of

the information Tate had shared about Adam's past mentioned him having lived there.

The lanky guy leaned close to her again, and Sabrina instinctively jerked back, wanting to get away.

"He didn't warn you, did he? He let you think he was some kind of stand-up guy, but the truth is he's a rat who's only loyal to himself." He gave her a crooked smile. "Sorry, honey, but you're going to pay for it."

"I didn't even know who he was until a week ago," she insisted, even though the dread building in her chest told her this wasn't about Adam at all.

The bulky guy shrugged, standing again. "When you found out, you should have run."

"Wouldn't have mattered," the lanky one put in. "He loves her, so it doesn't matter how she feels about him." Then he told his friend, "Get the ropes off. Camera is ready to go."

As his friend reached for her hands, Sabrina tried to wriggle away, but he yanked her arms upward, making her gasp at the sharp pain across her shoulders.

"Stay still." The blade of a knife slid too close to her wrists, and then her arms fell loose.

She wanted to wrench them in front of her, use them to claw at the guy's eyes while he was close to her, but they dropped uselessly, pain pricking like a thousand tiny pins.

How long had she been restrained and unconscious? How far away from Tate's house had they taken her?

The knife sliced again, this time through the bonds at her ankles, and then her feet were free, too. The sharp pains dancing across her feet at the sudden blood flow brought tears to her eyes.

"Get her up," the lanky guy said. "Remember, he'll probably take this to the cops, so no talking."

The bulky guy pulled her to her feet, but they were still asleep and wouldn't hold her. He grabbed her before she hit the ground, rolling his eyes as she tried to get her body to work.

She wiggled her toes and fingers, trying to get the blood flowing properly again, and just as she was starting to feel more stable, the guy let go. She swayed and fell backward against the cold concrete wall.

Glancing up, she saw more concrete above her. Where the hell was she?

The lanky guy stood across from her by the camera, against another wall. On either side of her, the space narrowed into what looked like hallways without doors to block the way. But there was only darkness, so she had no idea where either led.

"Let's do this," the bulky guy said, drawing her attention back to them as they both slid the masks over their faces again.

Panic struck. She knew she wouldn't make it, but she had to try. Shoving herself off the wall, she veered toward the hallway farther from the men, but her feet still weren't working properly, and the run she'd expected was an awkward stumble.

The lanky guy caught her easily and shoved her back into the wall.

She bounced off it, righting herself before she fell again.

"Sorry, honey. You sealed your own fate when you hooked your future to Tate Donnoly."

This was about *Tate*? The nonsensical words ran through her mind as she tried to process the wrong

last name they'd used. Had they confused him with
someone else?

Then the red light on the camera flashed on, and they
both stepped purposely toward her.

Sabrina backed up, then she hit the wall again, and
they were still coming. She threw her hands in front of
her face, her mind whirling. Tate had grown up in the
Midwest. He'd never mentioned Boston. But these men
must have seen him picking her up at the hotel, dropping her at his house. They'd seen his face, so presumably they knew him.

"Please don't," she begged as they took another step
closer and the lanky one smiled.

Panic overtook her, sending her heart rate into over-
drive. "Tate doesn't care about me! It was all a setup.
We're not really dating."

The bulky one snorted and then threw a punch that
smashed into her cheekbone. It lifted her feet out from
under her and made bright flashes of light strobe in
front of her eyes.

She hit first the wall and then the ground, slamming
into the hard concrete with a force that stole her breath.
The sound seemed to echo in the hard-surfaced room,
worsening her already-shaky equilibrium.

The other one swung a boot at her ribs, and she
rolled, but not far or fast enough. It connected, sending new pain through her chest, and she curled into a
ball, hoping to protect herself.

But one of them yanked her to her feet, only to hit her
again, this time a punch to the other side of her face near
her lips that made blood splatter across her face and fill
her mouth. She flew backward, slamming into the wall.

Her head bounced against it, and her vision went dark, so she didn't see the next hit coming.

It landed under her chin, snapping her head back into the wall yet again. Her legs crumpled, and she threw her hands out to try and catch herself. Then, she hit the ground face-first, and the whole world blessedly disappeared.

"You've got some explaining to do," the chief told him, hands planted flat on Tate's kitchen table as he leaned over it toward Tate. "And I want the whole truth right now. No more lies. I need to know what we're dealing with here. I need to know *who* we're dealing with."

Noise from his fellow officers reached him from a distance. The officers were in the mudroom near his back entrance, dusting around the broken window where the assailants had entered. It was where Charlie had been found, facedown in a pool of blood, his hand still clutching his cracked cell phone.

Others were upstairs, dealing with evidence near where Max had been killed and Sabrina had been taken. Evidence of a struggle both inside and outside the bathroom suggested Max had locked her in there before he'd been killed defending her. The smashed lid from his toilet suggested Sabrina had grabbed the only available weapon and tried to defend herself. The blood on his bathroom floor said she'd paid for it.

"I'm sorry," Tate said, and his voice came out a pained whisper. "I never thought my past would catch up to me like this. If I had—"

The chief put up a hand. "We don't have time for regrets right now. What we need is a plan to move for-

ward. So give me what I need to make an informed decision here, Emory."

Tate flinched at the use of his fake last name, at all
of the mistakes he'd made. If it could help save Sabrina,
he'd gladly give up all of his secrets, even if it landed
him in jail.

"My real name is Tate Donnoly."

The chief leaned back, as if pushed by the force of
his surprise, then nodded for Tate to keep going.

"I was a police officer back in Boston before I came
here. I was...able to create a fake name and start over
in Alaska." He left out mention of his family friend in
Witness Protection and the role his former chief had
played, but the way Chief Griffith's eyes narrowed, he
knew there was more to it.

"Back in Boston I witnessed three fellow officers
taking a payoff from a crime lord. I reported it, and
the whole situation was under investigation by the FBI
when there was an attempt on my life." Tate blew out
a heavy breath, remembering how close he'd come to
dying that day. Jim Bellows, Kevin Fricker and Paul
Martin were trained to take down an opponent fast and
efficiently. He'd had the same training, but all Sabrina
had was two years of running and trying to stay ahead
of the threat against her.

Trying to focus, he told his chief, "The crime boss
and one of the officers ultimately went to prison. But
I never actually *saw* Kevin Fricker and Paul Martin
try to kill me that day, only Jim, who fired the shot
that hit me. And the FBI could only find a money trail
to Jim. So Kevin and Paul got off. They stayed in the
department until the stain got too bad, then went on
to other departments. Other officers didn't trust them.

They didn't trust me anymore, either. I knew that I'd gotten lucky and that Kevin and Paul might try again. Kevin made a threat on his last day, and I didn't want to risk my life or the people I loved so I took on a new name and started over here. Went through the academy again, came in as a Desparre PD rookie. I kept tabs on them over the years, but it seemed like I was safe here."

The chief nodded slowly, his gaze still assessing, probably seeing a lot more than Tate was saying. "Then that news article went national."

"Yeah," Tate agreed. "And we made a big show of how I fell for Sabrina."

Lines creased the chief's forehead, an understanding that since the Boston officers had gone after Sabrina instead of Tate, it meant they wanted to hurt her to get to him. "So what's their next step? Are we waiting for some kind of ransom note? A request to make a trade? You for Sabrina?"

"I sure hope so," Tate breathed. "But I think that's a best-case scenario. They blame me for all of it. Not just one of their closest friends going to jail and them being ousted from the Boston PD, but I cut off their second source of income—their payoff. Not to mention that I destroyed their reputations. They've hopped from one two-bit department to the next ever since."

"I'm not sure that's on you," Chief Griffith said. "Sounds like they may be doing it to themselves."

"But they blame me," Tate reiterated. "I thought if they ever came after me, it would be a bullet in the head in the middle of the night or maybe out on a re-mote call somewhere. But this…" He stared hard at the chief. "No matter what happens, Sabrina is the priority. I take responsibility for myself. If they want me, they

can have me. Just please get her out." He glanced at
Sitka, who whined and shuffled her feet, nudging him
hard. His voice broke a little as he added, "And please
take care of Sitka."

The chief nodded slowly. "You know civilians are
always our priority. And we look after our own. Sitka
is one of us."

From the front of the house, Officer Sam Jennings
yelled, "We've got a delivery!"

Tate turned to run for the front yard when the chief
added, "You're one of us, too, Tate."

He nodded his thanks, knowing how much of a show
of faith that was, given how he'd lied and broken the
law to get here. Then he hurried to where Sam stood,
gingerly holding a manila envelope with gloved hands.

"How did it arrive?" the chief demanded from right
behind Tate.

"Someone tossed it out of a van, then took off," Sam
said. "Lorenzo and Nate went after him, but we all recognized the van. It's Old Oliver."

"Shit," Tate breathed. Old Oliver was Oliver Yardley,
the dad of Young Oliver, who was equally eccentric.
Old Oliver lived up in the mountain somewhere and periodically came into town and scared the newer locals
with his long, untamed hair and beard and constantly
darting eyes. He thought the government was spying
on him, that anyone could be working for them, and
even though the Desparre PD considered him gener-
ally harmless, half the time he didn't make much sense.

"Open it," the chief said.

"I got it," Tate said, grabbing the envelope from Sam.
"After Paul left the Boston PD, he got training as a
bomb tech at a different department." Ignoring the looks

of confusion from his fellow officers, Tate walked far enough away that if it was a bomb, it wouldn't take out anyone else with him. "Stay!" he warned Sitka when she tried to follow.

She plopped onto her butt, but glanced up at his chief as if waiting for him to overrule Tate.

She whined when the chief ignored her, leaning forward as Tate took a deep breath and ripped open the envelope. What fell out wasn't a bomb but a flash drive.

Dread hit like a punch to his chest as he hurried wordlessly back inside and upstairs to his laptop. He tried not to see the huge bloodstain in his hallway, tried not to imagine Max's prone body there, but it didn't work.

He fit the flash drive into his computer, then braced himself as he felt the chief and several of his colleagues crowd behind him.

The audio came on first, Sabrina's terrified voice pleading, "Please don't!" Static covered most of her next words, but he heard his name. Then the video flashed on his screen, two men in all black partially blocking the camera as they stepped toward Sabrina. One of them laughed at her, then smashed a fist into her face.

Tate cringed, clenching his hands as she hit the floor hard and then got kicked in the ribs as she tried to roll away. They yanked her up, hit her twice more, sending blood flying before she crashed into the ground and didn't move.

Then the shorter, bulkier guy walked toward the camera, a self-satisfied smile showing through the mouth hole in his ski mask. Tate knew that smirk. Paul Martin.

Paul's hand reached toward the screen, showcasing bloody knuckles, before the video went dark.

A couple of the cops behind him swore, and the chief's hand clapped on Tate's shoulder as the camera flashed on again, this time facing the wall, where a piece of paper had been taped. Tate had to squint to read the sloppy, angry writing.

You did this to her. You want her pain to end? Go downtown and shoot yourself in the head. Otherwise, we'll get her back to you eventually. In pieces.

"We'll find her," the chief said softly as Tate's mind whirled and his stomach threatened to bring up the coffee he'd sipped at the cabin by the glacier.

"Old Oliver isn't giving us much," Lorenzo announced as he burst into the room. "He got paid to do it, says he doesn't know the guy who asked him to drop it off. We can pick him up again, but he's a dead end."

"Hey, I know that place," Nate said, pointing at the image frozen on the screen, all concrete around the single piece of paper.

Tate grabbed the young officer by his shoulders. Nate had grown up in Desparre, and he often complained that he'd run out of things to do here. "Where?"

Nate jerked slightly at the force of Tate's desperation. "It's an old army fort at the base of the mountain, near Luna. It's deserted and boarded up, but when I was a teenager, you could slip through the boards at the main entrance if you were thin enough. It used to be a place to go drinking."

"Let's go," Tate said, moving toward the door.

The chief stepped in his path. "We need a plan."

Tate stared him directly in the eyes. "I know these men, Chief. They're going to keep making tapes. They know I won't actually shoot myself, because *I know* they wouldn't let her go even if I did. But eventually, she won't be able to take any more." His voice broke, and he paused for a breath. "We need to hurry."

The chief nodded. "Okay. We'll plan on the way. Tate, you're with me. Sam, Lorenzo, Nate, you three follow." He turned to the final two officers present. "You two, continue securing the scene. And call the state PD or the FBI and tell them we need a bomb tech immediately. Don't stop calling until we get someone who will meet us there now."

Then the chief led Tate and Sitka down the stairs to his SUV, and the other officers followed on their tail. During the hour-long drive, the chief put the other officers on speaker, and they went over details.

According to Nate, there was only one entry point. "There is a maze of rooms in that fort," Nate insisted when Tate pressed him on it, "and I think at one point, there were multiple exits. Windows, too, but those have long since been closed up solid or collapsed. The actual entrances are all blocked off now or buried against the mountain and the forest that grew into it. There's only one way in."

The news made dread churn in Tate's gut. Kevin and Paul weren't the kind of guys to trap themselves anywhere. Did they think the fort was so out of the way, old and unused, that no one would recognize where they were? Or had they banked on Tate and his fellow officers recognizing it? Had they already moved somewhere else and left the single entrance rigged?

He shared his fears with the chief, who got back on the phone and confirmed the FBI bomb tech was already en route via helicopter and would probably beat them there.

They beat her, but only by five minutes. As soon as she arrived, she donned a massive bomb suit and waddled up to the boarded-up entrance of the fort.

"We've got a bomb," she confirmed grimly less than ten minutes later.

The entrance was set against the side of the mountain, hidden off an old, overgrown trail that seemed to lead nowhere now that the fort was defunct. The building was derelict, pieces of it crumbling around the entrance. The structure itself went on seemingly for miles, disappearing into the side of the mountain and within the forest that seemed to have swallowed most of it up.

"How long to defuse it?" the chief asked.

The bomb tech, a tiny Black woman with sharp eyes and sure fingers, shook her head. "Probably a couple hours."

Tate swore. Maybe that was Kevin and Paul's ultimate plan. Let him get here with enough time to save her but spend so long trying to get into the fort that it was too late. Because one thing he knew for sure: in a couple of hours, Sabrina would be dead.

Chapter 22

The first thing Sabrina felt was an intense pounding in her head. It radiated down her neck and along her jaw. Even her eyes hurt.

She wanted to groan, but couldn't summon the energy. She cracked her eyes open, and they refused to go any farther. It wasn't exhaustion, she realized, but swelling.

Swallowing the moisture that had gathered in her mouth, she almost choked as she discovered it was blood.

The two men huddled across from her didn't seem to notice. They were arguing, their words echoing too loudly in her ears, intensifying the agony in her head.

Sabrina gently moved her jaw, trying to figure out if it was broken. New pain jolted up to her ears and down her neck, and tears blurred her vision.

Blinking them away, she looked down at herself. There was pain along her spine, and her hands and feet still throbbed. But she was still dressed, and no one had bothered to retie her bonds.

"What if he really *doesn't* care?" the bulky guy snapped.

"Relax, Paul," the lanky one replied. "You saw them at the hotel. He couldn't keep his hands off her. He'll come. And if he doesn't, we send another video." He shrugged. "Or we do what we threatened."

He glanced her way, and Sabrina closed her eyes, her heart thundering. But no footsteps sounded, at least not any she could hear over her pounding heartbeat and throbbing head. Finally, she eased her eyes open again. They weren't looking at her.

Paul's shoulders twitched, and there was discomfort on his face. "Or we just kill her. Drop her on his doorstep."

"Cops are there, moron," the lanky guy said.

"I didn't mean *literally*," Paul answered. "Geez, Kevin. But *I'm* not cutting her up. You want to do it, that's on you."

A shudder raced through Sabrina, violent and unstoppable, making her legs and arms twitch.

Both men glanced at her but immediately turned back to each other.

Her eyes were so swollen her captors couldn't tell they were open. The knowledge was only mildly comforting in the sea of panic swallowing her.

Her breathing hitched, threatening to make her choke on blood again, and Sabrina tried to tune out the men and focus on staying calm, on formulating some kind of plan. But she wasn't sure she could stand if she tried, and she certainly couldn't outrun them, even if she knew where to go.

Tears flooded again, and this time, she couldn't blink them away.

"You think Tate will recognize this place?" Paul asked, and Sabrina tried to focus again.

"If not, I'm sure one of the locals will. Stop second-guessing this. That local guide said the back entrance has been boarded up for a decade, and everyone knows it's impassable. There's no one out here to notice that we blew through those boards. We're good. They'll go to the main door, and they'll get themselves blown up."

Sabrina jerked at that, and Kevin looked her way, a slow smile on his face that told her he'd realized she was awake. Beyond enjoying her fear, he didn't seem to care, because he turned back to Paul and said, "Just relax. It'll all be over soon, and no one will ever know we were here." Then he pulled out his phone and focused on that.

Paul rolled his eyes, sank to the floor and leaned his head against the wall, staring upward.

Sabrina wiggled her toes in her shoes, bent her fingers. Her toes moved okay after a minute, but her fingers felt stiff and swollen, and she realized she'd thrown her hands up to block at least one blow. She'd probably taken a hit there. Or maybe she'd smashed them when she fell to the ground. She didn't remember falling again, but the ache across her face and chest and the way she was lying on her stomach, with her face twisted to the side, told her she had.

She needed a plan. Even if it was just to find her way to the door and blow it up herself before Tate could get there and trigger it. She didn't want to die like this, at the brutal fists of two men with some agenda she didn't understand. If this was the end, she wanted to go out fighting. Or at least saving the man she'd fallen for.

Trying to shift her body even slightly, maneuver her arms and hands out from underneath her, was surprisingly hard. It made new pain flash through her body and drew a groan she couldn't stifle.

The men barely spared her a glance, which told her she looked as bad as she felt. She kept trying, lifting her head to get a better look at her surroundings. Her neck made a terrible cracking sound, and the throbbing in her head amplified, obscuring her vision until she lowered her cheek down against the cold concrete.

Dizziness overwhelmed her, and she could feel herself being sucked under again. She tried to fight it, but the darkness claimed her.

It had been too long.

Tate shuffled from one foot to the other, watching the bomb tech—Njeri was her name—in her massive bomb suit meticulously working. He and the other officers were waiting at a distance.

The chief was continuously on the phone, digging up intel. He'd connected with Tate's old chief back in Boston, who'd been shocked to learn Tate had returned to Alaska and had expressed more worry than anger over Tate's illegal name change. Chief Griffith had also spoken with multiple police chiefs in Massachusetts who'd worked with Kevin and Paul. And he'd touched base with the officers handling the crime scene at Tate's house.

So far, he'd uncovered that a string of problems like unwarranted aggression and some suspected dirty dealing had followed Paul and Kevin from one department to the next. He'd found a general lack of surprise that they'd come after the man they'd apparently spent a lot of time railing against to their coworkers. But from their current departments, Chief Griffith's questions had been met with only careful statements that both men had taken personal time off. The chief had hung up those calls cursing about people covering their asses.

Tate's colleagues were on their own phones, following up on other connections the chief had dug up on his calls. Only Tate was left out of the work, since it seemed many of the people being contacted would either know him or know of him. Depending on what they'd heard from Kevin and Paul, that might not be good.

When the chief hung up his latest call and ran a hand over his eyes, Tate stepped closer to him. "There has to be another way in."

The chief shook his head. "Nate doesn't know of one, and he knows the mountains of Desparre better than any of us. I called the park service. They say normally this place might have become a tourist attraction, but the remote location and the fact that there are health concerns with it has kept it boarded up and off-limits. The fort originally had at least three entrances. One of those caved in a long time ago. The other was boarded up ages ago, but it might still be accessible. Unfortunately, they don't know where it is because the fort has been defunct since the end of World War II. The forest grew in around it. They're tracking down some local guides and are supposed to get back to me."

"I'm going to see if Sitka can sniff anything out."

At the sound of her name, Sitka jumped to her feet. She ran a tight circle around him, wagging her tail.

The chief glanced from him to Sitka, then back

again. He nodded slowly. "Okay. Just keep me in the loop—and I mean every fifteen minutes, Tate. If you weren't Sitka's handler, I'd send someone else with her right now. As it is, I need the rest of my team here, ready to go as soon as the bomb is defused. Njeri is making faster progress than she'd initially thought."

Tate nodded, then walked Sitka up next to Njeri.

She spun to face him and demanded, "What the *hell* are you doing?"

"We just need a quick sniff," he answered as Sitka put her nose to the thick layers of wood nailed across the entrance. Whatever gap had existed when Nate was a teenager had apparently been boarded over, because there was barely enough room for air to pass through now.

The boards looked relatively new, but whether Paul and Kevin had nailed them in place themselves after trapping Sabrina in there and rigging the place or whether someone had done so years ago, Tate wasn't sure. The only thing he knew was that if the crooked cops were still inside, they would have had to go in another way.

Sitka sniffed a line across the boards, then her nose came up. She sniffed the air and started moving around the side of the building. Tate followed, with Njeri's curse trailing after him.

Sitka stuck to the edge of the building as it disappeared into thicker woods, until Tate could no longer see his fellow officers. Then she veered right, away from the mountain, and started running.

Tate hesitated, then ran after her. She'd been right when they'd searched the woods behind Sabrina's house. He had to believe she could do it this time, too.

Hold on, Sabrina, he willed her, as his hand instinctively rested on his pistol. Besides the Taser and pepper spray, it was his only weapon. He had no doubt that Paul and Kevin had more. Hopefully, he wouldn't come across them too abruptly and be forced into a firefight before he could get backup.

As the forest closed in around him and Sitka, she slowed on a trail big enough to hold a four-wheeler and then veered left. Tate unsnapped the top of his holster. Last fall's dead leaves crunched under his feet, but he couldn't hear his fellow officers anymore even if he strained. All he could hear was Sitka's sure footsteps as she raced forward, leaping over a fallen log.

Tate ran around it, trying to keep up. He almost went down as his feet slid across a pile of smaller sticks on the other side, and then his breath caught. Up ahead was more of the fort, emerging from the mountain and surrounded by debris that looked like pieces of plywood, broken and splintered. Beyond it, possibly…a door?

Sitka turned her head toward him, and before she could bark, Tate put his hand to his lips and whispered, "Sitka, quiet."

She complied, her tail wagging frantically.

His pulse doubled as he crept forward. When he glanced down, he realized he'd pulled his weapon out without conscious thought.

After a few more steps, he was certain. Sitka had found the other entrance.

It was no longer boarded up. Apparently, Kevin and Paul had blasted their way inside with another bomb. Now it was a clear entrance they'd probably assumed no one would find.

Tears rushed to his eyes as he stepped up next to his dog, petted her head and praised her. "Good girl!"

She thumped her tail, and he urged her over to the side, around the corner from the door, in case Paul or Kevin stepped outside. Then he pulled out his cell phone and sent the chief a quick text about where he was, hoping the chief would be able to follow his directions.

Tucking his phone away, he glanced back the way they'd come. He tried to gauge how long it would take for his fellow officers to get here. His stomach churned at the delay, especially as his mind put Sabrina's beating on replay.

"Stay with me, girl," he told Sitka. "We're going to work."

From somewhere inside the cavernous fort, a voice echoed. "I think it's time to cut our losses and get out before they find us. Let's kill her now."

He recognized that voice. Paul Martin.

Saying a quick prayer, Tate stepped inside. Sitka slipped in next to him.

After the bright sunshine outside, his eyes took a minute to adjust to the long, dark hallway. It smelled dank and stuffy, like no one had used it since World War II.

He tried to will his heartbeat to normalize, to treat this like any other police callout. But this wasn't like any call he'd ever been to. This was Sabrina.

As his eyes started to adjust, Tate slipped his finger alongside the trigger. He raised his weapon and slid along the wall, toward the sound of Paul's voice. Sitka stuck right on his heels.

"Don't wimp out on me now." Kevin's voice reached him. "Don't you want to hear the explosion?"

Paul's response was muttered and sounded like a curse.

Beside him, Tate could feel more than see the fur on Sitka's back rise as there was a thump, and then Sabrina groaned in pain.

His whole body tensed with anger and shared pain, and then he was standing next to an open doorway. Gesturing for Sitka to ease in beside him where she wouldn't be seen, Tate peeked carefully around the corner.

Kevin was leaning against the wall diagonal from him, standing near a tripod as he scrolled on his phone. There was a pistol tucked into the waistband of his black pants and a length of rope near his feet.

Tate heard Paul from the opposite wall, muttering. He was pretty sure Sabrina was over that way, too.

Lowering himself slowly, silently to the floor while Sitka remained motionless beside him, Tate edged millimeter by millimeter until he could see around the corner.

Paul stood next to Sabrina's prone form, his hands fisted and his gun within easy reach at his waist. There was a foldable knife clipped to his waistband, too.

Sabrina was lying on her stomach, her arms tucked underneath her. Her legs were curled slightly inward protectively, her neck twisted so she wasn't facedown. There was dried blood caked to her lips and chin, and her eyes were swollen and bruised.

The sight made nausea and fury mingle in his belly. He might not have thrown the blows, but this was his fault.

Focus, he reminded himself. Forcing his gaze off her, Tate darted one more look toward Kevin, who was still on his phone, seemingly oblivious to Paul's fury. Then he slid carefully backward.

There was no good way in.

Kevin and Paul were too far apart. Even if he sent Sitka after Paul while he shot Kevin, it would be dicey getting through the doorway fast enough. Paul and Kevin might have time to pull their weapons, especially Kevin, who had one of the fastest draws Tate had ever seen.

Was his team close? Risking a glance at his phone, he saw that he had no bars. The text he'd sent the chief was marked Unable to send.

A curse built inside him, along with new fear. Did he turn back? Risk the chance of them hearing his retreat? Risk them deciding to get rid of Sabrina before he could make the trek to his team and back?

His pulse thundered as sweat slicked his hands. There was really no decision. He had one chance to get this right.

But if he and Sitka were even the slightest bit off their marks, Sabrina would be the first to die.

Chapter 23

"They're here!"

Paul's shout roused her. It took all of Sabrina's energy to force her eyes open again. This time, she could see even less. Just a sliver of the room, partially obscured by her eyelashes.

It seemed like Paul had just stepped over to the doorway on the left a second ago, but now he was moving toward her again, a nervous grin twitching on his face. "They're trying to defuse the bomb."

Hope blossomed beneath her pain until he added, "It'll happen soon. They'll think they've got the bomb defused and trigger the secondary device."

Fear erupted, overriding her pain, and Sabrina tried to stare down the long hallway, estimate how far it was to the door. But she could only see the first few feet, lit up by a lantern they'd set at the edge of the room. Beyond that was darkness. And she wasn't sure she could stand up, let alone run to the door before they caught her.

If Tate and his teammates were already working on the door, her trying to set off the bomb wouldn't save them, anyway. It would kill everyone.

Frustration tensed her chest, sent a new wave of pain through her body that she ignored. She refused to lie here and wait to die. But what options did she have?

She sucked in a deep breath, trying to clear the haze in her mind as well as give her body strength. The faint scent of dog and sandalwood filled her nose, and she couldn't stop her loud exhale, which sounded like something between laughter and a cry. She must be in bad shape if she was hallucinating Tate and Sitka nearby.

Kevin glanced her way, but she didn't hold his interest long before he was back on his phone, muttering to himself, "Soon, soon." Then he paused and glanced at Paul. "You sure we're safe here?" He looked up at the ceiling, which had crumbled in places and was stained from years of neglect and moisture. "I'm not sure how structurally sound this place is."

Paul grinned, seeming suddenly in his element. "We're fine. This fort has been standing since World War II. Besides, it's a directed charge. It'll blow out, not toward us. While they're cleaning up body parts— assuming anyone was standing far enough back not to get hit—we'll go out the back way."

Kevin nodded as he pushed away from the wall, tucked his phone in his pocket. He looked a lot more alert, anticipatory.

Sabrina took another deep breath, and the imaginary scents were gone. She wedged her hand underneath her chest and shifted slightly, getting a better angle for her neck. Then her breath caught and her eyes widened enough to realize she wasn't hallucinating.

That was Tate's head she'd just seen disappearing around the corner, down low, on the ground like her.

Hope and fear mingled, made her heart race. But as her gaze swept Paul and Kevin, she realized there was no good way into the room, even if Tate had a lot of backup.

She thought back over the almost two weeks she'd spent stuck in that hotel room, the times Tate had stopped by and they'd talked about anything and everything. He'd given her some insight into how police officers worked, the precautions and the dangers.

Something that had stuck out to her then because she'd never considered it was the danger of doorways. It made you exposed, gave a prepared criminal an easy spot to focus their weapons on and just wait. If you had to go in, you moved fast and got out of the doorway immediately.

If that was Tate's plan, who was with him? Only one officer could fit through the doorway at a time, and Kevin and Paul were at opposite sides of the room, Paul having taken up his typical spot near her.

They might not know Tate was here, but since Paul's announcement that officers were working to get past the bomb, they were alert. Kevin's hand had settled on his gun, and he kept licking his lips, like he couldn't wait to use it on someone. Paul was pacing back and forth, and he'd pulled his knife out, kept flicking it. Open, closed, open, closed.

If Tate came through that doorway, even if he had the element of surprise, could he really take out both Paul and Kevin before one of them killed him? Or her?

Fear cramped her stomach and tunneled her vision,

and she closed her eyes, tried to think. She needed to help. She needed a way to distract them.

Hoping to clear her mind again, she took a deep breath and gagged on something, maybe even more of her own blood. She tried to breathe through it, but it just got worse, choking her as she erupted in a fit of coughing.

"Get her up," Kevin snapped from what seemed like far away. "We might need her. Don't let her choke."

Paul gave a loud sigh, then tucked his knife back into his waistband. Then he stepped closer, grabbed her arms roughly and flipped her to her back.

It only made the coughing worse, and she tried to lean forward to get some air as he dragged her toward the wall. Tears obscured her vision and ran down her face as he propped her against the wall, then started to straighten.

This was it. This was her chance.

Fighting through the coughing that wouldn't stop, Sabrina lunged toward him, blinking back tears as she made a grab for the gun at his waistband.

"Hey!" Paul yelled, startling Tate as he climbed to his feet.

He peered around the corner and saw Kevin, wide-eyed and pulling his gun from his waistband.

From the other side of the room, he heard a scuffling, then a thump and Sabrina's yelp of pain.

He'd run out of time.

"Sitka, go get!" he commanded. Then he lifted his weapon and lunged into the room, breaking right.

Kevin already had his weapon up toward Sabrina, but at Tate's entrance, he swiveled, redirecting it at Tate.

Tate slid his finger under the trigger guard, his heart

thundering, his breathing erratic, his movements desperate. Kevin was one of the best shooters he'd ever seen. He was fast, too fast.

From his peripheral vision, Tate saw a blur of fur and lean muscles as Sitka raced past him, then launched herself into the air, straight at Paul.

Tate fired, and the blast of his bullet leaving the chamber echoed and echoed. Too late he realized it wasn't just his own bullet sounding.

His left arm screamed in agony as he flew backward, landing hard on the concrete floor, then sliding into the wall with a dull thud. *A matching scar for the other side.*

To his left, Sitka slammed into Paul, knocking the muscle-bound man to the floor. His gun, which Tate suddenly realized had been in a tug-of-war between Paul and Sabrina, skidded toward Tate.

Sitka shook her head, biting down hard on Paul's arm as the man screamed and twisted, trying to get away.

Ignoring the blood sliding down his left arm, Tate lifted his gun again. His right hand shook as he redirected at Kevin, who'd taken a bullet, too.

It had slammed the man into the wall, but he was recovering faster than Tate, even though Tate could have sworn his bullet had headed for center mass.

He had a vest on, Tate realized as Kevin swung his gun up again, too, hatred in his eyes.

Wasting precious seconds to lift his arm higher, up from center mass where he'd been trained to shoot, Tate fired again, once, twice.

Kevin's eyes widened as a cloud of blood erupted from his neck. He slid down the wall, his gun hitting the floor first.

From the opposite direction of where Tate had en-

tered, a distant *bang, bang, bang* sounded. The sound
of a battering ram. His colleagues were coming, breaking through the boards at the entrance. They must have
gotten the bomb defused faster than expected.

Pivoting back toward Paul, Sitka and Sabrina, Tate
swore and shoved to his feet.

Paul had yanked the knife off his waistband. As Sabrina launched herself toward Paul's gun, groaning as
she slammed into the concrete again, Paul flicked the
knife open.

He lifted his hand back to drive it into Sitka.

Sitka kept shaking her head, biting down harder, ignoring the threat and never giving up on her target as
the knife arced toward her.

Tate didn't have a shot. Sliding the gun back into his
belt, he jumped forward, praying his vest would take
the stab if he misjudged his aim.

He landed hard, smacking against Sitka and making
her yelp. But she still didn't let go.

His injured arm screamed in protest, sending spikes
of pain through his head. He twisted, trying to get a
hold of Paul's knife, which had been pushed backward
at the force of Tate's landing.

Then the knife was up again, coming for Tate's bad
arm. The arm he couldn't move well enough or fast
enough to block it.

He gritted his teeth, preparing for the pain even as
he fought for a grip on the man's arm. He grabbed hold
with both hands just below the elbow, his arms shaking
as he tried to keep the knife at bay.

Paul's overly bulky muscle wasn't for show. The man
was *strong*. He let out a deep, sustained yell as Sitka
kept biting, kept shaking him, but still he forced the

knife downward, changing direction so he was aiming for Tate's face.

Then he slammed his forehead into the side of Tate's head, letting out another scream as he made contact.

Tate's head bounced sideways with a crack, and his grip loosened.

The knife surged toward him, nicking a line across his cheek before he regained his hold.

Sitka growled low and deep, and Tate let out his own yell as he forced his injured arm to work harder, pushing the knife away.

From a distance, footsteps pounded toward them, but the knife was moving forward again, and Tate's injured arm started violently shaking.

"Drop it. *Now!*" The voice was weak, but the tone was deadly serious.

Tate's gaze jerked up to where Sabrina stood, swaying on her feet, blood dripping from her face. Paul's gun shook in her hands, but she had it angled well, lined up with Paul's face through the gap behind Tate.

Paul's gaze darted from her to Kevin and back again.

Tate took advantage of his momentary distraction to launch sideways, using his weight on Paul's arm as he grabbed the man's wrist and twisted.

Paul yelped, his muscles engaging too late as the knife clattered to the ground.

Tate kicked it aside and pushed to his feet.

Then his colleagues rushed the room, and Tate told Sitka, "Let go!"

She opened her jaw and dropped Paul's arm, then moved out of the way, letting the other officers do their jobs.

Tate could only stare at Sabrina. She'd dropped her

arm to the side, but she still held the weapon. She stared back at him through badly swollen eyes, and a wave of intense relief and residual terror and realization washed over him.

She was alive.

She blinked a few times, then the gun clattered to the floor, and she collapsed.

Rushing forward, Tate caught her before she landed. His arm gave out, and he slid to his knees, trying to take her weight.

"Get an ambulance." The chief's voice rang in Tate's ears as he fumbled to see Sabrina's face, to check her breathing.

Arm shaking, he managed to get a hand on her neck and feel for a pulse. Tears rushed to his eyes when he found one.

Then the chief warned him not to move her. "She probably has internal bleeding. We'll get the medevac."

They were closer to Luna and the hospital than they would have been back in Desparre, but they were deep in the woods, in the bowels of an old fort. A helicopter couldn't land here.

Fear once again gripped him. Had he gotten to her in time, only to lose her anyway?

Chapter 24

It had been almost thirty-six hours since Kevin had been declared dead at the scene and Paul had been taken into custody. Not only had the Desparre police defused the bomb he'd built, but apparently the secondary device Njeri had spotted was something Paul had trained on only the month before. They were already building a rock-solid case against him. The chief thought maybe this time they'd dig deep enough to find the money they hadn't located the first time around. Paul was unlikely to ever again step outside a prison.

Tate blinked at his watch, then rubbed sleep from his eyes and leaned over to pet Sitka, who was snoring on the hospital floor. Technically, she wasn't supposed to be here, but she was a police K-9, so they'd made an exception.

His left arm ached at the movement, but it was dulled by the painkillers they'd given him after they'd stitched him up. The bullet had passed through the muscle in his biceps and gone out the other side. He'd need physical therapy, just like last time, but he would recover. And the plastic surgeon who'd closed up the cut on his face had told him he probably wouldn't have a scar.

In the hospital bed, Sabrina twitched and then let out a whimper in her sleep.

He leaned toward her from the chair the hospital staff had pulled in, along with coffee for him and a bowl of water for Sitka. Once they'd gotten Sabrina into a room, he hadn't left her side.

But she still hadn't woken up. As soon as she'd arrived at the hospital, doctors had rushed her in for CT scans of her brain, facial bones, neck, abdomen and pelvis. She'd been wheeled away from him, looking small and battered and helpless in that hospital bed, a far cry from the determined woman who'd stood, blood-covered and swaying, and saved his life.

At the time, overhearing snippets of the doctors' conversations, phrases like *check for a fractured skull* and *could have an intracranial hemorrhage* had terrified him. They'd gotten him stitched up only by assuring him they'd tell him if there were any changes to or any news on Sabrina's condition.

Hours later, they'd told him either she was very lucky or her assailants had known exactly how to hit to cause a lot of visual damage but not to kill her. They said she had a couple of fractured ribs that luckily hadn't punctured her lungs. But she had a lung contusion that would need pain management. Amazingly, despite the massive swelling and bleeding on her face, she hadn't broken any of the bones there. But she did have a brain contusion. The doctors had called it minor, said the microbleed would require a longer stay in the hospital. It was also what was keeping her unconscious.

She was medicated, needed time to heal, but every moment her eyes stayed closed made him more anxious. Her doctors planned to keep her in the hospital for at least a week but said she would most likely make a full recovery within six months. But *most likely* wasn't good enough.

Somehow, in the time he'd spent with her at her hotel room and pretending to be her boyfriend, he'd fallen for her for real. Or maybe it had happened long before that, when she'd first come to the police station asking for help. Or even before that, when he'd run into her in town and felt an instant connection he wanted to pursue.

"Tate."

The whisper came from the doorway of Sabrina's room. After giving her one more glance to be sure she wasn't waking, Tate forced himself to his feet. His whole body ached as he hobbled toward his chief.

"How's she doing?"

"Nothing new," Tate told him. His fellow officers hadn't left the hospital until a few hours ago, exhausted. Luna police had taken over, stationing an officer at each of the two hospital entrances to protect both him and Sabrina. At this point, they all assumed Adam had left, that finding him would become a longer-term investigation. But they weren't taking any chances.

Tate hadn't realized his chief had stayed.

"I've got an update on Charlie."

Worry clamped down on his chest until the chief said, "The surgery was a success. They stopped the internal bleeding. He's got a lot of healing ahead, but he's going to make it."

Tate let out a relieved breath.

"And so are you."

When Tate shook his head, not understanding, the chief said, "The two of us have a lot of paperwork ahead, getting your personnel file in order. And there's a suspension in your future because I can't just pretend this didn't happen. But obviously, the threat against you was real. So, I'm willing to accept that you did what you had to do."

Relief loosened the tension he hadn't even realized he'd felt underneath his worry for Sabrina. "Thank you."

"You're a good officer, Tate. We want to keep you." He held out his hand as Sitka jerked upright, then ran over.

Tate shook his hand, then the chief bent over and petted Sitka. "You, too. You make one hell of a K-9 unit."

She gave the chief's arm a slobbery kiss, and he smiled, then stood.

He turned to leave, then twisted back toward Tate. "Don't give up," he advised, nodding toward Sabrina.

"Doctors said—"

"I know what the doctors said," the chief interrupted. "I'm talking about you. Don't give up on her. Believe me when I say I know what I'm talking about." Something wistful and sad flashed over his face as he said, "This kind of connection doesn't come around often. When you find it, hang on as long as you can."

"Thanks," Tate replied when he finally found his voice. By then, the chief was already striding away.

He glanced down at Sitka, who looked from him to Sabrina.

Tate's gaze followed, then he jerked in surprise. Her eyes were open, staring at him. She looked groggy, but far more aware than he would have expected after all she'd been through.

Rushing back into the room, with Sitka keeping pace, he carefully took hold of her hand. "How are you feeling?"

"Like a couple of assholes beat me up," she rasped.

Relief made his laughter come out sounding like a half sob. He stroked his thumb over the skin on her hand, mottled purple with bruises. "You're going to be fine."

The words seemed to reassure her, but her eyes closed again. They didn't open again for several long minutes. When they finally did, a nurse came in and listened to her heartbeat, then checked her pupils and helped her sit.

She gave Sabrina some water, then patted her arm, above where Tate still held her hand. "I know you don't feel so great now, but you'll be all right. You press your call button if you need me, okay?"

When Sabrina gave a shaky nod, looking a lot more alert, the nurse smiled at both of them, then left them alone.

Sabrina stared at the open doorway for a long moment. Then her lips pursed, lines forming between her eyes as she turned back to him, her expression one of wariness and distrust. "Who were they? Why were they trying to get back at you?" Her tone turned accusatory as she demanded, "And why did they call you Tate *Donnoly*?"

"I'm sorry." His voice came out barely more than a whisper, so he cleared his throat and tried again. "I'm sorry." He gave her the short version of the attempt on his life and his subsequent name change and return to Alaska.

Her gaze shifted to Sitka. "You didn't grow up in the Midwest." She looked back at him. "You grew up in Sitka, Alaska, didn't you?"

His dog let out a soft woof, then laid her head on the edge of Sabrina's hospital bed.

"Yes."

"You lied to me."

"I had to. I was trying to keep you safe. I was trying to keep *everyone* safe. I swear to you, Sabrina, I thought that article had gone unnoticed. Just in case, I was planning to leave after I helped you find your stalker. If I thought there was an immediate threat, I never would have—"

"You dug into my life without my permission," she cut him off. "And I get it. You did it to help me. But I told you *everything* afterward. I was really honest with you. Not just about what happened but about my *life*. About my family and my friends and who I really am. The whole time you were lying to me."

He clamped his lips shut as she spoke, letting her talk. But then he couldn't keep quiet anymore. "I tried to be honest with you."

She let out a huff. "When?"

"With everything. I told you more about myself than I've shared with anyone since I left Boston. Yes, I hid some of the small details that I thought were dangerous for you to know—like the fact that I used to be a cop in Boston, that I'd grown up in Alaska. But the rest of it? All the things I shared with you about my family and my dreams for my life? That was all true."

"The things you left out weren't small details," Sabrina said, her voice too calm now, like she was tired of it all. Tired of him. "You hid pretty important pieces of yourself. Including a threat. And I paid for it."

"I know." He slid his hand over hers, and she frowned, pulling her hand free.

Dread built up, the fear that he'd messed up so badly there was no coming back from it. But the chief was right. He had to try.

"I'm so sorry, Sabrina. I can't take that back. If I had suspected what would happen, I would have left."

She flinched a little at that, and it gave him hope.

He leaned closer and stared into her eyes, hoping she could see the truth there. "I love you, Sabrina."

Her lips parted as she stared back at him. Then tears welled up, and she blinked them away. Her voice was a whisper when she said, "I don't think I can forgive you."

Sabrina woke with a start, her heart thundering in her chest, her head and ribs aching. She blinked, trying to get her bearings.

She was in a dark hospital room. Not a hidden concrete fort, trapped in by crooked cops, thinking her only option was how she might die. By bullet, beating or bomb.

Taking a deep breath, she glanced around. Tate was asleep in a chair across from her bed. When she strained, she spotted Sitka sprawled at his feet, lightly snoring.

She didn't remember drifting off to sleep again, but the stiffness in her body that turned into sharp pain at any movement, told her it might have been a while. She did remember the doctor coming in, giving her a whole lot of medical speak that had made her head spin, then summing up with "You'll be okay. Your brain and your ribs need time to heal, but you'll get there."

Then she'd been alone with Tate again, struggling to figure out what else to say. He'd told her he *loved* her. But it didn't matter how she felt in return, not if she couldn't trust him.

He'd hidden his past from her. Hidden the threats against him. After she'd spent two years running from a stalker, he should have known how much of a difference the right information could make. Instead, he'd left her in the dark, clueless about the additional danger she faced.

Her fists clenched, and the movement tugged on her IV, stinging. But the pain was a welcome distraction from her building anger.

If he'd been totally honest with her, maybe she wouldn't have done anything different. Maybe she would have felt the same way he had about the likelihood of his past coming to get her. But at least then she wouldn't have this sense of betrayal that hurt worse than all of her injuries combined.

She loved him.

The realization hit with the force of one of the punches she'd taken to the head. She huffed out a humorless laugh, and her chest started to ache.

How hadn't she realized it earlier? Of course she'd fallen in love with Tate, no matter his last name. He was sweet and smart and funny, and all the struggles of the past few years had seemed lighter when she was with him.

When Jessamyn had joked that maybe she'd meet

her soul mate in that bar two and a half years ago and Sabrina had rolled her eyes, she'd thought about how her married friends liked to tell her that when she met the right one she'd just *know*. Adam had spotted her in that bar, begun his unnatural obsession that had led her to Desparre. That had led her to Tate. And now, suddenly, she *knew*.

But did that matter if she couldn't trust him?

Squeezing her eyes closed, she tried to imagine going home and never seeing him again. The idea was painful, and she didn't want to face it. When she opened her eyes again, a silhouette in the open doorway made her jump.

She almost didn't recognize him, with his hair dyed darker, the glasses, and the hospital scrubs. Obviously the Luna cops watching the entrances hadn't recognized him. But when he stepped inside, there was no doubt.

Fear mingled with a deep sense of betrayal. Adam had spent more than two years destroying her life, then convinced her to see him as a friend.

Adam smiled with a darkness in his eyes as he put a finger to his lips. Then he twisted toward Tate, his expression shifting into a possessive fury. His arm twitched, drawing her attention to what he held. A gun.

Sabrina's gaze went from him to Tate, asleep on the chair.

She didn't think. She just leaped.

The IV ripped out of her hand, and her bruised ribs set off a ferocious, searing pain that nauseated her. Her head jostled, and it felt as if her brain was bouncing inside her skull.

Then everything seemed to happen at once.

She smashed into Adam, propelling him back and

pushing the gun sideways. Adam's gaze locked on hers, a mix of jealous rage and sinister intent that sent goose bumps across her neck. Then his hands shifted, ready to shove her back.

Before he could move, Tate jumped out of his seat, awakened by the noise. He knocked over his chair as he pushed his way between them, smashing Adam's gun hand into the wall, and making him drop the weapon.

Then somehow, Sitka was there, pressed up against her when she might have swayed and fallen.

Tate spun Adam face-first into the wall, yanked handcuffs off his belt and slapped them on as nurses and doctors rushed toward them and Tate told them to call for backup.

"She's mine," Adam snarled, trying to twist out of Tate's grip.

Tate pushed him back into the wall as he turned his head to look at her. "You okay?"

She stared back at him, at the intense protectiveness in his eyes, at the love she could see there.

The love she felt in return made her chest ache, made the words want to burst free.

Instead, she managed to nod as tears filled her eyes. She gave him a shaky smile to reassure him she really was okay and that she hadn't reinjured herself badly.

When Sitka whined, Sabrina stroked her fur, still staring at Tate. She didn't take her gaze off him, even when a pair of officers rushed into the room and pulled Adam away.

It was over.

After two long years of running and hiding and thinking she'd never have her life back, they'd caught her stalker. She could go home, return to the life she'd made for herself there.

So, why did her chest suddenly ache so badly over all the things she was giving up in Alaska?

Epilogue

Sabrina pulled back the curtains on her living room window, exposing the glorious view she'd fallen in love with the moment she'd stepped foot in this cabin.

She took a deep breath, smiling when her ribs gave only a slight twinge in protest. She'd spent a full week in the hospital, while doctors gave her medication to help her manage the pain and tests to check her neurological state. Then they'd declared the small bleed in her head healed enough to release her.

For the next three months at least, they'd told her to expect her symptoms to persist. Ringing in her ears maybe or some dizziness or just not feeling quite right. They wanted her to have regular follow-ups with a neurologist back in New York. But they'd cleared her to travel.

Her bags were already packed. She'd left New York

two years ago with a trunk full of belongings. She was returning with two duffel bags.

But she was also returning with a feeling of safety. Adam was in custody. He had admitted to killing Dylan. He'd admitted to setting the truck on Sitka. He'd even admitted to giving her a shove in the woods, then grabbing her arm to ostensibly save her.

Apparently, he'd searched for her for over a year and a half without success after she'd left New York. Then she'd started her online jewelry business. She didn't remember it, but years ago, she'd posted something on social media about her dreams of designing jewelry, even shared a drawing of a necklace. A friend had shared that post. Then in Alaska, Sabrina had finally made that necklace. Adam had spent so much time obsessively trying to trace her online that the single post had eventually led him to her, through the PO box she used when she mailed out the jewelry.

She shivered at the deviousness, the obsessiveness he'd demonstrated. But it was over now. She straightened, pushing Adam from her mind as she looked around the place she'd come to call home.

She was going to miss this cabin. She was going to miss this town, miss the people.

A familiar pain clamped down on her chest, and she pressed a hand against her heart. After Adam had been arrested, she'd told Tate to go home, that she needed time. She knew how she felt about him, but she didn't know if she could do anything about it.

She hadn't told him she loved him. She wasn't sure she ever would. But meeting him and Sitka, coming to love him and Sitka, made leaving Alaska painful.

Glancing around the cabin one more time, she

reached for her duffel bags. Lifting them sent a searing pain across her ribs and caused her head to swim.
She closed her eyes and breathed through the pain until
it eased up. Then she moved slowly toward the door.

No matter what she decided, she'd call Tate once she
got to New York. She'd debated stopping by his house
on her way to the airport, but worried if she did, she'd
break down. She wanted time to feel more whole, to
have more distance from the attacks in the army fort,
before making any big decisions about her future.

She might come back here someday. Might see Tate
and Sitka again. But maybe they both needed to return
to the lives they'd left behind before they could decide
what their futures held.

Pulling the door open, she drew in a hard breath.
"Tate."

He stood on her porch, his hands twisted together
like he'd been wringing them. He looked serious and
determined and exactly what her eyes wanted to see.

Woof!

A smile trembled on her lips as she looked to his
side, at the beautiful dog. "Sitka."

"I know you wanted time," he said, his gaze going
to the bags she carried. His lips tightened briefly, then
his gaze returned to hers. "But I just needed you to
know something."

Sabrina nodded slowly as she took a step backward,
never taking her gaze off him. Her chest felt like it
swelled with all the emotions battling inside her: hope
and fear and love.

He stepped inside, into her personal space like he
had just under a month ago, when she'd felt like she was

taking such a big step letting him into her cabin for the first time. Sitka followed, tail wagging as she pranced next to Sabrina, nudging her leg.

Sabrina couldn't help but smile as she put down her bags and stroked Sitka's fur. She couldn't stop the smile from fading into something more serious as she looked up at Tate, breathed in his familiar sandalwood scent.

"I love you, Sabrina."

Her throat clenched, her own words of love wanting to escape past the barriers she'd put up.

But she'd spent two years being afraid. Two years keeping people at a distance. As much as she wanted it to, that fear didn't just magically disappear simply because the threat of her stalker was gone. The ability to trust again wasn't easy.

Was she keeping Tate at a distance because he'd broken her trust? Or because she'd become afraid to trust her own gut, trust her own feelings?

"I messed up," Tate continued. "And I will forever regret not being more honest with you."

He reached out, took both of her hands in his, and she felt the contact all the way down to her toes.

She had to be honest with herself. In the week she hadn't seen him, she'd missed this man desperately.

"I know you care about me," he said, his tone as intense as his gaze. "I *know* you do."

She felt herself nodding, saw a brief smile tip the edges of Tate's lips.

Then he was serious again. "We're right together, you and me. If you need more time, I understand and I'll give it to you. But I don't want to wait any longer."

He paused, as if waiting for her to speak, but she couldn't seem to form words before he rushed on.

"I'll do whatever it takes to regain your trust."

She stared up at him, thinking of all the opportunities she'd missed to be with him while she'd lived in Alaska. Thinking of how she'd tried to do what was best for her family, even though it hadn't been what they'd wanted. Of how she'd snuck out in the middle of the night, without a goodbye, so they wouldn't try to follow.

He'd made mistakes, too. But she knew he thought he was protecting her by keeping his past from her. And every time she'd needed him, he'd shown up.

She loved him. She was angry with him, but if she hadn't fallen for him so completely, she wouldn't have been so mad or felt so betrayed.

She couldn't deny what she felt any longer. She didn't want to let her own fear hold her back and lose him. Didn't want to spend the next part of her life missing someone else she loved.

"Whatever you need," Tate repeated, stepping even closer, so she had to tilt her head back to keep staring into his dark, serious gaze. "I know we both need to re-connect with the lives we had to leave. But I want to do it together. I want to see my family again, *finally*, and not feel like I'm compromising their safety or my own by doing it. I want to introduce you to them."

She jerked at the words, at the implied commitment there, and he spoke even faster. "I know you need to go home to your family in New York. I want to meet them. If you want me to," he added. "Whether it's now or later. I want to be with you, whether it's here or in New York or it's long-distance for a while." He glanced at Sitka and added, "The chief has agreed that whatever you want, if you'll let me be with you, Sitka can come, too."

Woof!

He smiled at his dog, then turned his serious gaze back on her. "You can think about this as long as you need. But I won't give up on us. I love you too much, Sabrina."

He let go of one of her hands to cup her cheek. "If you decide you want me to go and leave you alone, I will. But I'll always be waiting. I'll wait as long as it takes."

She stared up at him, words caught in her throat and fear still lodged in her chest.

She loved him. She didn't want to lose him. But was she ready to make such a big leap of faith?

He nodded, gave her a sad smile as he dropped his hand and backed away.

He'd started to turn for the door when she grabbed his arm, gripping tight, knowing it was time to truly move forward. And she couldn't have the life she wanted without him in it.

He turned back, his gaze filled with surprise and a sudden, fierce hope.

"I love you, too, Tate," she croaked, then suppressed a laugh at how tearful she sounded, how joyous she felt. "I love you, too."

Woof! Sitka nudged her again, and Sabrina gave in to the laugh ready to burst inside her. "I love you, too, Sitka."

Then Tate stepped closer, lowered his lips to hers and gently kissed her.

His lips only touched hers for a brief moment, careful of the bruising still coloring her jaw. When he lifted his face again and gave her a huge, brilliant smile, she felt better than she had in more than two years. They'd figure out the details, but she knew one thing for sure: she'd gotten two amazing gifts out of her two years on the run—him and Sitka.

And she wasn't going to ever let them go.

* * * * *